I0665930

The **Plains** *of* **Chalmette**

A **STORY** *of* **CRESCENT CITY**

JACK CALDWELL

WHITE SOUP PRESS

THE PLAINS OF CHALMETTE: A Story of CRESCENT CITY

For information, address Jack Caldwell, 3140 Sunset Beach Drive, Venice, FL, 34293.

http://www.cajuncheesehead.com/
http://whitesouppress.com/
http:// austenvariations.com/

ISBN: 978-0-9891080-2-7

Maps courtesy of: The Department of History, United States Military Academy
                    at West Point

Front Cover: *Battle of New Orleans*, 1856, Dennis Malone Carter
Back Cover: photo by Jack Caldwell, design by Ellen Pickels
Book layout & design by Ellen Pickels

Dedication

To Barbara
She is far more precious than jewels.

In Appreciation

To Debbie Styne, Catarina Cotic Belloube, and Ellen Pickels
for their endless hours editing this work.

Author's Note

The Plains of Chalmette is a work of fiction about the invasion of Louisiana during the War of 1812. In this novel, original characters interact with historical figures. Great care has been taken to accurately portray the events as they happened two hundred years ago.

For purposes of storytelling, certain actual actions and words have been given to the fictional characters. This is not meant to slight the men on both sides who fought, suffered, and died on a muddy plantation outside of New Orleans. This book is intended to honor their courage and sacrifice.

May there always be peace and friendship between the people of the United States and the United Kingdom.

— Jack Caldwell
Venice, Florida, November 2014

Introduction

President Thomas Jefferson never intended to buy Louisiana. It's just that Emperor Napoleon Bonaparte offered him a deal that was too good to pass up.

The growing population of the infant United States was moving ever westward in search of land and natural resources. The vast area west of the Appalachian Mountains proved rich in furs, timber, coal, and farmed produce, but there was no easy way of shipping these treasures eastward. The mountain passes were high and difficult, and the insufferable British controlled the Great Lakes to the north. The best way to move goods was by water, and that meant the Mississippi River.

President Jefferson knew that the new lands to the west all drained into the Mississippi basin and the city of New Orleans controlled the mouth of the river. He who owned the Crescent City controlled most of North America. For the United States to free itself from the restraints of both geography and enemies, the nation had to have New Orleans, so the president sent representatives to Paris to buy the city for ten million American dollars.

What Jefferson and his agents did *not* know was that the Emperor of the French had realized the impossibility of his dream to reestablish a French Empire in the New World.

The slaves of Haiti, inspired by the French Revolution, had revolted, leading to more than a hundred thousand deaths. For a time, the French Republic and the later French Empire tried to incorporate the newly freed blacks into the fold. But when Toussaint

L'Ouverture tried to make himself governor-for-life, it was too much for Napoleon. A free Haiti was a threat to his plans. He had bullied Spain, his former ally, into returning the vast Louisiana territory to France the year before, but he could not hold it without a secure naval base in the Caribbean, and that base was to have been Haiti.

Unfortunately for the Master of Europe, French troops dispatched to the island were defeated. Haiti was free, France had lost its last major base in the Caribbean, and Louisiana was redundant. If France could not defend the place, they would lose it.

Napoleon needed money to fund his long-dreamed-of invasion of England, and the upstart Americans were in France, trying to buy New Orleans. Why not sell them Louisiana? Such a sale would infuriate the English—always a good thing—and the emperor could use the cash. Conquering the world was an expensive business.

Consequently, to the shock of the Americans, France offered not the city but the *entirety of Louisiana*—all 828,000 square miles —for the fire-sale price of fifteen million dollars. At three cents an acre, it was the greatest real estate bargain in history!

There was some opposition in Washington to the treaty. The question was asked whether the president even had the authority to buy the territory. However, when it became apparent that the treaty effectively doubled the size of the United States, Congress knew a good deal when they saw it. They ratified the agreement on October 20, 1803 and, most importantly, authorized the funds.

Not everyone was happy with the transaction. The people of New Orleans felt betrayed. They had long desired a return of French rule, and that desire was now dashed. The Spanish were outraged, for they had agreed—under duress, mind you—to return Louisiana to France three years before for *nothing*, and the final exchange had yet to take place. How could Napoleon sell something that did not belong to him?

The British Crown agreed with Spain and was furious. Once the United States took possession of Louisiana, British plans to establish a Native Indian border state between the US and Canada under the Crown's "protection" would be blown to bits. The United States, not Great Britain, would be master of North America.

Huffing and puffing by the British accomplished nothing. The United States took possession of New Orleans on November 30, 1803 and the rest of the territory on March 10 of the following year.

The British were livid, for they could clearly see the balance of power shifting in the New World. A new force was rising, a force Britain was not prepared to respect or fear. It was an impossible situation, and eventually, something would have to be done about the arrogant former colonies.

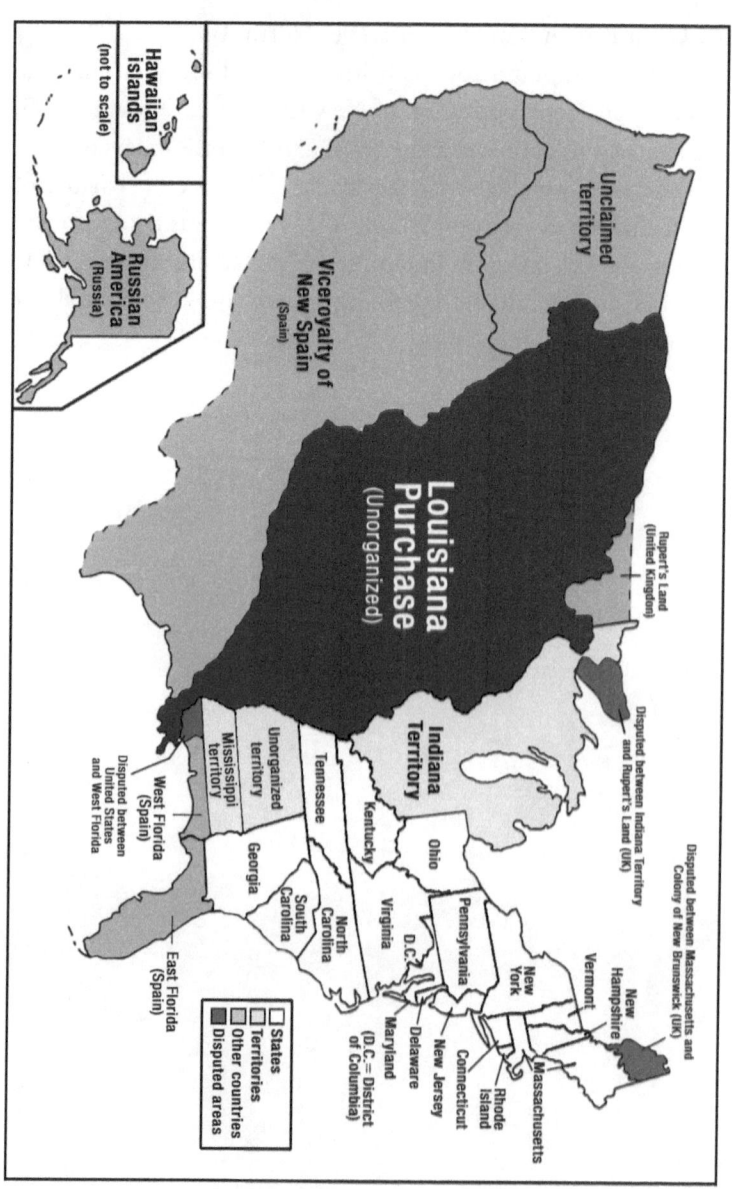

States and Territories of the United States of America

April 30, 1803 to March 27, 1804

The **Plains** *of* **Chalmette**

A **STORY** *of* **CRESCENT CITY**

Who are we? And for what are we going to fight? Are we the titled slaves of George III? The military conscripts of Napoleon the Great? Or the frozen peasants of the Russian Czar?

No! We are the free born sons of America. The citizens of the only republic now existing in the world. And the only people on earth who possess rights, liberties, and property which they dare call their own!

— Andrew Jackson, 1814

Dramatis Personae

Note: [*] designates a historical character.

AMERICANS

Major Matthew Darcy, US Army: native of Baltimore, Maryland, a
      member of the Federal army serving with General Andrew
      Jackson

Major Jacob Harville, US Army: Major Darcy's friend and
      comrade, native of Tennessee

Emile Dansereau: planter and trader, owner of Dansereau
      Plantation in St. Charles Parish upriver of New Orleans

Anne-Marie Girard Dansereau: M. Dansereau's only daughter and
      heir

Clementine: a slave, Mlle Dansereau's personal maid

Samson: a slave from Dansereau Plantation

Philippe & Madeline Melançon: Attorney, M. Dansereau's in-laws,
      residents of the *Vieux Carré*

Henri Herbert: owner of Buena Tierra Plantation in St. Charles
      Parish and land investor in New Orleans, nephew of M.
      Dansereau

Carmen Bellevue: a *mestee* (mulatto) lady, lover of Henri Herbert,
      and proprietress of a boarding house in the *Faubourg
      Marigny*

Wallace Anderson: American emigrant and trader

13

*William Charles Cole Claiborne: first elected Governor of
Louisiana, native of Virginia, resident of New York and
Tennessee, and former Territorial Governor

*Edward Livingston: American jurist and statesman, one-time
mayor of New York City, born in New York, brother of
Robert R. Livingston (who with James Monroe negotiated
the Louisiana Purchase), moved to Louisiana in 1804,
advisor to Governor Claiborne and *aide de camp* to
General Jackson.

*Major General Jacques Philippe Villeré, Louisiana Militia: planter,
politician, a leader of the Creoles, and owner of Conseil
Plantation

*Major Gabriel Villeré, Louisiana Militia: son of General Villeré

*Bernard Xavier Philippe de Marigny de Mandeville: French
Creole planter, land developer, gambler, and politician,
best known for introducing the English game Hazard
(now known as Craps) to America

*Commodore Daniel Todd Patterson, US Navy: commander of the
New Orleans Squadron ("Commodore" is an operational
title; his line rank in the US Navy at the time was
"commander.")

*Lieutenant Thomas ap Catesby Jones, US Navy: commander of
the Lake Borgne gunboat squadron

*Jean Lafitte: privateer and smuggler of goods and slaves, primarily
against the Spanish, leader of the Baratarians; well read,
well dressed, and very cultured for a pirate

*Dominique You: another chief of Lafitte's band, assumed to be
a half-brother of the Lafittes *Major General Andrew
Jackson, US Army: lawyer, planter, politician, duelist,
and soldier, born in the Carolinas, served as a boy in the
Revolutionary War where he developed a hatred for the
British, and commanded American forces during the
Creek War

*Major General William Carroll, Tennessee Militia: Jackson's friend, comrade, and successor as leader of the Tennessee militia after Jackson accepted his commission in the federal army

*Brigadier General John Coffee, Tennessee Militia: close friend and former business partner of Jackson, his brigade consisting largely of free blacks and Choctaw Indian warriors

*Brigadier General John Adair, Kentucky Militia: adjunct commander of the Kentucky militia in the Louisiana theater, accused before the war of collaboration in the Aaron Burr scandal and later acquitted of treason

*Brigadier General David B. Morgan, Louisiana Militia: commander of American militia companies on the West Bank

BRITISH

Major James Fitzwilliam: British army staff officer

Margaret Fitzwilliam: wife to Captain Fitzwilliam

Captain Walworth Elliot, RN: captain of *HMS Imprudent*, 50-gun, fourth-rate, *Portland*-class ship, used as an armed troop transport

*Vice-Admiral Sir Alexander Forrester Inglis Cochrane, KCB: commander-in-chief, North American station, architect and commander of the naval forces at the Battle of New Orleans

*Major-General Robert Ross: with Cockburn, burned Washington on August 24, 1814 after the Battle of Bladensburg and was killed on Sept. 12 during the Battle of North Point near Baltimore

*Major-General Sir Edward Michael Pakenham, GCB: in command of British land forces at New Orleans, brother-in-law, comrade, and friend to the Duke of Wellington.

*Major-General John Keane: commanded the Third Brigade, was initially commander of British land forces until Pakenham's arrival

*Major-General Sir Samuel Gibbs, KCB: saw most of his service in India, and was Pakenham's deputy

*Major-General Sir John Lambert, CB: served under Wellington in Portugal and Spain, and deputy commander of British land forces at New Orleans

*Colonel William Thornton, Eighty-Fifth Foot: fought with General Ross at Washington and Baltimore, was wounded, held prisoner, and paroled

*Lieutenant-Colonel Alexander Dickson: commander of artillery

*Lieutenant-Colonel Sir John Fox Burgoyne, CB: chief of engineers, illegitimate son of the British general who surrendered at Saratoga

*Lieutenant-Colonel Thomas Mullins, Forty-Fourth Foot: fought under General Ross at Washington and Baltimore

*Lieutenant-Colonel Robert Rennie: regimental infantry commander

*Major Duncan MacDougall: senior *aide de camp* to General Pakenham

Prologue

There are many reasons the United States and Great Britain went to war in 1812. The British, contemptuous of their former colonies, never truly accepted American independence. England embargoed U.S. trade with Europe and impressed —or more accurately, kidnapped—their sailors. They sold guns and weapons to native tribes in an effort to stop western expansion by the new country. And they dismissed American complaints with a wave of their snuff-stained handkerchiefs.

As for the angry, ambitious Americans, who chewed their tobacco rather than sniffed it, they viewed the territories to the north with a jealous eye. It took little to convince them that Canadians desired American-styled democracy rather than British rule. It never occurred to the Americans that some people might prefer a king to a Congress.

Though all these are valid reasons for conflict, what cannot be overlooked was that America had been embroiled in Europe's wars since 1754.

The Seven Years' War was the first worldwide conflict. Britain with their allies and France with theirs slaughtered each other across the globe: Europe, Asia, India, and North America. In the colonies, it was called the French and Indian War, and it was during this hostility that Britain won the majority of its spoils. The French were kicked out, and as a side note, so too were the Acadians—the future Cajuns of Louisiana.

Wars were expensive, and Britain tried to recoup their investment by taxing their colonies. However, the colonists did not take well to being taxed without representation, becoming one of the causes of the American Revolution. France sent ships and funds to help the Americans—not to defend freedom but to bedevil Great Britain. France was smarting from the loss of its colonies and eager for revenge.

America became free, and France became bankrupt. The French Crown tried to tax its way to prosperity, and that led to its overthrow. The successful revolutionaries, when not chopping the heads off their internal enemies, tried to export their homicidal republic, which led to the next round of European wars. The French Republic evolved into the French Empire, and the wars went on.

The United States tried to remain impartial, but their claim of neutrality was acknowledged by no one. America and France almost went to war in 1798 over trade. When in 1806 both Britain and France ordered blockades of each other's ports, America was caught in the middle. Its port cities suffered greatly. Warehouses were filled with rotting food and languishing dry goods. Men were thrown out of work.

So the pressure built. Great Britain would not let the puny United States trade with Napoleon's France and refused to recognize American citizenship for former Englishmen. The naïve Americans thought Canada would be easy pickings. The native tribes, armed by the British, fought new settlers from the east.

Finally, Congress heeded President Madison's call and declared war on Great Britain on June 18, 1812, fifty days after the new state of Louisiana was admitted into the Union.

The young, arrogant, and overconfident Americans soon discovered that, while an earnest militia—helped by a small number of regular Army troops—might win a defensive war and a new nation's freedom, it was next to useless as a conquering horde. Invasion after invasion of Canada was attempted, and by 1814, the only thing the United States had to show for it was the dubious satisfaction of burning York (modern-day Toronto). And while their new state-of-the-art 44-gun frigates like *USS Constitution* won spectacular battles against the renowned Royal Navy, America had nowhere near enough ships to break a crippling naval blockade.

Worse for the Yankees, time had run out. Hubris had been Napoleon's fatal flaw, and his ill-conceived invasion of Russia signaled his end. In London, the lords of the Admiralty and the generals in Horse Guards could now turn their attention to the irritating war in North America.

Great Britain decided it was time to rein in the upstart Americans for good. Veteran troops from Wellington's successful Peninsula campaigns would punish the United States and put an end to their plans of continental domination.

Britain's plan was simple and potentially devastating:

Step one: Avenge York's burning with a raid on Washington, DC. While America's attention was diverted, attack from the flanks.

Step two: March south from Canada, cut the United States off from the Upper Midwest, and establish the Indian border state.

Step three: Bottle up the Americans forever.

To fulfill the third goal, all that was needed was to take and hold one city: New Orleans.

Eyes right, my jolly field boys,
Who British bayonets bear,
To teach your foes to yield boys,
When British steel they dare!
Now fill the glass, for the toast of toasts
Shall be drunk with the cheer of cheers,
Hurrah, hurrah, hurrah, hurrah!
For the British bayoneteers.

Great guns have shot and shell, boys,
Dragoons have sabres bright.
The artillery fire's like hell, boys,
And the horse like devils fight.
But neither light nor heavy horse
Nor thundering cannoneers,
Can stem the tide of the foeman's pride,
Like the British bayoneteers!

The English arm is strong, boys,
The Irish arm is tough.
The Scotsman's blow the French well know
Is struck by sterling stuff.
And when before the enemy
Their shining steel appears.
Goodbye! Goodbye! How they run, how they run!
From the British bayoneteers!

The British Bayoneteers (author unknown), a British army song
from the Napoleonic Wars period, sung to the tune of the
seventeenth century marching song, The British Grenadiers

Chapter 1

At dawn, the small sailing skiff tacked for the last time and made for the rough wooden pier ahead. The crew had worked all night, sailing the little craft close inshore, past the looming British blockade, and into Lake Pontchartrain. Now, in the early morning light—a freshening breeze promising to battle the oppressive heat expected in these latitudes—the boat moved steadily in the calm waters.

Two men, dressed in the blue uniforms of the United States Army, stood in the bow, watching their destination draw closer. Both in their middle twenties, one was of medium height while the other was over six feet tall.

"That's Fort St. John? Ain't much to look at, Matt," drawled the shorter of the two in a thick Tennessee accent.

Major Matthew Darcy glanced at his friend and comrade. "Hopefully, appearances are deceiving, Jacob." His voice was more cultured with only a twinge of his native Maryland Tidewater.

Major Jacob Harville spat in the passing water. "Old Hickory sent us here to find out if'n these folks can defend themselves. Me, I ain't too sure."

Matthew was saved from responding when crewmen moved forward in preparation to dock. Within minutes, the boat was secured, and the two officers were on dry land. Immediately, a soldier in an outlandish costume approached.

"*Vos ordres, s'il vous plaît,*" he said imperiously, his hand out. His uniform was as French as his accent and hauteur.

"Ain't you the sight," commented Jacob as he and Matthew handed over the orders.

The young officer, who could not be older than twenty, glanced at them and shook his head. "*Elles sont en anglais,*" he spat. "*Qui êtes-vous?*"

Matthew stepped forward. "*Je suis le Major Matthew Darcy. Identifiez-vous!*" he barked, towering over the man.

The officer gaped before coming to attention. "*Mes excuses,* Major! I am Ensign d'Barrie."

"Your unit, Ensign?" Matthew demanded in French.

"Second company, Louisiana Militia, *monsieur.*"

Matthew turned to Jacob. "Militia. That explains the uniform," he said softly in English before returning to French. "Major Harville and I have orders to report directly to Governor Claiborne. You will take us there *tout de suite.*"

"At once, *monsieur!*" The young ensign dashed down the dock, shouting orders.

"Hoo-wee," laughed Jacob, "you got that one to jump."

Matthew allowed himself a small smile. "French is more than a language, Jacob. It's an attitude—a manner of acting."

"Ha! I thought he was gonna wet himself for sure. Good thing you understand the lingo."

Matthew said nothing, but he understood General Jackson's reason for sending him to New Orleans rather than to participate in the invasion of Spanish Florida. It wasn't just because he understood logistics; it was that he was fluent in French.

Jacob's mission was the more important one: inspect the defenses of the city and make recommendations for improvements. Jackson was convinced that the southern United States was vulnerable to a British invasion and was determined to defeat any such attempt.

The ensign soon ran back. "*Messieurs,* we have a wagon ready for you!"

"Excellent. We have baggage aboard the boat."

"Do not concern yourself, *monsieur*! My men, they will see to it. Right this way, *s'il vous plaît*."

THE WAGON MADE ITS WAY on a trail along the stream that gave the fort its name: Bayou St. John. The trail ended at a road called the Chef Menteur, down which the wagon moved before turning on Bayou Road. This led them into the city of New Orleans.

The road brought them in from the northeast, and the driver was very talkative. He gestured to points of interest, and Matthew translated for Jacob.

"That is the Esplanade Ridge to your right and the Gentilly Plain to the left," he said. "The *Vieux Carré* is right ahead."

"That is the central part of the city?" asked Matthew.

"*Oui.*"

"What's that over there?" Jacob pointed to some houses to the east. Matthew translated.

"Oh. That is the *Faubourg Tremé*," answered the driver.

"What th' hell is a *faubourg tremé*?"

Matthew smiled at Jacob. "*Faubourg* is a French expression for a neighborhood outside of the city." He turned to their guide. "What are the other neighborhoods?"

"The *Vieux Carré*, where the Creoles live. The government is there, too. That is the oldest part of the city. Most Americans, like you, live to the west, in the *Faubourg St. Marie*."

"Who lives in the *Faubourg Tremé*?"

"Freedmen and free men of color."

Jacob looked at the number of houses. "Must be an awful lot of 'em."

The soldier gave a rather Gallic shrug. "About one in three, *monsieur*." He pointed his whip ahead. "We are coming up to a new neighborhood to the east, the *Faubourg Marigny*."

"And who lives there?"

The driver gave them a sideways look. "Many people, but mainly the *placées* of the Creoles."

"What's *placée*?" asked Jacob.

"Mistresses," answered Matthew.

New Orleans

AS THEY TRAVELED DOWN THE *Rue de Quay* to the governor's mansion, Darcy could not help but notice the large number of Africans. Slaves he had seen before; the harbor of Baltimore was filled with slave labor. It was the same in New Orleans. But among the black faces were people well dressed—too well dressed to be slaves. They had to be either free men of color or freedmen.

"I've heard tell 'bout the mulatto women," said Jacob, "supposed to be real beauties. Wonder if that's true?"

Matt grinned. "What would your girl back home think about that?"

"Nothing, 'cause Fanny ain't gonna know. Besides, I've been faithful; you know that!"

"One of these days, I must meet your Fanny."

"If'n you ever get up to Tennessee after the war, you just look me up, an' there she'll be."

The wagon pulled up to the door of the governor's house. As the soldiers climbed down, the driver promised to deliver their belongings to the quartermaster at the *Place d'Armes*. They gave him a wave as they made their way inside.

A clerk sat at a desk just inside the door, writing on a paper. Jacob walked up to him. "Major Harville and Major Darcy, reporting for duty. We have orders to report to the governor."

The man asked them to wait, rose, and walked upstairs. A minute later, he came down again, announcing that the governor would see them for a few minutes.

"SO WHAT DID YOU THINK of Governor Claiborne, Matt?" asked Jacob as they left the governor's house, walking towards the *Place d'Armes*.

"About what I expected. He puts on a good show, but as for actually getting anything done? We'll see."

William Charles Cole Claiborne of Virginia had been the

territorial governor, tasked with bringing Louisiana into the Union. Knowing no French, he taught himself the language and made friends with the Creole elite. When statehood was granted, Claiborne was elected governor to everyone's surprise except Claiborne. He was hard working and ambitious.

He was also obsessed with his personal popularity and jealously guarded his preeminence. Yet, he was not a leader. He was not willing to upset any of the various factions in the legislature, so very little was done. He was well known for pouring out his frustrations in letter after letter to Washington; so much so, that the governor of Louisiana was regarded as a weak-willed, vainglorious fool.

"Yeah, I agree. So where do we eat?"

They were just passing a public house. "How about in here?" A delicious aroma floated out the door.

"Smells good. You got some money? Oh, that's right; you're rich. I keep forgetting."

Matthew laughed. "I wouldn't say rich, but I can pay for you and me."

"I'll make good next pay day," Jacob said as they walked in. Small and almost empty, the place was relatively clean. There were six tables, four of them unoccupied. Of the other two, three men sat at one, sharing a low, earnest conversation, while a single gentleman sat at the other, eating soup. They took a table next to the single man and waited for the proprietor.

It was not long before a fat man in a dirty apron appeared. "What I do for you gentlemen?" he asked in broken English.

Matthew replied in French, "Food and something to drink, *s'il vous plaît*. What do you have?"

The proprietor smiled, showing his missing teeth. "I have gumbo, *monsieur*—most excellent. For drink, I have ale and wine."

Matthew had no idea what *gumbo* was. His indecision must have shown because their neighbor said in English, "Try the gumbo, American, but stay away from the wine."

"What is this?" protested the innkeeper. "Why you say this, M. Henri? What is wrong with my wine?"

The stranger patted his lips with a napkin. "Nothing, my good sir, if you stopped watering it," he returned in French. "Get the ale, American."

The two officers were taken aback at the argument. For all the innkeeper's blustering, it seemed to be more of a good-natured teasing than anything else.

"Very well," Matthew said carefully, "a glass of ale, *s'il vous plaît*, and gumbo. Jacob?"

Jacob shrugged. "Guess I'll have the same."

The proprietor smiled and nodded, made some sort of rude gesture to the stranger, and disappeared through a doorway.

The gentleman leaned over and whispered, "Do not worry, sir. Thibodeaux is a friend, and I eat here often. But the wine is truly awful."

The man was about Matthew's age, well dressed, of medium height and a little heavy, with brown sideburns covering his cheeks. His face was open and friendly, and his French-accented English identified him as a local.

"Thank you. What is gumbo?"

The man indicated his own dish. "It is a thick soup, almost a stew." Matthew noted the bowl was almost empty.

"Major Matthew Darcy." The two shook hands. "This is Major Jacob Harville. Who do we have the honor of addressing?"

"My name is Henri Herbert. Your French is very good, Major Darcy, but it is clear you are not from Louisiana! Your accent is wrong."

Matthew shrugged. "As long as people understand me, I am content. I am from Baltimore. Jacob is from Tennessee."

Just then, mugs of ale and steaming bowls of gumbo were placed before them. "*Bon appétit, messieurs!*" said the innkeeper as he left. Matthew dug in and found that the gumbo was spicy and hearty, different from any soup he had ever had.

"This is some good stuff," remarked Jacob.

"Thibodeaux's gumbo is certainly acceptable, *mes amis*"—Herbert shrugged—"but there is better to be found."

Better than this? Matthew rather doubted their new acquaintance's claims, but he ate instead of arguing.

"And what brings you two to New Orleans?" Herbert asked after a few minutes.

Matthew took a sip of the ale. "Our assignment is to help Governor Claiborne build up the militia."

"Indeed? Do you really think that the English will attack us?"

"It's possible. In Europe, Napoleon is almost finished; he lost his entire army in Russia, you know. Once he's done, surely the British will turn their attention to us."

Herbert shook his head. "There are many who will be upset over the emperor's fall. Napoleon is popular among the Creoles, even though he did sell us to the Americans."

"*You* are now an American, Mr. Herbert," Jacob pointed out, "just like everyone in Louisiana."

Herbert laughed. "I do not feel American, *mon ami*! I am the same as I ever was. But it makes no difference, after all. *C'est la vie!*" He sobered a bit. "But others are not so sanguine, no. They resent you Americans. They will not join your militia."

"They will not fight for their homes?"

He shrugged. "Is anyone threatening us? I do not think so. If the English were at the gates, I would fight, but I cannot speak for everyone." Herbert got up to leave. "Perhaps I am wrong. I wish you *bonne chance, mes amis.*"

Matthew and Jacob were pleased with their accommodations. The walls were solid, the floors were dry, and the cots free of lice. For men who had slept in tents for the last two years, it was a relative paradise.

Jacob sat down to write a letter to his Fanny back home, while Matthew, having no one to write to in Maryland, decided to take in some air. Promising his comrade he would return soon, he left his quarters.

The heat of the day still hung in the heavy air. There was no sea breeze to refresh the soul, as there had been in Mobile. Matthew wandered up and down the streets of the *Vieux Carré*. The cobble-stone streets were wide enough for carriages to pass each other. The buildings were very different from those in Baltimore. These were tall—two and three stories—with galleries on the second floor. They had no front stoop to speak of; the houses were virtually on the street, set back only for the sidewalk. Oil lanterns lit the entrances. Matthew had heard that most had courtyards in the middle of the buildings so that the people could enjoy the air in privacy.

He glanced at a street sign. A strange name—*Rue Bourbon*. Bourbon Street, he mentally translated. He then thought he heard something, looked up, and saw an angel.

ANNE-MARIE DANSEREAU STOOD ON THE second-floor gallery of her Uncle Melançon's house overlooking Rue Bourbon as evening fell over the city, feeling very lonely.

She was not a classic beauty. Petite and curvy, her eyes were too large and her mouth too wide. At twenty-two, Anne-Marie was considered an old maid. However, when she smiled, it seemed her entire being glowed. Her black eyes sparkled, and her full lips parted to show lovely teeth. She was elegant and unassuming. These charms were lost on most young men, for they wished to court her for one reason alone: she was rich.

Anne-Marie's father, Emile, immigrated with his family to Loui-siana during *le Grand Dérangement*, the expulsion of the French Acadians from Canada by the British during the French and Indian War. Unlike the others, M. Dansereau smuggled a good bit of gold with him and, once in New Orleans, was able to buy land. That land was now the prosperous Dansereau Plantation in St. Charles Parish, just upriver from the city.

Wealth did not bring immediate acceptance of the Dansereau family from the Creoles in New Orleans. The newcomers were *Aca-diens*, country people, unworthy of associating with sophisticated society. When it was time for Emile to find a bride, most doors were closed to him. Only Marie Girard, daughter of a poor trader, would marry him. While happy in his marriage, Emile was not one to forget and forgive insults.

By the time the United States took position of Louisiana, Emile Dansereau had achieved enough wealth in his business dealings to be accepted, especially since his only child and heir was a daughter. However, Marie's death of yellow fever in 1805 intensified his bitterness and resentment. Scions of prestigious Creole families flocked to their door to court Mlle Dansereau, all in vain. Emile had vowed his girl would never marry a Creole.

Unfortunately, Emile's list of the people he hated was long. The English, of course, led the list. They had stolen the Acadians' homes and shipped them far away, many to their deaths. In addition, they were heathen Protestants. He considered most Americans to be really English and, therefore, worthy of his dislike. The Spaniards were devious. And for all his pride in his Acadian heritage, a poor farm boy was inconceivable for his *belle* Anne-Marie.

Anne-Marie spent a great deal of her time with her relations in New Orleans. Her father knew she needed female companionship, and as he had no interest in remarrying, his late wife's sister became her example of womanly virtues. This was agreeable to Anne-Marie, for she loved the Melançons with all her heart. Still, she was lonely for the company of people her own age.

So Anne-Marie, as was her wont, sat quietly in the shadows on the gallery outside her bedroom, thinking of nothing and everything. A noise from the street interrupted her musings, and she looked out to see a tall officer in a blue uniform.

An American, she thought. He had broad shoulders and dark hair, and he moved with an easy grace down the sidewalk. But most striking was his stature. *He is almost as tall as Samson, I think.* She shamelessly drank in his features.

Suddenly, the officer stopped dead in his tracks. To her embarrassment, Anne-Marie realized he had caught sight of her. The young man stood there, on the opposite sidewalk, staring up at her. Anne-Marie knew she should turn away, but she could not. His full face was visible in the glow from the oil lamps, and it was a handsome one. Moreover, his blue eyes captured hers, even from such a distance.

Anne-Marie forgot to breathe. For a time, the two simply stared at one another.

"Mademoiselle?" came a soft voice from behind.

Startled, Anne-Marie turned to her maid, a young slave named Clementine. "What is it?"

"It is late, *mademoiselle*. Do you not wish to retire?" Clementine's eyes darted to the figure below. She looked up with a smile. "He is handsome, *Oui*?"

Many others would severely reprimand a slave who showed such impertinence, but the Dansereaus were not like other people. They treated their servants and field workers like human beings, to the resentment of their neighbors. Perhaps that was why Dansereau slaves were more loyal than most. Anne-Marie only blushed and nodded. She looked over her shoulder to the street one last time.

The soldier was gone.

She sighed. *"Oui*—very handsome, indeed."

Chapter 2

Major James Fitzwilliam, British Army, walked to the side of the barge, straightened his dirty red uniform coat, and took hold of the accommodation ladder before him. With practice gained from doing this exercise countless times, he waited until the swell reached its zenith before he scampered up the ladder. He quickly reached the deck of *HMS Imprudent*, an old ship-of-the-line converted into a troop transport. There was no salute; they had come to the informal leeward side rather than the official starboard, and the ship's captain was nowhere in evidence.

Not that James gave a right damn about that. There was only one person he wished to see, and she did not disappoint.

"Jamie," cried Margaret Fitzwilliam before she embraced him openly on the deck.

Years before, James would have reminded his wife that it was unseemly for a lady to engage in such public displays of affection. And she would have reminded him that it was of no matter as *she* was not a lady. Now, James gratefully acquiesced to the ordeal of having his dear Margaret's arms around him.

"Meg, I am dirty—please," he murmured.

"And what do I care about that? You came back to me." In their present existence of army officer and camp follower, they had learned to speak in low tones, the only privacy assured from living in close quarters with others. "Come, love, we will get you cleaned up straight away."

Hand-in-hand, the pair made their way below decks, ignoring the stares—amused, offended, or resentful—directed at them. Soon they were in the relative seclusion of their cloth-walled cabin, where Margaret set upon divesting her husband of his filthy clothing. Naked, James stood in a shallow, wide tub submitting to a sponge bath with salt water. Once he was as clean as possible, Margaret directed her husband to their small bed, set hard against the hull of the ship. She then removed her own clothing and began his real welcome home.

LATER, AS THE PAIR LAY intertwined, James thought again of how fate had brought them there.

James Fitzwilliam was the youngest of the Earl of Matlock's three sons. He loved farming and longed to stay and help increase the prosperity of his father's lands. Unfortunately for James, that duty fell to his eldest brother, Andrew, the viscount, and since no son of an earl could be a steward, it was the army, the navy, or the church for James. He reluctantly joined the infantry like his brother Richard. Richard was very good at fighting and eventually became a colonel. But James saw the army as his duty, not his profession.

There was another reason James was loath to go to war: he had fallen in love. Margaret Smith was the pretty daughter of one of his father's tenants. She was a lively and lusty farm girl, but chaste, all the same. They became acquaintances as youths, James often meeting and talking to Margaret during his rides about the estate. Friendship flared into attraction as Margaret grew into womanhood. No shrinking violet was she; her frank and slightly challenging look as he appreciated her face and figure stirred him like no other woman. The vapid and simpering ladies the countess constantly threw in his way were but candle flames compared to the bonfire that was Miss Smith.

The events on the day everything fell apart were unintended but should have been foreseen. James had received his purchased captain's commission and orders for the Peninsula, and he only meant to say goodbye to Margaret. Both knew marriage was impossible, and both thought they were prepared for the final break. Both were wrong. Mutual love and mutual desire was too strong. They took each other's virginity in a shaded glen, calling out each other's name in their pleasure. The sweet caresses and lingering kisses afterwards only made discovery that much more painful, as a hunting party found them *in flagrante delicto*.

The families were outraged. The Fitzwilliams demanded James give up the girl and marry a proper lady as soon as possible. The Smiths were livid at their daughter's immoral actions and wanted to throw her out of their house. Margaret's family expected to receive monetary compensation for their loss of a daughter, and the earl was of a mind to pay it.

What shocked all was the couple's determination to stay together. James swore he would marry Margaret, and she would not leave him. Threats and cajoling did not move the young people. The die was cast. Finally, a decision was made: the two would marry quietly. James would receive the portion of his mother's dowry upon her death and his commission in the army. Other than that, not a penny more could be expected. As for the Smiths, in their shame of a daughter's fall and anger over the loss of funds, they declared their daughter dead to them and warned that any letter received would be burned unread. James and Margaret were on their own.

With no other option, Margaret Fitzwilliam traveled with her captain to Portugal and became, for all intents, a camp follower. The skills learned from her mother served her well, and she was in much demand as a seamstress. Rough living was no difficulty for her, and James knew many were jealous that he had his wife for company in his tent.

Through Portugal and Spain and into France, Captain Fitzwilliam fought under Field Marshal Wellesley, Marquess of Wellington. James's intelligence had caught the attention of his commanding officers, and those who were not concerned with offending Lord Matlock, such as General Robert Ross, used him as an aide.

James was happy with Margaret, and while the army was not always to his liking, he was satisfied with his success. James knew his rise was due to his abilities and not to any influence from his estranged parents. His connection with Andrew was non-existent. As for his relationship with Richard, it was complicated. *Colonel* Fitzwilliam was proud of his brother, but Richard Fitzwilliam, second son of an earl, could not acknowledge his brother's marriage. Their last conversation in France had been painful.

March, 1814: Orthez, France

CAPTAIN FITZWILLIAM HAD BEEN SUMMONED to Colonel Fitzwilliam's tent. He stood at attention, resolutely refusing to look his brother in the face.

Finally, Richard sighed. "Sit down, James. It is good to see you."

James sat in a chair opposite the desk. "This is new. You have not spoken to me in over three years."

"What would have been the purpose?" asked Richard. "Nothing has changed."

"Then what is the purpose of this interview?"

"I wanted to see how you got on. I have missed you."

James was incredulous. "You missed me? Not enough to seek me out."

"That was impossible before, with your—" Richard caught himself, but James knew he was going to say *your wife*. "Father has forbidden it."

"So what has changed?"

"My position, for one. A commander of a regiment can do things a lower ranked officer cannot."

"Including acknowledging his wayward brother?"

"Frankly, yes. Allow me to wish you joy on your promotion to major. I also wanted you to know everyone at home is well—Father, Mother, Andrew, Eugenie. The Darcys, too. By the way, Darcy has married."

James was surprised by how much he still cared that his family was in good health. "I thought I heard Darcy married and not to

Anne de Bourgh. Who is she?"

"No one of our acquaintance. The lady is from a small village in Hertfordshire."

"No society beauty? I suppose the family was outraged over that."

Richard colored. "No. The family quite likes her, actually—except for Aunt Catherine, of course."

All of James's resentment over his rejection returned. "So *Prince Darcy* gains approval while I am thrown out of the family!" James rose and stomped over to a window.

"Of course," Richard said in a louder voice. "Darcy's wife is the daughter of a gentleman while yours is not. Do you have any idea of the scandal your marriage caused? We tried to stop the gossip, but it still got out. Several of Father's friends will not so much as speak to him in the Lords."

James knew how important it was to his father to have influence in the House of Lords. "I did not know. You may not believe this, but I did not do what I did to inconvenience the family."

Richard held up his hand. "Let us not go into *that* again. I just wanted to see you before you left."

James calmed down a bit, and then a thought occurred to him. "You knew I was to leave the brigade and of my promotion to major. How?" A suspicion grew. "Did you have something to do with it?"

Richard would not meet his eyes, and that said volumes.

"I suppose I should thank you."

Richard shrugged. "General Ross wanted my opinion, and I gave it. I would just as soon see you safe."

"Safe fighting Americans?"

"They cannot be worse than Bonaparte's finest."

There was nothing else to say. "I must go and prepare for our departure. Believe it or not, it was good to see you again, Richard."

"Safe voyage, James. My best to your wife."

The acknowledgement was unexpected. "Thank you. Farewell, Richard. God keep you."

September 1, 1814: HMS Imprudent

"JAMIE," SAID MARGARET, BREAKING HIS recollections, "are you well?"

He smiled at her. "Very well, now that I am here."

She kissed him fiercely. "All I want is to have you in my arms forever, Jamie. Poor Mrs. Ross! Can you talk about what happened? We thought all was well when you took Washington."

James stared at the beams above their bed. She knew he liked to talk things out; it helped give him peace.

"Everything went wrong, Meg," he began. "The whole operation was to punish the Americans for burning York by doing likewise to Washington. But we overreached, and we paid for it.

"It started well. We faced a superior force at Bladensburg, but we routed them with the bayonet. Washington fell into our hands undefended. As ordered, we put their capitol and presidential mansion to the torch, along with other government buildings. None of the private houses, though; we had strict orders about that.

"However, a storm blew up—as fierce a storm as I have ever seen. Some said it was a cyclone, others a hurricane. All I knew is that it put the fear of death in all of us. It put out the flames, too."

"I know," said Margaret. "We were terrified; we all thought the ship would flounder."

"Thank God it did not!" He kissed her forehead and continued. "That should have been the end to it. We had avenged York with hardly any casualties. But that was not enough for Admiral Cochrane! Oh, no! He and Admiral Cockburn talked Ross into attacking Baltimore—said it would be easy pickings. How wrong they were!

"It was a two-pronged attack. The army moved northwards towards North Point and Baltimore while Cochrane's gunboats set sail for Baltimore Harbor. But the navy did not keep up with us. Before North Point, a sharpshooter with one of their infernal rifles shot poor General Ross. Colonel Brooke assumed command, and while we were able to drive the Yankee militia back at some cost to ourselves, Brook was no Ross.

"The next day, the navy finally began their bombardment of the Baltimore fort—Fort McHenry, I think was its name. Brooke had us advance to the Americans' next line of defense but only attacked halfheartedly. We fell back when it was apparent that Cochrane's bombardment was failing.

"Over four hundred casualties, Meg! Almost a hundred men killed, including General Ross, and all for nothing except a few burned-out buildings!" He lowered his voice to a whisper. "It was not a great day for Britain, I can tell you that."

Margaret hugged him. "Oh, Jamie, I'm so sorry. But what happens now? Do we go back to Bermuda or home? Do you know?"

James shook his head. "No, we are not going home. After the battle, I found out that the Chesapeake campaign was more than revenge for York. It was a diversion."

"What do you mean?"

"We are engaged in an invasion of America, love. Admiral Cochrane hates the Americans—they killed his brother at Yorktown during the Rebellion, you know—and he has convinced both the admiralty and the army to strike the Yankees hard. Sometimes, I think Cochrane wants to reconquer America, but I could be wrong.

"In any case, General Sir George Prévost is moving south from Canada into New York as we speak. The Chesapeake action was to keep the Americans' attention on us while Prévost attacks them from the rear."

"So, is the fleet sailing north?"

James was troubled. "No, that's the curious thing about it. Cochrane's got something else in mind for us, and I do not know what it is."

Saturday, September 3: Grande Terre, Louisiana

THE MISSISSIPPI RIVER BASIN IS the largest watershed on the North American continent. The Mississippi, Missouri, and Ohio rivers and their tributaries carry runoff soil from the Appalachian Mountains in the east to the Rocky Mountains in the west. Over the millennia during the annual spring floods, billions of tons of this runoff was deposited and became the extensive delta region that is southern Louisiana—the rich, dark clay farmlands, forests, marshes, and estuaries. The rest of the runoff flowed straight to the Gulf of Mexico into the endless deep off the Continental Shelf.

This material had an effect upon the waters of the Gulf. Rather than the crystal-clear blues and greens of the Caribbean, the seas off eastern Louisiana are a milky green, rich with nutrients that sustain and nourish the tidal marches and basins that are home to countess fish and other sea life.

This treasure attracted men to harvest that wealth. Many fishermen made their living through honest labor there, but others—like smugglers and privateers—took advantage of the numerous bays and coves to hide their illegal activities.

It was to thwart such men that the Royal Navy built ships like *HMS Sophie*. An 18-gun brig-sloop, she was fast, maneuverable, and powerful for her size. She could sail open oceans and coastal bays with equal ease and could give a good account of herself, even against a small frigate if well captained and crewed. She was the perfect weapon against pirates.

But when *HMS Sophie* dropped anchor one morning off the island of Grande Terre, its mission was not one of destruction but diplomacy.

The captain's gig was lowered into the cloudy seas, the heat of the day already building to near-oppressive levels. It meant little to Commander Nicholas Lockyer, the only master of the *Sophie* since its launch six years before. It would not do for an officer of His Majesty's navy to show discomfort, so he took his place in the boat, dressed in his Number-Two uniform, looking as unperturbed as if he were in the Downs off Foreland. Next to him was Captain McWilliams of the British army. The coxswain raised a white flag of truce and gave the order to push off for shore.

The gig had only gone a little way when they saw a small boat coming out to meet them. Once it was in range, a tall, well-dressed man called out to them from the pirogue.

"Gentlemen! Welcome to *Grande Terre!*"

Commander Lockyer was thankful that the man spoke English. He returned, "I request a meeting with the commandant of Barataria."

"For what purpose?"

"I bring him a proposition to earn freedom for all his people by entering into the service of Great Britain."

The man flashed a grin beneath his well-trimmed beard. "I see. Such important business is best discussed with a full belly. Come; allow me to have you as my guests for breakfast."

"Your guests?" Lockyer raised an eyebrow. "Do I have the honor of addressing Captain Lafitte?"

The man removed his hat and bowed from his seat. "Your servant, sir! Allow me to introduce my companion, Captain Dominique You." Captain You, a short, dark, swarthy brute, wore a scowl under his small moustache.

If Lockyer was surprised that this cultured man was the feared pirate Jean Lafitte, he did not show it. He nodded in acknowledgement, and the two boats pulled towards shore.

Chapter 3

On Sundays, Matthew's choice of church was simple. He was Roman Catholic, and St. Louis Cathedral was adjacent to the *Place d'Armes*. Jacob's decision was complicated. A Protestant, he found no choice of a house of worship other than with the Episcopalians, and they did not even have a church; their services were held in public buildings. Jacob's upbringing leaned more towards the Methodists, and he deliberated not going to services at all before giving in to his Christian duty.

At the appointed hour, the two comrades walked from the barracks together. Jacob made for the Cabildo, where Christ Church was performing services, while Matthew entered the cathedral next door.

Matthew sat in the rear of the church, allowing the Latin, spoken and sung, to flow over him. He could not help glancing about the place. The congregation, as expected, was mixed. Wealthy families sat in the front pews while the modest and poor were towards the back. A few slaves—personal servants, Matthew assumed—stood and knelt in the back corners. Except for the homily—in French —it was quiet and mysterious, just as Mass always seemed to him.

As Matthew approached the communion rail to receive the host, he noticed a familiar face in the forward pews. Henri Herbert knelt next to a very pretty young lady. With a jolt, Matthew recognized her as the girl up on the gallery from his first night in Louisiana. At that instant, she glanced up, caught his eye, and it was the scene in the street all over again. Fascinated by her dark, lovely gaze, he nearly tripped on the kneeler before the rail. He tore his attention away from the enticing siren long enough to receive the Eucharist from the priest. When he proceeded back to his place, the girl held her head down in prayer, so he could only enjoy her lovely profile.

Matthew was supposed to pray after communion, but all he could think about was having Herbert introduce him to the lady. His only apprehension was the nature of his new friend's connection to her. Was she a sister or relation, or was there a romantic link? Torn by hope and uncertainty, he was impatient for the service to end.

Finally Mass ended, and Matthew quickly made his way from the church. He watched the rest of the congregation exit, and fortune was with him. Herbert's party left by the main doors of the cathedral, and Matthew swiftly approached. As it turned out, Herbert was looking for him.

"Ah, Major Darcy!" he cried in French. "I thought I saw you."

"Indeed." The two shook hands. "It is good to see you again so soon."

"Let me introduce you to my friends." Herbert turned to his companions. Besides the enticing young lady, he was accompanied by a middle-aged couple, a portly gentleman, and a young slave girl.

"My uncle, M. Philippe Melançon, and his charming wife, Mme Madeline Girard Melançon. *Ma mère* was a Melançon, you see. This gentleman is my cousin and neighbor, M. Emile Dansereau, and this," he smiled, "is his daughter, Mlle Anne-Marie Dansereau. *Mes amis, je vous présente le* Major Matthew Darcy."

Matthew clicked his heels and bowed his head. *"Madame, ma-demoiselle, Messieurs, votre serviteur."*

Herbert laughed. "Ah, Major, you are showing off! I assure you we all understand English and speak it too." He turned to M. Dansereau. "Well, most of us."

M. Dansereau scowled. "Enough of your *folie*, Henri," he growled.

Herbert looked particularly untroubled by M. Dansereau's reprimand, and Matthew again wondered about their relationship.

Herbert turned back to him. "And where is your *bon ami*, Major

Harville?" Told he was at the Christ Church services, Henri laughed again. "I should have known he was a Huguenot!"

The others looked slightly embarrassed at Henri's exhibition. Mme Melançon changed the subject. "And what brings you to New Orleans, Major?"

"General Jackson sent us to see to the defenses of the city, *madame*."

M. Dansereau frowned. "He has concerns?"

Matthew was diplomatic. "He is being cautious, *monsieur*."

"Then you are welcome here, Major," cried M. Melançon. "Are you available for dinner this afternoon?" He looked to his wife. "Have we enough for another at table, Madeline?"

"Oh, Philippe, do not insult me so!" she said in good humor. "Of course, I do."

Matthew was taken aback. "I would not wish to intrude."

"Nonsense!" replied Herbert. "You must come."

"I am not alone. Major Harville—"

"Is invited, as well," Herbert interjected. "Is that not correct, Uncle?"

Melançon nodded. "We would be pleased to have you both join us."

"Please, Major," Mlle Dansereau spoke for the first time, "you are here to help us. Let us return the favor."

The lady's musical voice settled things for Matthew. "I am at your disposal."

Anne-Marie was at the dressing table of the bedroom she used when visiting her uncle's house, having Clementine do her hair for the third time. Normally Anne-Marie was not particular about her appearance, but today she wanted to look her best at dinner.

There was a knock at the door. "May I come in, *chérie*?" Herbert asked as he came into the room.

"There seems little reason to deny you, as you are already here," Anne-Marie observed, her attention fixed on her maid's work. "*Non*, it must be tighter, Clementine."

Herbert ignored her jibe. "You are spending more time than usual at your looking glass, *chérie*. Could it be you wish to impress someone?"

"Do not be foolish, Henri. *Non*, Clementine! The pearl comb, please."

Herbert leaned against an armoire, wearing a smirk. "Certainly I am a fool, but I am not blind. Major Darcy is very handsome, *n'est-ce pas?*"

Anne-Marie's blush was visible even with the rouge on her cheeks. "Is he? I did not notice."

"I will wager Clementine did." He turned to the maid. "What do you say?"

"He is very handsome," Clementine said with a giggle.

Anne-Marie huffed. "Very well! I will admit to noticing Major Darcy, and I suppose he is handsome enough." She turned to Herbert. "What good would that do me? You know how my father is."

Henri examined his fingernails. "Does not my good cousin return to Dansereau after dinner?"

"*Oui*, he does."

"And you remain here with our uncle." He raised his eyebrows.

"Henri! You cannot expect me to go behind Papa's back!"

"Did I say such a thing? But what he does not know cannot hurt him. I shall see you downstairs." Herbert bowed and left the room.

Anne-Marie huffed as she returned to her mirror. "Henri and his foolishness," she grumbled. "Ah, my hair will have to do, Clementine. Fetch my wrap, please."

The heat of the day was finally starting to fade when the two American officers were announced. Anne-Marie rose to her feet, her eyes seeking those of Major Darcy. How surprised she was to meet the tall, handsome soldier who galvanized her only a few weeks ago. Never before had she felt such an attraction for a young man.

A moment passed, and his blue eyes were caught by her dark ones. There it was—that strange connection! Like a charge, it ran through her. Her fingers tingled. She flushed so much she was certain she was red as a rose.

His eyes widened. Did he know? Did he feel the same?

Another instant and it was gone. Major Darcy paid his compliments to her aunt and uncle, as well as her father and cousin, before he reached her. By then, Anne-Marie could offer her hand in welcome with tolerable calmness, but she felt a heat course through their gloves. Did she imagine it?

"*Bonjour*, Major Darcy," she managed.

"*Bonjour*, Mlle Dansereau." He turned to the others. "Allow me to introduce my companion, Major Jacob Harville."

She tore away her gaze from Major Darcy. Major Harville was very different from the tall, serious, dark-haired officer who had haunted her dreams. The shorter gentleman had a ruddy face and sandy, unkempt hair. His air and grin were of confidence and amiability. Anne-Marie liked him immediately.

"Evening, Mrs. Melançon," he said in a strong drawl. "Erm… *bonjour, madame*." His French was horrible.

Anne-Marie could not help but laugh lightly, holding her hand over her mouth. From the corner of her eye, she saw that her father was not amused.

Her aunt put the poor man at ease at once. "Good evening, Major!" she replied. "Please, do not feel uncomfortable. Most of us speak English. You are very welcomed here."

"Thank you kindly, ma'am. Sorry I don't speak your language. Why, Matt here says I barely speak English!"

Matt? Anne-Marie thought. *For Matthew?* She smiled softly as she gazed at Major Darcy. *Yes, the name suits him.*

The group removed to the dining room almost immediately. M. Dansereau was to return to his plantation after dinner and wanted to leave while it was still light. Anne-Marie sat to her uncle's left, her father beside her. Across the table were the three young men, Henry flanked by the two American officers. Anne-Marie was pleased to see Matthew Darcy was directly opposite her.

As the soup was served, Mme Melançon asked Major Harville about his family. The Tennessean spoke at length while Herbert translated for M. Dansereau. He had a large family in Nashville; he claimed three brothers and four sisters. There was a sweetheart, too. A girl from a neighboring farm was promised to him.

"She must miss you," said Mme Melançon.

"She surely does, ma'am. I write Fanny every week, but it ain't —beg pardon, I mean, it is not the same." He took out a small miniature and opened the cover. "We had this done when I went off with Colonel Jackson—General Jackson, now."

Mme Melançon took it. "She is very pretty," she said as she passed it to M. Dansereau.

"Yes, ma'am. Prettiest girl in Davidson County."

The girl was pretty, Anne-Marie thought, but the cameo brought an unsettled conjecture to her. Did Matthew Darcy have a sweetheart back in his hometown—or worse, a wife?

"What is your mission here?" M. Melançon asked while the soup was replaced by their dinner. "We hear many rumors."

Harville grinned. "In the army, we call that intelligence. General Jackson is concerned 'bout the intentions of the British. New Orleans is an obvious target, so he sent Major Darcy and me to see how things were. Matt here's the expert in logistics and supply. Me, I know enough 'bout engineering to inspect the fortifications."

M. Dansereau leaned forward, concerned. "*Et qu'est-ce que vous avez trouvé?*"

Herbert offered a translation, and Harville repeated it around a bite. "What have I found? Not much so far, Mr. Dansereau, not much at all. Forts St. John and Petites Coquilles need more guns and men. I haven't been down to Fort St. Philip yet, but I'll wager things are pretty much the same there. There's nothing to the west of town, or east, neither 'cept Fort St. Charles, which is hardly worth its name. I hate to say it, but New Orleans is nearly undefended."

M. Melançon turned to Major Darcy. "And what have your inquiries unearthed?"

He set down his fork. "You have a small corps of militia, *monsieur*, nowhere near enough to mount a defense. You need more men and better training."

"I told you, Philippe!" cried Dansereau. "I said *les Créoles* would stand by and do nothing!"

"Emile," replied Melançon in a tone that indicated they had this discussion before, "I would remind you I am Creole, and I would do something if I were younger. I do not listen to Marigny."

Anne-Marie saw Harville and Darcy exchange glances.

M. Dansereau turned his attention upon Herbert. "And you, Henri, what are you doing?"

Herbert shrugged. "That remains to be seen, Cousin, as the English are not here. In the meantime, I have business that needs my attention."

"I suppose you mean your house in the *Faubourg Marigny*," he practically sneered.

The young Creole's face became frozen. "That is one of my concerns, *Oui*."

A quarrel was coming, Anne-Marie knew. She spoke up. "Major Darcy! Your friend has told us of his family, but what of yours? Where do they live?"

To her surprise, the young officer seemed hesitant to speak. "I was raised in Maryland, *mademoiselle*, on a farm not far from Baltimore. My half-brother still lives on the farm, and my sister married a man in Philadelphia. Our mother, you see, was my father's second wife. They both are gone now."

"We are sorry to hear that," said Mme Melançon. "Is that all of your family?"

"Yes," Darcy answered shortly.

Anne-Marie noticed a grim expression on Major Harville's face. *Oh, dear, I think we stumbled across a painful subject! Think of something else!* "Your French is very good, Major."

"*Merci beaucoup*. My mother spoke French, and I studied languages in college."

Harville barked out a laugh. "That comes in mighty handy 'round here."

"True enough," said Herbert dryly. "He translates Tennessean for us."

It took Harville a moment to catch on. "Ha! You're sure right 'bout that, Henri!"

The rest of the meal passed in pleasant conversation. The only member of the party who did not participate was M. Dansereau. Anne-Marie hoped the young officers would overlook her father's rudeness. She had long known of his abhorrence of the English and, by extension, their new American counterparts. She had to be happy that he did not start an argument with their guests. He had done so before.

Consequently, when she saw her father off in his carriage back to the family plantation, it was with unaccustomed relief. She hurried back inside her uncle's house, hoping to speak more with the young gentlemen, particularly Major Darcy. Unfortunately, her aunt had other ideas.

"*Ma chérie*, will you play for us?" The pianoforte was before her.

Anne-Marie suppressed a sigh as she took her place before the instrument. She decided on a simple country song she knew well. She did not want to make a mistake, for that would defeat her aunt's obvious intention of promoting Anne-Marie's accomplishments. Besides, she did want to make a good impression on Major Darcy!

The song completed successfully, if the applause was any indication, Anne-Marie moved to sit next to her aunt, which just happened to be the closest seat to Major Darcy's chair. The next half-hour was given over to their guests' impressions of New Orleans. Major Harville was very amusing, but it was clear he was not comfortable with the city.

"It's a strange town," he had said, "almost like they done sent me to a foreign land. It's nothing like Nashville, that's for sure!"

"You are right, Jacob, New Orleans *is* different," responded Major Darcy. "But I have to admit I like the place. The people, the culture" —he smiled at Mme Melançon—"the food. I find it fascinating."

Harville laughed good-naturedly. "That's because you're a Papist that speaks the lingo, Matt. Me, I'm a fish out of water."

It was time for the young gentlemen to leave. Anne-Marie said farewell to Major Harville, then turned to Major Darcy. "I enjoyed our conversation, Major. I hope we meet again soon.

His blue eyes grew dark. "I would like that very much, *mademoiselle*

—very much, indeed." He turned his head towards her uncle. "May I have your permission to call again?"

In answer to Uncle Melançon's questioning look, Anne-Marie gave a slight nod. "Of course, Major, whenever your duties allow."

Aunt Melançon jumped in. "Oh, the food the army serves must be dreadful! You must come back for dinner—you, too, Major Harville! Perhaps on Wednesday?"

Major Darcy looked so adorably surprised that Anne-Marie had to bite her lip to stop from giggling. "I...I would not want to impose—"

Harville clapped his comrade on the back. "Hold your horses there, Matt. Mrs. Melançon, we would be happy to come—right, Matthew?" This earned a laugh from Herbert.

Anne-Marie was thrilled that Major Darcy turned back to her as he said, "Thank you; we will come, if we can."

"And if we can't, we'll just sneak out!" Harville claimed. "You set a mighty fine table, ma'am!"

Herbert took his leave of Anne-Marie as the two officers were talking to M. Melançon. "Ah, I am overturned for a couple of Americans! You pain me, *chérie*!"

"You know you are welcomed too, Henri."

"*Non*, I would just be in the way. Enjoy your Major Darcy, Cousin."

"He is not *my* Major Darcy."

"But he could be." Herbert held her shoulders. "Seek your happiness, *chérie*."

"As you have done? Is it worth it, Henri?"

Pain flowed across her cousin's face. "I cannot live otherwise. Good night."

DARKNESS WAS FALLING AS THE two friends walked to the barracks.

Jacob interrupted his tuneless whistling with, "That Miss Dansereau is a right pretty girl, ain't she?"

"Yes, she is. What of it?"

"Don't play the innocent with me, Matthew Darcy! You couldn't tear your eyes off her the whole night. That's the first gal you've gone googley over since I met you."

Matthew said nothing, and Jacob added, "She likes you, you know."

"What?" Matthew cried. "How do you know?"

"Because she had the same look on her face that Fanny did when we was courtin'." He spat on the street. "Damn, I miss her. Gonna write her when we get back to our rooms."

"Why didn't you two get married when you had the chance?"

"Because she'd want to come with me, and she's too fine a girl to be a camp follower."

"It's not so bad here. You could have her come and get married in New Orleans."

Jacob grew very quiet. "I wonder if she'd come."

"Don't you think so?"

Jacob shook his head. "Of course, she'd *want* to come. But her folks, I'm not so sure they'd let her."

"Isn't she of age? Couldn't she come without their permission?"

"Yeah…maybe." The two walked on for a bit.

"Are you going to write Fanny and ask?"

"Gotta think it over. How about you? You gonna chase after that Miss Dansereau?"

"If she'll let me," Matthew admitted.

Chapter 4

A week later, Governor Claiborne's office was astounded to receive a letter from, of all people, the privateer Jean Lafitte. Attending a special meeting convened by the governor to deliberate the shocking news contained within were the governor's secretary, leaders from the legislature, and representatives from the military, including Matthew and Jacob.

Jacques Philippe Villeré, planter, Creole politician, and General of the Militia, had stood for governor in the last election. He took his loss to Claiborne like a statesman and generally worked well with the prickly governor. He was a leader of the legislature's Committee of Safety.

Edward Livingston, wealthy lawyer and businessman, was the brother of the man who helped negotiate the Louisiana Purchase. Resented by some due to his participation in the Mississippi steamboat monopoly enjoyed by his family, he was nevertheless a great legal scholar and Claiborne's most trusted advisor.

Two men of the navy were there. Commander Daniel Todd Patterson, Commodore of the New Orleans Squadron, was an exceptionally gifted sailor, known for his diligence and zeal. With him was his very able subordinate, Lieutenant Thomas ap Catesby Jones.

The crowded room was still as the secretary read Lafitte's words. For his part, Matthew was horrified. The British had tried to enlist Lafitte and his pirates to throw in with them and attack New Orleans from the south. He glanced at the map on the wall.

The island of Grande Terre, south of New Orleans, was the gateway from the Gulf of Mexico to Barataria Bay. The bay thrust northward, offering a route to the west bank of the Mississippi River. With a jolt, Matthew remembered what Jacob had observed: all of the city's major defenses were on the east bank or Lake Pontchartrain. Only Fort St. Leon at English Turn downriver of the city, a puny wooden stockade, stood between an invading army on the west bank and New Orleans.

Jacob noticed his attention. "The bastards could cut off Fort St. Philip or lay siege to it, our only strong point on the river," he whispered, "and they'd have the city at the mercy of their guns in the time it takes to skin a squirrel. This here is serious—if it's for real."

The secretary finished, and Claiborne spoke. "As you see, Lafitte wants to help defend the city. His price is pardon for himself and his men and to have the right to continue their activities with no interference."

"That is outrageous!" cried one of the legislators. "This audacious rascal plays us for fools! This is a ruse to have us release his brother, Pierre, from jail and make us look ridiculous!"

"What do you other gentlemen advise?" asked Claiborne. "He has sent not only his letter, but papers alleged to be from the British. Are these documents genuine, and if so, would it be proper for the governor to enter into correspondence with pirates?"

"Governor, Lafitte is no pirate," said General Villeré. "He is a privateer. He does not make war on our ships but on the English and Spanish."

"And that should be permitted?" cried another, a Creole of Spanish heritage.

"It is legal if he has letters of marque," Villeré explained. "Unfortunately, he cannot bring his prizes legally into the country. Their only crime is that they dispose of their prizes in violation of the law, and this he freely admits. The United States is their adopted country, and they see it threatened by an enemy they hate—an enemy we all hate." He pointed to the stack of papers. "These documents are true. We must trust the Baratarians."

"Bah! Lafitte never told the truth in his life!"

Commodore Patterson stood. "I must agree with the gentleman. I remind you my instructions from the Secretary of the Navy are to disperse the Baratarian association. The schooner *USS Carolina*, the most powerful ship in the squadron, has been sent here for that purpose. I fully intend to carry out these instructions." He retook his seat with great finality.

Claiborne's eyes turned to Livingston. The chairman of the committee cleared his throat. "It is tempting to believe this tale, but Lafitte is charming and deceitful always. Besides, these broadsheets are incredible." He picked up one. *"Assist us in your liberation from a faithless, imbecile government… Europe is happy and free, and France is now Britain's ally with the tyrant exiled."* He chuckled. "Now, Europe may be many things, but free? With all their kings and princes, I think not." He picked up another broadsheet. "Look at this one, for the people of Kentucky. *After the experiences of twenty-one years, can you any longer support those brawlers for liberty?'* Outlandish! I cannot believe these are from the British."

Matthew saw Jacob look up.

Livingston concluded, "My friend Villeré, I must disagree with you. These cannot be the genuine issue. These are counterfeits, and so is the pirate's offer."

Villeré protested, and the meeting continued in debate, but the outcome was not in doubt. A vote was taken, and except for General Villeré, the committee rejected Lafitte's proposal and ordered Commodore Patterson to clean out the pirates at the earliest opportunity.

As the two army officers returned to barracks, Matthew saw that Jacob was troubled. At his inquiry, Jacob frowned.

"While Mr. Livingston read that there broadsheet, I recollected the British officer we captured during the Creek War. I was the one who interrogated him, and he said something that struck me strange. He pointed out that most of us Tennesseans came from England and Scotland. He was puzzled, you see, and asked, bold as brass, how we could support those 'brawlers for liberty from

Massachusetts.'"

A chill went down Matthew's back. "He said that?"

"Them very words." Jacob looked at his friend, concern clear on his face. "I should've said something, but I felt it wasn't my place."

Matthew nodded. Junior officers did not offer opinions unless requested.

"I'm afeared we made a mistake, Matt. That broadsheet was for real, and so was that pirate's offer."

Matthew was grim. "So, what do we do?"

"We ain't got enough men to guard every entry point; you know that. We got to be vigilant, I reckon."

Friday, September 16: Grande Terre

TWO WEEKS HAD PASSED SINCE the Royal Navy's uninvited visit to Barataria. Jean Lafitte knew his time was almost up. He could put off the British no longer. They were to return to Grande Terre, he knew, and he did not plan to be there when they did.

So when a flotilla of warships dropped anchor off Lafitte's outpost, the famous buccaneer was not in residence, having fled with many of his people, most of his arms and ammunition, and all of his treasure. Left behind to welcome the British was the redoubtable Dominique You and his best gun crews.

But, to the Baratarians' surprise, the flags flying from the sterns of the ships were not the Union Jack; they were the Stars and Stripes. Commodore Patterson had come calling, and he was not of a mind to leave a single building standing when he left.

Dominique You reacted immediately. He had planned to give as good a fight as he could against the Royal Navy before withdrawing. Now, things were different. The Baratarians wanted peace with the Americans, and many looked forward to the day when they would give up the sea. Louisiana was to be their home, but they needed pardons from the government. Opening fire on American gunboats would be a very poor manner of inspiring trust and forgiveness. Dominique You would not shoot at Patterson's squadron.

Instead, he and his men set their warehouses and boats on fire and waited for the American authorities. He and eighty of his men were taken prisoner. Patterson's men were as resolute as their commander. Working quickly, they were able to salvage several of the Baratarians' boats and their precious cannons. The Americans then completed the job of destroying Lafitte's base on the Gulf before returning to New Orleans with their captives.

Ironically, the British never returned to Grande Terre. Having waited far offshore for two weeks and receiving nothing from Jean Lafitte but silence, Captain Lockyer came to the realization that the pirate had played him for a fool. He turned his back on Louisiana and set sail for the Spanish port of Pensacola, never knowing of the American Navy's destruction of Lafitte's empire.

Monday, September 26: New Orleans

JACOB TOSSED HIS HAT ONTO his cot as he strode into the room he shared with Matthew. "Damn if'n I wasn't right. We're in for it now."

Matthew looked up from writing his latest report. "What are you talking about?"

"Remember Patterson burning out Lafitte a week ago 'cause we thought he was lying?" Jacob sat heavily on his cot. "Well, Mr. Livingston got ahold of a letter from Havana—word is he got it from that Lafitte fella—and this letter says the British are planning an invasion along the Gulf. Massing men and ships, it says. Mr. Livingston's raising hell 'bout it."

"Good God. Could it be a forgery?"

"Mr. Livingston says no." Jacob rubbed his face. "We ain't ready, Matt. We couldn't hold this place from a bunch of Papist choir boys, much less the British Army."

Matthew's throat grew tight. "Are they definitely coming here?"

"That's 'bout the only good thing; it don't say where they're going. If I were a redcoat general, I'd sail right for Mobile—that's the best port on the Gulf—take it, use it as a base, and march overland to New Orleans."

"Oh, hell. General Jackson's in Florida taking on the Spanish and the tribes. I had better put this in my report to him."

"Knowin' Old Hickory, he left a good rear guard in Mobile. We'll scratch up a copy to him."

MATTHEW'S AND JACOB'S EFFORTS CHANGED after that. Rather than inspecting the Crescent City's capabilities in defending itself from a hypothetical invasion, they now energetically labored to build up its defenses against an expected British attack. In this they were joined by Edward Livingston, General Villeré, and other local leaders of the American and Creole factions.

Unfortunately, not everyone believed there was a threat. This skepticism and mistrust crossed ethnic and cultural lines. Creoles, like Bernard de Marigny, considered fears of an invasion overstated and accused the government of fear mongering. Some even secretly hoped for an American defeat, putting their trust in British promises to return Louisiana to France or Spain.

As for the American skeptics, many had a simple reason not to support the government.

"Well, Major Darcy," drawled Wallace Anderson, an American emigrant and trader in his office in the *Faubourg Saint Marie*, "you spin a fancy tale. But I don't see how it affects me."

"I do not understand your opposition, Mr. Anderson. Our country is under attack."

"And whose fault is that?" the trader shot back. "Mr. Madison and the Warhawks started this war, and all it's done is destroy our trade." He pointed out the window. "I have a fortune in cotton and other goods rotting in my warehouses. The Royal Navy's blockade is so tight a rowboat can't get past it. I'm losing money, sir. It's why everyone is buying from that damn pirate Lafitte; he's the only one who can get goods into the city."

"Mr. Lafitte sees the danger, Mr. Anderson. He had alerted us to British intentions. He is with those who wish to defend the city."

"You think he's some sort of patriot? He's just looking out for his neck. The British hang pirates, Major. We only put them in jail —the lesser of two evils and all that. There was no reason for the president to declare war against the greatest power in the world, and we're paying for it."

Matthew lost his temper. "No reason, sir? I suppose the fate of American sailors means that little to you?"

Anderson dismissed his argument with a wave of his hand. "Impressment? They were Englishmen, deserters from the Royal Navy."

"Not all, sir. And they were American citizens."

"Naturalized, perhaps. So for a handful of sailors, we endanger the country? That's a bad bargain for me."

Matthew had one last argument. "What about your fellow New Orleanians? You know what the British will do if they take the city. Remember, they burned Washington."

"My family will be safe."

"And the rest of the city? Not everyone has a plantation to flee to."

"Why should I care about them? They don't care about me," Anderson cried. "You know what they call Canal Street between *Faubourg Saint Marie* and the *Vieux Carré*? The *Neutral Ground* —the dividing line between these so-genteel Creoles and us! We're not good enough to darken their doors. Freedmen, Spaniards—oh, they're fine! To us, it's stay on your side of the Neutral Ground." Anderson spat in a spittoon. "I'll give a damn about them when they give a damn about me. Now, you'll have to excuse me, Major Darcy, I've got work to do. I'm sure you can see yourself out."

Sunday, October 2

MATTHEW ENJOYED AN AFTER-DINNER CIGAR in the Melançon courtyard with his host while the ladies sipped a bit of wine, carefully sitting upwind of the gentlemen. Matthew had become a regular fixture at dinner in the Melançon household. He could be found there several nights a week and after Mass on Sunday, and it was not because of the quality of Mme Melançon's kitchen. It had far more to do with Mme Melançon's niece.

"Major Harville, he is well?" asked M. Melançon. By common agreement, everyone spoke English during Matthew's visits.

Told that he was, Mme Melançon added, "I am sorry we have not seen him recently. You must tell him he is welcomed here, as well."

Matthew's ears reddened as he recalled Jacob's recent remark about visits to Rue Bourbon. *"Nah, you go on without me. Matt. I don't want to get in the way of your courtin'. Hope you appreciate my sacrifice. Mrs. Melançon sets a mighty fine table!"*

He glanced at Anne-Marie. He could not lie to himself. He was courting Mlle Dansereau, and he was very pleased with his progress. It was the highlight of his day to see her pretty face and dancing eyes. Her bright smile every time he walked through her uncle's door did away with any frustration he carried due to the lack of progress in his official duties. He knew he was falling in love with her and hoped she was doing the same.

"I'll be sure to tell him that, ma'am."

"Has the major heard recently from his intended in Tennessee?" Anne-Marie's sweet voice seemed to float in the air.

"He has, Mlle Dansereau. He got a letter just yesterday. Fanny writes regularly."

"This lady, she is very devoted. Major Harville is fortunate."

Matthew nodded. "Devotion is necessary to preserve affection, particularly when one is far away. Nothing lifts a soldier's spirits like a letter from home."

"Devotion must go both ways if the parties involved are to resist temptation." Mme Melançon lifted an eyebrow. Matthew knew a message had just been sent, but he knew not the reason.

"Yes, *madame*. It would not be right for a soldier to expect his wife to be faithful while…err, taking advantage of opportunity, you might say."

Anne-Marie frowned. "Opportunity? What opportunity may tempt a soldier far from home?"

There was no way Matthew was going to answer *that* question. But to his surprise, M. Melançon replied conversationally, "Camp followers, *chérie*. Cooks, laundresses, seamstresses, and the like. Many are wives and families of the soldiers, but many are not and think nothing of offering…comfort to lonely men. They have been with every army since time immemorial—eh, Major?"

Matthew coughed. "Yes, that is true." Apparently, the Creoles were far less circumspect about sexual affairs than most people.

Anne-Marie lifted her chin. "But a righteous man would resist temptation."

For the right woman, he would, Matthew thought, looking Anne-Marie in the eye. "Devotion and righteousness go hand-in-hand, I think."

"And do you value those attributes, sir?"

"Anne-Marie!" her uncle cried. "How can you expect our guest to answer such a question?"

The young beauty lowered her head, and Matthew took pity on her.

"*Mademoiselle* teases me, I think." Matthew gave the girl a big smile. "She knows a gentleman cannot answer her with any satisfaction. Who but a fool or rogue would dismiss those virtues? Yet, a scoundrel would praise them to the skies, all the time leading a life of dissipation. No, *mademoiselle*, I shall not fall into your trap! I shall live my life as I always have, and you must decide for yourself whether I am a villain or an honorable fellow."

Anne-Marie pursed her lips. "And do you have any advice on what to look for to see if a man is upright?"

Matthew relished their banter. "Of course! His profession, for one. I have found officers in the United States Army to be a superior collection of gentlemen."

Anne-Marie laughed. It was not the tightly controlled twitter of the society girls of Baltimore but a full, healthy display of mirth, issued by a lady open and transparent. Matthew's admiration for the girl grew further.

The Melançons shared a look. "Major Darcy, would you be so kind as to join me in my library?" his host asked as he rose to his feet. "There is something I must discuss with you."

"Uncle!" Anne-Marie appeared mortified, and Matthew had an idea what the good man had to say to him.

"I am at your disposal, sir. Ladies." Matthew bowed and followed the gentleman into the house. Once M. Melançon closed the library door behind him, he began.

"Normally, Major, this task would fall to a young lady's father, but as my niece is here under my roof and her father is not, the duty is mine. After *that* exhibition, I must ask your intentions towards her."

Matthew swallowed and felt like a schoolboy called on his bad behavior. "I am sorry, sir. It was not my intention to alarm or insult anyone. I am afraid I got carried away." He gathered his thoughts. "I do admire Mlle Dansereau exceedingly. If things were different, I would have approached M. Dansereau by now. As things now stand, with the enemy possibly targeting the city, personal desires must be set aside."

"I see." The man paced the room. "Are you aware of Anne-Marie's situation?"

"I…no." Matthew was confused. "I know she is an only child, her mother passed away some years ago, and her father owns a farm outside the city."

"Hmm. Young man, Anne-Marie is the only child of a very wealthy man. I understand where you come from it is exceedingly rare for a daughter to be the heir to a great fortune. Here, it is not unusual. There are many who pursue Anne-Marie not for her charms but for Dansereau Plantation."

Affronted, Matthew shot back, "M. Melançon, I do not like your insinuation. I know nothing about this, and I would not give it a moment's thought if I did."

Melançon seemed amused. "Very noble, Major. Tell me, if you were successful in your pursuit of my niece— Ah, do not deny it! Your attentions have been obvious, particularly with regard to the recent conversation in my courtyard tonight!" Matthew could say nothing. "To continue, assuming you won Anne-Marie's affections, how would you support her? Do you plan to take her away to Maryland?"

"I will not return to Maryland. It is not my home any longer."

"Indeed? I thought your family had a farm there."

"My brother has a farm there—or I should say, my half-brother, John. In Maryland, many follow the old practice of leaving the property to the eldest son. My mother was my father's second wife, and my half-brother, jealous of his mother's memory, resented her. Nothing changed when my sister, Mary, and I came along. John disliked us intensely. He refused to accept us no matter how strongly my father admonished him. For a time, he had to be sent away to his mother's family. That did nothing to endear us to him. Once my parents died, John felt free to cut any relationship with Mary and me."

"I am sorry to hear that there is ill will between you and your brother," said Melançon compassionately. "Shall you then live with your sister?"

"I do not think I will. Mary married a good man, and I would be welcomed, but her husband and I do not agree on politics. I support Mr. Jefferson and Mr. Madison, while he, a Federalist, is against all I believe." Darcy offered a small smile. "He is very passionate about his beliefs, and disagreements would be unavoidable. Distance would guarantee a cordial relationship. My sister should not have to choose between us."

"Then what shall you do?"

"Buy a farm, probably in Virginia. My father left me a bit of money."

"So you will take her to Virginia." Melançon stroked his chin. "I must be blunt. You can afford to buy a farm?"

"Yes, I can." Matthew said coolly.

"Your father left you more than a bit, then."

"Twenty thousand dollars."

Melançon gasped. "So, I see you are a wealthy man, too."

"The money came from my mother. Unfortunately, my brother, John, is of the opinion that everything should have gone to him and has pursued my inheritance in the courts. He has been unsuccessful so far, and I have been forced to hide my money in a bank in Virginia under an assumed name. I should be safe from him in Virginia."

"The law is different here," Melançon pointed out. "You would be very safe in Louisiana. Such a suit would be thrown right out of our courts. Many Americans have come down here and bought land for their plantations."

"I have not considered that," said Darcy. "What is raised here?"

"Sugar and indigo, mainly, and more are planting cotton. All these crops require many hands to work the fields, and slaves are expensive." Darcy frowned, which caused Melançon to add, "Does the expense trouble you, or are you uncomfortable with our *peculiar institution?*"

"Both, I think. I grew up with slavery; many large farms have slaves in Maryland. But my family did not, and I admit to some ambivalence about it. So many slaves are cruelly treated."

"I am well aware of that," said Melançon. "My brother-in-law, a kind and generous man, does not mistreat his people, yet he is condemned as a fool by the other planters. *C'est la vie.*" He thought for a moment. "Not all farms require slaves to be profitable. You could raise beef. Meat is always in demand, and you would not need many hands to manage a herd."

"M. Melançon, I thank you for your advice. I had always thought of settling in Virginia when I left the army. I know the people and climate well. I did not know much about plantations in Louisiana, and you have given me much to think about."

"You are a clever man, Major Darcy. I am satisfied you are no fortune hunter."

"I thank you for that." Matthew tried hard not to sound sarcastic.

"Do not take offence, young man! If you knew how many bucks prowl around Anne-Marie, you would appreciate my concerns." He thought for a moment. "I must talk to my niece. For now, you may continue to visit my house, Major Darcy, but I make no promises. The final decision falls to M. Dansereau."

"That is fair. When all these troubles are past, then we can talk of more pleasant matters." He rose and shook hands with Melançon. "Please call me Matthew, or Matt."

"I like you, Matthew," said the older man. "I wish you good luck."

Matthew let himself out of the library, eager to be in Anne-Marie's company again. He did not hear M. Melançon mumble to himself, *"Je crains que vous aurez besoin de chance.[1]"*

---

1 "I am afraid you will need luck."

NIGHT WAS FALLING, AND IT WAS time for Major Darcy to return to his barracks. Anne-Marie silently begged with her eyes to see the officer out alone. After a moment, her aunt nodded her permission. At the front door, she handed Major Darcy his hat.

"Shall we see you on Sunday, Major?"

To her surprise, he took his hat in one hand while holding her hand with the other. "You shall." She held her breath as he raised her hand to his lips. The touch of his kiss upon her knuckles caused her to gasp. "Until Sunday, *mademoiselle*."

"Anne-Marie."

His eyes were as dark as night. "*Excusez-moi?*"

"Anne-Marie," she repeated in the same soft tone.

The decision to request that he call her by her Christian name was impulsive and extremely forward. But something deep within Anne-Marie told her to give Matthew some encouragement. She was losing her heart to him. Did he feel the same? He would not —could not—speak of love unless he was assured she would not be harmed.

His smile lit up the night.

She was relived he was not offended, but the intensity of the moment forced her to turn away. Still, she squeezed his hand. The world stood still.

"Thank you," he breathed. "Until Sunday...*Anne-Marie*."

She thought her heart would burst in her chest. "Until Sunday...*Matthew*."

He kissed her hand again and was gone.

Chapter 5

James Fitzwilliam had just sat down to enjoy the simple dinner Margaret had prepared when there was a knock on the front door of their lodgings. Frowning, for it could only be something serious at that hour, James hurried to answer. He was surprised at his visitor.

"Ah, Major Fitzwilliam," drawled Captain Elliot. "May I come in?"

James stepped aside to allow the man to enter, amazed that a navy captain would call upon him. "To what do we owe the pleasure, sir?"

Elliot ignored his question. "Good evening, Mrs. Fitzwilliam. Oh, I hope I do not disturb your dinner." He smiled. "A fish pie! I have not had that since I left Plymouth."

Margaret bobbed a curtsey, directing a look to her husband. "Would you care to join us, Captain?"

"I have never turned down a fish pie in my life, madam. Thank you." He removed his hat and made himself at home at the table, taking James' place.

Margaret quickly set a new place for James while he poured the wine. "It's not much, sir," Margaret explained. "I have more bread—"

"Capital! Butter, too, if you please."

James noticed Margaret's wince. Butter, like most staples, was dear in Bermuda, something Captain Elliot knew damn well. What was the man about?

Elliot dug in, forcing the Fitzwilliams to do the same. He did not say much, only a few comments about the unseasonably warm weather. Just when James thought he might have to throttle the man, superior officer or no, he got to the point of his visit.

"By the way, Fitzwilliam, we set sail in two days."

Elliot's command, the *Imprudent,* was an old, 50-gun, fourth-rate two-decker, fit only for transport. "I see. Can you tell me where we are bound?"

Elliot patted his lips. "Someplace even warmer than here—Jamaica. We join the whole squadron. Excellent pie, madam!"

The entire squadron? James considered Elliot's statement. *Moving the army to the Caribbean? Why? What is the target?*

The captain interrupted the major's ponderings. "Shall you be going with us, Mrs. Fitzwilliam?"

James jerked up as Margaret pointedly said, "My home is with my husband."

"Excellent. I hoped it would be so." He turned to James. "She plays a superb game of whist, Major, and I must have my partner. We shall continue our rout of the others, shall we not, Mrs. Fitzwilliam?"

Margaret colored as she answered. "As you wish."

The naval officer rose. "You undoubtedly have packing to do. Shame about your lack of servants."

"We manage, sir."

"My man, Caruthers, sees to such things," he said carelessly. "The privileges of rank." To James he added, "Be on board by tomorrow night. We sail with the morning tide." He took his leave and left the house.

James turned to his mortified wife. "What the devil was that about, Meg?"

She did not answer. She would not meet his eye as she cleared the table.

"Playing whist with Captain Elliot? Him inviting himself to our dinner? It's clear you don't like him. What is going on?"

She moved into the small kitchen. "Nothing to worry about—"

"Meg—tell me! Why is Captain Elliot paying you his attentions?"

Margaret turned, her face pale, hands still full of dishes. "You do not think I have anything to do with *that one*, do you?"

"Of course not. But there is something you have not told me. What is it?"

"I have no choice!"

James was astonished. "What do you mean, you 'have no choice'?" He grew angry. "Has he tried to force himself on you?"

"No! Nothing like that!" She placed the dishes on the table with a bang. "Captain Elliot likes to amuse himself by flirting with the officers' wives aboard ship. He did so the entire time the regiment was in Maryland. We keep him happy by teasing back. It's mostly harmless—"

"Mostly?"

Margaret stared out the window. "One of the ladies—Lieutenant Warren's pretty young wife, Elizabeth—was the recipient of his advances. She rejected him—gave him a right set-down it was said. Suddenly, she was moved from her cabin to a hanging cot among the sailors. It frightened the rest of the wives."

James cursed. "Was not the colonel of the regiment told?"

Margaret shrugged. "Who was there to hear our complaint? Poor Warren was killed in battle, and the colonel had more on his mind than some lieutenant's widow. Besides, Elliot's word is law aboard ship. You know that."

James racked his brain. "Meg, you're playing a dangerous game. Elliot is a right bastard. That scrub is a Post Captain of seven years' tenure, but his reputation is so bad the only command he can get is a transport. It took all his influence just to get the *Imprudent*! Men with less seniority are commanding frigates and ships of the line." He paused. "I don't think you should come with us this time."

"No! Don't leave me behind!" She clutched at him. "I want to be with you!"

"Meg, I don't want you on Elliot's ship."

"Don't you trust me?"

"I said I do! It is Elliot I do not trust."

"I do not trust him, either; nor do the other wives. We stay together; we are never alone with him. After Mrs. Warren, we are determined that it should not happen again."

"I do not like it."

"Please do not leave me behind. You promised we would never be apart. You *promised*."

"Meg, I know, but—"

Margaret smiled. "Besides, I know where we are going."

"What? How?"

"All the ladies know; it is New Orleans. We talk amongst ourselves. 'Beauty and booty,' all the sailors say." Margaret narrowed her eyes. "If you think I will leave you alone with all those Creole beauties, you best have another thought!" She touched his arm. "We will be rich when you take the city. Can you not see me dressed like a real lady?"

James had to admit he would like to see that very much if only to stick his success in the face of his estranged family. Still, he had doubts. "Are you sure you will be safe with Elliot?"

"I have been so far," she assured him. "Besides, being a farmer's daughter has its advantages. First of all, I'm too lowborn for him."

James flinched.

"It is true, Jamie. You know it, and it is not such a bad thing. Second"—she grinned—"I know how to geld a bull." She flicked her hand through the air. "That's for him!" She looked into his eyes and grew serous. "My life is with you, Jamie. Do not leave me behind. I beg you."

James knew further argument was pointless. She was determined, and he could deny her nothing. "Very well, Meg. But you must promise you will never be alone with Captain Elliot."

"A promise easily made, love," Margaret exclaimed happily. She gave him a quick kiss. "Now, I must see to the packing."

As his wife dashed to their bedroom, James wondered whether he was making a mistake.

Wednesday, October 12: New Orleans

MATTHEW AND JACOB WERE SURPRISED to find Anne-Marie alone at the pianoforte when they were shown into the Melançons' parlor.

"Your relations are not here?" asked Matthew after he kissed her hand in greeting.

"A friend has taken ill, and they have gone to visit for a short while. It is my aunt's custom to bring a basket of food for the family at such times. They will return in time for dinner." Reluctantly releasing Matthew's hand, she turned to welcome Jacob.

The major glanced between his friend and the young lady with a knowing grin. "Miss Dansereau, I've a hankerin' for a chew. Knowin' Miz Melançon don't cotton to that in the house, I'll just take myself to the front porch if you don't mind."

"Of course not. Enjoy your tobacco, Major."

"Thank you kindly." Jacob winked at Matthew and left the way he came.

Matthew was taken aback. Jacob was leaving him alone with Anne-Marie! Anxiously, he watched to see her reaction. She was clearly nervous, but she had not stepped away from him, and a shy smile graced her lips.

"How was your day, Matthew?" She looked at the pianoforte, the window, anywhere but at him. "Were you able to gather more supplies?"

This was an opportunity he was not going to let pass by. "Anne-Marie." He reached out and gently took her arm. "Please look at me. You do not want to know about my day, do you?"

She licked her plump lips. "No."

He ran his fingertips along her cheek. "You are the most beautiful girl I have ever seen."

She sighed and leaned into his hand.

He drew close, his mouth aching for hers. "Please…"

Her answer was to close her eyes and part her lips. She breathed heavily, her breasts moving enticingly in her gown. A moment later, Matthew tentatively caressed her mouth with his. He drew back a fraction, and her moan in response was all he needed to return and deepen this, their first kiss. He held her by her elbows. Her hands cupped his cheeks. He could feel the heat of her body only inches away. It was the most exquisite torture.

"*Well, howdy, Mr. Melançon—Miz Melançon! Pleasant evening, ain't it?*"

The lovers broke apart at Jacob's warning welcome to Anne-Marie's relations. Matthew walked quickly to the open door of the parlor while Anne-Marie scampered to the pianoforte. Taking a few deep breathes to steady himself, he shot a quick glance at Anne-Marie. To his relief, she was not angry or distressed, only flustered. She returned his gaze with a heart-filled smile.

Matthew grinned, winked, and turned just in time to welcome the Melançons.

THE CITY OF NEW ORLEANS faced the greatest crisis of its existence, but for two people who walked its streets, the dangers were a world away. October brought some small relief from the sweltering heat of a Louisiana summer. The evenings were mild and fine, and the days long enough to enjoy a stroll along the city's avenues. For centuries, poets called young love the sweetest of all, and Matthew and Anne-Marie would never dispute it.

In the halcyon weeks that followed, the lovers were as inseparable as Matthew's duties would allow. He ate at the Melançons every night and attended Mass with them as if he were already part of the family. The two would take long walks though the *Vieux Carré*, the maid Clementine serving as a very inattentive chaperone. The pair spoke of matters great and unimportant, learned each other's histories and favorites, and shared dreams and plans.

Anne-Marie was horrified to learn of his mistreatment at the hands of his stepbrother. Matthew consoled her over the loss of her mother so many years ago. She leant a willing ear for his complaints and frustrations over his efforts to supply the army. He placated her worries by sharing his plans to establish his own farm.

And, when opportunity presented itself, the pair behaved scandalously, stealing kisses and caresses in darkened alleyways, Clementine keeping a sharp lookout for onlookers.

Matthew and Anne-Marie were not stupid people. They knew well the parameters of their class and the expectations of society.

They were breaking the rules; they were aware of it and did not care. The lovers told themselves they were cautious. Anne-Marie was willing, but they never crossed the ultimate barrier. Besides, no one saw them. In the folly of youth, they thought they would never be caught.

Of course, they were.

Monday, October 31

ANNE-MARIE WAS WRITING A LETTER in her room when her aunt came in. "*Ma chérie*, please come downstairs. Your father wishes to speak with you."

"Papa is here? Such a coincidence! I am writing to him." Anne-Marie then noted her aunt's worried countenance. "My dear aunt, what is amiss? Is Papa ill?"

"No, he is well. Come, you must not keep him waiting. He is in your uncle's study."

Puzzled, Anne-Marie made her way to the study. There she found Emile Dansereau seated behind Uncle Philippe's large desk.

"*Bonjour*, Papa!" she said as she moved to his side. "How wonderful to see you! What brings you to New Orleans?" She kissed his cheek, only to receive a cold look in return.

"Sit down, Anne-Marie." He gestured to an armchair close by.

She did as she was asked. "Papa, what is wrong?"

M. Dansereau grimly stared at a paper before him. "I have received a very alarming note about your behavior with a young gentleman."

Anne-Marie blanched.

"It says you have been walking unescorted through the town on the arm of an American officer—Major Darcy, to be exact. There is more here, but I would know if this is true."

Anne-Marie would never lie to her father. In any case, her guilt was plainly written on her mortified face. "Major Darcy has become a very good and special friend, Papa. *Oui*, we have spent time together walking, but Clementine is always with us."

Emile Dansereau closed his eyes in pain. "This letter says you have been doing more than walking, Daughter! Tell me, is he your lover? Are you still a maiden?"

Anne-Marie reeled as if struck. "Papa, how can you ask that? We have done nothing… He is not… I am not…" She broke down in tears. "How can you accuse me of such a terrible thing?"

"I have a right to know!" he barked. "Do you remain a maiden?"

She nodded, her face in her hands.

"*Dieu Merci*," he breathed. "You shall not see him again."

"What?" Anne-Marie dropped her hands from her tear-streaked face and stared at her father. "You forbid me to see Matthew?"

"Matthew, is it?" he growled. "Just what have you done?"

"Papa, I have done nothing but be with the man I love!"

"Love? Him? An *American*? I forbid it!"

"But why? He is welcome in this house. He attends Mass with the family."

Her father softened his voice. "Because you are meant for better things, Anne-Marie. You are my only child, and I love you more than my life. You are also my heir, and I have done everything in my power to protect you from the young Creole dandies that have flocked around you since you came out. Your grandfather and I built Dansereau Plantation with our bare hands, all the time enduring the scorn of our Creole neighbors. Your sainted mother and I swore they would not get *un sou* from us. When it is time for you to marry, I shall choose a good, devout Frenchman for you." M. Dansereau darkened. "Shall everything I have done, everything I have sacrificed, be undone by this…invader? This *anglais*?"

"Matthew is not an Englishman! He is an American soldier, sent to protect us, his fellow Americans!"

"I am not an American, nor are you!" he roared. "*Tu es une acadienne!*"

"We are not Acadians, Papa. We are in Louisiana, and this is part of the United States."

"You reject your heritage? This…this is the result of my leniency! The Melançons have betrayed me! I never should have allowed you to stay here!"

"Papa, Acadia was a long time ago. I know it was painful, but you must give up this hate. You must forget."

"You sound like the priests. The English took everything from us. *Non*, I shall never forget. I shall never forgive them."

"Matthew is not English."

"He is not French, either. Bonaparte, the upstart, betrayed and sold us to the Americans. But we shall never accept it. French we are, and French we shall remain. That is your heritage."

"But he is a good man."

"A man who would take you away. Yes, I know more than you think. I have talked to your Uncle Melançon. I know all about Major Darcy's plans to return to Virginia. He is either playing with your heart or will steal you away. Your destiny is Dansereau Plantation, Anne-Marie."

"But Papa, perhaps Matthew can be convinced to remain here. We can live at the plantation together—"

"Is that what he suggested? Then he *is* a fortune hunter!"

"*Non*, Papa! He said nothing of the sort! I just thought—"

M. Dansereau gently took Anne-Marie's hands. "*Ma chérie*, can you not see? It cannot be both. Either he is an adventurer looking for a wealthy wife, or he is not. If Major Darcy is all you say he is, then he will leave. He is not one of us. He *will* go back to his own people, and…and if you marry, you…you will leave your poor papa all alone." Tears ran down his winkled face.

Overcome, Anne-Marie embraced him. "Oh, Papa, do not weep!"

"You would break my heart if you went away, little one. I could not bear it. I have already lost your mama. If I lost you, I would surely die."

Anne-Marie broke down. "I will never leave you, Papa. Never!"

Chapter 6

I t was a cloudy day with a threat of rain. An irritated Matthew Darcy glanced at the sky as he turned his horse off the levee road to Dansereau Plantation house. This was a visit unexpected and disconcerting.

Matthew had gone to the Melançons the evening before for dinner and Anne-Marie's company as he had done almost daily for the last month. To his disappointment, she was not there. Her father had taken her back to their plantation home upriver in St. Charles Parish. M. Dansereau's request that Major Darcy call upon him at his earliest convenience was both surprising and disturbing.

When asked the subject of this proposed meeting, M. Melançon would say nothing about it or his brother-in-law's state of mind. Instead, he advised the young officer to go as quickly as he could manage, given his duties.

"M. Dansereau loves Anne-Marie very much," he had been warned. "He is very correct in dealings concerning his daughter. He demands respect for her and for himself. You would do well to remember this when you call upon him."

Matthew tried to remain calm as best he could. "Sir, you know no one respects Mlle Dansereau more than I. Has anyone said different? Tell me their names, and I will make them see the error of their ways."

Melançon's response was an ironic smile. "Matthew," he gently scolded with the familiarity their close interactions had produced, "your behavior lately has not been above reproach, and neither has Anne-Marie's."

The major had the decency to color. "My intentions are honorable, *monsieur*."

"I know this, or else you would find my door barred to you. But I want you to recall that M. Dansereau does not know you."

Now, as Matthew approached the plantation house, he paused and took in his surroundings. The rough driveway was framed on each side by a line of live oaks, each tree about ten feet tall. The main house, set back from the road and placed to face the Mississippi River, was a large, two-story, wood structure, covered by a hip roof. A gallery, held up by narrow pillars, ran along at least three sides of the house, offering a huge porch beneath. Numerous French doors lined the walls. Several slaves could be seen working in the garden next to the house. Matthew expected there were many more in the fields.

As he dismounted, two slaves approached. One, a barefoot young boy, was clearly a stable hand. The other, a giant of a man, wore a livery of a sort—a too-short blue coat over a white shirt and loosely tied cravat. Buff breeches and worn black shoes with stockings completed the costume.

"Do not unsaddle my horse," Matthew told the stable boy. "Should matters change, I will send word." He then turned his attention to the other slave.

"Please, may I ask your name and business, *monsieur*?" The giant—a footman or butler, Matthew did not know—had a gentle voice for one so large.

"I am Major Darcy, and I am here at M. Dansereau's request."

"You are expected, Major. Please come this way."

Matthew and the slave entered the mansion. Like most houses of the period, there was no hall; they simply walked through one of the French doors into a sitting room. To Matthew's surprise, it was not M. Dansereau who awaited him. It was Anne-Marie.

"That is all, Samson," she dismissed the tall slave. "*Bonjour*, Major Darcy."

Matthew smiled as he walked over to the girl. "Samson? That is a fit name for him. How are you, my dear?" He reached for Anne-Marie's hand, only to have her turn away. "Anne-Marie, what is wrong?"

Anne-Marie walked over to the French doors, her dress as dark as the threatening clouds without. "Thank you for coming, Major." Her voice was cold and flat. "I have enjoyed our acquaintance." She paused and gave a little sniffle. "But I am afraid I have inadvertently given rise to expectations that cannot be fulfilled. I believe you to be everything good and honorable, but I think it best we should not meet again."

Matthew was stunned. He had anticipated that M. Dansereau would raise objections to his courting Anne-Marie, and he had spent half the night preparing his rebuttal. But not in his worst nightmares did he dream that Anne-Marie would reject him. He felt as if he had been struck in the gut.

"Not meet again? Why?"

She refused to look at him. "It was not my intention to give you pain, *monsieur*. This is not an easy thing to do. But we must be realistic. We are…we are not the same."

"What is this?" demanded Matthew, his voice rising. "Is this about money? About status? Do you think my motives are mercenary?"

"*Non*, of course not! I doubt neither your honor nor your intensions. Major Darcy, can you not see that this is impossible?" She gripped the back of a chair.

"What is impossible?" Matthew moved closer to her. "Tell me!"

"Us!" she cried. Anne-Marie shook her head and continued. "We are different people from very different worlds. Once this crisis is over, you shall return to your people, and I shall remain here with mine. It is best we end this now before we cause each other greater pain."

"*My* people? You mean in Maryland?"

"*Oui*. You have told me about your home, your family—"

"My family is nothing!" Matthew spat. "My brother has cast me out! I have no family."

"But what of your plans for a farm in Virginia? You have told me of your dreams."

"Yes, but only to show how I had the means to care for you! I would have you come with me."

She bowed her head. "And leave Louisiana? Leave *mon père*? I cannot."

"Why not? It is the way of the world that a woman leaves her family for her husband." To Matthew, her argument made no sense. "If you married a local man, it would be the same."

"No, it would not. This house, this plantation, is my destiny. My family built this place themselves with no help from anyone. We are Acadians. We received nothing from the Creoles in New Orleans or our Germans neighbors here."

"Germans?"

"You did not know that *les Allemands* immigrated here? It is true, though many married into the Creoles.

"Nevertheless, I am heir to Dansereau Plantation. The care of this house, these fields, and our people will one day fall to me. I have known this all my life. Here, I was born, and here, I will rest." She stared out the French doors. "You, of course, would want to be with your fellow Americans. It is natural."

Matthew felt he was losing a contest of which he was ignorant of the rules. "You are American, too," he pointed out, belatedly realizing that it would make no difference.

"Am I? Is anyone in Louisiana truly American? I do not think so. This place is French and will always be so." She paused. "I am truly sorry, Major Darcy. More sorry than you know."

"You are sending me away?" Matthew asked in a low, even voice, struggling to hide his anguish.

"You will forever be in my prayers," Anne-Marie said to the window.

"Will you not even look at me?"

She shook her head.

Defeated, Matthew moved to leave. "I love you, you know."

Anne-Marie choked on a sob.

"God bless you. I hope you find your happiness." Matthew knew *he* never would. He reached for the latch on the door—

"Matthew!" Anne-Marie cried. An instant later, she was in his arms. Matthew had no idea what was happening except that Anne-Marie was weeping on his chest. He held her sweet body close, her perfume surrounding him, and mumbled words of comfort to her —words he would not be able to recall later. All that mattered, all that he knew, was that Anne-Marie was holding him—that she loved him still.

Finally coherent, Anne-Marie turned her tear-stained face to his. "Matthew! Matthew! I cannot do it. *Je t'aime! Je t'aime tellement!* Do not leave!"

Nothing could stop him from kissing her with all the love and passion he had, and she returned his kisses with a need as great as his. Matthew was lost to everything but Anne-Marie until he heard footsteps and opened his eyes. There, outside the French doors, was Samson, taking in the scene with an inscrutable expression.

Matthew's breath caught in his throat. As he pulled back from Anne-Marie's lips, she looked about and beheld the servant with a gasp. The two broke apart and retreated further into the room, Samson's gaze locked on them.

"What are we to do?" Matthew worried. "He will report us to your father."

"No, he will not." A small smile graced Anne-Marie's swollen lips. "Samson is *my* servant. I taught him to read and write. In return, he is devoted to me. He shall not betray us." She walked over to the door and said through the glass, "Samson, *tout va bien. Laissez-nous, s'il vous plaît.*[2]"

Samson nodded quickly and walked away. Once out of sight, Matthew drew Anne-Marie back into his embrace. "Anne-Marie, I am confused. One moment you try to dismiss me, and the next—"

She laid her cheek against his chest. "I am so sorry! This interview was my father's doing. He learned of our courtship and demanded

---

2 All is well. Leave us please.

I send you away."

"But, you love me. Why did you agree to this?"

"*Oui*, I love you, but I love my father, too. Oh, Matthew, everything I said to you was true. I am tied to Dansereau. I thought my father was right, that it would be easier if I set you free, but I cannot! I cannot bear to be without you."

"Then you will come away with me!"

"Matthew, please—" Suddenly, a door closed nearby. Anne-Marie's face showed panic. "My father! Quick, you must leave! He must not know I have not sent you away! Go now!"

In a moment of bravado, Matthew cried, "Let me face him."

"It would do no good," she snapped as she propelled him towards the French door. "Go!"

He realized that she was right. "But what are we to do? When shall we meet again?"

She touched his face briefly. "I do not know, my love. I will get word to you, somehow. *Vas-y, et je prie que Notre Dame veille sur toi.*³" A quick kiss on the cheek and Matthew found himself outside the plantation house. Confused and upset, Matthew again considered ignoring Anne-Marie's request and returning inside to confront M. Dansereau.

He jumped when a hand descended on his shoulder. "Come with me, *monsieur*," said a low voice.

Matthew saw it was Samson. "No, I mean to return inside."

The slave shook his head. "*Non, monsieur.* I heard *la mademoiselle*. You are to leave. Come, your horse is waiting." The man's grip was like iron.

With no choice, Matthew shook off Samson's hold and stalked around the house. Sure enough, the young stable hand held his horse's reins. Matthew mounted and turned to Samson. "If I give you a message for Mlle Dansereau, will you give it to her and no one else?"

The slave's face was impassive. "*Oui.*"

---

3 Go, and I pray that Our Lady watches over you.

"You will not report it to your master?"

"Only if *la mademoiselle* orders me to."

Just then, it began to rain. Pulling a cape from a saddlebag, Matthew knew the message would have to be short. "Tell her to have faith. I will think of some way that we can be together," he said as he fastened the cape about his shoulders. "Tell her I love her."

The pouring rain did nothing to dim Samson's broad smile. "I will tell her, *monsieur.*"

Matthew nodded and began his ride back to New Orleans.

Tuesday, November 8: Port Royal, Jamaica

A MIGHTY FLEET WAS BEGINNING to assemble in Port Royal. Troop ships, bomb ketches, and warships of all kinds filled the harbor. The target of this host should have been secret, but it was not. New Orleans was on everyone's lips. Officers and men openly talked of the beauty and booty awaiting them in Louisiana. Major Fitzwilliam was disgusted by the lack of safety measures, but there was nothing he could do about it.

Admiral Cochrane called a meeting of the officers in his cabin. "Due to the loss of General Ross in Maryland, Whitehall has appointed Major-General Sir Edward Michael Pakenham Commander of Land Forces for the Louisiana operation. He has set sail from England, along with Major-General Sir Samuel Gibbs and several thousand men. We have more men who will also join us. Major-General John Keane is sailing from Ireland, and Major-General Sir John Lambert shall follow. With the strength we have gathered here already, added to the host England is sending, this enterprise cannot fail. New Orleans will be ours."

"When shall General Pakenham arrive?" was asked.

"That is the difficulty. It is my understanding that they are making all speed, but they must be here by the twenty-fifth of November. This fleet shall set sail by high tide on the twenty-sixth, at the latest. If General Pakenham is late, he will just have to follow." He smiled. "That is assuming we even need Pakenham. Surely, we can swat a few raggedy farmers aside. All the more glory for us."

The army officers smiled at Cochrane's boast, but James recalled what a bunch of raggedly farmers accomplished before the city of Baltimore.

Another voice in the room was heard. "What of the American commander, General Jackson? He has been causing great consternation in Florida."

Indeed, thought James. *Jackson has been beating our arse proper in Florida.*

"Success against red Indians certainly cannot be an indication of great leadership," Cochrane sneered. "We did not have enough men at our abortive invasion of Mobile Bay, and Jackson's attack on Pensacola has, in a great measure, retarded this service. The Spanish proved poor allies. We shall not make that mistake again. Besides, General Jackson does not know our true target is Louisiana. While he is busy guarding Mobile, we shall be taking our ease in New Orleans."

The admiral stood, ending the meeting. "See to your duties. The fleet must be ready to depart on the twenty-sixth. That is all."

As the others began filing out of Cochrane's cabin, James allowed his eye to fall on the map of the Gulf Coast laid out upon the table. James admittedly knew little about navigation, but it was obvious that Mobile Bay was the best anchorage on the coast. New Orleans was a hundred miles up the Mississippi River. Where the devil did Cochrane plan to disembark the troops? Did he intend to sail up the bloody river?

James left the cabin, hoping with all his heart that General Pakenham arrived before the fleet set sail.

Chapter 7

"Think Henri will have a letter for you from Miss Anne-Marie?"

Matthew almost fell out of his saddle. "Jacob, sometimes you say the damnedest things!"

His comrade smirked. The two rode through the late afternoon streets of the *Vieux Carré* towards the *Faubourg Marigny* and their appointment. Both had been invited to dine at Henri Herbert's house.

"Aw, don't give me that look. He's her cousin. Who else would she use?"

Matthew turned away. "There may be no letter." It had been a week since the lovers' painful and passionate confrontation. Matthew tried to have faith in Anne-Marie's declaration, but there had been no word. It was not surprising, he kept telling himself. How could she send a letter to him? But doubts grew, doubts he had shared with his best friend.

Jacob patted his shoulder. "She'd send you one, Matt, believe me. I reckon she's like my Fanny. She told you she'll go against her paw. You can't ask for much more than that. Now, let's go get them vittles."

Evening had just fallen when they halted their horses before a boarding house. "Is this the place, Matt?"

"We followed the direction in Henri's note," Matthew said as he dismounted.

"Strange place to live, if'n everything I've heard about the *Marigny* is true."

The house was a wooden, two-story, square structure with a gallery across the front. With no stable hand to help, the horses were secured by their reins to one of the pillars. The two officers approached the single door in the center, lit by an oil lamp. But before Matthew could reach for the knocker, the door opened.

"*Bonsoir, mes amis!*" cried Henri Herbert. "Welcome, welcome. Come into my home." The two were greeted by their Creole friend warmly. Henri then indicated a woman in the room. "Allow me to introduce your hostess, Mlle Carmen Bellevue."

Matthew was taken aback. Mlle Bellevue was an extraordinarily beautiful mulatto woman. Of medium height, her curvaceous body was adorned in a gown of white with gold trim. Gold necklaces and bracelets gleamed against her *café au lait* skin. Her most arresting feature was her blue eyes. She wore no kerchief in her curly brown hair.

"*Bonsoir*, gentlemen." Her voice was like warm honey. "M. Herbert has told me much about you. Please follow me into the parlor. Dinner will be served very soon."

Bellevue— Yes, she is a beautiful sight, Matthew thought. She was perhaps the most striking woman, white or black, he had ever seen. *This woman is no slave.*

He then saw that Jacob was frozen in place. "Remove your hat," he said *sotto voce* with a jab of the elbow to his ribs. The parlor was a comfortable room with a pair of settees by a fireplace and a pianoforte in the corner.

By the time everyone was seated, Jacob had remembered his manners. They exchanged stiff small talk about the weather and the city. Jacob had recovered his wits enough to compliment Herbert on the house.

"*Merci*—thank you. But all credit must go to Carmen," said Herbert. The two shared an open look of affection, and a piece of the puzzle fell into place.

A maid announced dinner, and all repaired to the dining room. The furnishings were like the sitting room: fine, but not overly ornate or expensive. Matthew knew Herbert was not rich, so he wondered how he could afford two households—unless he did not have two households.

As the soup was served, Herbert asked about the war. "We understand your General Jackson has lately won a great victory. But why has he attacked Pensacola?"

Matthew sipped his sweet wine, made from local Muscatine grapes. "As you have certainly heard, the British tried to invade Mobile. But when General Jackson held them off at Fort Bowyer, the enemy retreated to neutral Spanish Florida."

"Old Hickory was fuming 'bout that, for sure," interjected Jacob.

Matthew continued. "He and General Coffee marched the army to Pensacola. Once there, he accused the Spanish governor of violating their neutrality. Jackson demanded the surrender of the forts that guard the bay and the expulsion of all British forces."

Jacob took up the tale. "'Course, the Spaniards turned the general down and prepared to fight. But Old Hickory fooled 'em and good. He set camp to the west of the town, but he circled around and hit 'em from the east. The dons and the redcoats never saw him coming. The British set sail and ran after blowing up all their powder at Fort Barrancas."

"Does the general remain at Pensacola?" asked Herbert.

"No," answered Matthew. "Without Fort Barrancas, Pensacola is indefensible. He and the army have returned to Mobile."

Herbert frowned. "Are we now fighting the Spanish as well as the English?"

"It does not seem so. By pulling out, our attack becomes an excursion—chasing a fleeing enemy—not an invasion. We crossed their borders, but we did not remain. They can complain, but they have no lasting injury."

Jacob swallowed a bite of his food. "The dons' hands ain't clean, anyhow. Taking in the British ain't being neutral."

"I am sure you are correct," Herbert observed, "however, the entire enterprise seems very risky. Your General Jackson is a bold man."

Jacob chuckled. "That's for certain."

Mlle Bellevue had been listening silently to the discussion. That it had been entirely in English told Matthew of her accomplishments. Now that the talk of war had ended, she turned to Major Harville. "Are you enjoying the meal, Major?" Her English was perfect.

Jacob seemed startled at being addressed. "Yes, ma'am, it's very good." His response was short, almost rude. Except for a glance, he did not look at her.

Matthew strived to cover any *faux pas*. "The meal is excellent, *mademoiselle*. In fact, we have yet to have a truly bad meal here. New Orleans' reputation for food and hospitality is well deserved. But tonight is exceptional." *What the hell is bothering Jacob?* he wondered.

"Ah, thank you, Major," she said with a brilliant smile, "but all thanks must go to Mama Susan, our cook." She turned to Herbert. "She has been with you for how long, Henri?"

Herbert gave a Gallic shrug. "I cannot remember when she first came to us—before my parents died, of course. I would not give up Mama Susan for the world."

The conversation for the rest of the meal turned to the officers' impressions of the city, with Matthew carrying the burden of the discussion and Jacob saying little. After the last plate had been taken away, the party returned to the parlor, where Mlle Bellevue entertained them on the pianoforte. Once the performance was done, she remained for a short time before excusing herself.

"I know you gentlemen need to speak of many other things," she announced as she rose from the settee next to Herbert. She took her leave of the party and left the room, a figure of grace, closing the door behind her. The room seemed darker without her presence. Their host passed around cigars and poured more wine.

Herbert leaned back as he puffed. "Now that Carmen has left us, we may speak frankly. What is your opinion of this business in Florida? For me, it seems that Mr. Livingston's warnings have been proven correct by this attack on Mobile. The eyes of the English have fallen on the Gulf Coast, and New Orleans is the obvious prize."

"General Jackson shares that opinion," Matthew admitted. "That is why he is in Mobile."

"Sure," added Jacob, his spirits recovered now that Mlle Bellevue had left them. "Mobile's the best port on the coast. We hold that, an' there ain't many places for the British to land."

"Cannot the English simply sail up the river or attack from Lake Pontchartrain?"

"They'd be mad to try the Mississippi," Jacob declared. "The current's against them, an' we've got two forts guarding it. They know that, an' I figure that's why they tried to bribe that Lafitte fellow."

"So Jean Lafitte told the truth?"

"We think so," said Matthew. "I know not everyone in the government agrees."

"Bah!" cried Herbert. "Everyone knows Governor Claiborne loathes the Lafitte brothers. So, the British cannot come up the Mississippi, and they would be lost in the maze that is Barataria without guides. What about the lake?"

"That could be trouble," Jacob allowed. "The shortest route into the city is from Fort St. John, but the road is awful narrow an' easy to block. Besides, Lake Pontchartrain's shallow, ain't it? Maybe too shallow for the British ships. I'm certain they have boats to ferry their troops, but that's a long pull. The best way in is either along the Chef Menteur Road in Gentilly or from the west through Baton Rouge."

"Can the city be defended?"

Jacob frowned. "Henri, it's hard to say. Sure, the city can withstand an attack. Like we said, there are only a few land routes around here an army can use. A good sized force can block these routes."

"And therein lies the trouble," said Matthew. "With two good routes, we would have to block them both. But do we have the men? I'm sorry to say we do not. I am not sure we have enough to block even one of them. We have had a hard time raising a decent militia."

Herbert shook his head. "I am not surprised. The Creoles, they are quick to defend their honor; we have duels every day—some days three or four! But to take orders like a soldier? It hurts their pride."

"What will *you* do?"

Herbert looked about the room. "I am not a brave man, *mon ami*. Do you know I have never fought a duel? *Le lâche Herbert* I am called—Cowardly Herbert. *C'est la vie*." He waved his cigar. "But this is my home. Give me a musket, and I shall do my best."

You will not go to that farm of yours?"

"My plantation? *Non*, Jacob. I am no farmer. My cousin M. Dansereau leases the land from me. My investments are all in the city, like this place. Ah"—he slapped his forehead—"how foolish I am! Forgive me, Matthew; I had forgotten! I will be but a moment." Herbert hurried out the room, only to return a moment later, bearing a letter. "This is for you," he said to Matthew with a grin.

Matthew instantly saw that his name written on the outside was in Anne-Marie's hand. He almost snatched the letter out of his friend's grasp. "Henri, I cannot thank you enough."

"It is no bother, *mon ami*. I know what it is to be separated from the one you love." He returned to his seat while Matthew tucked the precious letter into his pocket to be read later in privacy.

Jacob gave Matthew a knowing smirk before turning to Herbert. "Don't we all. I miss my Fanny somethin' awful."

"At least you can marry your love," Herbert mumbled as he took a puff of his cigar.

"Who is she, Henri? Is she promised to someone else?"

"*Non*, and you have met her."

All the pieces came together in Matthew's mind. "I take it you refer to our hostess tonight?"

Herbert gave him a sad smile. "You are clever, *mon ami*." He them turned to the other officer in the room. "You are shocked, Jacob?"

"Ahh, er...no," Jacob lied, drawing a laugh from their host.

"Ah, you Americans! So typical—so hypocritical! I mean no offence, of course."

Jacob was rather insulted. "Then just what do you mean?"

"Let me ask you this. What do you think this place is? Do you not think it is rather large for just Carmen and myself? Surely, you have noticed there are other entrances."

Jacob fidgeted and Matthew knew he was struggling not to say something that would insult Herbert. "Why don't you tell us, Henri?"

"This is an apartment house—one of my investments. We rent apartments and we have a common area where Mama Susan serves food for our residents." He took a puff. "You know of *placées*?"

"We have been told they are like mistresses," Matthew said cautiously.

Herbert shrugged. "For some, particularly the Americans. For the Creoles, it is different. Some of the women are slaves, but most are free mulattos or *mestee.*"

"*Mestee?* I am not familiar with that word."

"A mulatto is the child of a slave and a white. A *mestee* is the child of a mulatto and a white. It is a custom among the Creole planters when they are young to take a lover in town. Most marriages are arranged later in life, and the wives remain in the country. For some, the relationship between the Creole and the *placée* is for a short time. For some, it is not. Ah, I see I must explain our custom of *plaçage*.

"*Plaçage* has been referred to by you Americans as 'left-hand marriages.' It is more formal than that. Many years ago, under the old *Code Noir*, marriage between the races was forbidden. Yet men wanted wives, and white women were in short supply. It was not uncommon to take a slave as a lover. The children of such relationships were often emancipated along with the mother. The law required that the man support the woman and children, even if he had a legal marriage with offspring.

"Later, as more white women came to Louisiana, the custom remained. This became so common that the rules of *plaçage* became formalized. Once a man takes a lover, he is required to establish a household for her and any children. The children are free and often take the father's name. They also participate in the father's estate once he passes, though not to the extent of the man's legal children. So you see, the women, the *placées,* are not whores; they are faithful to their lover for life."

"That sounds like bigamy to me," observed Jacob.

"The white wives certainly agree with you," said Herbert with a smile. "*Plaçage* is understandably not popular with them. But this is a man's world. *C'est la vie.*" He took a sip of wine, and his face darkened. "Not all men want to marry a white woman once *plaçage* is established. Some lovers desire a true marriage, but the *Code Noir* prohibits it. In the old days, a bit of gold could arrange things differently if the *placée* was *mestee* and could pass for white. The officials could be convinced to look the other way. There are more mixed-race Creoles here than you know.

"Of course, this option was only open to men. White women can never marry *mestee* men or establish *plaçage* under any circumstances. It is unthinkable. As for *mestee* men, they may only marry *mestee* women, or buy a slave for a wife. They resent it, of course.

"Everything changed once the Americans came. American law forbids any marriage between the races, and this is strictly enforced. For once, bribes cannot help. There is no longer any opportunity for a white man to marry his *placée*."

Carefully, Matthew asked, "I take it you speak for yourself?"

Pain and disappointment flowed over the affable man's face. "The heart is a strange thing, *n'est-ce pas*? I will marry no one but Carmen." He threw back his wine. "Your friend, Mr. Anderson, has established a mistress here. That is why I said Americans are hypocrites, Jacob. He mocks our ways, yet he participates in our customs in his own manner." Herbert smiled again. "I charge him a higher rent. Call it a surcharge for dissembling."

The three sat in quiet contemplation, each lost to his thoughts. Finally, Matthew stirred.

"It is time for us to leave, Henri." The men stood. "Thank you for your hospitality, and please let Mlle Bellevue know how much we enjoyed dinner." They shook hands.

To Jacob, Herbert said, "Good night, *mon ami*. I hope our talk did not cause offense."

Jacob's face was neutral. "I always said folks down here were *different*. Thank you kindly for the vittles."

At the front door, Herbert took Matthew's arm. "A moment,

mon ami. I wish to speak about your letter."

Matthew nodded and told Jacob to gather their mounts. He then turned his attention to his Creole friend.

"I know not what is in Anne-Marie's letter," Herbert said softly, "but my cousin has spoken to me of this matter at length. To say she is at odds with herself is no exaggeration. There is an intense loyalty between my uncle and cousin, for it has been many years since my aunt's untimely passing. Yet, you have won her heart most completely. She would go with you to Virginia if not for Dansereau Plantation. This is tearing her apart."

"What are you suggesting—that I should go away?"

"*Non!* Not at all! Such grief she would suffer! I do not think she could recover from it."

"Then, what?"

"I tell you these things so that you know the entire state of affairs. You must be wise, *mon ami*; you must think of her and her desires as well as your own. *Bonne nuit et bonne chance!*"

THE TWO SOLDIERS RODE BACK TO THEIR BARRACKS IN SILENCE, Matthew's mind occupied by his romantic troubles as well as Herbert's. Once back in their rooms, he wasted no time opening Anne-Marie's letter. As he read it, a wave of relief washed over his tortured soul. She assured him of her love and her determination that somehow they would be together soon. It was enough to soothe him.

"Everything all right, Matt?" asked Jacob.

"Yes." Matthew closed his eyes briefly. "You were right." He then changed the subject to the other matter in his mind. "Now, may I ask just what the devil you were about tonight?"

Jacob seemed surprised. "You have to ask?"

"Yes! My God, man, you were downright rude to Mlle Bellevue! You are fortunate Henri did not toss you out in the street."

His friend scowled. "Well, I'm sorry 'bout that. Didn't mean to be rude, but Henri's lucky I didn't just up an' walk out of there. That whole sinful setup don't sit right with me."

"Look, I admit that I was a little uncomfortable, too. Their circumstances are unorthodox."

"Matt, you can use whatever fancy words you want, but it don't change nothing! That there's a den of corruption, an' you know it! Men lying with women outside of marriage…an' colored women, to boot! It's a sin against God!"

Matthew did not want to get into a theological discussion with Jacob, but he needed to make a point.

"Henri would marry his mistress—or *placée*—but the law will not let him."

"That's the least of his sins! But I'll say this: the Lord made the different races for a reason. It's unnatural to mix the races; that's a fact!"

"Jacob—"

"I like Henri Herbert—he's been good to both of us—but I can't remain on friendly terms with a man that runs a whorehouse, no matter what he calls it."

Matthew found himself conflicted. Much of what Jacob said was true. *Plaçage* was nothing more than organized bigamy, which was against the laws of men and God. But was it truly a sin for a white man to love a black woman? Relations between the races were not new to either of them. Mixed-race children could be found in both Maryland and Tennessee. Was it right to have a law against marriages of mixed blood? It was not a choice he would make for himself, but Matthew could not doubt the open affection between Henri and Carmen, and he trusted they would marry if they could.

Jacob calmed down. "Look, Matt, I know you've got to be on good terms with Henri. He's your contact with Anne-Marie. I promise I'll be cordial next time I see him. But I hope you'll understand why I'll never darken that door again."

Matthew was grateful for the escape Jacob offered. He shook his hand. "It is late, Jacob, and we have an early morning before us. It is time to sleep."

His comrade agreed, and soon the lantern was extinguished, but Matthew got little sleep between his thoughts of Anne-Marie and Henri.

Chapter 8

In the early hours of the morning, Anne-Marie crept out of her bedroom, her maid, Clementine, close behind, both carrying carpetbags. They were dressed in traveling clothes, their hooded cloaks giving them a mysterious aspect. It was pitch dark, the cool air having just a touch of the winter to come. The ever-present frogs and crickets, singing their nighttime songs, accompanied their squeaking footsteps.

The pair made their way along the gallery to the stairs in the front of the house. While M. Dansereau's bedroom was in the back of the mansion, they took no chances and moved slowly down the staircase, one step at a time.

Anne-Marie's grim face hid her inner turmoil. She was torn between her duty to her father and her deep attachment to Matthew. She loved them both, but she had come to the realization that a choice had to be made.

Oh, she had tried to find the middle way! For two weeks since her meeting with Matthew Darcy, she had tried to gage the extent of her father's opposition to the American officer. Knowing better than to openly challenge him by hints and offhand comments, she raised the subject of Major Darcy. She probed his mind, remarking how sad it was that Matthew came from so far away. She remarked how few men owned his intelligence and sense of duty. And she wondered aloud whether it was not still possible for a young immigrant to establish himself in New Orleans as many had done before.

To all this, Emile Dansereau had been obstinate. Matthew Darcy was an American—practically a hated Englishman—and therefore, unacceptable.

Two nights before, Anne-Marie tried one last argument. Her father had many good reasons to be suspicious of the local gentry, she admitted, given the indolence of many Creole dandies, and he was right to reject them as her potential suitors. Yet, Anne-Marie must marry to produce heirs, and the search for a proper husband had proven fruitless. Was it not better, she speculated, to take a young man of good character, a newcomer hundreds of miles from his birthplace, free from local faults, and mold him into an acceptable gentleman?

"I do not believe it is possible," her father replied. "A man is fixed upon his birth and cares only for his own people."

"That is not so, Papa," she had responded. "Why, look at the young men who have traveled here to protect us from the English."

Dansereau snorted. "It is one thing to parade about in shiny uniforms; it is quite another to face the guns of the enemy. Why should a stranger risk his life so far from his home? We are nothing to them, and I do not think they will fight for us. That assumes that the English attack us, and of *that* happening I am not convinced."

There was no moving her father, Anne-Marie determined. Therefore, between duty and love, she had chosen love.

At the foot of the stairs stood a tall figure in dark clothes. "Samson," she whispered, "is everything ready?"

"*Oui, mademoiselle.* The carriage is nearby—on the grass where it will make no sound."

Within moments, their belongings were stored in the carriage. Clementine climbed in, but Anne-Marie hesitated.

"Samson, are you certain about accompanying us?" She placed a hand on his arm. "I can manage the horses. You can stay here. You will not be in trouble."

Samson's face could have been made of ebony. "*Non, mademoiselle.* Please do not leave me behind. M. Dansereau—he has been a good master, but I owe too much to you. You taught me to read and write. From you I learned my figures. You saw that I was baptized. My duty is to protect you, so my master says. M. Dansereau is my master, true, but *you* are my mistress and my friend. Where you go, I will go."

"*Mademoiselle,* we must hurry," whispered Clementine. "The dawn is but hours away."

Anne-Marie capitulated. The two joined the maid in the carriage and stole away from Dansereau Plantation, the house in which she was raised—the house she loved.

She had resolved not to glance back as she left. She knew if she did, she would weep. This was not a time for grief. She would not weaken. She would resign herself to her fate. She would ride into her future.

New Orleans

The dawn had been less than three hours old when Philippe Melançon was called to the back door of his house by his butler; he received the shock of his life.

"*Anne-Marie*! What are you doing here?"

His niece and two slaves stood shivering at the back door. "Please, Uncle, may we not come in?"

"Of course, of course!" The trio hurried into the house, and Philippe noted that the large male slave carried a pair of carpetbags as well as a knapsack across his shoulders. He turned to Anne-Marie. "May I ask what this is all about?"

She met his incredulous stare calmly. "I seek sanctuary, Uncle Philippe."

Melançon frowned deeply. He opened his mouth to speak but then closed it again and turned to the two slaves. "I am certain you both are hungry. Leave your burdens here. The cook in the kitchen out back will serve you." He said to his butler, "Tell her I sent them."

Once the servants left through the back door, Philippe took his niece's arm. "Have you been harmed at all?"

"Oh, no, Uncle. We are just cold. You see, we misjudged the ferry across the river, and we sat in the carriage for almost two hours."

"The ferry? You mean to say you came all the way from Danse-reau...in the *dark*?"

Anne-Marie simply nodded.

"I think you have a story to tell me, Anne-Marie. Come to my study. Our breakfast will have to wait."

After a brief conversation, Philippe sent for his wife. Upon her arrival, Anne-Marie repeated her reasons for taking the enormous step of fleeing Dansereau Plantation for her uncle's house in New Orleans. Her relations listened in silence until she was done.

Philippe paced the room, a hand on his forehead. "Let me plainly understand you, Anne-Marie. Your father has rejected Major Darcy as a suitor and requested that you tell him so. Instead, when the major comes to Dansereau, you reaffirm your love to him. Since you were unable to change your father's mind, you have left his protection in the middle of the night to seek succor here."

"You make it sound so foolish."

"It *is* foolish, *chérie*! Emile is your father! You owe him obedience."

She lifted her chin. "*Non*. I owe him my love, deference, and respect. But my life—my future—is mine. I do not wish this choice between duty and love, but my father will not listen. If I can have only one, if I must choose, I choose Matthew Darcy."

Philippe grew red in the face, but his wife forestalled him. "Has Major Darcy proposed, then?"

"He has declared his love for me, and that is enough."

"Ah, *chérie*, when a man says he is in love, he may not be refer-ring to marriage!"

"I am well aware of that, but I trust Major Darcy. He will not propose to me until the danger is past."

Calmer, Philippe sat next to Madeline. "You know the major speaks of returning to Virginia once the war is over. Would you leave Louisiana?"

"I would rather not, but if Matthew leaves, I will go with him if he will have me."

"He is a soldier. Have you considered this?"

"What do you mean, Uncle?"

Philippe sighed. "He may not survive the coming battle."

Madeline clutched his arm. "Have you heard something, Philippe?"

"The streets are full of rumors." He turned his eyes to Anne-Marie.

She was pale and shaken, but she spoke calmly. "All the more reason I must be here. I must be with him as much as I can in case…" She could not finish.

The Melançons shared a look. At her husband's shrug, Madeline reached out and took Anne-Marie's hand. "Go to the dining room and get some breakfast, *chérie*. Your uncle and I must talk."

She stood. "You would not send me away, would you?" Her aunt shook her head, and a relieved Anne-Marie kissed them both on the cheek before leaving the study.

Philippe sat back. "Ah, how can you promise her that, Madeline? She is Emile's daughter, not ours!"

Madeline glared in righteous anger. "And have we not agreed that we do not like the way Emile shields her from New Orleans? How he hides away at his plantation? That is no life for a young lady!"

"I know. Emile hates a great many things. He cannot forgive the Creoles for rejecting his family when they first arrived."

"Bah! Are we not Creoles? Was not my sister a Creole? He does not hate us. I think Emile makes excuses to hide his real purpose. I do not think he means for Anne-Marie to marry at all! I think he selfishly wants to keep her with him at Dansereau forever!"

Philippe respected his wife enough to contemplate her theory. "Emile never remarried, even though there were ladies who were willing. I know he loved your sister dearly, but Anne-Marie needed a mother. He *should* have remarried."

"That would have been my sister's wish. Instead, he used *me* to act as her mother, to explain to Anne-Marie things about being a woman that he could not. It is the only reason he allows her to visit us. He wants all of Anne-Marie's loyalty and affection for himself. I say again, Emile is selfish."

Philippe paused to consider her words. "I believe you are right. Still, I do not like coming between a man and his child."

"We are only providing a room and safety for now. It is for Emile and Anne-Marie to decide this matter."

"I do not think Emile will see it that way. Besides, there is a third person: Major Darcy." He chuckled. "Two against one, I think. Who would you have your money on?"

Madeline pursed her lips. "I do not wager." Then, smiling, she added, "But if I did, it would be with Anne-Marie. There is much of my sister in her. My sister was the only one able to tame Emile Dansereau!"

Her husband gallantly kissed her hand. "As you have humbled me, *ma chérie*. Let us join our niece." As they left the room, he added, "I foresee much excitement in our future. Who will start the fireworks first, do you think, Emile or the English?"

RETRIBUTION WAS NOT LONG IN COMING. Before the afternoon was gone, an incensed Emile Dansereau was at the Melançons' front step. It was thought best to have him brought instantly to the study before he knocked down the door.

"Where is Anne-Marie?" he demanded.

"Good afternoon to you, too, Emile," responded Philippe dryly. "Please sit down. Anne-Marie is well. I am always happy to see my brother-in-law. Would you care for a glass of wine?"

Emile slammed a fist on the desk. "I want to see her this instant!"

"You have forgotten your manners, Emile."

"Manners be damned! You will produce my daughter right now!"

Philippe was unfazed. "Emile, you will see your daughter very soon. Please remember this is my house, I set the rules here, and in thirty years, you have failed to browbeat me even once. I suggest you sit down."

Emile mumbled something about lawyers as he took his usual chair.

"*Merci, mon ami.* Let us proceed to the matter before us. Anne-Marie has sought sanctuary with us." He held up a hand as Emile objected. "Emile, your blustering will not help matters. You know as well as I that Anne-Marie is of age. You cannot order her about as if she were a child."

"She is a good girl. She will listen to me!"

"Not in your present state. She is determined to marry Major Darcy—"

Emile leapt from the chair. *"Je l'interdit!"*

Philippe shook his head. *"Mon ami*, you cannot forbid it. I tell you such statements will do nothing but drive her into Matthew's arms and leave you estranged from your only child. Sit down and calm yourself."

"So! He is 'Matthew' to you, eh! You are in league against me!" he accused as he sat down.

The attorney rubbed his eyes. "It is *Anne-Marie's* welfare that most concerns me. I seek to settle this in a way that satisfies all parties. Let us look at this reasonably. Anne-Marie is sincerely attached to Matthew Darcy, whom I find to be an honest, intelligent, and reasonable young man. He is everything you have wanted in a son-in-law except that he is not from Louisiana."

"He is an Englishman who will take *ma belle* Anne-Marie away from me!"

"Emile, he is no Englishman; he is an *American*. He is here to *fight* the English." Philippe leaned back in his chair and crossed his arms. Philippe knew that Emile Dansereau viewed the world through a very narrow, limited perspective. Language, culture, and identity were all connected in his mind. There was a great deal of truth to that, Philippe conceded, but he knew that politics and shared experience could change people. That was a concept Emile had trouble grasping.

Emile spoke French; therefore, he *was* French, and all things French were superior. England was France's ancient enemy, and it was the English Crown that expelled the Acadians from Canada. That made all things English inferior. It was as simple as that. Ignored were the slights, pains, and disappointments Emile's family had suffered at the hands of French officials. He separated the crimes of the various French governments from the imagined glory that was France, Philippe knew.

In a like manner, Emile supposed that all Americans were, in truth, Englishmen because they spoke English and retained many British customs. The American Revolution and the current conflict were dismissed. For some time, Philippe tried to convince Emile that the Americans were becoming a new nation—a new cultural identity—with little success.

But perhaps it would be easier to persuade Emile that an individual man can be forced to change, given the amount of indignities he had suffered. Philippe thought it was worth the attempt.

"Do you know Matthew's background?" Philippe sat up in his chair.

"*Non.* Why should I?"

Philippe almost smiled at his brother-in-law's confused expression. "You should because he may become your son-in-law."

"Not if I can help it!"

Philippe held up a hand. "Let me tell you what I know."

ANNE-MARIE NERVOUSLY WAITED IN HER room, her Aunt Madeline keeping her company. She tried to do needlework, but she could not concentrate. All she could think about was that her father was downstairs. She knew he was there to take her back to Dansereau, and she was determined that she would remain in New Orleans.

She rejoiced when her uncle declared that she could stay in his house and trusted he would be true to his word. Clementine and Samson belonged to Papa. He could take them back. Would she lose her servants? Faithful Samson was her protector, and Clementine was more confidante than slave. How would she manage without them?

A knock on the door interrupted her musings. "Anne-Marie, it is time to speak to your father," said Uncle Philippe upon opening the door.

As Anne-Marie exited her room and walked along the gallery overlooking the courtyard in the middle of the house to the staircase, she wondered whether prisoners facing the guillotine felt as she did. Only moments later, she was in her uncle's study. Philippe shut the door as he left her with her father.

Emile Dansereau sat behind the desk, head in his hands. He said nothing even though he must have understood she was there.

So, he expected her to begin. Well, he would see no fear in *her*. Anne-Marie had made her decision, and she would not balk from it. She took a breath to quell her trembling.

"Good afternoon, Papa."

Her father dropped his hands, and Anne-Marie was taken aback at his expression. She expected he would be angry, even outraged, perhaps sly and conniving, hoping to manipulate her feelings. She did not expect him to be like *this*—resigned and defeated.

"I am happy to see you safe, my daughter." He paused, pain in his face. "So, it has come to this. You have chosen another over me."

Anne-Marie knew she had hurt him, but she pushed aside a twinge of remorse. "It is the way of the world, Papa, that a maiden should cling to her family until the time to start her own." She would not feel guilty for loving Matthew. She would not.

"That is true, but could you not have come to me to tell me of your choice?"

"I did, Papa, but you would not hear me."

He rubbed his face, obscuring his expression. "Ah, but did you have to choose *him*—an American?"

"Matthew is a good man, Papa. He is brave and honest and he loves me. And he is a good son of the church."

"At least he is *that*! Your uncle spent an hour extolling his virtues." He threw up his hands. "And you are to go to Virginia with him?"

This hurt most of all. "If he asks me to, I will."

"I cannot change your mind?"

"*Non*, Papa. It breaks my heart to say so, but—" She choked back a sob.

"Do not say it," Emile cried. "To hear you say you will leave me would kill me!"

Anne-Marie walked over to take one of his hands in hers. "I do love you, Papa, but I need to be with Matthew." Tears ran down her face, her resolve not to cry broken by his pain.

"Will you come back home?"

"*Non.* I must be close to him. You must understand."

Emile sighed. "*Oui.* I was young once, too. You have my permission to stay."

Anne-Marie kissed his cheek. "*Merci*, Papa." She left him, wiping her tears with her handkerchief, thankful for her father's understanding.

PHILIPPE ENTERED THROUGH THE DOOR Anne-Marie had left open. "I am happy you have seen reason, Emile. You are not the ogre you pretend to be. Would you now care for some wine?"

Emile grunted as he wiped the tears from his cheeks. "Enough, Philippe! I may have accepted this, but I still do not like it!" He took the glass Philippe offered and promptly drained half of it. "Major Darcy is undoubtedly as good a man as you claim, but he still plans to take my child far away. I hold out hope she will change her mind."

"Perhaps." Privately, Philippe doubted it. "But there is still something we can do if she does not."

Intrigued, Emile leaned forward. "And what is that?"

"Arrange things so that Major Darcy does not leave."

A WEEK LATER, THE GOVERNOR received a message. General Andrew Jackson and his army were on their way to New Orleans.

Friday, November 25

TWO DAYS LATER, AT HIGH noon on a clear, pleasant November day, the governor stood with Majors Darcy and Harville, reviewing the colored battalion as they marched about the *Place d'Armes* in a goodly fashion. For militia, they did well, and Matthew could see the governor was pleased. He had changed his mind about using freedmen and free men of color to defend the city, and in reply to his letter of intent, General Jackson heartily recommended using such troops.

The general was no stranger to non-white soldiers. He had used

Creek Indians as militia troops in the Creek Civil War. His crushing of the rebel Red Sticks had made Jackson famous and led to his appointment to the United States Army. Jackson cared not whether his men were white; he demanded only courage, competency, and loyalty.

The local planters strongly disagreed. They were more frightened of a slave revolt than a British invasion. It was thought that, were muskets issued to the colored battalion, it would encourage an uprising, which was why this militia marched unarmed.

It is foolish, thought Matthew. *Some of those free men of color own slaves themselves. They would no more want a revolt than the whites.*

After the exercise, Jacob shook his head. "I'll tell you true, Matt: it's a strange thing indeed to see coloreds in uniform, but they're about the best I've seen here. Them Creole regiments could learn a thing or two from 'em."

"Yes," Matthew agreed. "There's too much pride amongst the Creoles. They do not want to take orders from people they think are beneath them."

There was a cough. "What *les Créoles* lack in discipline on the parade grounds they make up for in ability," General Villeré stated confidently as he walked by, his son, Major Villeré, at his side. "No one fights like *les Créoles*; you will see."

Jacob displayed a rather open incredulity at the general's boast. Fortunately, the two Creoles did not see his reaction as they continued on their way.

Matthew hid his skepticism better. *I have been in the army too long not to know that discipline wins battles. Discipline and loyalty make a man stand his ground when the shooting starts.*

Jacob spat on the ground. "General Villeré had a devil of a time raising his division. Division, hell—he barely got together a couple of regiments! I swear the folks 'round here don't want to defend themselves. General Jackson won't like that!"

"General Villeré and Mr. Livingston have been doing their best. The problem is some are afraid, and others don't consider themselves Americans."

"That puts us in a pickle, now don't it?" Jacob took a last look at the departing colored troops. "Damn, it looks like we're gonna need them fellows. Ain't that something?"

Matthew did not pay attention, for he saw two people on the edge of the parade ground—a man and a woman—a very familiar woman.

"Say, Matt, ain't that Miz Anne-Marie with Mr. Melançon?"

Matthew paid no attention to his friend. He was already making his way to Anne-Marie's side.

Her smile was breathtaking. "*Bonjour*, Matthew!"

Matthew, splendid in his blue dress uniform, was before her. He longed to take her into his arms. He could not—not in public and not before her uncle. He had to be content with taking both of her hands in his.

"You came."

Her soft voice was for him alone. "I said in my letter I would find a way. Are you pleased?"

"Of course, but I can hardly believe it." Anne-Marie's hands trembled in his, drawing Matthew's concern. "What is wrong?"

"Nothing, *mon chéri,* nothing at all." She punctuated her claim by squeezing his hands.

Matthew finally acknowledged the amused Philippe Melançon. "Thank you for bringing her, *monsieur.* How long will Anne-Marie be here?"

"As long as she wishes, providing it is safe."

Matthew looked at his beloved. "But your father!" Turning to her uncle, he added, "Will he not object?"

Philippe laughed. "Oh, he indeed objects, you are most correct about that! But our Anne-Marie can be stubborn, as he well knows. She cannot be moved to return to Dansereau, so he comes to her."

"What do you mean? He is here, in the city?"

"Ha! He is in my study, I have no doubt, drinking my wine and sulking! He means to keep an eye on her. It seems, if we are to enjoy my niece's agreeable company, we must suffer my petulant brother-in-law's presence as well!"

Négril Bay, Jamaica

MAJOR JAMES FITZWILLIAM LEANED AGAINST the railing of *HMS Imprudent*, gazing at the assembled fleet. He felt a presence at his elbow.

"An impressive sight, what?" drawled Captain Elliot. "Sixty-odd ships, from pinnaces to men-of war. A thousand guns all together, I'll wager."

James could never fathom why Walworth Elliot kept seeking him out. All he knew was it was not out of friendship. "I have never seen such a fleet," he admitted.

"The Americans have nothing like it. Should they challenge us, we shall sweep the sea of them."

"No doubt." *Then why all the firepower?* James wondered. *How will those thousand guns help us once we are ashore?* "At least Keane's fleet got here."

"General Keane does not command a fleet, Major," said Elliot testily. "The ships bearing him and his men are under the command of—"

"I am aware of that, Captain," James cut him off. "The point is: much of our army has arrived."

Elliot sniffed. "Just in time, too. We set sail tomorrow."

James turned. "Tomorrow? But what of Pakenham and Gibbs and the three thousand troops with them?"

"They will just have to follow after us." He gestured at the fleet. "Do you not think we have enough for a few savages and backwoodsmen? I will tell you something, Major: I hope they are too late. That way, they won't be able to share in the glory!"

Elliot returned to the quarterdeck while James studied the enormous fleet filling the bay. He swallowed. *We thought we had enough men at Baltimore, too.*

He shook his head. *Where does this melancholy mood come from? For all his boasting, Elliot is right. We have thousands of troops. We can take New Orleans!*

He glanced over to see Margaret and the other wives coming up from below decks to take in the spectacle. Forcing a smile, he walked over to join them.

Chapter 9

A huge crowd gathered along the streets of New Orleans on the first day of December, for the word was out: General Jackson had arrived! Salvation was at hand!

Over the last month, anxiety had grown among the people. Details of the burning of Washington became known, as well as tales of rape and murder committed by the monstrous redcoats at Hampton, Virginia the year previous. The threat of war had changed from a mere inconvenience to deadly danger, and now their deliverance had come.

Given such high expectations, reality was a blow. Major General Andrew Jackson rode at the head of his army after a leisurely eleven-day march from Mobile. The famous general was not at all what the Creoles expected. The tall officer, sitting ramrod straight in his saddle, was gaunt and frail. Months of campaigning and dysentery had left the great man emaciated. His lead-grey hair made him appear older than his forty-seven years. The fifteen hundred troops following included three hundred regulars from the Forty-Fourth Infantry, but the vast majority were militia from Tennessee and Kentucky, dressed in buckskins and rags, their rifles and muskets almost their only possessions. This was no great army of gleaming brass and hard iron, marching smartly in immaculate uniforms to a martial beat. This was nothing more than a barely organized mob.

The crowd was shocked! *This* is the titan who would save them?

These are the men who would protect their families and homes?

The parade made its way to the *Place d'Armes*, where the men were dismissed to set up their tents. The general and his staff were greeted by the governor, who personally escorted them to a three-story building on Rue Royal, designated for the general's headquarters. The crowd followed, some crying out for the general to speak.

Inside the building, Jackson greeted Majors Darcy and Harville. "I thank you for your reports, gentlemen," he said in his stately voice, "but only so much can be committed to paper. We must discuss the defenses of the city, and I hope you have better news than what I read."

Before either Matthew or Jacob could answer, Edward Livingstone approached. "General, the people want to hear from you."

The general shook his head. "I have no time for that; I have work to do."

The governor interjected. "Please, General, the people have been very concerned. It would be well for you to speak. It will strengthen their hearts and soothe their worries."

"That is fine and good, sir, but I do not speak French."

Livingston, an old friend and congressional colleague of Jackson, volunteered to translate, and the general was convinced. The party made its way to the second-floor gallery, and General Jackson emerged to great cheers.

Matthew was not dismayed by his commander's aspect. When it came to Jackson, always severe in appearance, he had learned to watch the man's eyes to gage his feelings. Matthew was pleased to see the general's usual calm, clear, confident gaze. The Old Man was well, and for that, Matthew was happy.

Jackson's fiery speech was beautifully crafted to stir the crowd's hearts—so much so that Matthew thought Jackson's prior reluctance was but for show. The old politician had them in his hands.

"I pledge to drive our enemies into the sea or perish in the effort!" his voice echoed down the street. The crowd cheered then again louder at the translation. "Good citizens, you must all rally around me in this emergency, cease all differences and divisions, and unite with me in patriotic resolve to save this city from dishonor and disaster which a presumptuous enemy threatens to inflict upon it!"

Yes, thought Matthew, *the Old Man must have prepared a speech. He even remembered to mention the divisions in the city from our reports. The crowd is inspired.*

Matthew peered intently at the mass of humanity filling Rue Royal and spotted the face he longed to see. *Yes, there is Anne-Marie —and she sees me!* Only military discipline prevented him from gesturing. *Is that her father next to her?*

Sure enough, Emile Dansereau stood next to Anne-Marie, arms crossed, listening intently.

It is! Will wonders never cease!

That was all Matthew saw, for General Jackson had finished his speech and returned indoors, his entourage quickly following. He glanced over his shoulder to catch Anne-Marie's wave, and the curtain closed.

Jackson was so pleased with Livingston's performance that he requested he join his staff as personal aide and private secretary. Livingston accepted without hesitation, and the staff met directly with the city's committee of defense. The first and only order of business was strategy: From which direction would the British attack if not overland from Mobile?

The two most likely routes were determined to be up the Mississippi River or down from Lake Pontchartrain. Fort St. Philip guarded the river, and there were two roads from the north: Fort St. John on the south shore of Lake Pontchartrain and the Chef Menteur from Lake Borgne. Commodore Patterson reported he had already stationed a squadron of gunboats to block the pass into Lake Borgne.

General Jackson immediately ordered that Fort St. John and Fort Petites Coquilles be reinforced and that any water routes from the lakes to the north be blocked with felled trees. Major Villeré was given the latter task. Jackson also ordered that troops guard the Chef Menteur, a mission that should take few men as the entrance into the Plain of Gentilly was very narrow.

"We have more men coming, gentlemen," the general informed the committee. "General Carroll is coming down the Mississippi from Tennessee. General Coffee will guard our western flank at Baton Rouge, supporting General Thomas and his Kentuckians at Bayou Lafourche. General Morgan is raising more men in Kentucky as we speak. We shall give a good account, I assure you, with the local militia by our side."

Jackson's quick grasp of the situation impressed the committee of defense, and they left the meeting relieved.

General Jackson was not so sanguine. "We must inspect Fort St. Philip," he said to Major Harville, "and we shall do so after we review the local militia tomorrow. What are your impressions?"

"They need training, General, and lots of it," Jacob replied. "The best group they've got is a colored battalion."

"I hope they are treated well," Old Hickory growled. "I so told the governor, when he wrote to me. Our country wants soldiers to fight her battles. Colored troops are inured to this harsh climate and would make excellent soldiers. We must engage them with rights and privileges equal to white men. Otherwise, if they are mistrusted, they become our enemies."

"Our Creek allies proved very loyal in the late war," pointed out one of the aides. "They are with Coffee."

"Yes, sir," said Jacob, "but a lot of the locals ain't keen on the idea of colored soldiers armed with muskets."

General Jackson's long face grew hard. "It would be better if they attended to their own corps. I understand they have raised but three hundred Creoles? We must do better than that. What of guns, balls, and powder?"

"In short supply, General," reported Matthew. "The British blockade is tight. Everything must come down the Mississippi."

"General," injected Mr. Livingston, "there may be another source. The Baratarians can provide men, weapons, and powder."

Old Hickory was aghast. "What? Do business with those hellish Banditti? Out of the question!" He turned to the staff. "We must redouble our efforts to raise men and ammunition. Prepare to dispatch local troops to Fort Petites Coquilles and"—he looked down at the map—"Chef Menteur. Hmm, a puzzling name for a road. And see that our men are quartered. That is all."

Sunday, December 4

A FEW DAYS LATER, MATTHEW was shown into the study of M. Melançon. Sitting at the desk was not the owner of the house, but his brother-in-law. Matthew unconsciously came to attention. He did not expect this interview so soon or for it to be pleasant.

"You asked to meet with me, *monsieur.*"

M. Dansereau was grim. "*Oui.* I thank you for coming. You were not at Mass today."

"I attended an earlier service."

"Ah, I see. I do not take you away from your duties, I trust."

Actually, he did, but Matthew could spare an hour. He would just have to forgo his midday meal. Matthew stood silently, waiting for Anne-Marie's father to begin. He supposed that he was going to order him away from his daughter, a request that would fall on deaf ears. Matthew was determined to make Anne-Marie Dansereau his wife, and only she could send him away.

M. Dansereau absently ran his fingers across the fine wood of M. Melançon's desk. "Your general, he is a passionate man, *n'est-ce pas?*"

A slight frown marked Matthew's otherwise blank features. "General Jackson speaks his mind; that is true."

The older man picked up a broadsheet. "I doubt it not. This is a copy of his proclamation to the people. If you will forgive me, I shall read a little from it.

"'*Louisianans! The proud British, the national and sworn enemy of all Frenchmen, of all Americans, and all freemen, has called upon you by proclamation to aid her in her tyranny and to prostrate the holy temple of our liberty. Can Louisianans, can Frenchmen, can Americans ever stoop to be slaves or allies of Britain?*'"

He set the paper down. "Your general continues in this vein. My question, Major, is does your general believe this, or is this just empty words from a foreigner?"

Of course, he believes this, thought Matthew. *Obviously, he does not know Jackson!* That thought gave Matthew an idea.

"*Monsieur*, allow me to tell you a story about Andrew Jackson. It is well known to us, but you may not have heard it.

"During the Revolutionary War, a young Jackson, living in South Carolina, volunteered to help fight against the British, having lost his eldest brother to battle. He and his surviving brother were wounded and captured by the British. The story goes that a British officer demanded that Andrew Jackson clean his boots. Jackson refused, and the enraged officer stuck him on the head with his sword. He was but fourteen years old at the time. General Jackson wears that scar to this day."

Dansereau nodded thoughtfully. "He hates the English. *Bon.* But the rest of you Americans—would you truly lay down your lives to defend us—to defend Frenchmen?"

"It is our duty to defend the United States." As Dansereau tried to interrupt, Matthew forestalled him. "*Monsieur*, New Orleans and Louisiana are part of the United States. You are Americans whether you like it or not. And yes, we will defend you to the death."

"We did not ask to join your United States. We were betrayed."

"Betrayed by Frenchmen, I believe."

Dansereau looked like he swallowed something bitter. "It is not the first time my people have been betrayed by Paris. It is why we fled *Normandie* and *Bretagne* for *L'Acadie*. We could not trust our own kings. They betrayed us again when they did not defend us. They surrendered us to the English, who threw us out of our homes." He peered at Matthew. "You are familiar with the story?"

Matthew nodded.

Dansereau cocked his head. "Darcy. It is much like *D'Arcy*. You have French blood?"

Matthew almost smiled. It had taken a while, but he finally figured out what Dansereau was dancing around. Apparently, Anne-Marie could not be moved to give up her lover, and the older man was trying to save face. "I am told my ancestors came over from *Normandie* with William the Conqueror."

"*Normandie. Bon.* Why did your family immigrate to America?"

"There was a spilt in the Darcy family. Some accepted the Church of England, but my forefathers stayed true to the old faith. It caused a rift, and finally, after the ascension of William of Orange, we left England for the Maryland colony, where Catholics were not persecuted. We did well enough there, becoming farmers."

"Philippe tells me there is another rift in your family."

"That is true. The son of my late father's first marriage has rejected the children of the second. I must make my own way in the world now."

Dansereau became grave again. "I am told you plan to go north after the war, to Virginia. That is very far away."

"*Peut-être. Peut-être pas.*"

Dansereau looked up. "What? What do you mean with this 'perhaps—perhaps not'?"

"I mean to farm, *monsieur*. I spoke of Virginia because it is close to Maryland. I know the climate, the crops." He took a chance. "Let us speak clearly. I love your daughter, *monsieur*, and she says she loves me. If I survive this war, I mean to marry Anne-Marie. I know she loves you, and she loves her home. But she has said she will come with me wherever I go. That is well, for a wife's place is with her husband.

"That does not mean a husband's place cannot be also his wife's place. I want her to be happy above all else. If I can farm here—find land here—then here I will live. Not for me—for her."

Dansereau was quiet for a time, staring hard at Matthew. "What do you want from me? Money? Land?"

"I will assume you did not mean to insult me. I have funds, and I have prospects. For example, I have talked to your cousin, Henri Herbert. He might be willing to sell his land at the right price."

"Have you enough?"

"We have not discussed money as yet. I shall not, with battle in the offing. But M. Melançon assures me I have enough."

The older man frowned again. "You have spoken to many people about this, but not to me. It is *my daughter* who is in the middle.

This is not well done."

"I beg pardon, *monsieur*, but would you have listened?"

Stung, Dansereau sat back. He stewed for a while as Matthew quietly watched. Finally, the planter sighed. "You will not keep secrets from me any longer?"

"Will you allow me to court your daughter openly?"

"Hah! You are a bold man, indeed! Very well, Major, but chaperoned. Closely chaperoned, *n'est-ce pas?*"

Matthew knew Anne-Marie's father was within his rights. "Of course." He extended his hand.

Father and suitor shook hands, and then Dansereau offered Matthew a drink, which he refused. "*Merci beaucoup*, but I must be going. My duties cannot wait."

"I have Mme Melançon's permission to invite you to dinner if you are available. Your American comrade, as well."

Matthew was pleased at Dansereau's more genial attitude. "That is very kind. I am sorry that Major Harville is unavailable to attend. He is accompanying General Jackson as he inspects the defenses, but I shall be there. My compliments to Mme Melançon, and please remember me to Mlle Dansereau."

When Matthew returned to Rue Bourbon that evening for dinner, he was greeted cordially by M. Dansereau, his beaming daughter looking on. All of Anne-Marie's dearest wishes had been granted now that her beloved was beside her—welcomed by *all* of her family—and that her dear Papa had finally agreed to their courtship. Now, she longed for time alone with her Matthew.

Conversation at the Melançon's table was far more relaxed than it had been the last time M. Dansereau shared a meal with Major Darcy. Relaxed, but not pleasant, for most of the talk was about the state of the city's defenses. According to Matthew, New Orleans was in a sorry state. They lacked both men and guns to stop a determined enemy. While reinforcements were on their way from the north, no one knew when or from which direction the British would strike.

"Using the troops we have, the general placed them in the best possible position," Matthew reported. "Major Plauche's Creole militia is stationed at Fort Petites Coquilles while the colored battalion has been placed under Major Lacoste and sits astride the Chef Menteur, blocking the Gentilly Plain. Meanwhile, Commodore Patterson's gunboats control the entrance into Lake Borgne. Still, we need more men and, most importantly, guns and powder."

"Are not Generals Coffee and Carroll bringing arms and ammunition with them?" asked Philippe.

Matthew assured him that they would, but more would be required. "Besides," he added, "Coffee is to protect our western flank from Baton Rouge."

During the discussion, Dansereau said little except to express his disgust at the lack of martial enthusiasm among the Creoles. Otherwise, he seemed to be thinking.

After the delicious meal, the men retired for a time to the study. When they emerged, Anne-Marie was happy to see her father chatting amiably with Matthew. They shook hands, and her beloved walked over to her.

He took her hands. "I am sorry, Anne-Marie, but I have to get back to my quarters." He thanked her aunt for her hospitality, and in her turn, Madeline announced that the major was welcome to dinner every night he was free.

Anne-Marie announced she would walk Matthew to the door, and she was glad when the others turned their backs to give the couple a bit of privacy.

"I am so grateful you and Papa have settled your differences." She caressed his fingers, earning a heated look from Matthew.

"I hate to leave, my love, but I will return in a few days." At her frown, he added, "Sadly, the general takes precedence over you for now, *ma chérie*." He kissed her hands.

"Keep safe, Matthew."

"I will." Just as he opened the door, he added, "I did not know your father was acquainted with the pirates Lafitte."

Anne-Marie raised an eyebrow. "Many of the planters are. Why do you say this?"

He glanced over her shoulder. "He mentioned them. We were talking of the supply shortage. Have you met them?"

"*Oui*. The brothers are handsome and rather charming, particularly Jean." She laughed as Matthew's face darkened. "Do not worry, *mon chéri*, I have not fallen under his spell. He is too charming by half." She rolled her eyes and then whispered as she placed her hand on his chest, "Besides, I like my men in uniform." Her reward was a sharply drawn breath.

"Good night, my love." A kiss on her hand and he was gone.

Chapter 10

In the following days, the energy shown by General Jackson, inspecting and improving the defenses of New Orleans, delighted the frightened citizenry. The tall, painfully thin Tennessean was everywhere: Fort St. John and Fort Petites Coquilles overlooking Lake Pontchartrain, Fort St. Phillip near the mouth of the river, and the plains of Chalmette and Gentilly. By his side were his staff engineers, Commodore Patterson, and a local man of immense reputation.

Arsène Lacarrière Latour, a French engineer in Napoleon's army, had immigrated to New York in 1804, where he met Edward Livingston. M. Latour followed his friend to Louisiana, established himself as an architect, and helped to lay out the town of Baton Rouge. Jackson immediately recognized the engineer's worth and enlisted M. Latour into the army's service at the rank of major. The events that followed would prove this to be one of the most important decisions ever made by Old Hickory.

General Jackson's tour showed that Fort St. Phillip near the river's mouth wanted enhancement, and Fort St. Leon, just downriver from New Orleans at English Turn, was dangerously weak. Fort St. Charles at the eastern gates of the city was dilapidated. All three strongholds, plus the forts by the lake, needed repair and improvement to the fortifications and, most importantly, more cannon. Jackson wanted to abandon Fort St. Charles, but Major Latour changed the general's mind.

The most frustrating state of affairs was his army's lack of manpower. There were simply not enough men to go around. Jackson's own troops were stretched to the breaking point, and reinforcements had not yet arrived. Old Hickory needed greater participation by the locals.

Heeding Jackson's request for laborers, the legislature called upon the planters to provide as many slaves as could be spared for rebuilding the forts. The general also needed to build a larger militia, and he didn't care where the men came from. The appeal went out to the patriotic locals: Creoles, Spaniards, Frenchmen, transplanted Americans, immigrants from Germany and Ireland, Jews, freedmen, and free men of color. Almost anyone would do, and the stern protector of the city would not stand for dissent. When a local paymaster objected to enlisting men of color, the general thundered, "Be pleased to keep to yourself your opinions upon the policy of making payment of the troops with the necessary muster rolls, without inquiring whether the troops are white, black, or tea!"

The men who came forward either brought their own weapons or received arms by the generosity of the citizens. Adult men who were unable or unwilling to fight donated their ammunition and guns, mostly hunting rifles. Locals with military experience taught rudimentary drills to the others and formed them into companies.

There was one last problem that became intransigent of solution. Jackson lacked artillerymen, both for the forts and for Patterson's squadron of boats. Civilians with limited instruction could become tolerable riflemen, particularly in defensive positions, but cannoneers were a different matter. It was a skill that took much practice to master, and Jackson had neither time nor powder to train raw recruits. General Jackson needed men with experience, and he could not find them—at least, none that he found suitable.

"The general won't hear of it," complained a weary Jacob as he tossed his hat onto his bed. It had been a long day in a string of long days, and Matthew knew his friend was as exhausted as he. "He won't talk to that Lafitte feller or take any of the pirates into the army."

"I thought Commodore Patterson was going to speak to him."

"He did, an' so did Mr. Livingston. Hell, the whole defense committee, led by Mr. Marigny, swore up and down guaranteeing Lafitte's loyalty, but the old man still refused. He won't deal with banditti, he says." Jacob half fell into his bed and threw one arm over his face.

Matthew was amazed at his commander's obstinacy. "I thought sure he would listen to Patterson. After all, the commodore was sent here to root out the Baratarians. If *he* finds them suitable now, why not the general?"

"You know the old man," said Jacob. "Stubborn as a mule when he put his mind to it. He wants the legislature to press men into the boats."

"What? Jacob, British impressment is what started this war! The legislature is not going to do that!"

"I reckon you're right. I hope General Carroll's bringing artillery with him. We'll be in a sorry shape if he doesn't."

Matthew sat back, taking in all Jacob told him. They needed Jean Lafitte and his Baratarians, not just for manpower but also for the stores of guns and powder the pirate was rumored to have. If Matthew could get confirmation of the stockpile, that might change Jackson's mind. But who did he know that knew Lafitte?

He sat up straight. He *did* know someone.

BERNARD DE MARIGNY AND THE rest of the Louisiana legislature were not deterred by General Jackson's intransigence. In the Louisiana way, they simply went around him. They negotiated with the local federal judge and came up with a scheme. The lawmakers passed a resolution suspending any action against the Baratarians for four months. The judge immediately ordered the federal district attorney to cease prosecution of the Lafitte brothers and to release Dominique You and the other privateers from custody. The Lafittes also received safe conduct from the judge.

So, the Lafitte Brothers could walk the streets of New Orleans without fear of arrest. That did not mean General Jackson would meet with them. Something would have to be arranged.

Wednesday, December 7

MATTHEW, HAT IN HAND, WALKED into Philippe Melançon's law office and addressed the gentlemen assembled.

"M. Dansereau, Philippe, thank you for meeting with me today at such short notice." He saw that Philippe was openly curious, while Emile Dansereau was apprehensive. Refusing a glass of wine, Matthew took his seat.

"You are a very busy man, Matthew," said Philippe carefully, "so I think it wise we dispense with formalities and get right to the reasons for this meeting, *n'est-ce pas?*"

"I agree." Matthew turned to Dansereau. "*Monsieur*, how well do you know Jean Lafitte?"

Dansereau was clearly taken aback. "No more than any other planter."

"Are you able to contact him quickly?"

Dansereau's eyes darted about suspiciously. "Why do you ask? It is not a crime to know such people."

Matthew leaned forward. "Please, *monsieur*, it is vital to the safety of the city that my message reaches Captain Lafitte. Can you help me?"

"Ah." Dansereau's mistrust turned into curiosity. "*Certainement, mon* major. What is this message?"

Matthew held up an envelope. "Is Captain Lafitte sincere in his desire to defend Louisiana? And if so, would he be willing to meet with General Jackson?"

Philippe frowned. "I had heard that the general has refused to meet with Lafitte many times."

"General Jackson is a stubborn man, but he is not immune to reasoned argument. He is very proud and must be allowed to save face. The men I represent understand this and seek to promote a meeting that preserves the general's honor—a chance encounter at a dinner, perhaps, or some other coincidence. It is most important that it not appear a capitulation by the general, or everything will be lost."

"Hmm," mused Dansereau, "this scheming sounds like Marigny."

Matthew smiled. "Mr. Livingston, actually."

"Hah! Give me your message, Major"—Dansereau reached over—"and I will see that it is in Captain Lafitte's hands no later than tonight."

Matthew handed him the document. "I thank you for your cooperation, *monsieur*."

"I am happy to help." Dansereau tucked the envelope into a pocket. "I must admit that, when you entered the room, I thought you wished to speak of another matter."

Matthew grinned. "That is for another time—once this crisis is over, God willing."

Dansereau's gaze was thoughtful. "You continue to surprise me, young man. It must be your French blood. Shall we see you at dinner tonight?"

"My duties will not allow it." He turned to Philippe. "Please give my regrets to your wife and your niece and tell them I hope to come tomorrow. I shall send word."

Philippe nodded.

"I notice you do not ask *me* to send your regrets to Anne-Marie," rumbled Dansereau, "but I shall do so, nonetheless."

"That is very kind of you. I thought you did not approve of me." Matthew shook Dansereau's hand, who gave another Gallic shrug.

"I do it for her. Her happiness is paramount."

"On that subject, *monsieur*," Matthew said evenly, "we are in perfect agreement. *Au revoir*."

Thursday, December 8: off the Louisiana coast

JAMES FITZWILLIAM MADE HIS WAY to the main deck of *HMS Imprudent* after the unpalatable dinner normally found on transport ships: boiled half-rotten beef with weevil-infested ship's biscuit. Other officers—those with rich families or money in the funds —brought their own provisions. All James could afford was a case of smuggled French claret. Margaret remained in their cabin while her husband attempted to walk off his indigestion and smoke a pipe.

The sun was just setting, and the ship glided through the calm waters and light winds. James clasped his coat close, chilled by the breeze.

The crew of the ship scampered to and fro, working the lines and stays, and responding to barked commands.

"One hundred feet by the deep!"

"Prepare to tack ship!"

"Haul courses! Make fast those lines! Smartly, now!"

"Come about; let fly!"

"Two points true, if you please!"

"Seventy feet! Hard sand!"

James had sailed with the Royal Navy many times, yet the orders still sounded like gibberish. Looking over the rail, he could see the fleet moving with the waves, the glow of ship's lanterns dancing in the twilight. There would be no stars that night, the skies being overcast. The waters looked as dark and muddy as the clouds. It was a cold, miserable evening.

"Ah, Major Fitzwilliam. Up to enjoy a bit of the crisp air, what?"

James turned to the sound of Captain Elliot's voice. "Good evening, Captain."

Elliot sauntered to the rail, a weather coat over his everyday uniform. "Same to you, Major. And how is the lovely Mrs. Fitzwilliam? Well, I hope?"

"No complaints, sir." None at all, except for the blasted chill in the cabin, heat being in short supply aboard ship. Still, it was warmer than above decks. "If I may ask, how far are we from the anchorage?"

"In this wind? Another day or two."

James frowned. "What about those islands there?" He pointed to a distant series of low, black objects on the horizon, just left of the bow.

"Those? Ah, the Chandler Islands. A great misnomer—they are little more than exposed sand bars."

"Are we near land?"

"Miles from it, such as it is. We are east of the Louisiana coast, over twenty leagues from New Orleans."

"But we are not landing there?"

"Well, I suppose we could," Elliot drawled "but the army would have a devil of a time of it. The Chandlers are useless, and according to our scouts and spies, the coast beyond is all salt marshes and quicksand, infested with crocodiles and vipers. Nasty place, what?"

"So, we are heading"—James got his bearings—"north?"

"Northwest, actually. Our destination is Cat Island at the mouth of Lake Borgne. Lake—hah. More like a bay according to the charts. Damned shallow, that's for certain."

"Have you orders where we are to disembark?"

"We must see if we can sail into Lake Pontchartrain. It is rumored to be but a dozen feet deep. Too shallow for us, but the admiral wants to make certain. If it is too shallow, we plan to use Cat Island to stage the disembarkation."

"I trust this Cat Island is more substantial than the Chandlers."

"It is to be hoped. Haven't seen the place, myself. Well, I must return to my duties. Enjoy your pipe, Major." Captain Elliot returned to the quarterdeck while James puffed thoughtfully.

Salt marshes, quicksand, and crocodiles? Is Elliot serous, or is he mocking me again?

He watched the sailors going about their necessary tasks. It was hard, backbreaking work. Surely, the fleet would not put forth all this effort unless it was required for their mission. James turned to once again take in the Chandler Islands as they faded from sight in the gathering darkness.

Just what manner of place is Louisiana?

Friday, December 9: New Orleans

IN A REMARKABLE COINCIDENCE, GENERAL Andrew Jackson was "accidently" accosted on the corner of Rue St. Phillip and Rue Royale by none other than Jean Lafitte and Dominique You. Of course, this meeting was as accidental as a military review. Much planning behind the scenes had given the pirates of Barataria their opportunity, and they made the most of it. The two privateers launched into a passionate appeal to be allowed to fight for their adopted country. Their enthusiasm and aggressiveness impressed Jackson, and he was heartened by their promise of cannons, shot, and powder.

Andrew Jackson was, above all things, a patriot, and nothing could move him like an appeal to patriotism. He was also a man who put much stock in another man's bearing and courage. In the late Creek War, his enemy, Chief Red Eagle, boldly walked into Jackson's camp to surrender after losing the Battle of Horseshoe Bend. The general did not summarily execute him, as many others would have done in his place. Instead, he spared Red Eagle and sent him back to try to convince the other rebel Creeks to lay down their arms and end the war.

Now, Jackson acted similarly. He accepted the pirates' assistance and gave them their orders. Jean Lafitte was to deliver the war materiel he claimed to possess, while Dominique You was to raise three companies of artillery.

Thus began the legend of the alliance between the aristocratic General Jackson and the dashing Captain Lafitte. It was all a complete fantasy, of course.

Jean Lafitte was not some romantic buccaneer forced into a life of sea-bound larceny due to crimes against his family or in revenge over a lost love. He was raised by his mother and merchant stepfather, and he became a pirate, thief, smuggler, and slave trader by his own volition. He cheated the government out of taxes and duties, and pocketed that gold for his own enrichment. While not a murderous animal like Edward Low or Blackbeard—in fact, he was known to release his captives, and even their ships, unharmed—he ran his empire of Barataria with an iron grip. His courtly manner was all for show. Lafitte was a criminal because he was good at it.

Andrew Jackson, with his patriarchal manner, gave the appearance of a steady, by the book, career army officer. It was a calculated invention. Nothing could have been further from the truth. A farmer's son, born in the Carolinas and orphaned in his teens, Jackson became a lawyer, planter, land speculator, and merchant after moving to rough-hewed Tennessee. He had been a congressman, senator, and judge of the Tennessee Supreme Court, all before the age of thirty-seven.

Jackson's first major military action was as commander of the Tennessee militia during the just-concluded Creek War. To say he had an unusual affinity for martial activities would be an understatement. It was well that Jackson's natural abilities made good his arrogant self-image, for most of his activities in the Creek War were against expressed instructions issued by the government in Washington. That his decisions proved correct and successful, despite orders to the contrary, did not escape Jackson's notice.

There was no shared command at New Orleans. That was impossible. Lafitte had no military training or experience. As for Old Hickory, only he would give the orders. He jealously shared that responsibility with no one—not even with the governor of the state he was protecting.

So the stage was set. The defense of the most strategically vital city in North America was entrusted to an ambitious amateur general, a career criminal, a nervous governor, and a barely trained, volunteer army made up of farmers, native Indians, backwoodsmen, merchants, freedmen, pirates, and puffed-up grandees who spoke different languages than their allies.

What chance did they have against the greatest military power in the world?

Chapter 11

There were three types of spies and informants in the early nineteenth century. The purest were members of the diplomatic corps: the ambassadors and their staff. More effective were the agents or spies, and they came in two flavors. The volunteers were patriotic adventurers, fighting for king or country. The rest were paid scum who loved nothing but gold and would sell their own mothers if the price was right.

The third player in the game of intelligence was not motivated by flag or gold. Hate was enough. The enemy of one's enemy was his friend, and this type of unofficial spy was known to send unsolicited information to his adversary's foe.

It was fortunate that these men existed because the United States at the time had no formal means of intelligence gathering. With a tiny diplomatic corps, she depended on admirers in foreign countries to keep an eye on America's enemies. This irregular service proved quite useful and curiously timely, as if some great hand controlled the destiny of the world—something greater than coincidence or luck.

General Jackson was bombarded with reports from the Caribbean. He and the American government knew a great armada had set sail from Jamaica. No one could misunderstand the signs. The British were going to invade the Gulf Coast of America. The ultimate target was obviously New Orleans. The only question unanswered was where they would land.

All the Americans could do was to wait for the hammer's fall. It would not be long in coming.

December 12–14, 1814: Lake Borgne

BRITISH VICE-ADMIRAL SIR ALEXANDER COCHRANE was not a happy man. He had requested flatboats and shallow-draft ships to help transport the troops ashore when he landed along the Gulf Coast. But his appeals went unanswered.

He hoped to sail directly into Lake Pontchartrain, but once he got to the mouth of Lake Borgne, he found two obstacles. One was a large sandbar, just underwater, that stretched the width of the lake. The other was the fact that the lake itself was twelve feet at its deepest. It was impossible for the fleet to get any closer to the city. There was no choice but to drop anchor off Cat Island and row the army ashore in small boats and barges.

To the admiral's consternation, scouts reported numerous armed gunboats in Lake Borgne, guarding the entrance into Lake Pontchartrain. Damn those Yankees! Surprise was gone, and valuable time had to be used to eliminate those gunboats.

AMERICAN LIEUTENANT THOMAS AP CATESBY Jones was an anxious man. His mission was to guard the approaches to New Orleans from the sea. Now before him was a mighty armada of threescore ships, and he had but five gunboats to stop them.

Following orders, he fell back towards Fort Petites Coquilles, which guarded the Chef Menteur Road. He planned to block the Rigolets Pass into Lake Pontchartrain and lure any British craft into the range of the fort's guns. He did not worry about the enemy's large ships; their hulls could not clear the numerous sandbars infesting Lake Borgne.

Unfortunately, the meager five feet of water the American gunboats drew were also too much to clear the bars. Catesby Jones's little fleet grounded itself right at the Rigolets. The lieutenant could not flee, so he prepared to fight. With shear muscle, his men pulled their beached boats broadside to the lake. The squadron was now a wall, and the sailors could only wait for the onslaught.

Thirty-six hours later, it was upon them. At first, Catesby Jones thought the barges heading towards him were troop transports.

He was wrong. Admiral Cochrane had forty-five barges armed with cannonades and nearly a thousand men rowing to destroy the American gunboats. Just out of range of the Yankee guns, the British barges stopped so their crews could eat dinner.

When they did finally press home the attack, both sides fought valiantly. Catesby Jones's men kept up a steady fire with their heavier cannons, but they could only shoot broadsides. The enemy could dodge and move, the light cannonades making perfect bow chasers. The Americans were easy targets. The battle lasted forty-five minutes, and while the British suffered ninety-four dead and wounded versus forty-five for the Americans, Catesby Jones's squadron was overrun by superior numbers and tactics.

It was a catastrophic defeat. Eighty-six Americans were captured, including the wounded Catesby Jones. All the gunboats were put to the torch. The British had swept Lake Borgne clean of the American Navy.

With the loss of the Lake Borgne squadron, the Americans had only three ships left of Commodore Patterson's fleet, and *USS Louisiana* was unmanned.

First blood belonged to the British. The Royal Navy could now operate without fear of interference.

December 14–15: New Orleans

THE NEWS THAT THE BRITISH fleet had wiped out Catesby Jones's gunboats electrified the city. Panicked horsemen rode through the city, crying that the enemy was at their very gates. The governor was unable to calm the masses.

Only one man could: Major General Andrew Jackson. Assuming the steely demeanor he had developed during his lifetime, he set to work, giving speeches and orders. The entirety of the reserves was called up. Troops were sent to reinforce Fort Petites Coquilles and guard the Chef Menteur Road. Interestingly, Jackson chose his Creek and Choctaw fighters as well as a company from the colored battalion. The citizens drew courage from this tall, thin, rock of a man.

Jackson's cool energy belied his fury. The British had outsmarted him. His eyes on the coast were blinded. The invasion could come from anywhere: through the Gentilly plain, Fort St. John on Lake Pontchartrain, or even from Baton Rouge in the west, assuming the British landed on the Mississippi coast and marched overland around the lake. And while Jackson had calmed the citizenry to a certain extent, rumors were flying everywhere—many of them coming from members of the legislature.

The only good news to come from the debacle was that the British had shown their hand. They intended to directly attack New Orleans rather than land at Mobile and cut Louisiana off from the rest of the country.

Dispatches were sent to Coffee in Baton Rouge and Carroll in Natchez, urging them to push to the city without delay. The day did provide a welcome surprise: the steamboat *Enterprise* arrived from Pittsburg with a cargo of munitions.

Still, the city was frightened and about to erupt into chaos. General Jackson knew he had to act decisively.

Friday, December 16

Matthew and Jacob sat down for their first meal with the Melançons in a week. Their hosts peppered them with questions.

"Is it true that General Jackson has declared martial law, Matthew?" asked Philippe, in English for Jacob's sake.

"Yes, he has. He is unhappy with the legislature. Their failure to suspend *habeas corpus* leads him to believe their support of the army is halfhearted. He does not trust them. He is also concerned with spies. The general knows that not everyone in the city accepts Louisiana's purchase by the United States"—Matthew turned to M. Dansereau—"present company excluded."

Anne-Marie quickly translated and asked her own question. "What do you mean by 'martial law'?"

"By this order, Miz Dansereau," replied Jacob, "the general's runnin' the city. The governor, the legislature, the mayor—they all have to answer to him. The general can call up any able-bodied man to serve in the army or navy. An' nobody can come in or out of the city unless they get permission from the general's staff."

"I see," said a pale Anne-Marie. She repeated Jacob's words to her father in French.

"I think it well done by the general," Emile Dansereau declared. "I do not trust the politicians, especially Marigny."

Philippe threw up his hands. "Why must you always disparage Bernard de Marigny, Emile? He is no traitor, I tell you. He has been helpful in this crisis."

"And I say Marigny cares only for Marigny!"

"He looks out for self-interest, but so do we all. That he disagrees with what the general has done does not make him disloyal." Philippe turned to Matthew. "It so happens I agree with the legislature. I do not see the need for martial law."

Matthew said nothing. What would it accomplish to say he supported the general's actions except to offend his host? The political situation in New Orleans was unstable. With their rulers changing three times in less than four years, a half-dozen languages spoken in the street at any given hour, and mistrust and loathing between the Creole and American citizens, local politics was quarrelsome during the best of times. Now that the British were at their doorstep and rumors of a slave revolt running rampant, the city was at the breaking point. General Jackson's leadership might well be the only thing holding New Orleans together.

"The general's plan is workin', you've got to admit. The city seems calmer," Jacob pointed out.

"It is," said Madeline Melançon, "but there is much fear, also."

"General Jackson has ordered a grand review of the troops in the *Place d'Armes* on Sunday the eighteenth," Matthew informed them. "He hopes that, once the people see their army, it will strengthen their hearts."

Madeline nodded. "He understands us. There is nothing the people love more than a parade."

"What of the English?" Emile demanded. "Where will they land?"

Matthew glanced at Jacob before answering in French. "That is a good question, *monsieur*, and we wish we had an answer. We have reinforced our defenses along the Chef Menteur. It is the logical approach to the city, but it has its own difficulties. Lake Borgne is shallow—too shallow for their ships—and it would take a great deal of time to ferry them via barges." He gave Jacob the gist of his statement.

"Matthew's right, sir," added the Tennessean. "They might still land in Mississippi an' march overland to Baton Rouge."

"I thought the general had recalled General Coffee from Baton Rouge," said Philippe.

"That's so. Coffee'll leave a small detachment to be a lookout, though."

"But what if the British do march to Baton Rouge?"

"Let 'em." Jacob grinned. "It would be a trap. The British won't find anything of use; Coffee will take all the war materiel with him. The redcoats will stretch their supply lines to the breaking point. They'll be that much easier to whip."

Matthew thought his friend's bravado a bit much but chose not to contradict him.

They were interrupted by the butler. "*Monsieur*," he reported to Philippe, "there is a soldier at the door for *les majors*. They are requested to return to headquarters, *tout de suite*."

Both officers immediately got to their feet, politely declining Madeline's entreaties that they at least finish their meals. They were making their farewells when Anne-Marie took Matthew's hand.

"Please, *chéri*, wait a moment." With that, she disappeared from the room.

Meanwhile, Jacob spoke to Philippe. "Are y'all staying in the city?"

"I do not wish to be away from my business, but"—he glanced at his wife—"we shall go to Dansereau Plantation if the need arises."

Emile approached the two Americans with an unreadable expression. He requested that Philippe translate. "You will fight the English when they come?" He stared hard at Jacob.

Jacob Harville was puzzled. "That's what I came to do, Mr. Dansereau. Don't you worry none. Matt an' General Jackson an'

I'll give them redcoats a proper whipping."

To everyone's surprise, tears welled in Emile's eyes. "*Pardonne-moi.* I was mistaken about you. *Vous êtes mes bons amis.*" He paused and in his heavily accented voice, repeated in English, "My good friends —good luck to you!" He embraced them both, Jacob first, then Matthew, bestowing a kiss on their cheeks. The planter then mumbled something and walked off, wiping his face with a handkerchief.

Jacob, stunned, rubbed his cheek. "First man to kiss me since my granddaddy."

Madeline seemed to be fighting her own emotions. "He said he would pray for you, as will we all. Take care of yourselves, my boys!" She then repeated Emile's gesture, as did Philippe.

Matthew tried to convince Philippe to take the others and leave the city soon when Anne-Marie returned, a small object in her hand. A moment later, she was at his side, handing it to him.

"I had this made for you," she said softly.

Matthew looked at the miniature of Anne-Marie in his hands. It obviously had been quickly done; it barely resembled the girl. He did not care. He knew what this represented.

He stepped closer to his beloved. Slowly, deliberately, he kissed the miniature and placed it in the pocket closest to his heart. "When this is over, I am going to commission a portrait of you to hang on the wall of our house. I want our grandchildren to know just how beautiful you are."

Sobbing, Anne-Marie threw herself into his arms. "Oh, Matthew, take care!"

"Anne-Marie, I want you to leave the city."

"No, my love, I will not go."

Matthew wanted to argue, but the messenger, a sergeant, broke in impatiently. "Major Darcy, the general is waiting."

There was nothing else to do but give Anne-Marie a quick kiss. "Thank you, my love." He released her and beseeched her father and uncle to take the family and flee New Orleans. The two officers then followed the sergeant out the door.

Moving at a quick step along Rue Bourbon towards the *Place d'Armes* through the late afternoon, the sergeant expressed regret for interrupting their meal, but a staff meeting had been called. "There is no urgent news—no reports of landings or anything of that nature."

"Thank God for that!" Matthew said crisply. "Do not apologize, Sergeant. We both understand the gravity of the present situation. There is no time for socializing or fine dinners. We have much to do."

"I'll tell you one thing," growled Jacob. "That's probably the last fine dinner we'll have from Miz Melançon until this unpleasantness is done. Them damned Britishers will hear from me 'bout that!"

Off Cat Island

THE ENTIRE STAFF GATHERED IN Admiral Cochrane's grand cabin aboard the flagship. It was a surreal scene. The room was crowded, but only the admiral, General Keane, the fleet captain, and Lieu-tenant-Colonel Thornton of the Eighty-Fifth Foot sat at the table along with a civilian—a short, swarthy, filthy fisherman dressed in foul-smelling rags. The rest of the staff stood about in their fine uniforms, jammed shoulder-to-shoulder, closely attending every word that dropped from the fisherman's lips.

The fleet captain leaned over the table. Fluent in Spanish, he conducted the interview. "You will lead my men to this outpost of yours on Bayou Bienvenu?"

The fisherman was a Spaniard by heritage with no love for the Americans. He nodded and smiled, showing several missing teeth. "*Sí, señor.* I will take you there. You will see it is a good spot. The Americans, they do not know of it."

Major James Fitzwilliam was standing next to Lieutenant Colonel Sir John Fox Burgoyne, Chief of Engineers for the expedition. Like most in the room, he wore an impassive expression. The two excep-tions were Admiral Cochrane and General Keane. Sir Alexander was pleased and relaxed, but Keane was tense and concerned.

The general spoke to the fleet captain. "Ask him again about the enemy's strength." The question was asked and the Spaniard turned to Keane.

"They have many soldiers, *señor*," the fisherman replied. "Fifteen thousand, twenty thousand—I think. I cannot count that many. But, you have many more, *sí*?"

James struggled to hide his alarm. *Twenty thousand? We have but three thousand! They outnumber us six-to-one? If what he says is true, we must withdraw!*

The questioning ended, the fleet captain dismissed the fisherman, ordering that he be held under guard but treated as a valuable ally. Once the man left, general discussion began with Admiral Cochrane.

"The navy has won a great victory against the American gunboats, but surely the enemy has been alerted to our arrival. By now, they have moved whatever forces they possess to the more likely landing sites. The most dangerous portion of this enterprise is in landing the troops. This man"—he gestured at the door of the cabin—"has given us the opportunity to surprise the Yankees. We can steal a march on them and find ourselves enjoying the hospitality of New Orleans within a few days if we are bold."

General Keane was clearly cautious. "You place a great deal of faith in this fisherman, Sir Alexander."

"And why should we not? The Spanish are our allies. Bonaparte and the Americans have stolen Louisiana from them. Of course, we will scout this village of his, but"—he smiled—"I see no reason to doubt his honesty."

"And the number of troops he claims the enemy has?"

Cochrane smiled indulgently. "Stuff and nonsense! I would be surprised if the Americans have a tenth of that! And what sort of troops are they? Wild men, shopkeepers, the dirtiest rabble to inhabit the Earth. Certainly not proper gentlemen." He patted Keane on the shoulder. "You were not with us when we swept the field before Washington City. Show them a bit of the bayonet, and they will take to their heels.

"Besides, the people of New Orleans will welcome us as liberators! They are all French and Spanish, you know, and they know they have been imposed upon by these uncouth brawlers for liberty.

Our fisherman friend is but an example. "

The admiral turned to the staff. "Comments, gentlemen! What difficulties do you foresee in transporting the troops ashore?"

Major-General John Keane seemed mollified by the admiral, James saw. He recalled what he knew of the general's background. A second son of an Irish baronet, he had joined the army at the tender age of eleven. His rise through the ranks was propelled by purchased commissions and patronage. It did no harm that his wife was the daughter of a lieutenant-general. Keane did not see his first action until he arrived in the Peninsula as a newly minted lieutenant colonel in 1810. He gave good, if uninspired, service, earning the Gold Cross. Now at the age of thirty-three, he was a major-general and temporarily in command of all land forces facing New Orleans. Nothing in his background could have prepared Keane for this.

As for Vice-Admiral Sir Alexander Forrester Inglis Cochrane, KCB, commander of the Royal Navy's North American Station, he was justly renowned for his actions off Egypt and in the Caribbean. The fifty-six-year-old son of the Earl of Dundonald, he was talented, courtly, and competent. He had earned his rank and awards. Sir Alexander had many friends—and enemies, too. The Cochranes had squandered their heritage; his brother Lord Archibald, the current earl, had lost the family lands to bad investments. It was said the remaining Cochrane brothers served in the King's forces as much for gold as glory. They were rumored to be fraudsters and corrupt.

The great British admiral, the Earl of St. Vincent, once wrote that, *"The Cochranes are not to be trusted out of sight. They are all mad, romantic, money-getting, and not truth-telling, and there is not a single exception in any part of the family."*

Sir Alexander also developed an intense hatred for Americans. His brother Charles died at Yorktown. Sir Alexander never forgot or forgave. It was the reason he executed his plan to burn Washington City with such zeal.

Now his sights were set on New Orleans, and James wondered whether the admiral's judgment was not a little affected by his antipathy for the enemy.

The general turned to James's companion. "Colonel Burgoyne, have you anything to add?"

Sir John shook his head. "Nothing, sir, except to request joining the navy's scouting party. Once I have inspected the landing site, I shall report to you."

James took in the look on Cochrane's face. He doubted that any opinion except the admiral's would be heeded. Besides, the chief engineer was the illegitimate son of the infamous General John Burgoyne, the man who lost the Battle of Saratoga in 1777. Sir John escaped much of his father's disgrace by losing his father at age ten and being raised by the Earl of Derby, a relation of his late father's wife. The thirty-two-year-old officer had served, like many in the room, under Wellington in the Peninsula, where he earned his knighthood. His hard work had earned the respect of his fellow army officers, but the men of the navy only knew of his rather low birth.

Admiral Cochrane patted the table. "The die is set, gentlemen. We shall inspect Bayou Bienvenue as soon as can be arranged. Meanwhile, begin the process of disembarking immediately. We have identified an island west of here that shall serve as a staging area for the army. We shall begin with the West India regiments. The black man is used to this climate and should prove useful in enlarging the road from the landing site." He turned to General Keane. "With your permission, of course."

It did not matter whether Keane cared or not. James knew he would not overrule the vice-admiral. "Granted, sir."

Admiral Cochrane replied, "Splendid! Gentlemen, return to your ships and your duties."

Chapter 12

There was a great sense of relief when General Coffee's troops arrived from Baton Rouge. With them were one hundred fifty Mississippi Dragoons. General Jackson now had a mobile force capable of covering an immense amount of ground during their patrols. The next day, General Carroll's eight hundred Tennessee and Kentucky riflemen reached the Crescent City on flatboats, bringing with them much-needed ammunition.

The city was as ecstatic with the near doubling of the army as they were distraught only days before. The great families threw open their homes to their deliverers, only to be startled by the rude behavior of the rustic frontiersmen. The Tennesseans and Kentuckians were polite enough, even though they spoke not a word of French, but their clothes were a disgrace. They looked like beggars, not soldiers. Having no true uniform, they wore whatever their relations back home made for them. Dark, dirty-colored hunting shirts, resembling ponchos, were a common choice. They had loose-fitting pants instead of proper breeches. Their oversized slouching hats were of fur, animal skins, or leather. They had rarely shaved or bathed.

The worst thing about them in the eyes of many a Creole matron was that these dirty-shirted ruffians lacked civilized manners. Why, after eating, they had the gall to rest their feet on the table while chewing tobacco! Still, these brave strangers were there to protect them, so the foibles of these backwards backwoodsmen were tolerated with relatively little complaint.

Still, could such rabble really defeat the British? The inhabitants of the city were rational people. They smiled and waved and said all the right things, and meanwhile quietly armed themselves, the ladies with sharp scissors.

General Jackson now had about four thousand men under his command. Considering his strengths, he had a large number of battle-hardened veterans, and he knew the position of the enemy. There was no chance of an attack via Mobile.

But Old Hickory faced many more challenges and uncertainties. His navy was decimated, the local militia was suspect, and language and race were problems. Except for Livingston and Latour, the local leaders were either weak or unproven. The Baratarians were untrustworthy.

Worst of all was the lack of cannon and ammunition. Supplies were desperately needed. The Lafitte Brothers kept their promise and turned over all the supplies and materiel they stockpiled. It was considerable but, to Jackson's mind, not enough. He had word that another shipment of supplies had yet to come down the river from Natchez, and that rumor picked at the general's already irritated thoughts.

Acknowledging all these considerations, General Jackson made his dispersions. He sent the trustworthy Coffee to guard the Chef Menteur Road. David Morgan was made a brigadier general and was assigned to Fort St. Leon at English Turn. General Villeré was charged with training the locals and blockading as many landing spots as could be identified. Jackson had not lost his suspicion of the Baratarians, so they were assigned to Fort St. Charles, where the general could keep an eye on them.

The bulk of his men he kept near New Orleans. There were three reasons for this. First, it provided him with great flexibility. He could respond quickly to any landing by the enemy. Second, the presence of so many troops gave an air of security to the skittish civilians. Third, Jackson felt he needed his men in the city for a more unpleasant reason. The general did not trust the politicians, hence his declaration of martial law. There was always the possibility he might have to enforce his will if a panicked legislature tried to surrender the city.

Wednesday, December 21

The human mind is a strange and wondrous thing. In the face of uncertainty and calamity, it can be diverted by the most mundane of matters—such as shopping.

So it was on a cold and damp December afternoon that Madeline Melançon and Anne-Marie Dansereau, accompanied by the slave Clementine, strolled along the Rue Royale, viewing the wares offered in the shops. Mme Melançon's excuse for venturing out with war in the offing was to purchase a small but vital number of necessities, and she desired her niece's company during this strenuous undertaking. That Anne-Marie took the opportunity to shop for items suitable for a bride's *trousseau* was pure coincidence.

Anne-Marie and Madeline had just exited a modiste renowned for making scandalous lingerie, Clementine following dutifully behind, when they heard a voice.

"Mlle Dansereau?"

The ladies turned to behold a tall, fashionably dressed *mestee* woman approaching them. She, too, had a female slave attendant.

"*Excusez-moi, s'il vous plaît,* but you are Mlle Dansereau, are you not?" Her voice was rich and low.

Madeline Melançon took a step forward. "Who are you to ask?" she demanded.

"My name is Mlle Carmen Bellevue. I am...a friend of your cousin."

Anne-Marie could not help but stare at the mulatto lady. She had seen *placées* before, of course. Their money was just as good in the shops as anyone's. But she had never met one, much less had one address her. It was highly improper. The issue of race aside, the white women's hostility for *plaçage* was almost universal.

Still, she had to admit Mlle Bellevue's loveliness. She envied the woman's exotic appearance: statuesque carriage, creamy, light-brown skin, and azure eyes. Anne-Marie felt short and plain in comparison.

So this is Henri's lover. What does she want from me?

Madeline seemed irritated at Mlle Bellevue's audacity of approaching them on a public street. "I am very happy for you, but you must excuse us."

Something made Anne-Marie touch her aunt's arm. "Wait, Aunt. I would speak to her."

"Anne-Marie, you must not," Madeline hissed. "This person can have no business with you."

Anne-Marie turned to Mlle Bellevue. The *mestee's* beseeching expression made up her mind. "Mlle Bellevue, you seem to know who I am."

"*Oui*. M. Herbert has described you and your aunt very well."

"And you wish to speak to me?"

"*Oui*. I have been told you plan to remain in the city during these dangerous times."

Anne-Marie frowned. Henri had eaten dinner at the Melançon house the evening before, and she assumed he was the source of Mlle Bellevue's information. "You are well informed." Her voice was neutral

"*Merci*. I have been given to understand you have a connection with the Ursuline Sisters?"

"I know them." In fact, Anne-Marie had volunteered to serve in the hospital the nuns had set up for wounded soldiers. If Matthew had to fight, she would help to heal the injured. She had revealed this to Henri last night. "Do you wish an introduction?"

Mlle Bellevue shook her head. "I doubt the good sisters would tolerate my presence. No, I want to ask for your opinion. I, too, wish to be of service to those who defend us. Have you any suggestions?"

Anne-Marie's estimation of this woman rose to an extent she hardly would have believed but a moment before. "That is very good of you, *mademoiselle*! I think many of the soldiers who have journeyed here lack coats and blankets."

The lady smiled, which made her even more beautiful. "*Bon*! I can speak to the others in the *Faubourg Marigny*. We will collect what we can and will make what is lacking. *Merci beaucoup.*"

To Anne-Marie's surprise, her aunt spoke up. "Send a note to my husband's office. He will forward it to the quartermaster, easing your way. Your assistance is much appreciated."

"Oh, yes," said Anne-Marie. "He would be happy to help."

Mlle Bellevue thanked her and made a small curtsy in farewell. Anne-Marie returned the gesture, thinking the lady deserved the courtesy, *placée* or not. War was not a time to stand on tradition.

Friday, December 23: Lake Borgne

JAMES FITZWILLIAM SAT IN THE bow of the rocking landing barge, holding his cloak tightly around his body against the sharp, damp, cold wind. The hundred or so infantry troops jammed about him grumbled, and their commanding officer demanded to know why the barge had stopped right in the middle of Lake Borgne.

"Begging your pardon, sir," the midshipman addressed the infantry officer with thinly disguised contempt, "my men have been at the oars these five hours. Surely, you cannot begrudge them a rest and a bite of breakfast. We shall arrive at the landing spot as soon as may be."

The infantrymen were hungry too, and freezing as well, the officer pointed out. "How much farther to shore?"

The midshipman glanced at the cloudy sky. "In this wind, another four hours, I should think."

The groans redoubled.

James well knew the frustration of the infantry officer. A week earlier, the army had been ferried piecemeal thirty miles from the fleet anchored at Cat Island to a windswept spit of sand known as Pea Island. The place was barren of wood or shelter, so the men sat in the open with no fire to warm their bones or cook their food. No tents had been brought, for it was expected the conquest of New Orleans would take only a few days. Worse, they were plagued by cold, torrential rains, the likes of which none had ever experienced. It was beyond misery for the English, Scots, and Irish in the army, but at least they were raised in a hardy clime. No such upbringing prepared the troops from the West Indies for killing frosts, and many succumbed to exposure.

Now, a barge filled with wet, cold, and hungry soldiers bobbed offshore, hours from relief. Theirs was not the only one. Scores of boats dotted the surface of the water, but there was nothing for it. The sailors were the ones pulling at the oars. They had rowed an army thirty miles through the sea only days before, and now they had to move that army another thirty miles to land. The only benefit to the seamen's pitiful lot was that the drudgery of rowing kept them warm.

The downpour at dawn had finally ended, leaving them in a light fog.

Where had this weather come from? James knew from maps that New Orleans was on the same latitude as Alexandria in Egypt. Cold like this was expected in England, but this was the tropics! It should be warm, or at the very least pleasant, even in December. It was a wonder ice did not cover their bodies.

James silently gave thanks to his wife's foresight. Meg had insisted that he take his heavy weather cloak. Many others had no winter gear among their belongings, and they eyed the garment jealously.

Finally, the midshipman recalled his men to the oars. With herculean effort, the sailors dug into the water, forcing the barge forward. Stoke after stoke, the boat moved faster, momentum helping the oarsmen's exertions. Slowly, the Louisiana coast grew closer.

HOURS LATER, JAMES LEARNED THAT Captain Elliot did not exaggerate the condition of the coast. They rowed for miles along a reed-infested shoreline, a few odd cypress trees or short bushes here and there breaking the monotony. James could not believe there was any dry land in that green, swampy wilderness.

Finally, a single pole with a red flag could be seen. Closer inspection proved it was the entrance to an inlet about a hundred yards wide. His barge followed the other boats into the inlet and up the bayou. Still, there was no dry land in sight. The flotilla continued up Bayou Bienvenue some distance, the channel becoming too narrow to allow more than one barge at a time, before grounding on the mud. The bayou was barely more than a creek now, branching out in several directions.

Admiral Cochrane's pendant flew from a pole erected beside a crude series of huts. Once James disembarked, he made his way to one of the naval officers overseeing the operation.

"Where may I find General Keane's headquarters?" As the man was a naval lieutenant, equal to his rank, salutes were not exchanged.

"Inland, Major," the lieutenant said. "Just follow the troops up the road. You will find him in a plantation house, close to the Mississippi." The man turned back to his tasks.

James had been in one of the last barges of the Ninety-Fifth Foot, the Eighty-Fifth Foot being in the vanguard. Keane had gone with the Eighty-Fifth, along with most of the staff. James hurried to report to headquarters. Surely, the advance on New Orleans was imminent.

The going was incredibly difficult. The road was no better than a path through reeds and brush—and a wet, muddy one at that. Men sometimes had to move in single file, bringing the expedition to a near halt. Soldiers slipped and fell into the muck and water, only to get up and trudge on, leaving the path in a worse state than before. James stepped as carefully as he could, keeping Elliot's warning of crocodiles and vipers in mind.

About a half-mile in, the reeds gave way to a swampy forest of cypress trees and palmettos, growing close together. For two miles, he continued, and just before breaking into solid wood, he came across a party of soldiers working to improve the road. There, he saw Lieutenant-Colonel Burgoyne, overseeing the work. James made for him.

He saluted. "My compliments, Sir John. Where is headquarters?"

Burgoyne returned the honor. "Good to see you, Fitzwilliam. Welcome to Louisiana. Damnable place, ain't it? You are just in time for a noon staff meeting. Come, we shall go together."

As they walked through the hardwood forest, James vented his spleen. "Are we certain that bloody Spaniard told the truth? I have never seen such miserable excuse for a road in my life!"

"Indeed. I have no idea whether it can carry any guns heavier than nine-pounders. But the way was unguarded, and we are less than ten miles from New Orleans. We have prisoners at the plantation house, including officers." Burgoyne lowered his voice. "A word to the wise, Fitzwilliam. You should keep such opinions to yourself. Your conduct has been noted."

"*What?*" hissed James. "Of what have I been accused?"

"Nothing—not that it matters. Fitzwilliam, I know your worth. We were in the Peninsular together. General Ross thought the world of you. But Ross is dead, and Admiral Cochrane is in charge, no matter what General Keane thinks. He knows nothing of you, except your...condition in life. You have no influence, and you are not Royal Navy. That is all that counts to a scrub like Cochrane. To be truthful, he hardly thinks better of me. Just watch your words in public, and give your opinion to Keane in private—when asked, and not before."

It took a moment for James to cool his Fitzwilliam temper. "Thankee, Sir John. I shall keep your good counsel in mind."

The colonel patted the major's back. "We shall soon be in New Orleans, and all this will be forgot." The forest parted before a broad, open farm. "Ah, there is the headquarters now—that long, white house. They call it Conseil."

Conseil Plantation

"GENERAL, WHAT IS THE ARMY doing?" demanded Admiral Cochrane. "You must march on New Orleans immediately."

"My men are in no condition to move forward, Admiral. They are exhausted." General Keane appeared as drained as his troops, James thought. "The Eighty-Fifth Foot is bivouacked forward with picquets, and the Fourth and Ninety-Fifth have just arrived. I understand the Twenty-First will be here soon."

Cochrane turned to a naval captain at his side. "The Twenty-First Foot should land at dusk, General," he reported.

"There you are. By tonight, I shall be able to muster two thousand in the field. Tomorrow we shall see what the enemy is about."

"General, I must respectfully disagree." Lieutenant-Colonel Thornton of the Eighty-Fifth spoke up. "The enemy does not know we are here. We should take the city by *coup de main* this afternoon. We will shock them with one swift, bold attack."

General Keane would not be moved. "Colonel Thornton, may I remind you of Fort St. Charles and their cannon? We have nothing larger than three-pound field pieces. The prisoners said General Jackson has twenty thousand under his command."

"Sir, surely they lied about the number. Besides, they are militia, not trained regulars."

"No doubt, but it does not mean that we outnumber them. Numbers count, Colonel, militia or not. The navy is bringing heavier guns as we speak. To be blunt, sir, this army is in no condition to fight. They must rest and eat. Gentlemen, we must form foraging parties for firewood and food. New Orleans can wait."

"The Americans are nothing but rabble, in any case," agreed Cochrane. "We shall chase them off the field as we have done before."

"Indeed, Sir Alexander," said Keane. "Gentlemen, you have your orders." He turned to an aide. "Have someone stoke that fire. I'm chilled to the bone."

James walked out with one of his fellow aides. "Who is interrogating the prisoners?"

"The militiamen? They know nothing."

"And the officers?"

"Haven't you heard?" was the response. "The buggers jumped through a window not an hour ago and ran for the river. Last we saw, they were making for the other side in a dugout canoe."

"What?" James came to a dead stop. "Prisoners escaped?" *And Keane does nothing? No wonder Thornton is in such a mood!* "Why are we not moving forward?"

"Did you not understand? The army is dead on its feet. Besides, the cowards are on the wrong side of the river from the city. They are probably soiling their trousers hiding in the swamps. There is nothing to worry about."

New Orleans

GENERAL JACKSON'S HEADQUARTERS ON RUE Royal was abuzz with activity. Since the defeat on Lake Borgne, every day had brought a new report of a British landing. Each report was investigated, and each one was disproved.

This day had been no different. Boats had been seen on Lake Borgne, but not towards the Rigolets Pass. It did not make sense, but Jackson sent out scouts to reconnoiter. The general's eye was on two areas: the Chef Menteur Road through the Gentilly Plain and Baton Rouge. He thought the British landing to the north and marching around Lake Pontchartrain most likely, but he worried that they might try the shorter route. Major Latour announced he wanted to conduct his own inspections and had ridden out that morning.

It was half past one in the afternoon when there was a commotion at the front door. In rushed Major Gabriel Villeré, Colonel Laronde, and M. de la Croix, a member of the city's public safety committee. All three were stained with mud.

"General!" cried de la Croix, "Important—highly important news! The British have arrived at the Villeré plantation! Here is Major Villeré. He was captured, but escaped and will now tell you his story!"

Major Villeré spoke only French, so de la Croix had to translate. The gist of the report was that the British had surprised the detail at Conseil Plantation and were now encamping there, only nine miles east from the city, on the Chalmette Plain.

Both Matthew and Jacob were shocked. No one had anticipated an attack from the east; their attention had been on the north and west. This was a disaster.

General Jackson rose from his chair, incensed. He slammed a fist on the desk. "By the Eternal, they shall not sleep on our soil! Gentlemen, the British are below. We must fight them tonight!"

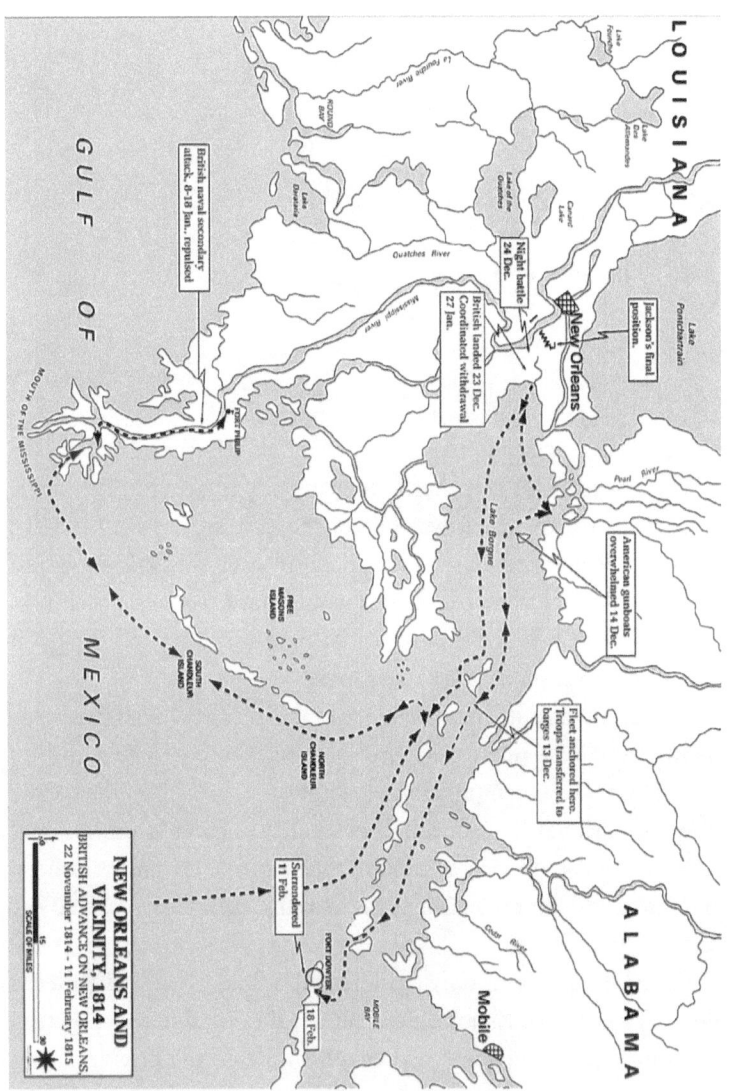

Campaign Map: The British Advance on New Orleans

Map courtesy of: The Department of History,
United States Military Academy at West Point.

Chapter 13

A t five o'clock in the dusky afternoon, Matthew Darcy stood next to his commanding general, preparing to do battle. It helped that it was one of the shortest days of the year; the sky was growing dark. Like much in war, this was good and bad. Both attacker and defender would have troubling seeing in the nighttime. The Americans would have the initial advantage: if a man was in front of you, shoot him.

The scene about him was encouraging. The watchword was silence, and to a man, the army obeyed. Over sixteen hundred troops had taken their positions five hundred yards from the enemy picquets with hardly a sound. The Americans had few professional soldiers—most of General Jackson's men were merchants, farmers, and lawyers—but no regiment in the world could have formed the line better or quieter.

Four hours before, only minutes after Major Gabriel Villeré's electrifying report, Major Latour returned to headquarters. Acting on intuition, he had gone east and encountered the British setting camp at Conseil Plantation. The wily Latour was able to creep close and reconnoiter the enemy camp for an extended time. He presented for his general's pleasure details of the encampment: numbers of troops, types of arms, and location of companies and picquets.

This had been valuable intelligence indeed! The Americans knew the location of the enemy, his strength, and dispersions. This courtly

Frenchman had accomplished a great service, possibly the saving of New Orleans.

In contrast, the brash young Creole Major Villeré failed to carry out the most basic of orders. He let his command be taken by surprise, something that would not have happened had he blocked Bayou Bienvenue and set a guard. The furious Jackson ordered Villeré's immediate arrest, and General Jacques Villeré had to watch in pained silence as his son was taken away in disgrace.

The intelligence given to General Jackson was beneficial but incomplete. He could not be sure whether the landing at Chalmette was the main thrust or a diversion for a larger force headed for Gentilly. He had to divide his command, something Matthew knew no soldier would find comfortable.

Old Hickory was itching for a fight, however, and he wanted his best men. He recalled Plauché's Creoles from Fort St. John and Dacquin's free colored battalion from the Chef Menteur Road. In their place, he sent Governor Claiborne and three companies of the state militia. The untested Baratarians guarded Fort St. Charles.

Jackson's plan was ambitious. Using Major Latour's intelligence, he proposed to attack the British from three sides. A small, mobile force under the trusted General Coffee would flank the enemy from the left along the marshy cypress forest. Jackson kept the majority of his strength under his hand; he would hit the British straight on. Artillery would move forward with him along the levee to support the advance. Meanwhile, *USS Carolina* was assigned to move downriver in the darkness and blast the invaders from the right. The schooner's first broadside would signal the start of the fight at about seven-thirty, well after dark.

Matthew's assignment was to see that the cannons' ammunition kept up with the advance. He wished Jacob was at his side, but Jacob was tasked to General Coffee's service.

"Back with your Tennesseans, eh, Jacob?" Matthew had observed as they prepared to leave Fort St. Charles two hours before.

"Can't say I'm sorry, Matt." Jacob grinned. "Them good old boys can knock over a fly with their rifles, if'n they have a hankerin' to do it. Them redcoats'll never know what hit 'em."

Matt patted his shoulder. "Leave some of the redcoats for us, and I will see you afterwards."

"Yeah, we'll get us some more of that fine cookin' Miz Melançon puts out. Think she'd share some of her cook's recipes for Fanny? I ain't gonna miss much about New Orleans when this is over with, but I'll miss those dinners!"

Recalling his leave taking of Jacob also brought back the march out of the city. The citizenry were wild from both fear and enthusiasm, the ladies, in particular—crying and cheering at the same time, Anne-Marie among them. Like her, the ladies showed no inclination to flee the city. Of course, it did not hurt that the general, through Mr. Livingston, claimed that the British shall never get into the city so long as he held the command.

A confident boast, thought Matthew, *but can we do it? Just what sort of command do we truly have?*

He looked about him: federals in blue and white with stovetop hats, Creole militia in French uniforms, free men of color in civilian suits, backwoodsmen in buckskin and ponchos—almost two thousand men. Many did well against Creek rebels, but now they faced a British army almost as large as themselves—the vaunted Wellington's Heroes, who had fought and beaten Napoleon's best.

Matthew nervously checked his pocket watch. *Five-fifteen*. The sun was setting, and the skies were somewhat clear. *There will be a moon tonight. Good and bad. We will be able to see to some extent, but so will they.* He ground his teeth. *So be it.*

He turned to inspect the ammunition carts in the rear.

New Orleans

AFTER VIEWING THE DEPARTURE OF Major Darcy and the army from the city, Anne-Marie hurried to the Ursuline hospital. There, she joined the sisters and other volunteers preparing the place for the arrival of the inevitable casualties from the upcoming battle. Their work done, the women retired to the convent's chapel for prayer and Holy Mass.

Rosary in hand, Anne-Marie knelt with the others, reciting the Hail Mary.

"Ave Maria, gratia plena, Dominus tecum. Benedicta tu in mulieribus, et benedictus fructus ventris tui, Jesus."

Before them, on the altar, illuminated by candlelight, was the statue of *Notre-Dame de Bon Secours*, Our Lady of Prompt Succor, the patron saint of New Orleans and Louisiana, to whom the faithful beseeched to intercede on their behalf.

Once before, there had been a miracle. In 1812, the Ursuline sisters had implored the help of Mary, Mother of God. A fire was ravaging the Vieux Carré, and it threatened the convent. "Pray for us, hasten to us, save us," the people begged, and Our Lady answered. The Lord spared the building.

Could the people's devotion to the Virgin save the city again?

"Sancta Maria, Mater Dei, ora pro nobis peccatoribus, nunc et in hora mortis nostrae. Amen."

Anne-Marie mouthed the familiar prayer, but her mind was not on the fate of the city. Instead, her attention was focused on the man she loved.

Oh, Mother Mary, I beseech you to remember Matthew Darcy. Keep him safe from harm in the days to come. Our Lady of Prompt Succor, hasten to help us!

Conseil Plantation

Just after seven, James Fitzwilliam left the Conseil Plantation house to enjoy his pipe. All about him, soldiers were cooking the first hot meal they had enjoyed in over a week. They had scoured the countryside for food and pots, and few armies were as good at foraging as the British. The slave quarters proved a good source of both, to James's surprise. Apparently, Louisianans allowed their slaves to prepare their own food rather than having meals doled out by their masters from a common kitchen.

The men reported enemy sightings during their scavenging, but the high command was not worried. Certainly, the Americans were aware that they had landed; it was impossible to keep that secret for long. But night had fallen, and in the safety of darkness, the redcoats could eat their fill and rest, preparing for the conquest of New Orleans on the morrow. Picquets had been deployed, of course, but it was more from routine than concern. No army attacked at night; everyone knew that.

James strolled over to the levee between the bivouacs of the Eighty-Fifth and Ninety-Fifth regiments. The air was still very cool, the sky was clearing, and the nearly full moon rose in the east. The smooth, Virginia tobacco was a fine after-dinner treat. It was the best night James had since disembarking from *HMS Imprudent.*

One thing the Americans can make is excellent tobacco! He puffed serenely. *Lord, how I have missed this in Spain.* That he had taken the tobacco from a Washington City store caused James not the slightest discomfort. Like his comrades, he considered it the spoils of war.

While mentally composing his next letter to Margaret, James noted that the picquets along the levee were acting strangely. Walking over to investigate, he saw they were waving at a dark shape on the river.

"What's this, then?" he demanded.

"Sir," replied one guard excitedly, "it's one of our ships! They must have gotten past the Yankee fort downriver." The solider turned back and shouted, "Good show, boys!"

James smiled. Finally, some good news! With the Royal Navy's firepower, New Orleans would fall into their hands like ripe fruit. Margaret would be there in days.

It was then James noticed something odd. The ship was moving downriver. Why? Shouldn't it be going upstream?

Seconds later, the night lit up in a blinding crash. The shock caused James to slip and fall on the muddy grass as grapeshot flew over his head by scant inches. The picquets were not so lucky—they were torn to bits. It took a moment for him to collect his wits.

My God, that is a bloody American ship! We are under attack!

EXACTLY AT SEVEN-THIRTY, COMMODORE PATTERSON's *USS Carolina* fired a devastating broadside directly into the British camp.

Matthew and the rest of General Jackson's command watched as the *Carolina* pummeled the enemy for fifteen long minutes. Musket fire could be heard over the din, but small arms could not hurt the schooner. Matthew was relieved that the redcoats were not shooting back at Patterson with cannon. The Americans' puny three-pound guns were surely the only artillery on the field and just might make the difference, he hoped.

At the appointed moment, General Jackson ordered the advance. The battles for New Orleans had begun.

THERE IS NOTHING NEW IN war, no matter how loudly armchair generals protest. The point of battle is to take land and have enough soldiers left to hold it. Sun Tzu's *The Art of War* was supposedly written five hundred years before the birth of Christ, about the same time Thucydides composed *The History of the Peloponnesian War.* Julius Caesar's various *Commentaries* are two thousand years old.

Brute strength is not always enough to win battles. From the beginning of time, innovative commanders have used strategy to overcome the odds, finding new and original ways of using their assets to confuse and defeat their foes. For instance, much of Napoleon's success was due to his mastery of logistics. Having trains of wagons filled with canned food following the army meant his soldiers spent less time foraging for sustenance than his opponents.

But often, the mind conceives what the hand cannot achieve.

General Andrew Jackson was a brilliant man and a natural solider. He knew that coming at the enemy from three directions often led an inferior force to beat a superior one. On paper, he should have routed the British from Conseil Plantation. General Keane was taken entirely by surprise, his men were cold and sleep-deprived, and they had no knowledge of the number of their attackers or their ability.

For hours, individuals and squads clashed in the cold moonlight on the Chalmette plain, often hand-to-hand. The British were stunned by the *Carolina's* broadsides, but as professionals, they reverted to their training, and they held off the advancing Americans. For their part, Jackson's dirty shirt amateurs fought as well as any of Wellington's Heroes.

However, confusion won the night. Coordination between Jackson and Coffee was impossible. Bullets and grapeshot filled the air, and how many brave men fell to friendly fire only the Lord knew. When Jackson got word that British reinforcements had arrived, the frustrated general knew he had to be satisfied with bloodying the hated invader, not annihilating it. He ordered a withdrawal, and the Americans fell back to their starting positions at Lacoste Plantation. The British did not follow. Fog had rolled in, and Keane feared a trap.

By nine-thirty, relative peace settled over the battlefield. The combatants licked their wounds and counted their dead, the silence broken by the sound of skirmishes and the occasional cannon fire from the *Carolina*. The British suffered more killed and wounded, and the Americans had slightly more of their men taken captive. No campfires would be lit again that night, and nervous picquets on both sides stood their posts uneasily.

Tactically, the Night Battle of December 23 would be considered a draw or even a minor British victory. After all, it was the Americans that had been forced off the field. In the days to come, from a strategic and psychological standpoint, it would prove to be the critical event of the New Orleans campaign.

Lacoste Plantation

FILTHY, WEARY, AND RELIEVED, MATTHEW leaned against an ammunition wagon. It had been a close-run thing at the end. The British were advancing, intent on taking the Americans' cannons, and Matthew was concerned they would succeed. If not for the order to fall back, they would have lost the guns.

He forced himself to move. He had to account for the powder and balls expended and to make sure the runners were ready to replenish the guns, should the British follow. That they did not counter-attack, he thanked God, for his men were exhausted. Matthew gave orders to the officers and ignored the hated glares sent in his direction by the drained common soldiers who would carry out his commands. He then set off to report to headquarters.

From the sound of his discussion with General Coffee and Major Latour, it was clear that General Jackson was unhappy with his position. The Frenchman was anointed chief engineer, and as such, he recommended a further withdrawal to a more defensible location. Jackson wanted no more retreat that night, hating the idea of surrendering more land to the enemy.

While they argued, Matthew gave his report to the quartermaster. Having done his duty, he approached General Coffee, who had stepped away for a drink of water.

"Begging the general's pardon"—Matthew saluted—"do you know where I might find Major Harville?"

Coffee turned, and his grim expression told the tale. "I'm sorry, Major Darcy, but I have to tell you Major Harville…fell."

Jacob dead? Matthew's gut clinched. He always knew something like this might happen, but not to Jacob. Jacob was invincible!

"How, sir?" he managed.

The general took a drink. "I wasn't there myself, but I was told he was with the colored battalion during the height of the battle. Those black fellows fought like devils and Harville too. He was shot, point-blank, during the action. We carried him back with us, but he passed before a surgeon could help. It's to be hoped he didn't suffer." He placed a hand on Matthew's shoulder. "Jacob Harville was a good man and a fine officer. I know he was your friend. I'm sorry."

A grieving Matthew forced himself to say, "I will see to his belongings, sir."

In his mind's eye, Matthew saw Jacob's laughing face before the battle, joking about the fight to come. After everything they had gone through—forced marches, long boring nights drinking in the tents, terrifying fights with the Creeks in the forests of Georgia and Alabama—his best friend could not die. Not before the final battle, a battle this skirmish only postponed.

Jacob had so much to live for—his family, his girl, Fanny, his farm in Tennessee! It is not right! I am the one who has nothing. It should have been me!

At that moment, General Jackson approached. "Darcy, I just heard about Major Harville. He was a fine officer and a true gentleman. He will be missed. Unless you have anything that merits my immediate attention, you go and get yourself some food. We shall speak in the morning."

"Thank you, sir." Matthew saluted and left, already trying to find the words to write in his letter to Fanny.

Conseil Plantation

The mood in the British command was one of shock and uncertainty. To a man, they knew how close the army had come to being routed. No one foresaw the attack. What civilized army fought at night? Just what sort of enemy were they facing? This was not like Maryland—or Spain, for that matter. If not for the timely arrival of the Fourth Regiment, things could have gone very badly indeed!

James shared his commander's opinions. The army was badly shaken and the navy, too, given the ashen expressions worn by Admiral Cochrane and the other naval officers.

"The prisoners were right," cried one staff officer. "The Yankees must have thousands of men."

"At least fifteen-hundred," agreed General Keane. "You see, gentlemen—you see we are in no condition to advance to New Orleans. We must rest and prepare."

"For how long?" demanded Cochrane. "Until Pakenham arrives?"

James flinched at the tone the admiral used in addressing the general, and he never wanted to strike a sailor more than at that moment.

For his part, Keane ignored the imperious Scotsman. "Double the picquets and interrogate the prisoners."

"Sir," put in Colonel Thornton, "we have to do something about that damned schooner. It is still shooting into the camp!"

"Our three-pounders can do nothing," the general pointed out. He turned to Cochrane. "We will need those larger guns as soon as may be, sir."

"Never fear, sir," Sir Alexander responded. "The guns are even now on their way. My tars will break their backs to get them here as quickly as may be. Those ruffians will pay for tonight, I assure you."

James had a bellyful of the admiral's boasting. This staff meeting could not end soon enough. He wanted to sleep badly, but there were stores to inspect. His cot was still hours away.

The Americans were a bad surprise, he thought. They had not run, as they did before Washington City, or hidden behind trees, like at North Point. *Colonel Thornton is right. We have to destroy that schooner, but we need to sit back and consider that this Jackson might be a better general than we thought.*

He glanced at General Keane. *A good man, a competent brigade commander, but not the leader of an army. We need Sir Edward Pakenham. I pray to God he gets here soon.*

Chapter 14

B y morning, General Jackson bowed to good advice and his own nagging instincts and ordered the withdrawal of his army closer to the city. Two miles to the west lay Macarty Plantation, separated from Chalmette Plantation by a shallow ditch called Rodriguez Canal. It was there Andrew Jackson chose to make his stand.

Major Lacoste was delighted with the new location. At once, the engineer set about building a substantial barricade hard against Rodriguez Canal. Teams of men scoured the local plantations and woods for building supplies. Carts of lumber, timber, cotton bales, and hogsheads of sugar returned to the site of the works. Major Lacoste immediately rejected the sugar casts; the sugar would melt in the wet mud, he explained. The rest he used.

His idea was to use the lumber and bales as a framework and cover it completely with a thick coating of mud. Louisiana's heavy, black clay was perfect for the job. Once dry, it would harden like stone. Wet, it would absorb the heaviest of cannonballs. The wall would be almost impregnable if properly built.

Lacoste's major difficulty was manpower. The battlements had to be thrown up quickly before the British could recover and attack. Slaves from all over were sent to help, but they were not enough. Jackson's army was forced to drop their guns and pick up shovels.

The regulars, colored troops, and out-of-state militia went about it with no complaint, but the same could not be said for the Louisiana militia. The proud Creoles were aghast! Dirty their hands with manual labor? Do slaves' work next to slaves? Impossible! Lacoste's appeals to their patriotism and Jackson's outright threats ultimately quieted the discontent.

Labor was its own reward, and the men's spirits rose along with the fortifications. The mud came from the canal, making it deeper and wider. That would make an assault on the ramparts even more difficult. The men realized it, which spurred them on with greater zeal. By nightfall, their work was hardly finished, but what they had accomplished in less than a day was incredible. Line Jackson had been established.

Major Lacoste was too much of a perfectionist to be satisfied, but General Jackson knew well to appreciate the industry of both his engineer and his army. Both leaders knew that relying on a single line was suicide, and the next day they would continue the work, as well as build a secondary line at Dupré Plantation, a mile behind, and a third line beyond that.

While the army toiled, the Mississippi Dragoons recovered their mounts and scouted the enemy camp. General Jackson was well informed of his opponent's activities. The same could not be said of the British.

Conseil Plantation

PATRICK McCURRY LEFT HIS FATHER's farm in Lancaster seven years earlier to join the renowned Fourth Regiment of Foot, known as the King's Own. He wanted a regular income, two meals a day, to see the world, and never to shovel manure again. As it turned out, his income and meals were irregular, he had been to Portugal, Spain, France, and America, and he only shoveled manure rarely and usually had people shooting at him. Despite all that, he had never risen above the rank of private. His army career had not yet turned out the way he hoped.

Private McCurry stood picquet near a stand of swampy forest as the cool day faded to chilly evening. He was glad of two things

—that he was far from that blasted American boat that kept shooting at them, and that his best friend in the regiment stood guard beside him. Charlie Duncan was a Scot, good with a joke and a drink, and the two had gotten into more than one scrape in Spain and lived to tell the tale.

Clouds were moving in, promising a dark, miserable night. The temperature was dropping. McCurry hoped it wouldn't get as cold as it had on that damned island during the disembarkation. That had been the worst week of his life.

"I could go for some food, Paddy my lad," Charlie complained, his breath dancing in the air.

"Sure, an' they'll be some left, Charlie. Say, do ya think the ladies in New Orleans are as pretty as we've been told?"

"Women can wait. I could eat my weight and drink yours, I'm thinking. Hold—you hear something?"

McCurry cocked an ear. "No. Maybe a squirrel? There's an awful lot of 'em. Think they'd be good to eat?"

Duncan's only response was a grunt. To McCurry's horror, two arrows protruded from Private Duncan's red coat. His friend's eyes rolled up as he fell to the ground.

"*Charlie!*" Private McCurry whirred toward the woods, musket at the ready. He never saw the arrow that pierced his back. Screaming, he fell one way, his musket another. Desperately he rolled in the muck, whimpering, trying to get at the thing in his back. His last sight on Earth was a dark figure launching itself at him with a blade gleaming in the twilight.

Private Patrick McCurry's army career had unquestionably not turned out as he expected.

Sunday, December 25: Conseil Plantation
"THE AMERICANS ARE KILLING OUR picquets?" cried General Keane.

James Fitzwilliam grimaced. "Yes, sir. They killed four men last night. Two of them with these." He placed arrows on the table.

The others looked at the missiles in horror. "Savages," one breathed.

"Three more soldiers are missing," James continued, "either dead or captured."

"Damned barbarians! First, they attack after dark, then their bloody schooner fires on the camp night and day, and now our picquets are molested. Do these damned Yankees have *any* understanding of the customs of war?"

An officer sniffed, "It is obvious they are brutes and *not* gentlemen." The aide's tone indicated that this was the gravest of insults.

"Do you have any orders, sir?" Colonel Burgoyne asked.

General Keane eyed Fitzwilliam. "What are the conditions of our stores?"

"Very low, sir," James acknowledged. "The navy transported very little in the way of food."

A fleet representative objected. "It was to be expected that we would be in New Orleans by now. The transportation of food was considered superfluous."

"Have not foraging teams been utilized?" Colonel Burgoyne inquired.

James almost smiled, as Sir John already knew the answer and was trying to put the blame off the army and onto the navy. "Yes, Colonel, but we have already stripped the countryside bare. There is also the issue of our…guests."

"The prisoners?"

"No, General. It seems a large number of slaves have entered the camp, seeking refuge. They are under the belief that we will free them."

General Keane frowned. Most of the officers present were uncomfortable with the practice of slavery, and some truly hated it, but to win the local populace's support, Admiral Cochrane guaranteed that "personal property" would be respected by the Crown's soldiers. That promise included returning escaped slaves.

"I saw them—poor buggers," remarked another aide. "One had this spiked device locked about his neck. It prevents him from lying down to sleep. He said it was a punishment from his master."

"Barbarians, all of them," muttered General Keane. "Well, we must leave this matter for Sir Edward. His ship has joined the fleet, and he and General Gibbs should be here by the afternoon. Captain" —he turned to the fleet observer—"we must get more stores from the fleet. It is imperative."

The sea captain, as dirty and haggard as the rest, nodded. "I am told that the additional victuals have been sent for and should arrive this day."

"Excellent," General Keane replied halfheartedly. James expected that the good man was as anxious as the rest of those assembled for General Pakenham's arrival. All these problems would then fall to Sir Edward. "By the way, Happy Christmas, gentlemen. You are dismissed."

New Orleans

THE ATMOSPHERE THAT CHRISTMAS DAY at the Melançons was gloomy and distressed. Anne-Marie's relief that Matthew had survived the battle was tempered by the knowledge that Jacob had not. Matthew had written them the tragic news, and the entire household found it hard to accept. The brash young officer had been befriended by all, even Anne-Marie's father.

Matthew's duties required that he return to town to see to the transportation of stores and ammunition to the army at Line Jackson. He also had time to attend a Christmas Day Mass and have a brief luncheon with his friends. It was the only bright spot to the holiday for the Dansereaus and Melançons.

At the dining table, Uncle Philippe offered to take on the responsibility of returning Major Harville's belongings to Tennessee.

"*Merci beaucoup*, Philippe," said Matthew, his left hand openly held by Anne-Marie. "I will rest easy, knowing Jacob's things will be in your capable hands. I will have them sent to your house. It was hard enough writing to Miss Fanny."

Anne-Marie's imagination was captured by the notion that *she* could have been the one to receive such a letter from Jacob. The pain *Mademoiselle* Fanny would feel upon receiving Matthew's note! It was almost too much to conceive.

Her choked-back sob was lost in her father's loud declaration. "I will write her, too! Major Harville left his home to fall in the defense of mine. I will remember and pray for him for as long as I live. I will tell her that and that her brave lover was my *bon ami*!" Emile started weeping as he repeated in broken English, "My good friend! He was my good friend!" He could say no more, as he was crying openly.

In a strange way, M. Dansereau's overwrought pronouncement seemed to bring some relief to a grieving Matthew. He offered Anne-Marie a small smile as he squeezed her hand. She returned the gesture before releasing him and attending to her father.

"Papa, please do not cry." She took his handkerchief from his pocket. "Here, use this."

Uncle Philippe leaned over. "Do you need more men, Matthew?"

"Philippe, *Non*!" cried Aunt Madeline.

"My dear, the crisis is upon us!" her husband answered. "If General Jackson needs me, I must go."

"I, too!" shouted Emile, dashing the tears from his face. "I will send Samson to get my gun!"

"Papa!" Anne-Marie looked at Matthew in horror.

Matthew held his hands up. "Gentlemen, I thank you for your enthusiasm, but right now the best you can do for the city is to protect our ladies. Philippe, you are working with the mayor and the legislature to organize additional militia, correct? Emile, it is vital that you spare a few of your slaves to help build the fortifications." He then turned to Anne-Marie. "I also ask that you take Anne-Marie back to Dansereau Plantation."

Anne-Marie glared at her lover. They had had this argument before. "*Non*! I am a volunteer with the Ursuline Sisters. I return there in a few hours." She lifted her chin. "You have your duty, and I have mine."

Matthew appealed to Emile, but he shrugged. "I have tried to have her see reason, but you see how it is? She is hardheaded, like her mother."

She hid a grin. "I will be safe, Matthew," she promised him.

Matthew had to be satisfied with that.

Luncheon ended soon afterwards, and Anne-Marie embraced Matthew at the door before he left.

"I am trying to be brave, *mon amour*," she said into his chest, "but with poor Jacob— Oh, please take care, Matthew! I am so frightened."

"Do not be. No harm will come to me. Be frightened for the enemy." Matthew's face was as grim as his mood. "The British took my best friend, and I'm mad for revenge. The whole army is fighting mad, too, from the general on down. We are confident. We hurt the redcoats badly two nights ago, and should they attack again, they will get a lot more than they bargained for. If they are smart, they will get back on their ships and go home."

"But they will not, will they?"

"No, Anne-Marie, they will not." He kissed her. *"Joyeux Noël, mon amour."*

Anne-Marie whispered a prayer as he left.

Our Lady of Prompt Succor, hasten to help us!

Conseil Plantation

JUST BEFORE NOON, GUNS WERE fired all over the British camp. Major-General Pakenham, the commander in chief, had arrived, along with his subordinate and friend, Major-General Gibbs. The chilled and hungry redcoat troops cheered them as well as the three thousand additional soldiers that sailed with them and were now landing on American soil.

Major-General Sir Edward Michael Pakenham, GCB, was a tall, light-haired second son of an Anglo-Irish baron, his family devoted to the British Crown. His early service included putting down the Irish Rebellion of 1798. He had made his reputation as a dashing and fearless leader of men in the Peninsula as adjutant to his brother-in-law, General Arthur Wellesley, now Duke of Wellington. He had earned the Knight Grand Cross of the Bath, the highest military award, for his actions at Bussaco, Salamanca, and Toulouse. He was respected by his peers and beloved by his men.

However he was honored, there were those who pointed out that the thirty-six-year-old general had proven a superb executor of the orders given by the genius Wellington. He had never before held an independent command. Pakenham was only at New Orleans because Wellington had declined it, recommending his brother-in-law in his place.

At forty-four, Major-General Sir Samuel Gibbs earned the Bath due to his service in India and the East Indies. His last action was as a brigade commander in the failed assault on the fortress of Bergen op Zoom in the Low Countries earlier that year. Gibbs escaped any blame for the defeat, was designated second-in-command at New Orleans, and was to lead a brigade under Pakenham. The two men befriended each other during the voyage, despite their age difference. Gibbs was known as brave and steadfast and was well regarded by his superiors.

The British assembled for a quick review, but Pakenham was more interested in the position of the army than its condition. For the next few hours, he inspected the Chalmette Plantation before calling for a meeting of the staff in his new headquarters. Joining them was Admiral Cochrane and his staff.

Pakenham wasted little time with pleasantries. Instead, he wanted to know who ordered the troops to land at Chalmette instead of Gentilly.

"I have looked at that field, and I must say I am astounded at its condition. There is barely a mile between the swamp to the right and the river at the left. The ground is low, muddy, and poor. The enemy controls the river, constantly firing cannonballs and shot into the camp and is building earthworks before us while we do nothing!"

The army officers assembled said nothing as Admiral Cochrane explained the change in plans. James Fitzwilliam flinched at Sir Alexander's courtly tone and snide insinuations. If the admiral was to be believed, the choice of Chalmette was both brilliant and necessary, and the failure to take the city lay completely with the exhausted army.

Cochrane finished his presentation in a confident manner.

"Recall, gentlemen, they are only militia facing us. They will take to their heels presently as they did at Bladensburg before Washington City."

Pakenham would not look at General Keane as he responded. "I regret the defeat of our forces due to the error made on the twenty-third of December." This was an obvious rebuke to the navy choosing Chalmette, but the army would not be spared, either. "Our troops should have advanced to New Orleans immediately."

Both Cochrane and Keane colored.

"I want plans made for the immediate withdrawal of the army from this place and its repositioning to the Chef Menteur Road in Gentilly."

The room exploded. Army and navy officers talked over each other, giving reason after reason why they could *not* retreat: They had fought a battle against the enemy and won. The men's morale would suffer knowing they were leaving a field sanctified by the blood of their comrades. The British tars manning the barges were exhausted. It was inconceivable to ask them to move the entire army again. No one knew whether the plains of Gentilly were in better condition than Chalmette. The Americans were building their defenses here, so they knew where the enemy was. It would be simple to determine its strength. Besides, the damned Americans would surely attack if they started to withdraw.

James was not part of the discussion. Junior staff officers did not speak unless requested. It was just as well. James was of two minds about the whole exercise. Yes, they were in a bad spot. General Keane should have marched straight into the city, but now that they were here—and the enemy knew that—how could they reposition without inviting attack? An invasion of Gentilly would be made piecemeal, the lack of barges guaranteed that, and they would be easy targets for any defenders.

James realized they would either fight at Chalmette or leave America.

General Pakenham clearly did not like the arguments given but said little to dispute what he heard. He seemed to be wavering when

Admiral Cochrane had his share of the conversation.

"It is incorrect that we were defeated," he claimed, "and there is nothing wrong with our position. If the army shrinks from the attack here, I will bring up my sailors and marines from the fleet. We will storm the American lines and march into the city." Disdainfully he added, "Then the soldiers can bring up the baggage."

The gross insult rang through the now-still air. Sir Edward stared at Sir Alexander. He was completely still, his face stony; the only evidence of his deep anger was a slightly shaking fist on the table. No one breathed for long moments.

"Very well," said the commander in chief evenly. "We will do our best to get us out of this jeopardy in which we find ourselves. We shall persist in the attack. Tomorrow I shall personally reconnoiter the enemy lines." He gave Cochrane a hard look. "I trust the navy shall do everything in its power to support this army which *I* have the honor to command?"

"Of course," the admiral allowed.

The die was cast, James realized. The fate of the New Orleans expedition would be decided on the Plains of Chalmette.

Chapter 15

The Americans had been doing more than building Line Jackson along the Rodriguez Canal. Commodore Patterson placed several cannons along the West Bank of the Mississippi River opposite the enemy. He also had the sloop *USS Louisiana* manned and gunned. Along with the schooner *USS Carolina*, he had three gun emplacements to bedevil the British camp. He used his guns with gusto, particularly at night. General Morgan was tasked with defending Patterson's position on the West Bank, for it was certain that the redcoats would eventually try to take them.

On the East Bank, Major Lacoste's Line Jackson was an impressive fortification. He ordered it built as tall as possible and had wooden platforms set into the embankment for the soldiers to stand on while they fired. Gaps were made for seven gun batteries, which forced the commander in chief to make a momentous decision.

Jackson had cannons but not enough artillerymen to operate them; Patterson needed his naval gunners on the *Carolina* and *Louisiana*. There was only one source of trained cannoneers left for the Americans, and General Jackson, against his better judgment, was forced to use them. The order was given: Bring Jean Lafitte's Baratarians forward from Fort St. Charles.

In quick order, thirty-six privateers arrived at Macarty Plantation. They were a scurvy, dangerous looking lot, led by the short, swarthy Dominique You and the more refined Renato Beluche. They were assigned to battery number three, close to General Jackson's head-quarters in the Macarty Plantation house and, more importantly, under his watchful eye.

New Orleans offered little in the way of arms and ammunition, but what the city did provide was just as valuable. The citizens threw open their larders and closets, providing needed food, coats, and shelter for their defenders. The generosity of the civilians did much to keep the army's spirits high.

The same could not be said of the British. They enjoyed little success reconnoitering the American works. The swamps frightened them, and the Mississippi Dragoons harassed any who ventured upon Chalmette Plantation. The dragoons were in their element, spying on the British and taking picquets prisoner when not killing them. At night, the Tennessee militia and native allies joined in the "sport." The redcoats were forced to take to the trees to spy on Line Jackson.

The army's custom of living off the land proved to be a terrible mistake. The invaders stripped the surrounding area of all the food and supplies that could be found, and it proved to be inadequate. The near-rotten food brought in by the navy was almost worse than nothing at all. Valuable manpower was wasted on dismantling structures for firewood and makeshift shelters, neither of which did much to deliver the men from the unexpected cold, wet weather.

Thanks to insistent assaults, relentless bombardments, bitter conditions, and persistent hunger, the British were growing increasingly frustrated and angry. They had been promised Christmas in New Orleans. Beauty and booty would be theirs. Instead, they were freezing on a swampy farm, and their food stores were beginning to run low.

General Pakenham was exasperated by the situation. In his first independent command, he was under tremendous pressure from within and without. He was expected to overcome the fixed works of an enemy of uncertain number and quality. His men were angry and miserable. He suffered conditions known to sap an army of its strength. Meanwhile, his ally, Admiral Cochrane, was constantly pushing him to throw his troops against General Jackson's battlements.

Pakenham was painfully aware of what he did not know. He did not respect the quality of the American soldier, but he was concerned over the quantity. How many men did Jackson really have? Deserters and prisoners gave conflicting numbers. Was it two thousand or twenty thousand? General Keane was convinced it was fifteen thousand, but if that were so, where were they? Hours of spying on Line Jackson gave no clue.

Pakenham's only consolation was the knowledge that Major-General Sir John Lambert was coming with two more regiments of infantry. Eventually he would have over eight thousand under his command. But he had no idea when he would arrive.

He did not choose this place and had no idea just how many foes he faced. Pakenham had learned from Wellington not to waste his men on foolish, costly assaults. As much as he hated the idea, he would have to tread cautiously.

So the British would continue to drill and plan. And do something about those damned American ships.

New Orleans

ANNE-MARIE HAD RARELY VISITED HER Uncle Philippe's law office. Therefore, she was surprised on receiving a note to stop by as she prepared to report to the Ursuline hospital. She made her way to her uncle's, the slave Samson by her side.

The city was filled with nervous anticipation. Armed men were everywhere. Members of the militia patrolled the streets while other soldiers conveyed supplies to General Jackson's command. Shopkeepers who had not volunteered to fight stood in the open doors of their shops for lack of custom. Everywhere was infested with fear as dreadful as the cold, damp air.

Anne-Marie was glad to arrive at the warm office. "Uncle," she greeted him, "good morning. I came as soon as you…" Her voice trailed off as she lowered her bonnet.

Philippe Melançon was a tidy and organized man; therefore, it was a shock to behold the state of his rooms. The place was filled with tall stacks of blankets and clothing—his desk, his chairs, and even his floor. One could scarcely see the walls. Her bemused uncle stood in the middle of the shambles.

"Uncle! What is this?"

"Do you not know, child?" Philippe laughed. "This is *your* doing."

"Mine? How can this be?"

"Did you not have a conversation with a Mlle Bellevue?"

Carmen, Henri's placée! "Yes, I did. Do you mean to say all this is from her?"

He stretched out his arms. "Indeed! A gift from the ladies in the *Faubourg Marigny*. Shirts, blankets, coats, and ponchos those Tennessee backwoodsmen seem so fond of. Quite the Christmas present, eh?"

She clapped her hands! "Oh, how wonderful! The soldiers, I know they will appreciate this!"

"I think they shall, but I must ask you one thing. Did you request that Mlle Bellevue deliver this to my office?"

Anne-Marie recalled the conversation. "Aunt Madeline told her to send a note to you. I only said that you would help."

"Ah. She apparently took that to mean something other than intended."

"Goodness! What shall we do?"

Philippe made his way through the piles of material to pat his niece's shoulder. "I have already sent a man to the *Place d'Armes*, requesting a wagon from the army. I just wanted you to see the fruits of your suggestion to Mlle Bellevue."

"She is very generous."

"Everyone is giving what they can—mostly everyone."

"Even Henri?"

"Every man must live with the consequences of what he does or does not do. Henri is exempt from the call-up, being head of his house. He is asked to volunteer, not required. I am the same."

"There is all the difference in the world," Anne-Marie shot back. "You—you do so much! You collect arms and supplies for the army!

You help run the city! Henri does nothing. He is young and you are— Oh! I beg your pardon, Uncle!"

"I know I am older, Anne-Marie, but I can fight if I must. I am not insulted. But I will not force Henri to enlist." Philippe stroked her hair. "You think of Matthew?"

Her heart clenched as she thought of the danger to her lover. "Of course, and of Major Harville, too. He came from so far away to help us, and now he is gone."

"The Lord has blessed us with these defenders. Our new country has given us many friends."

"*Oui.* Many new friends who have sent their sons to fight for us while our young men hide under their beds!"

"Anne-Marie! You know this is not so! Hundreds of the sons of New Orleans are at the line, standing with our Matthew. The cowards are few. Your grief and worry makes you bitter."

Anne-Marie saw the truth in his words. "I sound like Papa, is that what you say?"

Philippe smiled. "I did not say that, *chérie.*"

She returned the smile. "But you thought it."

"Eh, perhaps."

Anne-Marie turned to Samson, who had silently witnessed the entire conversation. "Samson, clear a place where we all may sit as we await the soldiers, *s'il vous plaît.*"

Tuesday, December 27: Chalmette Plantation

IN THE COLD, PRE-DAWN GLOOM, the British artillerymen stood to their guns, waiting for the signal. All night they had labored, the darkness occasionally violated by the flash of cannon from the *Carolina* or *Louisiana*. Missiles of death had rained upon their comrades as they sought sleep. The artillerymen ached to repay the upstart Yankees with their own coin. In a few moments, they would.

At about six o'clock, a voice yelled, "FIRE!"

The British did not have any heavy cannons. The six-pounders and naval carronades could do little damage to the sturdy oak sides of the American ships. The British knew that and planned accordingly.

Furnaces had been set up in the night to heat the cannonballs and shot for hours. The red-hot iron was quickly loaded down the barrels and the lanyards pulled. Again and again, flaming incendiaries rained down on the nearby *USS Carolina*. Fires broke out on the sails and decks. The Americans responded as swiftly as they could to save her, but it was for naught.

It soon became obvious that the blazing *Carolina* was doomed. Her captain ordered the schooner grounded and evacuated. Through herculean effort, the crew managed to salvage several of her guns. Not a soul was lost in the fight, but the valiant *Carolina* died a fiery death.

The British cheered their victory. The hated warship was destroyed. Surely, this was a foretaste of what Pakenham had in store for the Dirty Shirts, the new name the troops bestowed on the Americans. New Orleans would be theirs after all; they felt sure.

Conseil Plantation

"SIR." JAMES STOOD AT ATTENTION. "Major Fitzwilliam reporting as requested."

A senior aide to General Pakenham waved in the direction of a chair. "Sit down, Major. Have you seen last night's report of our picquets?"

"No, sir." Like most of the camp, he had watched the artillery battle against the Americans.

"We lost six more. At least four killed. One was wounded and able to tell us what happened. The Dirty Shirts came out of the woods with knives and arrows, attacking our people like highwaymen. General Pakenham is incensed at this clear violation of the customs of war."

"Yes, sir."

The aide indicated a sealed letter on the desk. "You are to advance under flag of truce to the American lines with General Pakenham's letter. You will protest the inhuman treatment of our picquets in the strongest terms and deliver that letter to General Jackson or his representative. Return once you receive an answer."

James stood. "Yes, sir."

"There are a few horses about. Take one and have a soldier go with you. That is all."

Macarty Plantation

AT ABOUT NOON, A LOOKOUT cried, "Sir, there's a party approaching under a flag of truce! Two men—one is an officer."

From his horse, General Jackson scrutinized the redcoat detail. "Request to parley, eh? What rank is the officer? Can you tell?"

The entire staff peered through their telescopes. "I think he's a major," one of them finally announced.

The general turned to Matthew. "Major Darcy, get a man and go see what the fellow wants."

Matthew requisitioned a sergeant from the regulars and had him fashion their own white flag. The two mounted horses, made their way through the earthworks and over the canal, and rode out to the waiting British detail, about five hundred yards away. They were not alone on the field. Patrolling about the plantation were a few of the dragoons, reconnoitering the enemy and making a general nuisance of themselves.

Matthew stopped about ten yards away from the enemy soldiers. The redcoat officer wore buff trousers tucked into knee-high black boots, a black bicorn hat upon his head. The major's red uniform coat was as filthy as Matthew's blue one, and a kernel of respect grew in his breast. This Englishman was no typical staff officer who sat at a desk with maps all about while others fought and bled. This man had seen action, and therefore, he was a dangerous opponent.

The British officer offered a salute, his palm facing forward. "Major James Fitzwilliam, British Army. I have a message from my commander in chief, Major-General Sir Edward Pakenham."

Matthew returned the salute in the American custom, palm down. "Major Matthew Darcy, representing Major General Andrew Jackson of the *United States Army.*" He placed particular emphasis on his last three words. He wanted this blasted trespasser to know he faced a patriot. "What is this message?"

"Darcy?" The British officer was clearly puzzled. "Did you say your name is Darcy?"

"I did." Matthew wondered what was so unusual about his name.

Major Fitzwilliam had an eager look on his face. "Are you from the North of England? Derbyshire, perhaps?"

"I am an American from Baltimore, Maryland, sir," Matthew snapped. "Perhaps you have heard of the place?"

"Err, yes." Major Fitzwilliam's face flushed, and Matthew suspected this man had taken part in the burning of Washington. The major continued, "But, your family—are they from Derbyshire?"

"What is so important about that?"

"I am related to the Darcys. They are my cousins. We might be distant cousins of a sort."

Jacob's death was still fresh in Matthew's mind. "I am no cousin to any damned Englishman, distant or otherwise! Give me your commander's message or leave."

Major Fitzwilliam lost all expression. In a cold voice, he stated, "I have been instructed to relay to your commanding general Sir Edward's disgust with the barbarous attacks on our picquets. It must stop. Here is his note."

"I beg your pardon?" Matthew took the note.

Major Fitzwilliam raised his chin. "It is well known in civilized nations that picquets are not to be molested. Neither do gentlemen fire upon encampments at night. Your people are acting as assassins and murderers. It is simply not done."

Matthew wanted to laugh in the man's face. Instead, he replied in a growl, "Yes, we know well how *gentlemen* from Britain fight. You kidnap innocent men from neutral ships. You give guns to the native tribes to slaughter farmers. You murder civilians and rape women."

"What?" cried Fitzwilliam.

"I speak of Hampton, Virginia," Matthew spat. "June, 1813. You do not know of it? I assure you we have not forgotten, not for a moment!

"I will convey your general's message to mine, but I will give you your answer now. We intend to extend to the entirety of your army the same courtesy we have shown to your picquets. You, sir, have invaded our country and seek to destroy our homes. I will have you know these are men you are facing, and we will fight you in any manner we choose. That is our answer."

Matthew began to turn away, but decided to get one last shot in. "Our last word to you is this: Leave this place, or we will kill you, one and all...*Cousin*." He turned to his companion. "Come, Sergeant."

With that, Darcy and the sergeant rode back to the American lines.

MATTHEW DELIVERED PAKENHAM'S LETTER TO General Jackson and briefly described his discussion with the British representative. He omitted the bizarre conversation about relatives in England, of course. It was not germane to the subject at hand, and the general preferred succinctness from his staff.

"Hmm, so we're irritating Wellington's Immortals, eh? Your answer, Major Darcy, will do for them. Well done." The general wore a sly smile, which appeared skeletal on his thin face. "Customs of war? Bah! The less those rascals sleep, the better I like it."

He changed the subject. "Gentlemen, the loss of the *Carolina* is a blow, certainly, but we shall make the best of it. Commodore Patterson, your report."

Patterson spoke up. "I remind you, gentlemen, we still have *USS Louisiana*. We have towed her upstream, out of range of their guns. For some of the finest cannoneers in the world, it was an inexcusable error for the British to allow her to escape. Not that I am complaining! We have lost half of our naval strength, true, but only half. Several of the guns from *Carolina* have been salvaged, and we have saved all of her crew. We shall re-arm *Louisiana* with as many guns as she can carry. Whatever is left shall be used on the line here or shipped to the West Bank."

"We were taken by surprise, gentlemen. We shall not make that mistake again!" Jackson vowed. "Coffee, make sure your 'visits' to the redcoats bring back intelligence as well as prisoners. We must know his plans.

"The enemy has the advantage of maneuver while we are behind this line. Neither our troops nor supplies are unlimited. We must husband them well and place them where they will do the most good. Pakenham must attack or retreat, and he shall not retreat. The question is where he will strike.

"Vigilance, gentlemen. Our eyes must be ever fixed upon those villains."

Conseil Plantation

"I delivered Sir Edward's message," James reported. "The American representative told me flatly that they intend to continue their uncivilized attacks."

Pakenham's chief aide, a colonel, rubbed his face. "I see. Well, at least we sank their damned schooner. We shall get some sleep tonight and discover whether the Yankees are so insolent tomorrow. In the meantime, double the picquets."

"Yes, sir." James turned but then hesitated. "Sir, do you know anything about Hampton, Virginia?"

The colonel eyed him. "What makes you ask?"

"Something the American major said about atrocities supposedly committed by us in June of '13."

"Oh, that." The officer sighed. "That wasn't us—Regulars, I mean. A couple of companies of foreigners, made up mainly of French deserters and prisoners who came over to our side, participated in a raid on Virginia. I believe they were looking for the home port of one of their frigates—the *Constellation*, I think it was. Damned operation was a bloody blunder, and when they got to Hampton, some of the foreigners went wild. It happens. The men were withdrawn from the Chesapeake and eventually returned to England, where the companies were disbanded."

"Was anyone punished?"

The colonel had returned to his paperwork. "Not that I know of," he said without looking up.

James was silent, his mind racing. In Portugal and Spain,

Wellington had been a strict disciplinarian. More than one soldier had been executed for stealing or rape. Hanging a few malcontents and criminals sent a strong message to the rest of the troops; else, it was said, they could lose the entire army. And yet, nothing was done to the perpetrators at Hampton?

"Leave this place, or we will kill you, one and all," Major Darcy had said. *The Americans probably believe we would act the same as was done at Hampton, should we take New Orleans,* James thought. He shuddered. He knew angry, scared men were the most dangerous enemy of all.

The colonel looked up. "Anything else, Major?"

James's attention returned to the man. "No, sir. I will see to the picquets straight away."

"Good. General Pakenham wants to see for himself what we are facing. With the damned schooner out of the way, we can act. The army assembles tonight, and we do not want the Yankees to know what we are about."

"A full assault, sir?" James knew the army wasn't ready for that.

"No. He plans a reconnaissance in force. But if the Dirty Shirts are as skittish as Admiral Cochrane believes, we could be in the city by this time tomorrow. Carry on."

Chapter 16

In the pre-dawn darkness, Major-General Sir Edward Pakenham assembled his host and prepared to cast a hazard.

At first glance, the terrain of Chalmette Plantation appeared as flat as a table. Having taken care to personally scout the terrain, Pakenham knew looks were deceiving. Paradoxically, the high point of the land was near the small levee protecting the farm from the Mississippi River. The ground sloped oh so gently towards a cypress forest that grew swampy and impassable.

In fact, the entirety of the field was damp and muddy. The near-constant rains the British had encountered since their arrival had turned the rich, black Louisiana dirt into a sticky, thick sludge.

To the British general's chagrin, General Jackson had chosen his position well. The plantation was shaped like a funnel from east to west. Cleared land extended almost a mile from the river where the British encamped, but narrowed to half that at Rodriguez Canal, where the Jackson built his works. There was limited area for the British army to maneuver.

Having been persuaded against withdrawing in favor of an approach through the Gentilly Plain, General Pakenham needed to know exactly what he faced. He had no idea as to Jackson's strength. According to spies and informers, the Americans numbered anywhere between a thousand men to ten thousand.

Time was of the essence. Pakenham could not sit and wait for

General Lambert's corps to arrive. They were in enemy territory, the weather was foul, supplies were limited, and the men were cold, hungry, and impatient. Any delay would also give the enemy time to resupply and reinforce. Waiting for reinforcements was ruled out, but a full attack, using suspect intelligence, was foolhardy.

So Sir Edward chose the middle way—a reconnaissance in force. The goal was to probe the American line, looking for weak points. The general was taking a chance, much like his men when they played the dice game Hazard.

If he "threw crabs" and the defenses were stout, Pakenham could withdraw with minimal causalities. If he "nicked it," however, and the opportunity presented itself, the army could rush to the weak spot, break the enemy line, defeat the enemy in detail, and enjoy dinner in the *Vieux Carré*.

General Pakenham decided to use two columns: his trusted friend General Gibbs on his right near the cypress jungle, and the disappointing General Keane on the extreme left along the levee. With the destruction of the hated *USS Carolina*, he expected Keane's men would suffer limited harassment.

As the sun rose and the mist floated away, General Pakenham gave the order. At about six o'clock, the host slowly moved forward.

Chalmette Plantation

TELESCOPE IN HAND, MATTHEW STOOD with General Jackson and the other staff officers, looking out the second floor of the Macarty House headquarters, watching the maneuvers of the enemy. It was quite a sight through the mist—flags flying, bagpipes playing, immaculate rows of scarlet coats marching in good order. It was a sight meant to terrify.

"It looks like they're on parade, General," remarked one staffer.

General Jackson closed his telescope. "Enough, gentlemen. It is time we saw to the men." As one, they descended the stairs and left the house.

The attack was not a surprise. Scouts had been spying on the British since their arrival and had reported the obvious preparations for action hours before. Jackson's rag-tag troops were already at their positions, guns loaded and waiting.

As the other officers hurried to their assignments, Jackson gave Matthew his orders, mounting his horse as he did so. "Major Darcy, you are to oversee the resupply of the right wing. I also require you to pay special attention to the Baratarians." He pointed at Dominique You and Renato Beluche overseeing the guns of battery number three. "We will see if these fellows are as good as Captain Lafitte claims."

On horseback, the general could easily see over the parapet, and he gazed at the maneuvering enemy on the far side of the plain, more than a mile away. "Those redcoat villains are yet out of range," he remarked. "Major, make sure those pirates hold their fire until the enemy is in striking distance, and then let their presence be felt. Carry on."

Matthew saluted as the general rode off to the center of his line.

IT TOOK SOME TIME FOR the regiments to move into position. The British high command's attention was fixed upon the American works, searching for points in the enemy line, both strong and weak. Meanwhile, soldiers dug furiously, building emplacements for the army's six and nine-pound cannons. It was nearly eight o'clock before the guns were ready to begin probing the Yankee fortifications.

However, it was the Americans who offered the first salute. A broadside of canister from *USS Louisiana* tore into General Keane's regiments. Surprised and enraged, the British immediately returned fire, both at the ship and Line Jackson.

They used a new weapon. Multiple jets of fire rose up in an unworldly screech of sound from behind the troops, arcing over towards the American lines.

"*Mon Dieu*! What the devil are those?" cried a member of the colored brigade.

"Congreve rockets," replied Matthew. "They used them at Baltimore. Makes one hell of a racket, but not much damage. They want to scare us."

"They are doing a good job of that, *monsieur*!" The man ducked low, crawling as close as he could to the wall of dirt protecting him.

"Never mind them! It is their cannons we have to watch for. Keep your heads down until your officers say otherwise."

Just then, a salvo slammed into the earthworks. Mud and dirt flew everywhere, but the wall held.

"Hah!" Dominique You slapped his thigh. "The mud, she eats up the cannonballs!" He squatted behind his gun, lanyard in hand. "Ready!" He stepped to the side and pulled, triggering the flintlock on the breach. The twenty-four-pounder leapt back with a crash of fire and smoke.

"*Pour vous, cochons d'anglais!*[4]"

New Orleans: Later that afternoon

"IT WAS A DIRECT HIT," a dirty Matthew said as he took his ease in the Melançons' parlor, a glass of wine by his hand. "The Baratarians are as good artillerymen as the army and navy boys. I think it was a rude surprise for the British."

His audience included the Melançons, Emile Dansereau, Anne-Marie, and Henri Herbert. While the men were enthralled, the ladies present were decidedly uncomfortable with the details.

"The columns facing me, near the river, were caught in the crossfire between our cannons, the *Louisiana's* guns, and Commodore Patterson's battery across the river," Matthew continued. "We raked them using canister and grapeshot. The redcoats took to ground, halting their advance. The few guns they brought forward did little damage to us.

"As for the columns on our left, they tried to turn our flank, but General Coffee ambushed them from the swamp. Rifle and arrow fire forced the redcoats to pull back. By noon, the action was essentially over, and the British withdrew in good order while we continued to harass them."

Herbert shook his head. "Indians fighting for us! I would never

---

4 For you, English pigs!

have thought it."

"They were stalwart allies during the Creek War, Henri"—Matthew turned to the others—"as was the local militia today. They were frightened at first, but they stood their ground. While the enemy never got into range of our rifles and muskets on our end of the line, I think the militia would have given a good account of themselves if matters came to that."

"So, the English, they are beaten?" asked Emile Dansereau hopefully.

"*Non, monsieur*, they are not." Matthew then explained the purpose of a reconnaissance in force. "They will be back, remembering the lessons they learned today. That will be the main battle."

Silence enveloped the room as his friends realized the import of his words. The worst was yet to come.

Philippe Melançon was the first to speak. "What do you need from us, Matthew?"

Matthew ran a weary hand through his hair. "What we always need: men, guns, and powder. Food, too. Lafitte has been true to his word. I do not think we could have held without his cache of weapons and gunpowder. His men, too—those Baratarians are fearless." He looked at Emile. "Thank you for your assistance there."

"I did nothing," Emile said with feeling. "You—you are the ones standing between us and the English." He threw a glare at Herbert, who avoided his look.

Philippe changed the subject. "I understand General Jackson has shut down the legislature. Why did he do that?"

"Word got to the general during the action that the legislature was ready to vote on surrendering the city to the British. He sent the dragoons to prevent that from happening."

Emile gestured at his brother-in-law. "I told you, Philippe! I told you Marigny and his friends would betray us!"

Matthew held up his hands. "Wait, *monsieur*. To be fair, the legislature sent a delegation to the general protesting the closure, and M. de Marigny was among them. They all claimed there was no move to surrender."

"I had heard a few days ago that some of the traders were frightened and sought peace," said Philippe. "Both Creole and American." He glanced at Matthew. "Wallace Anderson was one of the leaders. As for Bernard de Marigny, he has a reputation for scheming, but his name was not among those reported to me."

"Anderson—bah! It is always about money with that one. As for Marigny, I do not trust him and never have." Emile would not be moved.

"Is it true the general threatened to burn the city rather than surrender?" asked a worried Madeline Melançon.

"Yes, *madame*, he did."

Philippe looked him in the eye. "Would General Jackson really do that?"

Matthew paused, his gaze on his boots. "Knowing the general as I do, I think he would."

There were gasps around the room, overridden by a shout from Emile. "Hah! *There* is a man I can follow! The general, he is another Charles Martel! I cheer his name!"

"Emile! You would burn down New Orleans?" Madeline said, shocked. "This is my home! How can you say such a thing?"

"Think of all the people, Papa," added Anne-Marie. "Many would be killed."

"What? You would live under English rule?" Emile would have none of it. "Far better to die with honor! Or flee to the country; we have room. The city, she is nothing!"

Matthew thought things had gone far enough. "The army will make sure you do not have to make the choice between fire and surrender." He stood up sadly. "And I must return to the lines. *Merci beaucoup*, Madeline, for your hospitality. Philippe, M. Dansereau, thank you for your pledges of assistance."

Philippe shook his hand. "We will somehow find what you need, Matthew."

"Whatever I have, you shall have it, my brave major," Emile vowed. "*Bonne chance, mon ami.*"

Matthew never thought he would hear Emile Dansereau call him his good friend, and it took a moment to register. "*Merci beaucoup, monsieur.*"

"I shall call you Matthew, eh, my son?" Emile embraced him. "You come back soon, Matthew— *Oui?*"

The major thought he misheard but saw the older man glance in Anne-Marie's direction. *He accepts me? Will wonders never cease?*

Once released from Emile's grip, Matthew found himself face-to-face with Henri Herbert. His friend could not meet his eye. "You still need soldiers?" His voice was very low.

Matthew nodded.

"I have never fired a gun." Herbert paused. "I am a coward, *mon ami*, but I can learn to shoot, I think. I will come and do what I can."

"That is all we can expect from any man, Henri. Thank you."

Anne-Marie walked him to the door. For the first time that afternoon, they had a moment together. She picked at his dirty uniform coat. "Your orderly will need to clean this," she said in a distracted manner, her head down.

"I do not have an orderly, *ma chérie*. It is well; I have brushed my coat many times before." Placing his fingers under her chin, he lifted her face. "You should go back to Dansereau Plantation. It is not safe for you in the city."

"*Non.* If you are here, then I will be here. The sisters, they need me at hospital, tending to the wounded."

"I just want you safe."

"I know." Her eyes filled. "We have sent Major Harville's belongings to Nashville. I think of his Fanny, and I cannot help but weep." Her voice was urgent. "Promise you will take care. Promise you will come back to me."

"Anne-Marie, I will do what—"

"Promise me!"

He kissed her forehead. "I promise. I promise I will return."

"Oh, *mon amour.*" She wept against his filthy uniform, and they held each other for a time.

"*Ma chérie*, I must go."

Anne-Marie reluctantly released him. "I will pray to Our Lady to watch over you, *mon amour.* Remember your promise."

No one needed to tell James Fitzwilliam the level of General Pakenham's frustration over the day's events. It was obvious. Over two hundred dead and a like number wounded or missing, and the British had nothing to show for it. All knew the cause: Sir Edward had underestimated the Yankee artillery. He had indeed "thrown out."

It had been thought that, with the destruction of *USS Carolina* and its guns, the American line would prove as porous before the disciplined British troops as had the enemy's defenses at Washington. The number of enemy cannon that had appeared from nowhere was a rude shock, and the marksmanship of the gunners proved excellent. The Americans had also set up a battery on the far bank of the river, catching the British in a crossfire. The failure to sink *USS Louisiana,* now manned and armed, loomed large over the day's defeat. There was nothing for it but to eliminate the American artillery positions.

The army's six- and nine-pounders were inadequate for the job, and Admiral Cochrane's promised eighteen- and twenty-four-pounders had yet to arrive from the fleet. They were on the way, the navy vowed, along with cannoneers.

Meanwhile, dissention reared its ugly head within the council of war. Lt. Colonel Rennie, a brigade commander under General Gibbs, insisted he was about to turn the Americans' left flank near the swamp when he received the order to withdraw. He angrily defended his view from those who thought otherwise.

James was part of the latter group. He had seen the incredible marksmanship from the Yankee riflemen, who could kill at will a hundred yards or more beyond the effective range of British Brown Bess muskets. More so, the sight of Red Indian arrows decorating the coats of infantrymen was a horror for which the men were unprepared.

As for the navy, Cochrane insisted that the army attack the

Americans as soon as possible. The contempt in which the admiral held the army was almost as great as he held for the Dirty Shirt backwoodsmen who had barred their way into New Orleans.

There was another issue with which James was well acquainted: overconfidence. It was a given that the Americans were bad soldiers. This belief infected the entire command. They truly expected that they could just march into the city with little to no opposition.

This overconfidence was taking its toll. The troops were suffering terribly. The weather had proved to be unexpectedly freezing and wet. It was bad enough to work, stand guard, and drill in the cold rain; it was an unimaginable misery to try to sleep in the mud with nothing but a thin blanket to stave off the damp chill. Sleep could not be found in any case, for the enemy entertained themselves by bombarding the British camp throughout the night. Backwoodsmen and braves continued to assassinate the picquets. The continuous harassment was intolerable.

The greatest difficulty was lack of food. The same arrogance that left an army famous for logistics unprepared for an extended battle against an entrenched enemy had also left them short of food. Again, it was assumed the troops could forage for a day or two before entering the captured capital of Louisiana.

Now it was a week later. There was little food to forage. Their numbers were swelled with escaped slaves, and they had to be fed. The navy brought what they could, but it was not enough. The British army was down to eating horseflesh, and that only when it could be found. The high command's shortsightedness had left Pakenham's men freezing and staving. Morale was crumbling.

Thus, there were intense pressures on General Sir Edward Pakenham. Defeat was not in his nature, and withdrawal was unthinkable. If redeployment to the Gentilly Plain was unfeasible, the only road out of this bitter hell was into the Crescent City, and the commander in chief meant to take it. But if he did not conquer New Orleans forthwith, his army would fall apart.

Pakenham assigned his artillery commander the task of silencing the American guns once the navy cannons arrived. Meanwhile, the staff reviewed what they knew of Line Jackson. The wall of dirt and wood was not particularly tall, but ladders would still be required. A greater problem was the ditch before the line. It was too wide be crossed by men without assistance.

Fascines would be needed. There were warehouses nearby filled with sugar cane stalks. They would do nicely.

Chapter 17

"We must extend the line, *mon General*," Major Latour insisted.

A council of war had been called at daybreak by General Jackson to renew the current situation. In attendance were Jackson's divisional commanders, Generals Carroll and Coffee, Commodore Patterson, and a representative of General Morgan, who remained on the West Bank. All of Jackson's aides were there along with the local volunteers: Edward Livingston, Arsène Latour, and Majors Plauche, Lacoste, and Daquin of the local militia. Also in attendance were Governor Claiborne and Jean Lafitte.

Matthew Darcy and the other federal officers found themselves in the strange position of observing what amounted to a briefing of their general from local amateurs, particularly the Frenchman Latour. They had marched for weeks to come and save New Orleans, and this foreigner was telling them how to do their business. The Americans had been impressed with the line Latour designed and constructed. Results count, they all realized. So they stood quietly about, listened, and learned.

The atmosphere was serious. Yes, they had turned back the British the day before. However, the commander in chief was not one to rest on his laurels. Old Hickory would never underestimate a foe. The British reconnaissance-in-force had revealed near-fatal weaknesses in Jackson's defenses.

An immediate problem was with Line Jackson itself. Major Latour's engineering prowess was proven by the ramparts' resistance to British fire. But the wall of mud and timber needed to be taller, the Frenchman said. Worse, General Coffee reported that the earthworks on the extreme left had been nearly flanked and overrun the day before.

While *USS Louisiana* had fought brilliantly, the loss of the *Carolina* and its firepower hurt. Heavier guns were needed for the sloop and on shore as well. Stronger emplacements for the artillery had to be constructed on Line Jackson for the bigger guns coming from the shattered *Carolina*.

The general was well pleased with Commodore Patterson's battery on the West Bank, and he expected that Pakenham would expend great effort to eliminate those guns.

The entire staff gathered about a rough map of the line. Jackson pointed at the left flank. "How much further do you recommend, gentlemen?"

Coffee and Latour had already discussed this, Matthew knew. "Sir," said Coffee, "we need to extend well into the swamp."

"*Oui*," said Major Latour as he drew his finger across the paper. "We shall go this far, and then bend a little, where it is drier. The bend, she will be a strong point, you see."

Jackson voiced Matthew's concern. "Our men will be stretched, as well." The general did not wait for an answer. "Strengthen the gun emplacements at the center and left—Batteries 6 and 7. Bunch them close. I want the heavy guns from *Carolina* placed there and at Battery Number 5."

Major Latour rubbed his chin. "Those guns, they shall be very heavy, *Oui*? We must have good support to carry them, or they shall sink in the mud."

Matthew spoke up. "We found some hogsheads of sugar. Will they serve?"

The engineer dismissed Matthew with a wave of his hand. "*Non!* The sugar will melt. Useless! Cotton bales are what I need."

"There's plenty of bales in the warehouses around here," said another aide.

Jackson nodded. "Excellent. I want them all brought to the works at once."

"General, you are speaking of a fortune in cotton," Livingston warned. "The planters will not be happy."

"Would they be happier to have their cotton in the hands of the redcoats?" Jackson replied. "Let the planters be satisfied their goods will be used in the defense of the country." He returned to the French engineer. "Major Latour, the line on the West Bank must be strengthened."

"*Mon general*, I shall be occupied here. I cannot go to the other side of the river." Major Latour nodded at General Morgan's representative. "But I shall confer with this man and Commodore Patterson, and they will take my instructions back with them."

"We'll make sure all will be in readiness, sir," promised Patterson.

"Very well." Jackson turned to Claiborne. "Governor, General Thomas has informed me he is coming with his Kentuckians, but what of the locals? Are we to expect more Creole companies?"

Governor Claiborne assured Jackson that more men joined the militia every day. When Captain Lafitte was asked whether more Baratarians were available, the buccaneer replied that he had no more men.

General Jackson stewed for a moment. "We must do what we can with what we have. To your duties, gentlemen. Governor, Mr. Livingston, a moment, if you please."

Matthew knew they were to talk of the political situation in the city. By placing New Orleans under martial law, General Jackson was virtually a military dictator. He and the governor ruled a city of scared, distrustful civilians. Who knew how many traitors and agitators were among them? Another headache for the commander in chief.

Such subjects were not in Matthew's purview. He needed more men and equipment to build Latour's Line Jackson. There were cotton bales to requisition.

Conseil Plantation

A SIMILAR COUNCIL OF WAR was held in General Villeré's fine dining room. James Fitzwilliam could only imagine how the owner of this house felt, knowing British officers used it as their headquarters, barracks, kitchen, and personal treasure trove. The cabinets and furniture were broken, much of it used for fires. Anything of value was confiscated. Mud was tracked everywhere. The beautiful house was now a filthy hovel.

Three British generals, an admiral, and various other officers gathered about the dining table. Strewn all over it were maps and papers. The atmosphere was tense, filled with anger, disappointment, and restlessness. Gone was the polite sedateness usually found at these meetings. The officers' words were brusque and sharp, verging on open rudeness.

James had never attended a council like it. That was no surprise, for in his career he had never been with an army in such straights.

Because of mistakes and bungling, the army was in a terrible position. In unfamiliar, hostile territory, they were hemmed in on three sides. To the left was the immense Mississippi River; to the right an impassible swamp. Their only line of retreat was by a narrow, muddy road—barely worthy of its name—that snaked through marsh and open water.

Two miles westward was an unknown number of the enemy, safe behind superb fornications. The line bristled with guns and cannons. And that was not the worst of it.

"Gentlemen," said General Pakenham, "it was a grave misfortune that the American sloop was not destroyed when we sank their schooner. It seems the Yankees have placed many guns on the left bank of the river, and with the sloop, they have not lost the ability to shoot at us from two directions."

The commander of artillery, Lt. Colonel Dickson, pointed out that his small cannons could not be brought to bear on the *Louisiana* while they were engaged with the *Carolina*. By the time the schooner was aflame, the Americans had towed the sloop out of range.

"Indeed, Dickson. That is no reflection on you. We need larger guns." General Pakenham directed this last comment at Admiral Cochrane.

"The guns are coming, Sir Edward." Unlike the others, Sir Alexander was not ruffled in the least.

"Thank you, but can we carry them forward through the swamp?" The commander in chief turned to his chief engineer. "Colonel Burgoyne?"

"We have been seeing to the state of the road since our arrival, Sir Edward. It is poor and low—very wet, indeed. The mud eats up the trees we have felled. It is a hard business."

"You cannot fix the road?" asked the admiral disdainfully.

"Of course we shall," replied Lt. Colonel Burgoyne easily. "I merely speak as to the difficulties my men face. They have overcome many obstacles in the past; I expect this will be no different."

General Pakenham turned to Admiral Cochrane. "How much longer before the guns arrive?"

Sir Alexander waved a hand, and a navy captain stepped up to him, bending to whisper in his commander's ear. "Two days," the admiral promised when the captain was done, "perhaps less."

James saw Sir Edward was unhappy with the news and knew he would have to make the general unhappier still. "Sir, I must report that our stores of food are dangerously low."

"What of the foraging parties?"

"The local farms have been stripped clean. A couple of the ponies found in the barns have been slaughtered. As for hunting parties, success has been limited. There is a want of game, and to be honest, the men fear the creatures in the swamp, particularly the crocodiles."

"Alligators," corrected one of the naval officers. "There are no crocodiles in these waters, only alligators." The rest of the room stared at the officer. "The snout of the alligator is broad, you see, not narrow like a true crocodile—"

"Thank you for the naturalist lesson," interrupted General Pakenham. "Can they be eaten?"

The red-faced captain, belatedly realizing his *faux pas*, gave a simple, "Yes, sir," and stepped away from the table.

"The navy continues to ship stores?" asked the general.

The admiral was defensive. "It was expected we would be in the city by now. We are doing all we can. Guns—stores—we have only so many boats."

"I do not question the navy's commitment of support for this enterprise, Sir Alexander." Pakenham's reassuring tone fooled no one. Of course, he was chastising the navy, and everyone knew it.

"There is food aplenty in New Orleans," was Cochrane's silky answer. "I suggest we go get it."

The army contingent in the room recognized the insult. There was a low murmuring, cut off by Pakenham raising a hand.

"That is my intention, Sir Alexander. That is why I need those guns." He looked to Lt. Colonel Dickson. "Your assignment is to destroy the enemy's artillery positions." Dickson nodded. "Once that is accomplished, we shall break through their line and take New Orleans. You said two days at most, Sir Alexander?"

"I did, sir."

"December thirty-first," Pakenham mused. "Then we attack the next day. We'll give those Yankees a New Year's day they will not soon forget."

Chapter 18

The British preparations were complete long before New Year's Day dawned. Teams of men silently worked through the night, and six hundred yards from the American works, six batteries of five guns each had been completed. The powerful eighteen-pound naval cannons were manned by superbly trained and experienced soldiers and sailors. They had proven their skill in Spain, France, and on the high seas, to the woe of Napoleon, and now they meant to do the same to General Jackson. Each battery was filled with precious ammunition. On both wings, regiments of infantry waited to storm the enemy line once the earthworks were breached.

Everything was in readiness. The gunners stood by, cannons loaded, and gunlocks cocked. Troops fixed bayonets to their muskets. The hounds strained at the slips. Yet no order came.

For the day had dawned like so many others: cold, wet, and foggy. Visibility was barely twenty yards. Cannoneers could not hit targets they could not see, even at point-blank range. Frustrated, General Pakenham had no choice. He had to wait until the fog lifted.

Macarty Plantation

MATTHEW LOWERED HIS TELESCOPE, USELESS in the pea-soup fog. The noise from the night previous had proven a false alarm. The British would not come today. It was just as well. The men needed to celebrate, and General Jackson had called off all work and ordered a grand review.

The men ate a hearty breakfast and dressed in their finest. Civilians came with food and drink with an eye to make merry with their relations. Matthew was particularly glad to see one wagon.

"*Bonne année*, Matthew!" cried Emile Dansereau from the driver's bench. The tall slave, Samson, sat next to him, reins in hand. "Behold what I bring for our gallant defenders! Bread! Cheese! Wine!" He winked. "And something special for you!"

Anne-Marie smiled and waved from inside the wagon. She wore a pretty, white, somewhat low-cut dress, a wrap placed over her shoulders.

"You are just in time for the festivities," Matthew managed with a dry mouth as he helped Anne-Marie from the wagon. If his hands remained on hers longer than necessary, no one remarked on it.

"I see!" she cried gaily. Indeed, flags and standards were unfurled throughout the American camp. Citizens mixed easily with the soldiers. The "Marseillaise" and "Yankee Doodle" were played by the bands. An air of relaxation was all about.

Emile Dansereau slapped his leg. "What a sight! Our soldiers, so brave, so confident! The English have nothing superior to this! Let them come! We shall serve to them a dinner indigestible, eh, my dear boy?" He turned and waved his arm. "Samson! You may drive the wagon to the kitchens."

The vagaries of Emile Dansereau's sentiments continued to astonish Matthew. Only weeks before, the older man despaired for the deliverance of the city. Now he was spoiling for a fight! Once he was ill tempered and insulting, now he was outgoing and complimentary to a fault. And Matthew was his dear boy, not some mistrusted foreigner.

The fog began to lift, and the sun peeked out of the mist as the three walked over to the tables of food. Dansereau's wagon could be seen behind the nearby kitchen tent, Samson standing beside it.

"Matthew! Anne-Marie tells me you have no orderly. Is that true?"

Emile's *non sequitur* interrupted Matthew's contemplation of his beloved's *décolletage*. If she stood any closer to him, he could not answer for his actions. "*Oui, monsieur*. If I wish for a servant, I must hire one."

Dansereau shared a private look with his daughter. "We cannot have that—not for our brave Major Darcy. Samson! Come here." A moment later, the large black man was before them.

"Matthew, meet your orderly!" Dansereau gestured at the slave with a twinkle in his eye.

"I beg your pardon?"

Anne-Marie took his hand. "Samson will act as your servant as long as you are here, Matthew. Is that not so, Samson?"

The slave nodded, his face without expression.

Matthew was stunned. "Ahh…that is exceedingly kind of you, but I have no need for a servant."

Dansereau waved him off. "Nonsense! Officers are gentlemen, and gentlemen require a valet! You do not have one, so I bring one to you. *C'est fait*."

Anne-Marie drew close, and in English, whispered, "Matthew, to refuse would insult Papa. Please accept Samson, if but for my sake? He is strong and loyal and is to watch over you."

Matthew peered up at one of the few men taller than himself. "Let me speak to him for a moment."

Permission granted, the two walked out of the others' hearing. "Samson, truthfully now, do you wish to do this? I will not lie to you. It could prove to be very dangerous. If you have no heart for it, I will release you and not think the less of you."

Samson studied him as if taking his measure. It was unusual behavior for a slave. "My mistress, she cares for you very much. She asks me to protect you. Only for her would I do such a thing. I will do as *la mademoiselle* asks."

"You will obey my orders without question?"

His face grew impassive. "Slaves must obey orders."

"Here, you will not be a slave, but a soldier. You may have to fight."

A feral grin grew. "*Très bien*. The English come to hurt *la mademoiselle*. That, I will not allow."

"I will not allow that either while I live."

Samson nodded. "I will obey the major, then, without question."

Bemused, Matthew realized he had just gained an orderly. He patted Samson on the back, and they returned to the others.

"*Merci beaucoup*, M. Dansereau. I accept the services of your man Samson for the duration of hostilities." He turned to Anne-Marie. "I will do what I can to keep him safe."

"I know you will, Matthew." Anne-Marie pointed. "Oh, look! The fog has lifted."

Matthew turned. "Yes, you can see—" Shock stilled his tongue.

The mist had dissipated, showing British guns only a few hundred yards away. Guns that were not there the day before.

"Good God!" He turned to his friends. "You must leave —immediately!"

Just then, the British opened fire. It was ten o'clock.

Chalmette Plantation

JAMES WATCHED THE ASSAULT WITH relieved satisfaction. Apparently, the delay due to the persistent fog had not lessened the shock delivered by the British artillery barrage, for the Americans had been taken completely by surprise. The recently delivered naval guns belched fire and iron over and over again, pounding the wall of mud, the gun emplacements, and the buildings beyond. Congreve rockets leapt into the air with an evil hiss—like Satan's own snakes —to arc and explode over the breastworks, showering the defenders with shrapnel. Smoke half-obscured the grey and misty day.

The veteran British gunners worked their cannons expertly. Scores of balls tore into Macarty House. One, and then another of the American guns were struck. An ammunition wagon exploded with a satisfying boom. The Dirty Shirts were running about in utter confusion and failed to return fire. Finally some success!

James looked about. The troops were heartened by this demonstration of the power of Great Britain and were anxious to charge. The Americans had embarrassed them, and to a man, they longed to pay them back with interest. One could almost feel their impatience.

But now was not the time. The guns had yet to break down the American works. Another few minutes would make the difference.

LIKE THE REST OF JACKSON's troops, Matthew quickly shook off the initial shock of the bombardment. He hurried the Dansereaus into their wagon and sent them galloping back to the city with hardly a farewell. He was left with a haunting memory of Anne-Marie's despairing face as they joined the civilian pell-mell evacuation.

Matthew dashed towards Macarty House, cannonballs falling all around him. He soon found he was not alone.

"*Samson*! What are you doing here?"

Wide-eyed and sweating even in the cold, the big slave answered, "Where should I go, *monsieur*?"

Matthew had no time to ask why he did not flee with the Dansereaus. He pointed to the rear. "The supply tents! Go there, and do whatever you are told!"

"But I am to be with you! *La mademoiselle* said—"

"Not now, Samson!" In a calmer voice he added, "I will see you later. Now, go." Without waiting for a replay, Matthew continued to headquarters.

General Jackson and the staff had escaped from the building without injury, but the beautiful plantation house was now a shell. Matthew reported, and with the rest quickly took stock of the situation. The men had dashed to their posts, trusting that their labors had been worth the effort, that the earthen works would protect them from the maelstrom of iron. Most had sense enough to bring their arms. The artillerymen stood to their guns, waiting to respond. General Jackson was pleased.

"Ah! All is right, and we shall return their compliments presently." Old Hickory mounted his horse and rode off to inspect the entirety of the line, but Matthew's place was here, between the local militia and battery number three, the Baratarians' position.

The privateer gun captains were attempting to lay their guns on targets, but the thick smoke and mist defeated them. Dominique

You was cursing in French.

"We are to fire in rolling volley," Matthew informed the fiery buccaneer, who nodded and continued to urge his gunners to quicker action. All had to wait until the air cleared.

IT WAS NOT LONG BEFORE James sensed matters were going wrong again. The first clue was the lack of damage to the American works. Ball after ball slammed into the earthen wall, to no effect. The bloody Louisiana mud seemed to eat up the iron without consequence. Never, in all of James' experience, had he seen so much artillery fire with so little result.

A tickling fear started in the back of his brain. *Powder and shot are in short supply. How much longer can we keep up this expenditure before we are fatally low of both?*

The British gunners' rate of fire was slowing around him. Before James could see to the reason, the Americans decided to join the party with an earth-shaking crash.

James dove to the ground for his life.

THE ARMY BATTERY LOCATED HARD against the river fired first, and the others followed suit, one-by-one. Soon the firing became endless. Hundreds of pounds of iron rained on the British gun positions, and the marksmanship of the American proved just as expert as their foes. Ball, shot, canister, loose metal—anything would do. The British attack turned into an artillery duel between an ancient power and their upstart cousins. And to the consternation of the king's professional killers, the volunteer backwoodsmen and shopkeepers stood toe-to-toe with them, trading blow for blow without slacking.

This was not supposed to happen.

The British grew desperate. A contingent of soldiers was sent to probe the vulnerable left wing of Line Jackson, the spot where the British had what little success they enjoyed on December 28. But Coffee's men were ready for them this time. A furious counterattack drove the redcoats into the swamp, and the Tennesseans hunted their quarry mercilessly, killing those who could not flee fast enough. A few of them drowned in the murky swamp water.

The rest of the British regiments took what cover they could in the muddy cane field that was the Chalmette Plain, for the Americans did not spare them from the firestorm. Those who were brave, curious, or foolhardy exposed themselves for a look and found, to their surprise, that American marksmanship was really quite good. It was often their last mistake on this earth.

To add to their agonies, Commodore Patterson's hated battery on the West Bank added their firepower to Jackson's. The British again were caught in the crossfire.

The British artillerymen resolutely continued the assault. They were able to explode another ammunition caisson and wreck several more of the enemy's guns. But that came at a high price. The Americans lost ammunition, but so did the British, and they had less of it. The British guns could not rain death on the Dirty Shirts because of Major Latour's genius in building the enemy's defenses while the American guns were killing both infantry and artillery.

And, to their dismay, the British found their heavy naval guns ill prepared for the action. Superb and well manned, they still rested on naval trucks rather than proper big-wheeled army carriages, and the small wheels of the trucks were easily mired in the mud by the guns' recoil. No quantity of sugar cane bundles could stop the wheels from sinking. The sailors working them lost valuable time wrestling the weighty cannons back into position after every shot, leaving them exposed to return fire. Position after position had to be abandoned because of damage or lack of ammunition.

Two hours after the initial bombardment, it was clear that the Americans had won. Any assault on the enemy's line was forgotten. Still, the artillery would not stop. The battle had its own momentum. Pakenham foolishly allowed his gunners to run through the majority of his powder.

By three o'clock, the last British cannon sounded. Five hours of continuous bombardment had accomplished nothing but to expend precious ammunition and lives. The redcoats suffered a hundred casualties, including forty-four dead. After darkness fell, Lt. Colonel Dickson tried to recover his guns, but the rains returned to hinder the withdrawal. Five cannons had to be left behind. It had been a catastrophe.

Macarty Plantation

BEHIND THE AMERICAN LINES, THE exhausted men were jubilant. They had beaten the British again! True, they had lost eleven comrades, but many more redcoats surely had been killed. If they listened to General Coffee's Tennesseans, they would think hundreds had been sent to their eternal reward. Confidence swelled in the ranks.

The mood in Jackson's headquarters was more sedate though there was great satisfaction in the results of the day. The men had responded superbly, and Major Latour's engineering skills had stood the test.

But concerns remained. The British had failed, but they did not press their initial attack. That indicated this was not an all-out assault. Deserters had claimed that more soldiers were arriving every day. They also confirmed conditions in the enemy camp were deteriorating. Men were cold and hungry. The horseflesh found on their persons bore this out.

General Jackson knew this was good news and bad. The British were running out of time. He expected General Pakenham would not retreat; therefore, a desperate major assault was in the offing.

Matthew doubted they had enough men and ammunition to withstand an all-out attack. Not for the first time, he wondered why Washington sent nothing.

Conseil Plantation

THE AIR WAS GLOOMY AT Pakenham's headquarters. The carefully planned artillery assault had failed to knock out all the Yankees' guns. Worse, Dickson had lost some of the few cannons the British had. The situation was unsupportable.

Everyone in the room, save Admiral Cochrane, knew General Pakenham had only two choices before him: attack General Jackson's line or withdraw in defeat. The first would be costly, perhaps suicidal —the second, inconceivable.

Or was it?

James was shaken by the thought that had leapt into his head. *Defeat? Are we defeated? Have the Americans beaten us? No! We have beaten Bonaparte! We cannot lose to this rabble!*

"The enemy has been hurt," General Pakenham observed. "They have lost a ship and much ammunition. We must take advantage of this. Enough of doing things by half. We must prepare to assault the line in full." He looked about the room. "General Lambert shall be here soon with at least two regiments. Once they have landed, we will attack and smash them."

"Those guns on the far bank of the river have been the very devil," General Keane pointed out. "If we do not silence them, we must move forward in force on the right wing. Surely the enemy will see this and act accordingly."

"Why not turn those guns against the Dirty Shirts, gentleman?" asked Admiral Cochrane.

The others in the room turned to the courtly admiral, General Pakenham nodding. "My very thought, Sir Alexander. We will take those guns by a *coup de main*, turning them upon our tormentors, while our brave lads give the Yankees a taste of British steel."

"Bravo, Sir Edward!" cried Cochrane.

"Thank you, Admiral; I leave it to the Navy to conceive a method of conveying the required number of boats to the river. They shall ferry the troops to the right bank. Colonel Burgoyne will assist you."

"How many troops, sir?"

General Pakenham thought for a moment. "I believe two battalions should do for them with some light artillery."

Two battalions! That is fourteen hundred men! thought James.

"That would require sixty boats, General," pointed out a naval aide.

"As you say. Can you provide them?" Pakenham asked Cochrane.

"You shall have them, sir," said Cochrane confidently.

Macarty Plantation

AT NIGHTFALL, A DIRTY, WET Matthew slowly walked through the rain towards Macarty House, feeling his exhaustion with every step and wondering whether anything was left of his belongings. He had almost reached the house when he saw a tall, dark figure next to the ruined porch.

"Samson."

The tall slave moved to meet him. "You did not tell me what to do after the attack, *monsieur*, so I waited for you here." He was wearing a poncho over his clothes. A floppy hat kept the rain off his face.

To be honest, Matthew had forgotten all about him. "Have you had anything to eat?" Samson only shook his head. Matthew groaned. "Let us see if there is anything."

Fortunately, there was soup and bread awaiting them, and Samson insisted on serving him. "I am your orderly, *n'est-ce pas?*" The two sat on the floor, eating quietly.

Matthew did not want to think about what he needed to do. Already, he had sent a note to Anne-Marie that he was safe. His mental list for the next day was enormous, and he was sure Old Hickory would be adding to it. So to pass the time, he decided to talk to Samson.

"How is your soup?"

The slave shrugged. "Good enough. The food, it is better at Dansereau."

Matthew shook his head at the food-obsession of the locals. "What did you do today?"

"I brought powder and"—he paused over a strange word—"*canister* to the gunners. The cannons, they are very loud."

Matthew closed his eyes and leaned his weary head against the wall. "Yes, they are."

Samson finished his soup. "Do you want more, *monsieur?*"

Matthew shook his head and sipped a mug of water.

"So that is battle."

"Yes, Samson, that is battle."

"The English, they are beaten?"

"For now."

Samson frowned. "But they will come back?"

"I presume they will."

The black man was grave. "I need a weapon, *monsieur.*"

Matthew looked over in surprise. "You expect to fight?"

"Do you not think so, should the English return?"

"I suppose so. Have you ever fired a gun?"

He shook his head. "But, I have this." He reached over his shoulder and pulled a large, triangular blade from behind him. The metal gleamed in the lantern light. He hefted it as if it weighed nothing.

"What is that?"

"This is a cane knife. I have used it many times."

Matthew grew alarmed. "On people?"

Samson blinked and then laughed. It was deep, hearty sound. "Oh, no, *monsieur!* I use it in the cane fields during the harvest. But sometimes there are water vipers in the fields—black and nasty with a white mouth like cotton, they are. They can kill a man quickly. They make no sound, unlike the rattlesnake. I have used this on such snakes many times."

"Hmm. Sounds like a copperhead. Black, you said?"

"*Oui.* One should stay away from the water viper unless you have this." He gestured with the cane knife.

"Samson, I am not certain I can get a gun for a slave."

The large black man was quiet for a time. "Then I must use my cane knife. *C'est la vie.*"

"*C'est la vie,* indeed. The British will come at us with bayonets. They will not stop to reload their muskets. We will have to meet steel with steel: bayonets and swords"—he indicted Samson's tool —"and cane knives."

Samson pointed at Matthew's belt with the knife. "I see you carry a sword and a pair of pistols."

Matthew glanced down. "Yes, that way I may get off two shots before—" An idea struck him. "Samson, have you ever loaded pistols?"

"*Non, monsieur.*"

"You mean to fight?"

"By your side, if I am allowed."

"Samson, I believe the best way for both of us to stay alive is for you to load one of my pistols while I use the other."

Samson nodded slowly. "You teach me, *monsieur*; I will learn. We shall fight together."

"Done. Your lessons start tomorrow." Matthew groaned as he shifted positions. Samson quickly got to his feet and put away his knife.

"*Monsieur* is tired. I shall prepare your bed."

Matthew held up a palm. "You do not have to do that."

"I must." The giant grinned. "I am your orderly."

There was no arguing with the man. "In that case, you should refer to me as Major."

"*Oui, mon Major.*" He tried a salute and failed miserably. Matthew laughed, and Samson smiled in return. He told the slave where his belongings were, assuming they had not been destroyed. Once he was alone, Matthew took out the miniature of Anne-Marie and gazed at it for a long time.

Chapter 19

The New Year's Day artillery duel had been a rude shock to the Americans, and General Jackson vowed that he would not be surprised again. But first, he had to see to his defenses. Major Latour immediately had the men repair and enlarge Line Jackson. The gun positions were rearranged and strengthened. An eighth battery was constructed on the far left side near the swamp. Its job was to protect the left flank from an assault through the woods. General Coffee was glad for it. A bit of grapeshot was sure to discourage any more attacks against his position.

On the right, General Jackson suddenly decided that a redoubt was called for forward of the line, close to the river. Regular army troops were assigned to its construction. In the center of Line Jackson, the heaviest guns were placed. Major General William Carroll of the Tennessee militia was placed in charge, and General Jackson made it clear it would be his position, too. He suspected that this was the place the heaviest blow would fall, for it was out of range of Commodore Patterson's battery on the West Bank.

In the rear, new recruits for the Louisiana militia were receiving the most basic of training. They learned to march shoulder-to-shoulder, serenaded by the band playing "Yankee Doodle" and "The Marseillaise." General Jackson was glad for the reinforcements, and he anxiously awaited the arrival of General Thomas's Kentucky militia on its way from Bayou Lafourche.

Because of his position, General Jackson had been forced to react to the enemy's moves. His was a defensive battle. The key was where to place his limited men and materiel. For that, he needed better intelligence.

That meant increased spying on the British.

Conseil Plantation

IN THE WET, COLD DARKNESS, Matthew Darcy crept through the cypress swamp with all the stealth he possessed, imitating his Creek warrior escort. Directly behind him was his orderly, Samson, his eyes pale against his black skin. Samson had begged to come, and Matthew decided that the slave's cane knife might prove useful in the night. The entire party wore dirty-brown ponchos, the better to conceal themselves. That the clothing stank was the least of Matthew's concerns.

A Creek private raised his hand and everyone froze. A moment later came the sound of leaves crunching under footsteps. They had reached a line of British picquets.

Using the brush and trees for shelter, Matthew peeked out. He regulated his breath as best he could, remembering the Creeks' warning that vapor from breathing in cold weather would give them away. He saw little; there was no moon or campfires to illuminate the night. He heard the redcoat guard but could not see them.

For a long time, the party crouched in the woods—an eternity it seemed to Matthew—before the signal was given to move forward.

Thus it was for the next hour: skulking through the trees and underbrush like shadows, stopping on occasion to listen for or avoid threats, and then continuing on deeper into enemy territory. Danger and fear was every man's companion.

Matthew's scouting party had one ally. *USS Louisiana* had taken up the late *Carolina's* job of bombarding the British camp during the night. As not to give the sloop targets, no campfires were lit. Therefore, the redcoats sat shivering in the dark and wet while the Americans enjoyed nearly complete freedom of movement.

Finally, the group reached the rear of the British camp. Matthew used his telescope to survey the area.

A Creek soldier appeared at his shoulder. *Look there*, he gestured more than said, pointing to the far rear.

"What do you see?" Matthew whispered as his adjusted his 'scope.

"Many men working on a path through the woods."

In the murk, Matthew could barely make out figures with picks and shovels. They were widening the trail to Bayou Bienvenue and burying logs across it.

They are strengthening it. Why? he wondered. *For the arrival of reinforcements or to carry large cannons? Or do they plan to withdraw?*

Matthew started to stand to get a better angle for his telescope, when a large hand pulled him abruptly down again. In surprised anger, he twisted to see Samson holding a finger to his own lips.

"*Mon Major*, over there."

Matthew looked over to his right and saw a hundred yards away a group of people huddled together. It took a moment to realize who they were.

Slaves! Did the British capture them? No, there is no guard. They must have escaped…and are seeking refuge.

At that thought, he turned warily to Samson. The big slave must have come to the same conclusion. How would he react?

His orderly was grim, cane knife in hand. His expression gave no clue.

"Quiet," said the Creek. "They will see us."

Matthew nodded and scanned the area again. Learning nothing new, he put the instrument away. "Do you see anything else?"

"They gather piles of sticks and stacks of sugar cane," he reported.

Matthew contemplated what they had seen. The British must be making fascines to throw in the canal before the battlements. So it was an assault they planned and not a withdrawal. But that did not explain why they were making improvements to the trail. It must be for cannons—or something else.

"We go, Major," said the Creek.

"Lead the way."

The patrol began to make the long, hazardous journey back to

Line Jackson. Matthew noticed that Samson was unusually quiet during the trip, even for the taciturn slave.

Macarty Plantation

"FASCINES, EH?" MUSED GENERAL JACKSON. A single candle burned on the general's desk. Except for the fire in the hearth, there was no other light in the room. "That agrees with other reports I have received. Those red-coated rascals are planning another attack—a major one, I should think. I wonder about the road." He looked sharply at Matthew. "Are you certain of what you saw?"

"Yes, General. The enemy is working hard upon the Bayou Bienvenue trail."

General Jackson glanced down at a paper on the desk, lost in thought. "It is no secret that more ships have arrived at the British anchorage. Reinforcements, no doubt." He tapped a fist on the table. "Damnation! Where is Thomas? I need his Kentuckians." He looked back at Matthew, as if remembering he was there. "Good work, Major. Get some rest."

As Matthew turned to leave, he heard General Jackson muse, "But why labor so to improve that trail if only for reinforcements?"

"Perhaps they plan to bring in large guns, sir?" Matthew offered.

General Jackson's hard eyes gleamed in that cadaverous face. "Perhaps. But why did they not work upon it to carry the cannons they used yesterday? That road bears watching. Good night, Major."

"Will you not get some rest yourself, General?" Like the rest of the staff, Matthew knew their commander in chief slept little if at all.

"There will be sleep enough for me when this battle is done—one way or the other. Get to your bed, Major Darcy."

SAMSON WAS WAITING FOR MATTHEW beside his cot. The major was thankful that his orderly had acquired a basin of warm water. To wash one's face was a luxury.

Matthew dried his face with a towel provided by the slave. "Ah, this is fine, Sam. Thank you."

"I serve you well, *mon Major*?"

"You do. I could ask for no finer orderly." Matthew stripped off his coat as he sat on the cot, watching Samson dispose of the used water out the window. There was a tightness to the slave's shoulders Matthew did not like.

"Sam, come here."

The large black man moved to the cot, looming over the seated officer. "What does *le major* require?"

"Sit, Sam, please." The giant hesitated and then plopped down, crossed-legged, before him.

"Thank you. What troubles you, Sam?"

The slave frowned. "Have I displeased *le major*?"

"No, Sam, but something has displeased *you*." He paused. "Was it the slaves we saw in the British camp?"

Samson blinked, obviously surprised that the major had guessed. "I...it is difficult to say." He turned to the other officers in the room, some sleeping, others reading or smoking.

Matthew leaned over, arms on his knees, and lowered his voice. "You can trust me, Sam."

Long moments passed before the giant spoke. "I know I am fortunate in my master," he whispered. "M. Dansereau, he does not mistreat his slaves. Those we saw tonight have been beaten."

"I suppose you are right."

Samson's expression was resigned. "There is no life for an escaped slave. Every hand is turned against him. Those who are not killed... the punishments are terrible." He looked into Matthew's eyes. "Yet, who does not want freedom?"

Matthew could see both sides. What could he say to the slave? He knew Samson belonged to Emile Dansereau, but he felt pity for the gentle giant. There was nothing he could promise him—certainly not his freedom. All he could think of to say was, "I suppose you are right again."

Samson drew a heavy sigh and relaxed. "You are a good man, Major Darcy. You should rest. *La mademoiselle* would want it."

"You are a good man, too, Samson." Matthew extended a hand. Samson stared at the offered hand as if he had never seen one before. Slowly, he grasped it and the two men shared a handshake.

"You get some rest, too, Sam. That's an order." Matthew pointed at the bundle of blanket that served as the slave's bed before lying down. "Right here, next to me, as an orderly should. You have pistol-loading practice tomorrow."

Just before he closed his eyes, Matthew heard Sam say, *"Oui, mon Major."*

Wednesday, January 4

Two days later, Major General John Thomas finally arrived in New Orleans, leading his two thousand Kentucky militia. General Jackson's relief turned to consternation, for only one man in four carried a weapon. That was not the only problem. The unkempt Kentuckians wore little more than rags and suffered from exposure. Some were ill, including General Thomas.

A disappointed Jackson sent the five hundred armed men to Line Jackson and stationed the rest near the city. Immediately, the call went out to the citizenry of New Orleans for arms and clothes. Once again the Creoles threw open their cupboards and storehouses. In quick order, the fifteen hundred men had proper clothing on their bodies and warm food in their bellies. Guns were another issue. Few could be found.

In an amazing coincidence, the British received reinforcements on the same day. Major-General Sir John Lambert landed with two thousand men of the Seventh and Forty-Third regiments. The talented forty-two-year-old Sir John had served under Wellington in Portugal and Spain. Because of his seniority, he became second in command of the expedition.

The order of battle was now set. Major General Andrew Jackson had scraped together just under seven thousand men, but of that number, less than a thousand were Federal Army. The rest were Tennessee militia, inadequately trained local Creoles and free colored, Creek and Choctaw braves, unarmed Kentucky backwoodsmen, and Baratarian pirates of questionable loyalty. Only half of the militiamen had fired a gun in anger before December 23, and Jackson's only offensive operation had ended in a draw. Old Hickory was forced to fight a defensive battle.

Facing Jackson three miles away was Major-General Sir Edward Pakenham and nearly ten thousand superbly trained, battle-hardened veterans. Pakenham had the advantage of maneuver. His officers were educated in modern Continental tactics. Most of his regiments had fought against Napoleon, and several of them had seen action at Washington and Baltimore. It was an army of professional killers.

Sir Edward was confident in his troops and his strategy. In the grand tradition of European warfare, Sir Edward planned to use his mighty army as a battering ram. He would smash the American line and put the Dirty Shirts to the bayonet.

Chapter 20

"How is the work going, Colonel?" James Fitzwilliam asked Lt. Colonel Burgoyne.

The chief of the Royal Engineers grimaced. "Slowly, more slowly than I would like." He pointed at the mass of sailors and soldiers digging a huge trench, while others were cutting downed trees into poles. "The dirt is heavy with clay, which this incessant rain turns to mud. We must reinforce the walls of the canal with timber, requiring more labor." He paused to take in the progress. "Still, another day and we will be at the river."

James lowered his voice. "Why a canal? Why not simply roll the barges on rollers, as we did with the cannons? Boats cannot weigh nearly as much as guns."

"Admiral Sir Alexander Cochrane insisted upon it." Sir John Fox Burgoyne's inflection made the name a curse. "'Build a canal from Bayou Bienvenue to the Mississippi. Float the barges to the embarkation point and continue across the river,' he said. The other officers tried to talk him out of it, but the old man would not budge, and Sir Edward allowed him to have his way."

"And all the work conducted to strengthen the trail?" observed James bitterly. "Completely lost?"

The colonel turned to the major. "We must carry out our orders, not question them. As for the canal, it is not a bad idea, and the navy is renowned for pulling off impressive feats. Eleven years ago, *HMS*

Centaur hoisted two eighteen-pounders from the deck six hundred feet straight up to the top of Diamond Rock at Martinique. Each one of those guns weighed over two tons, and *Centaur* did it with cable and capstan. Two tons, sir! Sir Samuel Hood got the Bath for that."

"Would it be disrespectful to recall that the French drove us out of Martinique the next year?"

"No." Colonel Burgoyne paused. "Fitzwilliam, as I said before, you must keep such opinions to yourself. You do your career no good." He pointed at the laborers. "Cochrane is fully invested in this enterprise. Note the number of sailors digging out the muck." The colonel raised his voice and called to the workers. "Hold! That wall must be strengthened! Get more timbers—smartly now!"

The engineer returned to James. "We must follow our orders, Fitzwilliam, no matter what we think of them. I will finish this canal, for that is what I am commanded to do." He looked up to the sky. "Rain or no rain."

James berated his weakness in confessing to Burgoyne his misgivings, but it grew harder and harder to disregard his doubts. As a major, he had spent more time with the common soldiers than higher-ranked officers. He could feel the discontent and despondency of the men. Many had lived in pure wretchedness for a month and had nothing to show for it. And, unlike their betters, they did not discount the fighting ability of the enemy.

Meanwhile, the high spirits of the Americans could be easily perceived by their campfires and constant music. The smells of their kitchens rode on the westerly breeze, adding to the redcoats' envy. Anger was turning to despair, and James knew that each day fewer men answered the morning muster. "Desertion" was the word unspoken but present in every officer's mind.

James walked to the river, desperate for a pipe that the rain would not allow.

Why the devil are we here? he finally allowed himself to contemplate. *The government keeps claiming we did not start this war with the United States, that we did not want it. But they sent almost ten thousand troops to seize New Orleans. Why? Do the fools in London think we can refight the American Revolution? That we can conquer Louisiana? Why does no one question this?*

James recalled what he knew of the last war with the Americans. *In 1775, we had local loyalists—allies. It was as much a civil war as revolution. But we still lost. Today, things are different. There are no loyalists to the Crown here or anywhere else. There is no dissention among our adversaries. We are alone in an alien place.*

The other officers are blind. This is a mistake. We should not be here, Major James Fitzwilliam could no longer stop himself from thinking.

The proud British Army was starting to come apart, and James could not wonder at it.

New Orleans

ANNE-MARIE WORKED AT THE URSULINE Sisters hospital for a few hours each day. As a member of the gentry of New Orleans, she was not allowed to perform the more unpleasant business usually carried out in a house of mercy: changing bandages, emptying bedpans, or washing patients. Ladies were encouraged to talk or read to the wounded, lifting their spirits. Anne-Marie desired to do more, so she was permitted to help feed them.

As she was fluent in English, Anne-Marie attended the American patients, and she was encouraged by the sisters to visit the British wounded if she wished.

Most of the Americans in the ward were sick with common illness; colds of the chest were the most prevalent. Coughs and fevers were no stranger to Anne-Marie, and she bore the men's suffering with kind compassion. Those with grievous battle injuries were another thing entirely. The wounds the soldiers suffered were hideous and their cries of pain heart wrenching; only through strength of will did she not flee, screaming from the horror.

With fortitude and grace, Anne-Marie overcame her natural revulsion, and her respect grew for the nuns who chose nursing the sick as their calling. She quietly read aloud their letters to the soldiers, softly mopped their brows, and spooned soup with a smile. All the time, she battled not to imagine that it was Matthew she tended instead of strangers.

The hardest duty was accepting that the talents of the surgeons and nurses could not save them all. She held back her tears, allowing herself to weep later over the deaths as she prayed alone before the Virgin.

The British patients were housed in a separate wing, and to her surprise, Anne-Marie found herself there. She assumed it was the Lord's hand guiding her to show mercy to their enemies, and she endeavored to nurse the redcoat wounded no differently than she treated her countrymen.

Today, she sat next to the cot of a young man, barely more than a boy, half his face swathed in bloodstained bandages. She had not seen him before.

"Good morning," she greeted him. "I am Miss Dansereau. What is your name?"

Only one eye was visible, and it opened wide at her approach. "Billy Masters, miss," he managed, his voice a low croak. "Ah, Private Masters, I should say, beggin' your pardon."

Her instinct was to put the young man at ease. "Private Billy Masters, should I address you as Private Masters, or would you prefer Billy?"

He blinked. "Billy, if you please, miss."

"Where are you from, Billy?"

"Hertford, miss. My father is a vicar there."

Anne-Marie nodded. "A clergyman. Would you like for me to read to you, Billy?"

"I don't have anything for you."

"I can read from my Bible." She reached into her pocket.

Private Masters held up a hand to forestall her. The effort caused him some pain. "If you please, miss. My father... I suppose I've heard enough sermons for a lifetime."

Anne-Marie picked up a wet cloth from a bedside table and dabbed Private Masters' forehead. "Very well. Is there anything you need?"

"No, miss, but it would be a kindness if you just sat with me for a time. I..."

"Yes?"

"You are the prettiest girl I have ever seen, Miss Dansereau!" he blurted out.

Anne-Marie smiled. "Thank you, but I am sure there are many pretty girls back in Hertford." She assumed there was a bit of spirits in what the patients were given to drink as alcohol was the most plentiful sedative on hand.

"We were told the girls were pretty in New Orleans. They were right. Do you have a sweetheart, miss?"

She did not know if she should be amused or offended by his rude question. She decided to answer truthfully. "There is a gentleman in the army. We hope to marry once all this is done." There was a stab of pain as Anne-Marie's fears for Matthew's safety returned.

"Of course," Private Masters grumbled. "He's a Yankee, I suppose."

Anne-Marie made herself focus on Billy, setting her worries aside. "Yes, he is an officer and a very good man."

Private Masters colored. "An officer! Forgive me, miss. I meant no disrespect! I should have known you would be an officer's lass. You are far too pretty for the likes of me."

"I would love Matthew just as much if he were a private. But what of you? There are pretty girls back in Hertford, surely."

His face crumbled. "Yes, but…" He turned away. "They will never look at me now. Not after this."

"Why do you say this?"

He shuddered. "My face…my face is ruined."

Anne-Marie bent closer. "Billy, you will heal—"

"No!" He turned back. "I was knocked on the head by a splinter in the artillery fight and left for dead. The Dirty Shirts—I mean, the Americans—captured me and brought me here. I awoke to find my left ear torn off. The scars! I'll be scarred for life." He began to weep. "What woman would have me now? I wish I would have died!"

"Billy." She lightly touched his shoulder. "You must not despair." She waited until she captured his full attention. "You have been wounded badly. This is true. But you are alive, and the right girl will look beyond that."

"What kind of girl?" he demanded despondently.

"A good girl. A girl who sees a man's character, not his appearance. You are an honest man, are you not? Do you work hard and treat your parents well?"

"I am… I do," he said, his resentment gone. "I write my mother as often as may be."

"What of vices? Do you drink too much, or gamble, or patronize loose women?"

"Of course not!"

She smiled sweetly. "Then you need not fear. A good woman, a righteous woman—she longs for such a man."

"Are you sure?"

"*Oui*. Yes. I love my Matthew because he is these things. You will find your lady, Private Billy Masters. Of this I am sure."

Private Masters looked at her reverently. "This Matthew of yours is a lucky fellow. I hope he comes back to you."

"I pray to Our Lady that he will."

The British soldier was quiet for a time. "Miss Dansereau?" His voice was low and thoughtful. "If you please, could you read to me a little from your Bible?"

"If you wish." Anne-Marie turned to the Sermon on the Mount.

Friday, January 6: Macarty Plantation

GENERAL JACKSON SPENT ALMOST EVERY hour of daylight in the saddle, inspecting every preparation along the line. Major Latour's improvements were almost complete. Line Jackson stretched over one thousand yards, almost a half-mile, from the banks of the Mississippi northward, deep into the cypress swamp. New recruits for the Louisiana militia drilled in the rear, and supply officers scoured the city to provide for the Kentucky newcomers. Not the smallest detail had escaped Old Hickory's notice.

Matthew rode down the line to General Coffee's position. He knew his commander preferred the company of his friends, John Coffee and William Carroll. Sure enough, the fastidious Jackson was deep in conversation with the slovenly Coffee.

Matthew dismounted and saluted. "General, Commodore Patterson sends his respects and requests an immediate meeting."

The tall, long-faced general grew grim. "Gentlemen, we must repair to the house. The commodore would not waste a moment of our time. Major Darcy, summon the other officers of the staff. We meet within the half-hour."

COMMODORE PATTERSON'S NEWS WAS RIVETING. He had personally seen preparations for a river crossing in force by the British. Their objective was obvious: Patterson's gun battery on the West Bank. No one in the room had to be told of the implications for the enemy's move. Should those guns fall into British hands, they would be turned to enfilade the American line. Major Latour's masterwork would be useless.

"It is as I expected," announced the grave Tennessean. "Our eyes in Lake Borgne yesterday captured a boat full of British sailors. They revealed that the redcoats are digging a canal connecting Bayou Bienvenue with the river. Your report, Commodore, confirms this information. I now see how General Pakenham intends to attack."

Matthew remembered the work on the trail. *A canal! That's what they are doing!*

All gathered about a rough map of the area. "The British are here," Jackson pointed to Conseil Plantation, "and this is our position. Here is our line behind the canal. Pakenham intends to divide his force. He will send a detachment to attack and take the battery on the far side of the river, forcing us to abandon the line. Meanwhile, the rest of his army moves forward."

An officer present wondered aloud, "How many men does he have?"

"Ten thousand, I should think, for him to divide his army," replied General Jackson. He looked at Commodore Patterson. "Your guns must not fall into the enemy's hands, sir."

"They will not, General," said the naval officer confidently, "but General Morgan needs more men."

"I will send what I can, but I must have the bulk of the reserves here to hold my position. We can spare another regiment of your militia, General Villeré. I shall ship them over tomorrow along with some of the Kentuckians. Commodore Patterson, inform General Morgan I can send him no more and that he must hold his line at all hazards."

"Where do you think he will hit us?" asked the rough-hewn General Coffee.

"Pakenham cannot move against our right. The West Bank battery prevents that, no matter whose hand holds it. Commodore Patterson will rake his people, and should the British chase the Navy away and use the guns to shoot at us, any redcoats on the right would be hit, as well."

Jackson pointed to the center of the line. "Pakenham must strike here. He will be out of range of the West Bank battery, and the ground is firmer than nearer the woods." He turned to General Carroll. "Right at you, William."

General Carroll nodded. "Right at the bulk of our men and cannons, too, sir."

"Exactly right." He turned to Brigadier General John Adair. "With General Thomas's illness, the command of the Kentucky troops falls to you. You shall make up the reserve."

"Many of my men lack weapons, General," General Adair replied.

"Your opinion is noted. Only those men who are armed will be held in reserve. The rest shall be sent to Line Dupré in the rear." He turned to Mr. Livingston, General Villeré, and Captain Lafitte. "Are there any more guns to he had?" Told that there were none, the craggy general shook his head and addressed the entirety of the staff.

"We should consider this an opportunity, gentlemen. For the enemy to exert such effort proves that the battle shall be here and that they are not planning to steal around and strike along the Chef Menteur Road. Our covering force there may be reduced and troops bought here to strengthen the line. We shall place our trust in the Almighty, Major Latour's battlements, and each man's arm."

Matthew was nervous. With all the men on the West Bank or sent to the rear, they would have less than five thousand armed men at Line Jackson, even after the reinforcements. They were out-numbered two-to-one.

"When do you think they will attack, General?" asked Coffee.

"If they stay to schedule, and the redcoats are mad about schedules, I should think Sunday." General Jackson addressed his naval commander. "Commodore Patterson, what is your estimation of their progress?"

Patterson answered immediately. "Finishing the canal and crossing at night—and they would have to; in daylight, *Louisiana* would cut them to pieces—I think no sooner than nightfall Saturday."

"Then we should expect the British to move against us at dawn on Sunday, January 8."

LATER THAT DAY, DURING A BREAK in his usual activities, Matthew and Samson walked to the riverbank for target practice. Atop the low levee, stripped of trees and brush, the two could see *USS Louisiana* anchored against the current, her sailors going about the usual business aboard a warship.

Matthew hefted a flintlock pistol. "Are you ready, Sam?"

"*Oui, mon Major.*" Samson's fingers twitched nervously. In his hands, he also held a pistol.

Matthew nodded, turned to the river, and took aim at a tree on the far side. He could not hit it, for it was nearly a mile away, but he needed a target. He pulled the trigger, and the air was torn by the crack of the pistol's retort. Smoke billowed about as he exchanged pistols with Samson. With practiced movements, Matthew raised the second pistol to shoulder height, and once the barrel reached his line of sight, he fired again.

Matthew turned to exchange weapons. Samson was fumbling a bit. Matthew stood quietly, waiting for the exchange and saying nothing. Finally, Samson jammed the rod down the barrel, packing the ball and powder firmly, and thrust the gun into Matthew's hand.

The sequence was repeated. Matthew took careful aim, fired, and extended the empty weapon for a reloaded one. This time the fresh pistol was ready, and Matthew shot a third time.

Samson was not happy. "I was too slow."

Matthew handed him the smoking pistol. "The first pistol, per- haps, but you did much better with the second one. There is no shame to being uneasy, Sam. Learning how to load a pistol is one thing; doing it under fire is another. You did fine for a first exercise."

"I will do better next time."

Matthews patted the giant's shoulder. "I know you will. Clean those before you report to the quartermaster for further orders."

"*Oui, mon Major.*" He turned and observed, "M. Herbert is approaching, I believe."

Matthew looked to where the slave pointed. Sure enough, it was Henri Herbert, in a blue and red French Army uniform, walking towards him. The Creole waved as he walked.

"Henri, well met!" Matthew cried when his friend arrived. "I see you have joined the militia."

The Creole grinned. "*Oui, mon ami*! Private Henri Herbert at your service! I see I am not the only one to join our brave forces." He gazed at the tall slave. "Samson, is it not?"

Samson's size was formidable enough, but dressed in indigo and brown from the floppy hat on his head to his rather substantial boots, the man was pure intimidation, particularly when he was scowling.

"*Oui, monsieur.* Major Darcy, I leave you now." He saluted and walked towards Macarty House.

Henri laughed. "*Sacré bleu*! I thought he was going to bite my head off! So you have Emile's slaves working for you?"

"Samson is my orderly, Henri, and he takes his occupation seri- ously," Matthew said dryly. "He knows, for example, that privates salute when in the presence of a superior officer."

The amusement slid off Henri's face when he realized his friend was in earnest. Slowly, the Creole came to attention and offered a salute. Matthew returned it.

"Henri, this is not for show," he explained. "Military discipline might be the only way to keep us alive in the coming battle."

"Then the rumors are true? We will fight soon?"

"That is no secret. Those fellows over there are not here for a visit. Are you ready?"

"Ah, if marching for hours prepares us for battle, then we will conquer like Hercules! At least I have my father's gun; many have none. I hear they will send us across the river, *mon ami*. That should not be bad, eh?"

"As long as you do not get sick or fall out of the boat."

Matthew was sad to hear that his friend was part of the detachment tasked with supporting General Morgan's defenses. He would have preferred to have Henri here, on the East Bank, where he could look out for him. It was at times like these that Matthew missed Jacob terribly.

Just then, they were interrupted by Samson, running towards them and shouting. "Major Darcy! You must return to the house! *Le Général*, he has called a meeting! Hurry!"

"Thank you, Sam." He took his leave of Henri. "If I do not see you before you leave tomorrow, I wish you *bonne chance*. Farewell."

"Farewell, Matthew." Henri was unusually grave as they exchanged salutes. "Go with God, *mon ami*."

Chapter 21

For days, soldiers and sailors toiled shoulder-to-shoulder to construct Admiral Cochrane's canal. The rich, black Louisiana soil was thick with clay, all the better to grow rich crops but heavy to work. It was backbreaking, made all the more difficult with the recurring rains. The men sloughed through thick muck for hours, manhandling great timbers to shore up the walls of the canal, only to have one section after another fail and need to be rebuilt. By noon, it was clear that they were hopelessly behind schedule. A decision had to be made.

It was impossible to abandon the canal; too much of the shortest route to the river had fallen under the shovel and pickaxe. It was also impossible for the navy to provide as many barges as first imagined. The British would be lucky to carry half the thousand men General Pakenham had planned to transport.

Admiral Cochrane blamed Colonel Burgoyne for the delay, and Burgoyne complained that the navy overestimated what was necessary to be done and could not deliver. But General Pakenham was sanguine.

Sir Edward and the majority of his staff still held the fighting abilities of the Americans in contempt. The veterans of the burning of Washington related again and again how the Yankees fled at the first sight of British steel. The Seventh and Forty-Third regiments, which had arrived with General Lambert, were fresh and confident.

And Pakenham could find no flaw in his textbook plan.

This belief was reinforced by an American deserter. He told the British that the right end of Line Jackson was very weak and that twice before, on December 28 and January 1, it had nearly been overrun. This corresponded with Colonel Rennie's assertions of those engagements and gave great comfort to the British staff.

The adjusted plan was that a little over five hundred men would be used for Colonel Thornton's assault on the far bank of the river and the American gun battery located there. Pakenham decided that it should be done with proven veteran soldiers, so he reassigned the black West Indies troops to the diversionary assault upon the American redoubt, hard against the river levee. The confidant and aggressive Colonel Rennie had been given that task of taking the strongpoint.

The only worry was timing. Every soldier needed to be in his proper place before dawn on Sunday. When the signal rocket went up, the British juggernaut would move as one, crushing all before it.

Late in the afternoon, Pakenham and the staff inspected the works. The canal, if the low, muddy ditch could be called that, was barely adequate for the job. But the walls were holding, and the barges were half-dragged into place. The canal was closed up by a dam between the last boat and Bayou Bienvenu.

The plan was to line the barges in the canal right up to the uncut levee, fill the boats with the men, and cut the levee. The river was higher than the bayou, and to stop the boats from going backwards once the levee was cut, the dam would allow the canal to fill to the same level as the river. Then it would be a simple matter to float out and cross the river.

The party stood at the dam, the commander in chief eyeing it with suspicion. "Are you certain that the dam will bear the weight of water that will be upon it when the banks of the river are cut?" he inquired of Colonel Burgoyne.

"Perfectly," Burgoyne replied, adding with a glance at Admiral Cochrane, "I should be more so if a second dam was constructed."

James Fitzwilliam raised an eyebrow in disbelief. It seemed to him that Burgoyne was suggesting that things be delayed until another dam was built. That would put off the attack for at least another day.

But General Pakenham was unresponsive to his chief engineer's hint. "Ah, well, good! Come, gentlemen. The day grows short, and we must complete the inspection ere we retire for the night."

Macarty Plantation

Another long day was ending, but Matthew remained at the second floor window of what was left of the grand Macarty House. Weeks of war had left its mark—holes shot through the walls, plaster and glass shattered, and the floor covered in dust and filth. Here, General Jackson made his headquarters, and here, he and staff slept.

Matthew continuously scanned the battlefield and the enemy camp beyond, watching and listening to the British movements. The air was heavy with dreadful anticipation. The fever of impending battle had swept the camp, from the lowest private to General Jackson himself.

The commander in chief was even now spying on the British in the same fashion as Matthew, but he was a floor above, alone in a perch he reserved for himself. Did he see, Matthew wondered, the redcoats making fascines near the woods, as he did? Did he hear the sounds of great, unwieldy things being moved far away, either cannons or boats? Did he feel the same sense of dread?

Matthew had no idea whether he was going to sleep that night.

Earlier, the staff inspected the line, all sixteen hundred yards. At Gun Battery Three, Jackson pointed at the Baratarians. "I wish I had fifty such guns on this line, with five hundred such devils as these fellows behind them!" The privateers laughed and offered their general some of their coffee. Jackson accepted it readily, knowing its quality, and teased the Baratarians about their skills at smuggling.

At the end of the line among the federal infantry and marines, General Jackson stared at the redoubt he had ordered built days before. It seemed to Matthew the general had changed his mind about the outpost, for the tall Tennessean mused aloud, "That will give us some trouble." Of course, it was too late to do anything about it.

The inspection over, Old Hickory asked General Adair, who had accompanied him, "Well, what do you think of our situation? Can we defend these works or not?"

The fifty-seven-year-old Kentuckian looked out at the battlements and the hordes of men standing along them. "There is one way, and only one way, in which we can hope to defend them. We must have a strong corps of reserve to meet the enemy's main attack, wherever it may be. No single part of the line is strong enough to resist the united force of the enemy."

General Jackson agreed and ordered Adair to strengthen his reserve by calling up all armed men at Line Dupré. He also gave Adair authority to place those troops close to Line Jackson at the spot he thought best. The Kentuckian chose the middle of the line and moved his men directly behind Carroll's Tennessee militia and Jackson's federal infantry.

Now, all major preparations were done. The men were all at their stations. The reinforcements for General Morgan had been shipped over to the West Bank hours before. *USS Louisiana* moved downstream to take up its nightly position to fire on the British camp.

It was relatively quiet. The men moved, worked, and spoke in low, earnest tones, their voices betraying nervousness or fear. The temperature was dropping. It would be a cold, miserable night, soothed by the low campfires among the tents and the reassuring crash of the *Louisiana's* guns firing their nightly salutes of death at the redcoats.

Matthew was cold, tired, and hungry, but he remained at the window, staring at his enemies.

"Major Darcy?"

Matthew turned to see Samson behind him. His orderly wore a worried expression.

"You have not eaten, Major. Is it your wish I bring you food?"

"No. Wait a moment, Sam." Matthew made one last sweep of the battlefield. He then stepped away from the window, closing his telescope with a snap. "I am finished here. Is there food downstairs?"

"*Oui, mon Major.* Some soup and bread."

The pair walked to the stairs. "Is it any good?"

"I do not know, Major. I have not eaten." At Matthew's incredulous look, Samson added. "I wait for you, *monsieur*."

"Then we shall eat together."

Minutes later, the two sat on the steps of the ruined estate house, holding steaming bowls and cold bread in their hands; a bottle of wine, courtesy of Emile Dansereau, stood between them. The officer and orderly ate in silence.

BOOM! It was the *Louisiana's* cannon. Samson started at the noise. "The cannon, it does not bother you, Major Darcy."

"One gets used to it after a few years."

Samson chewed a bite of bread. "The battle, it is tomorrow, *Oui*?"

"We think so, Sam."

"I…I am afraid, *mon Major*."

Matthew looked at the tall slave. "I am afraid, too."

"You are afraid?" Samuel could not believe it.

"Every time. Fear is not always bad, Sam. If you do not give in to it, it makes you careful. That can keep you alive."

Samson stopped eating. He stared at the growing darkness, his white eyes stark against his ebony skin. "I do not want to die."

"No one wants to die. Do you want to go back? Just say the word."

The big black man turned and glared at him. "*Non!* I stay and fight by your side. I fight for *la mademoiselle*. I fight for my home."

"I fight for the same reasons, Sam." Matthew put down his empty bowl and picked up the wine bottle. Taking a swig directly from the bottle, he allowed himself to enjoy the sweet Muscadine wine before offering it to Samson. The slave hesitated before accepting the offering. He drank deeply before setting it down again.

"A good gift from M. Dansereau," Matthew observed.

"*Oui*. The wine, it is very good."

BOOM! This time, Samson did not jump.

"When this is over, *mon Major*, will you stay and marry *la mademoiselle*?"

Matthew noticed that Samson had already picked up the soldierly custom of speaking of *when* they survived a battle, not *if*. "If she will have me, *Oui*." At once, Anne-Marie's image was before him, dressed in a beautiful gown, her eyes filled with love and passion. He blinked to clear his mind. "And you? Do you wish to marry?"

"If I am allowed."

"Do you have someone in mind?"

Samson grinned. "Clementine, *la mademoiselle's* maid. She is very pretty, *Oui*?"

Matthew laughed. "I think you have picked out the prettiest one, Sam."

The man did not reply. He just smiled wider.

Matthew laughed again and picked up the bottle. "One more drink, Sam, and then to bed." He drank and paused. "It will be a long day tomorrow."

Samson just nodded and took the bottle.

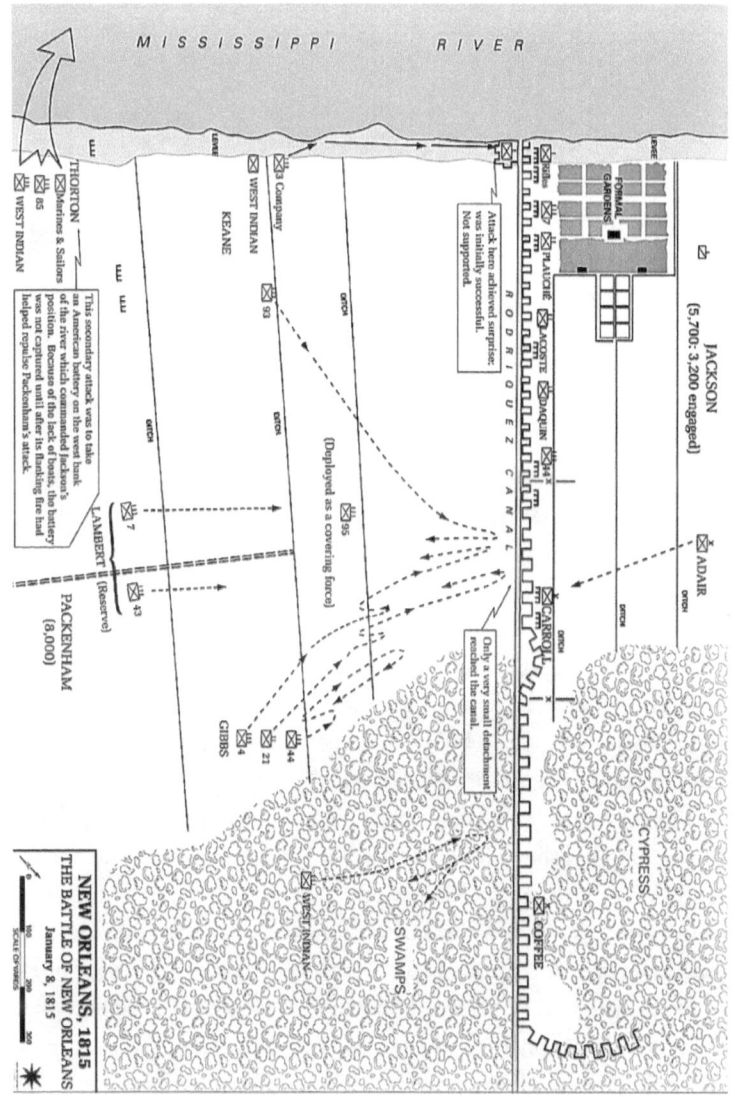

Battle of 8 January: Positions and Movements

Map courtesy of: The Department of History,
United States Military Academy at West Point.

Chapter 22

K nocking on the door of the room where the staff slept awakened Matthew.

"Who's there?" barked General Jackson.

A Louisiana militiaman by the name of Rezin Shepherd answered. "Commodore's Patterson's complements, sir. He reports that the enemy is crossing the river in force to attack General Morgan's position. The general fears this is the main axis of the enemy's advance, and he cannot hope to hold unless he receives reinforcements." It was plain that the man was frightened.

The words "in force" sent a chill ran down Matthew's spine. How large a force? If the British were moving the majority of their army to the West Bank of the Mississippi rather than a detachment, they would sweep Morgan's command aside like a fly and outflank Jackson's line here on the East Bank. New Orleans would be wide open with nothing and no one to stop them. It would be a catastrophe.

General Jackson rubbed the sleep out of his eyes. "Hurry back and tell General Morgan he is mistaken. The main attack will be on this side, and I have no men to spare. He must maintain his position at all hazards."

Shepherd hesitated. It was clear to Matthew that the general's response was not what he had hoped to hear. Collecting himself, the militiaman nodded and withdrew.

General Jackson swung his long legs off the couch and sat up.

"Gentlemen, we have slept enough. Rise. The enemy will be upon us in a few minutes. I must go and see Coffee."

Candles chased away the gloom of night. Matthew glanced at his pocket watch and saw it was a little after one. He stretched, barely rested from a few hours' sleep. Today was the day—the day of the great battle they all knew was coming. The British were coming soon, probably with the dawn.

The best army in the world, Matthew thought. *They beat Napoleon. They outnumber us two-to-one. And they are coming right at us. But we have rifles, and our artillery is better. We have beaten them three times, and we will beat them again if every man does his duty. We will send these red-coated bastards to hell!*

Matthew made his way downstairs in the dark. It was bitterly cold, his uniform jacket doing little to ward off the chill. The kitchen was a warm, welcoming place, where the female cooks handed out the chicory coffee he had grown to love. Sipping, he stepped out to the back and beheld Samson, already awake, with the other slaves, sharpening their cane knives.

"Do you ever sleep, Sam?" he enquired.

"The English, they are coming, *mon Major.*" Samson swung his cane knife. "We prepare a good welcome for them."

Matthew laughed as he slapped the black giant's broad back. "That is the spirit, *mon ami*! Come, walk with me." As they moved off to the supply tents, he whispered, "Stay close to me, Sam."

"*Oui, mon Major. La mademoiselle* would have it no other way."

Conseil Plantation

The Royal Navy's canal project was a disaster. The walls kept collapsing, forcing the men to dig out what they had already excavated several times before. They were behind schedule. The boats that were to ferry the soldiers at nightfall, had yet to leave now eight hours later. And there was worse news. Because there weren't enough boats, only four hundred fifty of the fourteen hundred men could be transported.

Colonel Thornton could afford to wait no longer if he was to attack the Americans in concert with Pakenham. At three in the morning, the levee was breached, the canal filled, and the British tars began hauling the little army across the river.

Immediately, things went wrong. The river's current was far stronger than anticipated and the fog too thick to see through. The flotilla was swept downstream, away from the riverbank.

James Fitzwilliam had slept as fitfully as General Pakenham. Finally, unable to stay abed, the commander in chief and the staff left the Conseil Plantation house to watch Colonel Thornton's embarkation. For about an hour, they stood along the fog-shrouded riverbank, straining to hear whether the troops had reached the other side, the fog being impermeable. They heard nothing.

At about four in the morning, General Pakenham huffed. "I will delay my own plans no longer." With that, he turned and rode back to camp, the aides following.

So we must force the enemy's lines without knowing whether Thornton is in position to flank the Americans, thought James morosely. The failed attack on December 28 remained fresh in his mind. He hoped the reinforcements that came with General Lambert were enough.

Chalmette Plantation

The two armies rose and stood to their positions at about the same time. For the British, it was the end of another cold, frosty, miserable night. To maintain surprise, no campfires were permitted. It was ship's biscuit and suspect water only for breakfast. As the professionals assembled in their ranks, their filthy uniforms soaked through, the thought of New Orleans's beauty and booty practically in their reach fueled the army's determination. They were in a murderous mood and in no mind to take prisoners.

For the polyglot Americans, it was another story. Bacon and cornbread were on hand and plenty of hot coffee. Yes, they were scared. Some added whiskey or other spirits to their drink, for they knew death or dismemberment could be a few hours away. They had won the skirmishes, but now the final battle was upon them, and no one had beaten the British before.

The two titans sat in the muddy, foggy fields, almost within sight of New Orleans, and waited for the dawn.

"Where is the Forty-Fourth?"

The British had moved into position, preparing for the assault. General Keane would be on the left, his twelve hundred men led by the crack Ninety-Third Highlanders. A small detachment of black West Indian troops, led by Colonel Rennie, would take the American redoubt next to the river. In the center was General Gibbs and over two thousand redcoats, the main axis of the attack. Led by Colonel Mullens' Forty-Fourth Regiment, they would punch through the American line close to the swamp, away from the enemy's cannons. General Lambert would be about a mile to the rear with the reserves.

It was a sledgehammer of a plan, one that depended on three things: first, that the early morning darkness and fog would mask the approach of the British almost up to the crest of the enemy's works. True, the Americans would know they were coming; cannons, Congreve rockets, and martial music would make sure of that, but it was all part of inflicting terror on the untrained militia. And, thanks to the mist, the enemy could not kill what they could not see. It was hoped that, like at Washington almost a year ago, many of the Yankees would simply break and run.

The second key was Colonel Thornton's men taking the American guns on the far bank of the river and turning them against Jackson's line.

Third and most importantly, the fascines and ladders had to be in the vanguard so the troops could scale the breastworks. This dubious honor had fallen to the veteran Forty-Fourth (East Essex) Regiment of Foot.

The trouble was that the Forty-Fourth was nowhere to be found. They were to be at the head of Gibbs' column. Without the fascines and ladders, the army would be helpless in the face of the enemy's resistance. An angry General Pakenham sent Major Sir John Tylden to find them. James and the rest of the staff sat on their horses, impatiently waiting for the report. Priceless minutes passed.

Finally, Major Tylden returned. The Forty-Fourth was coming forward at last.

"Do they have the fascines and ladders?" Pakenham demanded.

"Yes, sir, although they are moving in a very irregular and un-military manner."

"As long as they are at the head of the column, I am satisfied." He glanced at his pocket watch, frowned, and rode off.

"How late are we?" asked another aide.

James shook his head. "Late. It is nearly six."

"We were supposed to attack over an hour ago. It is almost dawn."

"There's nothing for it but to hope the fog remains." James turned to Sir John. "Did Colonel Mullens give a reason for the delay?"

"I did not see Colonel Mullens."

What? thought James. *Then who is leading them? Are they even at the vanguard?*

His doubts grew. The terrible weather had taken a toll on the men. American marksmanship had proved better than anticipated, and their cannons were handled by magicians. Thornton's assault had been delayed, and now the Forty-Fourth was late as well.

The plan is already in shambles, yet the general is determined to push on. He is overconfident. He does not respect or fear the enemy. He could afford to be reckless in Spain; Wellington was there to rescue him if needed. There is no Wellington here. I fear this is going to go badly.

Just then, a Congreve rocket was fired. The attack was on.

FOR TWO HOURS, THE AMERICANS stood nervously at their positions waiting for the British to advance. Matthew found himself between batteries two and three with the navy cannon and the US Seventh Infantry to the right and Major Plauche's Louisiana militia and the Baratarians to the left. Matthew was talking to Dominique You when the first Congreve rocket arced overhead.

"*Mon Dieu!*" cried Samson.

Dominique You laughed. "That is the English passing wind! The game, she has started!"

He and Beluche shouted orders to their men as Matthew and Samson ran the fifty yards to Lieutenant Norris's gun. Assured by the navy that they were well supplied with shot and powder, Matthew then returned to the Macarty House headquarters.

Matthew turned to Samson as they reached the steps. "You stay here. I am going up to the second floor and try to see through this fog."

"*Mon Major*, I must go with you. *La mademoiselle*—"

"Stay here, damn it! You must take orders from *me* now." Matthew handed Samson his pistols. "Make sure these are loaded. We shall see action soon enough."

Samson nodded, and Matthew felt his disapproving eyes on his back as he dashed inside. In quick order, he was at Jackson's favorite window, telescope in hand, peering through the murk. He was not alone. Two other officers were doing the same.

"Have you seen anything?" he asked his fellows.

"Nothing! You can hear the bastards, though!"

It would have been hard not to. The British had begun firing their artillery, drowning their drums and bagpipes. American guns answered almost immediately, and their band struck up "Yankee Doodle." British and American cannonballs flew all over the battlefield. Matthew saw the Baratarians working their twin twenty-four-pounders with great enthusiasm. He could swear the privateers were enjoying themselves. The noise of battle was tremendous.

Matthew ducked as something stuck the house with a crash. Wooden shards flew about the room. "Watch out," shouted a lookout unnecessarily. "They'll be trying to knock us to pieces!"

Matthew rose to look out the window again when something amazing happened. The fog suddenly thinned. If was as if God Himself had pulled back a curtain, leaving a bit of mist in His wake. There, before Matthew's eyes, were dark figures moving in the brightening gloom.

"There they are!" shouted the lookout.

Matthew caught sight of something out of the corner of his eye —a movement along the river levee. "The redoubt! The British are going for the redoubt!"

With an oath, Matthew made for the stairs.

BY THE TIME MATTHEW AND Samson reached the breastworks, the surprised New Orleans Rifles and the marines were fully engaged with the enemy on the other side. The artillerymen shifted their guns to fire into the redoubt, now overrun with British troops. Suddenly, several British officers appeared at the crest of the parapet.

"Hurrah, boys! The day is ours!" one redcoat shouted.

Instantly, a desperate volley of rifle fire cut them down, and they fell backwards into the ditch before the works. Immediately, yet another enemy officer climbed the earthworks, sword in hand. The redcoat knocked away a militiaman with the hilt of his sword and leapt towards Major Darcy. Matthew barely had enough time to aim his pistol before firing it, inches from the man's coat. The violence of the shot twisted the redcoat officer aside, and Matthew was stuck by his arm rather than his sword. An instant later, a militiaman emptied his musket into the redcoat's midsection. The British officer fell in a heap at Matthew's feet.

"Quick, Sam, a pistol!" demanded Matthew as he tossed the still-smoking pistol to Samson. Almost at once, his second gun was in his hands.

Rearmed, Matthew crawled up the earthen works and wood, peered over the top, and took aim. The scene before him was total confusion. Through the smoke, he could make out enemy troops —black troops, Matthew noticed—carrying guns or ladders. Some continued to move forward while others dropped their burdens and ran. Matthew fired into the mass of humanity, not knowing whether his shot had any effect. A moment later, he exchanged pistols with his orderly, but did not shoot. He did not need to.

The local militia had been joined by the regulars of the Seventh, and the firing was now constant. The cannons of Patterson's detachment across the river joined in, and the air before Line Jackson was filled with ball, bullet, and grapeshot. It was a slaughter. Through the smoke and fog, the British broke. Many ran back towards their starting point, only to be cut down by Patterson's guns. Others tried to take cover under the levee, which made them easy prey for the other batteries.

Gunfire slackening as the assault faded, Matthew turned away from the carnage, breathing hard. He then noticed that the British officer who had attacked him was still alive. He knelt beside him, examining the man's wounds. The officer groaned.

"Bear up, sir," Matthew gently told the suffering redcoat, stuffing a handkerchief into the worst of his wounds. "You are far too brave a man to die."

"No," the man managed, grimacing in agony, "it is too late for me. Tell them—" He shuddered. "Tell my superiors that I fell at the head of my men."

"I will. Hold on." Matthew turned to Samson. "Sam, lend a hand with this man."

Samson knelt down and reached for the officer, but after touching him, he sat back on his heels. "*Mon Major*, I think it is too late for this one."

Matthew returned his attention to the British officer. The man's face was now slack and pale. Matthew sighed.

"Carry this man's body away from the works, Sam. Treat him no differently than if he was one of ours."

"*Oui, mon Major.*"

JAMES KNEW NOT WHAT WAS happing on the left wing of the advance. His attention was fully engaged with the progress of Gibbs's troops on the right. It seemed they had gotten past the American outposts. The enemy's defensive works were almost in sight.

Then it was in sight far too soon. The fog was lifting!

The spectacular formations of the army, standards fluttering in the slight breeze, marched resolutely forward, regimental drums beating the cadence, the sound of bagpipes heralding the advance. Rockets and cannons fired towards the American works, and the call of the trumpets rung in the air. There were thousands of scarlet coats, an army invincible and unstoppable. Across countless battle-fields, such a sight had sent untrained opponents fleeing in terror.

But not this opponent. For over the magnificent noise of the advancing host, a strange sound could be heard. Cheering. *The Americans were cheering!*

Instantly, James understood. The Americans were not going to break and run. They were going to stand and fight. They *wanted* to stand and fight.

"Faster! Move faster, before they open fire!"

The troops did not, could not. British military practice taught that the men must move in disciplined close order—shoulder-to-shoulder, bayonets fixed. This required a slow, measured approach. Losses were expected, but the theory, borne out by hundreds of battles, had it that by the time the enemy reloaded their muskets and cannons, the army would be upon them.

Unfortunately for the British, the Americans did not fight that way.

The enemy artillerymen stood resolutely by their guns, waiting for the British front line to reach a predetermined point. The Americans had six guns aimed right at Gibbs's command, loaded not with cannon balls but with canisters of shot. A hideous weapon, it was made up by packing iron balls, each several inches in diameter, into a wire cage projectile. It resembled a gigantic shotgun shell. One round of shot could kill a dozen men instantly.

A minute later, three of the batteries opened up. The immaculate redcoat lines were torn asunder, instantly filled by men from the rear. But to the surprise of the British, the American's worked their guns quickly and expertly. Again and again, they fired. Again and again, men fell.

General Gibbs's men slogged forward, making progress through the firestorm. They stopped, reformed, and advanced again. They were but two hundred yards from Line Jackson. A few more minutes and they could silence those terrible guns.

James saw that the Americans had not yet opened up with their small arms. They had not run; he could see heads peeking up from behind the earthworks. James was impressed. Usually, militia fired their muskets at ranges too long to be effective. The enemy's extraordinary discipline was unexpected.

The army was still out of range of muskets. It was almost time for them to rush the barricade. It was time for the Forty-Fourth, with the fascines and ladders, to take to the van.

James glanced about in puzzlement. *Where were they?*

Just then, the entire enemy line erupted in smoke.

THE MAIN WEAPON OF THE Napoleonic era was the flintlock smoothbore musket. It revolutionized warfare. Battles would be won not by charging knights on horseback but by ordinary foot soldiers with muskets and bayonets. Since 1700, the musket dominated the battlefield.

At about the same time, gunsmiths invented an improvement to the musket. It was shown that if grooves were cut along the interior of a musket's barrel, the ball would fly further and with greater accuracy. An elongated bullet flew even better. The new weapon was called a rifle.

There were several significant differences between the two guns. The effective range of a musket was about twenty yards. After that, no one knew where the musket ball would go. A well-trained rifleman could easily hit a target at well over two hundred yards. Muskets were relatively inexpensive to make while rifles cost much more. Most importantly, a smoothbore musket could be reloaded in a matter of moments. The rifled barrel slowed down reloading considerably.

Like the other great European powers, Great Britain designated the musket as the primary infantryman's weapon. To offset the gun's inaccuracy, the soldiers marched in close order, shoulder to shoulder, shooting their muskets in a rolling volley, and thereby created a devastating wall of fire. Rifles were reserved as specialized weapons for snipers or elite assault troops.

For the Americans, necessity was the mother of invention. Because her fighting forces were made primarily of civilian militia, the United States army used whatever weapons were at hand. Most of the merchants, farmers, and backwoodsmen owned rifles because they were more effective hunting guns than muskets. As many a family's survival depended on the skill of the hunters, rifles were preferred, no matter the cost.

The result was that there were no better riflemen than frontiersmen from Kentucky and Tennessee. General Jackson had over a thousand such men behind his line, making up the core of his forces.

An army of muskets faced an army of rifles. The outcome would change warfare forever.

To the shock of the British command, scores of redcoats fell at the first of Jackson's volleys. Expecting inaccurate muskets, the British could not believe their eyes. They were well over a hundred yards from the enemy earthworks, a place where they should have been safe. Never before had they seen a rolling volley of rifles. Hundreds of men fell.

A bloodbath was occurring, but it was British blood that was spilled.

The main attack was already faltering, and the Forty-Fourth was still nowhere to be found. General Gibbs needed support, so the British high command rode to General Keane's position on the right. General Pakenham ordered Keane to reposition as quickly as he could to help Gibbs. The attack on the American right wing was over, and Pakenham was moving all his forces to bash in the left.

This would take time. Gibbs had to continue the fight until Keane arrived. Dodging cannonballs as they rode to confer with Gibbs, the command was startled to see British troops had halted. Some were even retreating.

An angry Pakenham demanded answers from the first officer he saw.

"The firing is murderous," he reported as bullets flew all around them. "We are easy targets for the Dirty Shirts."

"Easy targets? From this distance? What of the fascines and ladders?"

The aide shook his head. "We thought the Forty-Fourth had them, but we were mistaken. They were still carrying their muskets. I think they have gone back for the fascines and ladders, but—"

General Pakenham cut the man off, shouting orders for the others to turn back the fleeing men. They did not heed his cries.

"Lost!" cried Sir Edward. "Lost for want of courage!"

He announced he would find the Forty-Fourth himself.

BY THE LEVEE, THE SHOOTING had already died down. With the initial assault in retreat, the officers demanded that the men conserve their ammunition. Only the cannons kept firing.

In the relative quiet, there was time to see to the wounded. The American causalities, except for the men trapped in the redoubt, were almost nonexistent. The British were another story. Most were dead, but a few of the enemy who had attacked the earthworks were still alive, and when it was safe to do so, they were retrieved and taken prisoner.

"Sam, help bring these prisoners to the surgeons' tents," Matthew ordered his orderly. The slave nodded, took hold of a makeshift stretcher, and made for the rear with his bloody burden. The prisoners who could walk were taken under guard.

Matthew moved to the parapet, next to another American officer. "What are they doing?" Matthew asked, pointing at the enemy regiments hundreds of yards downriver.

"Don't know," replied his comrade. "Wait!" He adjusted his telescope. "They're moving to our left. Yes, it looks like they're repositioning to support the attack by the swamp."

"They are not coming at us?" Surprise and relief was mixed in Matthew's voice. He pulled out his telescope and studied the British formations.

"No. I can't say I'm sorry," remarked his comrade.

"We have to send a report to General— Hold!" Matthew looked up from his 'scope. "Look! They are not marching parallel to our lines. They are moving in an oblique."

"You're right. They keep that up; they'll soon be in range of our grapeshot." The officer turned to Matthew. "You go tell those pirates to open fire, and I'll report to the navy boys."

Chapter 23

Chalmette Plantation

Historians have placed considerable weight on the actions and inactions of the First Battalion, Forty-Fourth (East Essex) Regiment of Foot. This was no green outfit. The Forty-Fourth was a veteran fighting force that had served the Crown since 1741. They had fought with distinction during the French and Indian War, the American Revolution, and in the Peninsular campaign against Napoleon.

The First Battalion had been at Bladensburg and North Point in Maryland, but they had originally been under the command of Colonel Arthur Brooke. Brooke had been promoted to brigade command in Maryland and eventually took over for the fallen General Ross at North Point. Major Thomas Mullens was brevetted lieutenant-colonel and given the Forty-Fourth. The unit performed well, and Lt. Colonel Mullens was kept in command of the battalion.

The privilege of carrying fascines and ladders in battle was more of a horror than honor. The infantry needed these things to successfully scale barriers such as ditches and earthworks so as to take the fight to the enemy. Unfortunately, a soldier could not carry either ladders or fascines—large bundles of sticks or, in the case of New Orleans, sugar cane stalks—as well as their muskets, so the troops would be unarmed. As these men would be the first to the enemy's fortifications with no way of defending themselves, this type of mission was considered suicide.

Tales of unarmed troops staring down the gun barrels of the enemy while preparing the way for their fellows following was the stuff of legend. The high command thought the ordinary soldiers would eagerly anticipate the glory that would soon be theirs. Surely, remembrance of their feats of courage would warm many a veteran's heart in his sunset years—assuming he survived.

Thomas Mullens did not think many of his men would survive and thought such an "honor" poor payment for the battalion's good service in Maryland. His troops heartily agreed with him. What good would glory do if they were dead? It was no wonder then that the Forty-Fourth "forgot" where their deadly burdens were stored.

JAMES SPENT THE NEXT FEW minutes dashing about the field with the others, trying with limited success to re-form the retreating men, when he saw General Pakenham personally leading the Forty-Fourth forward towards the rampart. The command group and the soldiers turned to follow. Bullets and grapeshot filled the smoky air. Men fell all about, their fascines and ladders useless. The Forty-Fourth was being decimated.

Suddenly, General Pakenham was on the ground too, his horse dead. James and the others rushed forward to the stricken commander in chief. By the time they reached him, he was struggling to stand, his right arm bloody.

"Help me up!" the general snapped. "Captain MacDougall, I must have your horse."

The staff mounted General Pakenham on MacDougall's Creole pony, a puny steed compared to the general's warhorse. Sir Edward turned to James. "Major Fitzwilliam, my hat, if you please."

James quickly retrieved the black bicorne hat. General Pakenham put it on, his mud-streaked face failing to hide his pain. He surveyed the battlefield while his aides mounted what horses were left before the party continued its slow ride toward the American lines. Those without rides walked behind.

The closer the commander got to the vanguard, the worse the situation appeared. Dead soldiers littered the ground, most of the officers among them. The damned Americans were targeting the officers! Without leadership, the proud infantry was folding before the bullets and grapeshot. They continued to break.

"For shame!" General Pakenham shouted in an attempt to restore order. "Recollect you are British soldiers!" He gestured towards the American earthworks. "*This* is the road you ought to take!" The commander rode on to General Gibbs, trying to inspire courage by example. It was for naught; every moment, more and more redcoats took to their heels.

General Gibbs was beside himself with consternation. "I am sorry to report to you that the troops will not obey me!" he cried amid the din. "They will not follow me!"

Just then, the sound of "Monymusk" floated on the air. "The Highlanders!" cried an officer. "The Highlanders are coming!"

General Keane was marching to the rescue of Gibbs's column.

"WAIT, BOYS," WAS THE WATCHWORD along Line Jackson. "Wait 'til they get close." Their cannons reloaded with grapeshot, the left wing of the American line watched as Keane's Highlanders marched resolutely towards Gibbs.

The Ninety-Third (Sutherland Highlanders) Regiment of Foot was from the north of Scotland. Many of the men were related to each other and took great pride in the regiment. They were a splendid sight in plaid trousers and Tam o' Shanters. Beautiful uniforms are no protection against a hail of bullets, however. For reasons known only to him, General Keane sent the best the British had to their destruction.

The enemy moved in an oblique, diagonally across the field, rather than in parallel to it. It was a bold and desperate decision by General Keane. It meant his men would reach their comrades quickly, but it also required that his soldiers bear the fire of the entire American line. With every strep, they drew closer and closer to Line Jackson. The smoke and fog were not heavy enough to hide them. The Americans held their fire as the fog lifted more every moment.

The Americans finally opened up with artillery and rifles.

Hundreds of men instantly fell, their commanding colonel among the first. The Highlanders hesitated and slowed but never stopped. With incredible courage, they continued on. With every step, the toll grew. Finally, the endless torrent of hellish fire grew too much even for them. This was a deathtrap, every soldier now knew it, and military discipline could only carry a man so far and no farther.

After taking incredible losses, the Ninety-Third finally broke. Slowly, incredibly, inevitably, the Highlanders slowed, stopped, and began to fall back. Men dropped to the ground, hugging the mud in a pathetic attempt to save their lives. It was poor shelter, for the cry along the American line was now, *"Shoot low, boys! Rake 'em! They're coming on their all fours!"* The Highlanders had to use the lifeless bodies of their comrades as shields against the onslaught.

Some, from duty or desperation, dashed to the ditch before the earthworks. Their brave assaults all failed, and the survivors were forced to take shelter, half-burying themselves in the freezing muck. Others ran or crawled away.

The field became a shooting range for the Americans. Wagers were taken on who could hit the most officers. There was little fear in the lines. It was grand sport.

James looked about to see something he had seen only once before in his military career: defeat. The British were beaten—not "unsuccessful" or forced to fall back to "regroup" for another day. No, this was an utter rout—a complete catastrophe.

General Pakenham seemed to know it, too. "Order up the reserve!" he shouted. He turned to watch the Highlanders struggle against the hell-storm. "Hurrah, brave Highlanders!" He waved his hat with his good arm.

An explosion of grapeshot tore through the command. Once again by some miracle, James was unhurt. General Pakenham, however, was not. He was on the ground again, another dead horse by his side. As James dismounted to help him, the group was the victim of fire yet again, and the general cried out. Captain Mac-Dougal was the first to reach him, dragging his commander in his arms away from the murderous fire.

Agonizing moments passed as the general's aides carried their silent commander to an oak tree, out of range of the American guns. A quick glance at Pakenham's wounds told the tale. James did not need a surgeon's opinion to know that Major-General Sir Edward Pakenham would never see England again.

"Gibbs," said one of the others, tears running down his face, "General Gibbs must be told."

James spoke without thinking. "I will tell him." Keeping low, James dashed at a crouch through the mud toward the front lines.

Once he got there, the general was nowhere to be found.

"Where is General Gibbs?" he demanded of an officer. Directed closer to the line, James still could not find him. Bullets flew like bees about him. Then he spied a group bearing a figure to the edge of the battlefield. The group was made up of officers, and he knew the answer as the words left his lips.

"General Gibbs?" he asked as he reached them.

"Aye, badly wounded."

James followed the men to the rear, knowing his place was now beside General Lambert.

General Keane must manage things here until the reserves can come forward. The screams of the wounded were answered by cannon shot. *For all the good that will do.*

"I BELIEVE WE GOT ONE of their officers," Dominique You informed Matthew. "The man on horseback, he is there no more." He fired his cannon again.

Matthew was impressed with the zeal with which the Baratarians went about their deadly work. Their rate and accuracy of fire was as good as or better than the sailors and soldiers at the other batteries. The combined American artillery had devastated the British troops before them.

Samson, who had been commandeered to help haul ammunition to the guns, now returned to Matthew's side. He peered over the parapet. "*Mon Dieu!*" was his comment. "I do not think we will need my cane knife today, *mon Major.*"

"I think you are right, Sam," Matthew replied. "You have done good work."

"Ha! He is worth three men, that one!" cried Beluche. "I would buy him from you if you would sell him."

Matthew patted Samuel on the shoulder. "My *orderly* is not for sale, *monsieur.*" Samuel flashed a smile. The major turned to the pirate and asked, "How are you for shot?"

Dominique You fired his gun. "Get more. There are still redcoats in the field!"

"CEASE FIRING! CEASE FIRING!"

Up and down the American lines, the order was given. *Stop shooting. Waste no more powder. The enemy is in retreat. Stand to your positions and prepare for any new attack.* Only the artillery still fought, sending their missiles of death towards the massed British troop reserves over a mile distant.

Matthew now had the opportunity to survey the field without fear of being shot. What he saw shook him to his very core. The ground, once a prosperous plantation, was a slaughterhouse. Uniformed figures littered the flat, muddy ground. Most lay still, grotesquely disfigured, clothing half-torn off their bodies, while others, still alive, moved pathetically. The screams and moans of the wounded and dying floated over the field, punctuated by the roar of the cannons.

American soldiers and militiamen climbed over the parapets and onto this field of death, taking prisoners and seeing to the wounded. More than a few helped themselves to the belongings of the slain. The Mississippi Dragoons, previously held in reserve, now emerged and rode about the place, scouting the enemy's intentions and taking the opportunity of getting in a few shots themselves. It was truly hell on earth.

"*Mon Dieu!*" cried Samuel again.

"My God, indeed, Sam," said Matthew.

Before them was a sight from hell. The muddy, yellow-brown

farmland was littered with red-coated figures, hundreds and hundreds of them. In some places, the bodies were so close together a man could walk for some distance without touching the ground, only dead British soldiers.

He glanced at his pocket watch: half past eight. Only two and one-half hours had passed since the British rocket went up. It seemed a lifetime ago. With the joy and relief of victory, there was also horror at what they had accomplished.

"We destroyed the British Army in a little over two hours. There must be hundreds—no, thousands of men out there." Matthew made the sign of the cross. "May God have mercy on our souls."

BY THE TIME JAMES REACHED the reserves in the rear, he learned General Lambert had used his troops to cover the retreat of what was left of Gibbs's and Keane's brigades, rather than renew the assault. There were no general officers left on the field. General Keane had been grievously wounded leading the Highlanders. There was nothing to be done but pull back in as good order as could be expected, out of range of American artillery, and prepare to repulse any counterattack.

An exhausted James sat heavily on the muddy ground, gratefully draining a cup of filthy water given by an orderly.

This is worse than Baltimore, he realized. *There, we were in disarray because of Ross's death. But here, the damn Americans have killed Pakenham and probably Gibbs and Keane, too. We have left hundreds of officers and men on the field. Maybe thousands! They have wiped us out! Those bloody, Dirty Shirt sons of bitches would have done Bonaparte proud.*

He glanced at his fellow officers, dashing about in confusion. *Good God, if the bastards attacked us now, could we hold?* That uncertainty fueled what remained of James's determination. He struggled to his feet. The army command could not let this defeat turn into a catastrophe. They must be ready to save what they could.

He grabbed one of his fellows. "What orders have we?"

"Reform the men far enough out of range from those guns," he was told. "If Colonel Thornton can take their cannon on the right bank, we still might pay the Goddamns back."

James doubted that might be enough, but he sprang to work, restoring what order he could.

West Bank

THE RIVER'S CURRENT HAD SWEPT Colonel Thornton's assault troops over a half-mile downstream from their intended landing spot on the West Bank. They were in the midst of disembarking when Pakenham's single rocket went up. There was nothing Colonel Thornton could do but to carry on his mission as best he could. Speed was of the essence, so it was decided that they would attack the American's forward position with bayonets alone.

What followed was an example of British professionalism and American incompetence. The American leadership on the West Bank was divided. Commodore Patterson commanded the naval batteries at the river's edge, and they were trained on the British attacking on the East Bank. General Morgan's job was to protect those guns, and he had over a thousand men to do it. Unfortunately, the Louisiana militia assigned was poorly trained, and not all of the Kentucky troops were armed. All were green; none of them had taken part in the previous month's battles. A calm, skilled commander could still make use of all this, but Morgan was neither calm nor skilled.

He placed about two hundred men three miles forward of Line Morgan as an advanced guard, but not all were armed. Since they were a mixture of rough-talking Kentucky frontiersmen and French-speaking New Orleans Creoles, coordination was impossible, and two hundred men were not enough to hold the long line between the river and the woods. The guard was quickly overrun by Thornton's men, and the Americans had to flee back to Line Morgan.

Colonel Thornton then took the time to reconnoiter Morgan's main defenses. He set a three-pronged attack, again moved forward with steel alone, and after a sharp action, took Line Morgan and swept the Americans from the field. Commodore Patterson was aware of what was happening, but he could not bring his guns to bear on the attackers in time. Frustrated, he could only order the guns spiked before abandoning them.

When the British troops reached Patterson's disabled and inoperable cannons, it was ten o'clock. It was all for naught. By the time the British formed, moved upstream, and attacked the advanced guard, the battle on the East Bank had been over for almost two hours.

Colonel Thornton paid for his gallantry. Wounded numerous times, he lay near the guns he so brilliantly seized—guns that were absolutely useless. All he could do was send a message back to headquarters, not knowing that he had a new commander in chief.

Chapter 24

Anne-Marie had been up all night, again praying novenas with hundreds of others in the chapel of the Ursuline convent. At dawn, they could hear the distant cannon fire, rolling like thunder from a distant storm.

The vicar general offered Mass during the height of the battle. The consecration performed and *Agnus Dei* sung, the people moved forward to receive Communion. The roar of the great guns had lessened, but no one knew what it meant. Was it another spoiling attack or an artillery duel like before? Was the battle still raging, or was it over? If so, who won?

Anne-Marie groggily knelt before the rail, rosary in hand, and awaited the host, silently praying, when the doors of the chapel were thrown open. The place erupted in shouting. Anne-Marie could hardly understand what was said.

The English... What...? *Victoire? Mon Dieu,* victory? She leapt unsteadily to her feet.

"The English—they are beaten! *Victoire*! Our Lady of Prompt Succor has answered us!" People were shouting. People were crying. People were cheering.

Anne-Marie reached out to the communion rail to steady herself. *We won? But, what of Matthew? Was he spared? Oh, Holy Mother, please tell me he lives!*

"Everyone, please," said the priest with quiet authority.

"Communion is not done. Let us sing *Te Deum* in thanksgiving of this miracle when the Mass is concluded."

Almost falling to her knees, Anne-Marie received the host. Spots danced before her eyes as she crossed herself.

She stood and nearly fainted. The press of people was such that she was caught before she struck the hard tile floor. Carefully, Anne-Marie was helped to her pew as the hymn filled the church.

"Te Deum laudamus: te Dominum confitemur. Te aeternum Patrem omnis terra venerator."

Macarty Plantation

"Eight?" cried Matthew. "We only lost eight men?"

"I am astonished. It is almost incomprehensible," said General Jackson to an impromptu meeting of his aides in the center of his line. The commander could not remove himself from surveying the battlefield, so concerned was he over a new attack. "This has to be the most lopsided victory by any American army."

"The surgeons report seven wounded—a few might not live through the night—and we do not have a final report from General Morgan," said an aide. "Still, 'tis a wondrous thing."

The Mississippi Dragoons were thirsty for blood. "Sir, we've got the British on the run. Why not take this opportunity to destroy their entire army?"

"Because the British Lion is hurt but still outnumbers us. I shall not send men out there to give them targets to shoot. Not after, at the cost of less than ten men, I have accomplished *this*." He waved at the battlefield.

Matthew saw American figures walking about the fallen British. Coffee's native fighters were stripping the dead as were some Tennesseans and Kentuckians. He also saw that the wounded were unmolested and, in fact, offered water.

"Continue to collect prisoners and wounded, and stand to your guns," ordered Jackson. "This war is not yet over."

Conseil Plantation

"YOU *MUST* RENEW THE ATTACK, sir!" Admiral Cochrane demanded.

Major-General Sir John Lambert, the new British Army commander in chief, was in consultation with his staff and their counterparts in the Royal Navy. The army's reserve, along with the battered survivors of the assault on the American lines, remained in defensive positions, and Admiral Cochrane was not at all happy about it. He gave Lambert hell while his entourage of naval officers in their spotless uniforms looked on.

"With what, Admiral?" General Lambert's voice was as soft as Cochrane's was imperious. His uniform was one of the few of the army that was not spattered with mud and blood. "May I remind you that we have no general officers left? Sir Edward is dead, and Generals Gibbs and Keane are grievously wounded. I have reports that the field officers suffered most grievously, many of them dying at the head of their troops. All of our brigades have been badly mauled. Our cannons are nearly out of ammunition. All this blood and powder spent, and we have made no impression on General Jackson's line. *None.*"

"But our success on the right bank—"

"Colonel Thornton is badly wounded, and the guns he took were spiked, useless. Pressing on with his advance serves nothing."

"Are you suggesting that you retreat?" Admiral Cochrane sneered. "That the British Army is incapable of routing a few Dirty Shirt backwoodsmen?"

James was not the only army officer present who wanted to call out the insulting old bastard.

General Lambert would not be intimidated. "We are not retreating. We have pulled back out of range of the enemy's cannon, prepared to repulse any counterattack the Americans may launch."

"May I remind you, sir, that the point of this exercise was to take New Orleans?"

"At the present time, we cannot do that or hold the city if we did."

The patrician admiral continued to protest until Sir John raised his voice. "Sir, *I* am commander in chief of this expedition. You will follow my orders, or you may expect to explain to the Lords Commissioners why you did not!"

Admiral Cochrane, affronted, got to his feet, but the general was not finished.

"Sir Alexander, if you wish to take your sailors forward and lose a few thousand of them, I am certain my soldiers will find a way to sail the fleet home." He paused. "*You*, of course, will be at the head of your men like Sir Edward."

A deadly silence filled the space. Admiral Cochrane gave General Lambert a look of utter contempt before leaving the room, most of his officers following; two of the navy captains remained. Their dirty uniforms identified them as the officers charged with supplying the troops. Lambert began issuing orders.

"Recall our men on the right bank of the river," was his first instruction. "I do not believe General Jackson will be foolish enough to emerge from behind his wall, but we must be prepared for any occurrence. See to the wounded, and prepare to bury the dead. And hang that informant! Certainly he was a spy for the Americans." He turned to the naval officers. "We must begin planning for the safe removal of the army."

James and the others all knew it, but to have the words spoken aloud was devastating.

Evacuation. Retreat. Defeat.

"What of our men forward?" an officer inquired.

General Lambert sighed. "I must draft a message for General Jackson."

Chalmette Plantation

AT ABOUT THREE IN THE afternoon, an American lookout spied a small group of horsemen flying a white flag, crossing the Bienvenue Plantation, heading towards the American lines. Behind them was a train of wagons.

"Major Darcy, go see what they want," ordered Jackson. "Remember my instructions."

Matthew mounted a horse, rejecting Samson's pleas to go with him. "It is all right, Sam. That white flag means they want to talk."

"I do not trust the English, *mon Major*," Samson growled. "Be cautious."

Matthew and two other officers rode out to meet the delegation. The two groups halted in the middle of the Chalmette Plantation.

Matthew Darcy recognized his opposite number. "We meet again, Major Fitzwilliam."

A visibly tired James Fitzwilliam nodded. "Yes, Major Darcy." Each introduced the remainder of their parties. "We request an end to hostilities to collect our wounded and bury our dead." He gestured to the wagons of surgeons and teams of men armed with only shovels.

"My general agrees," Matthew stated. "There is a ditch here, just behind me. Advance no farther than that, and you shall not be molested."

"And what of our men before your lines?" demanded one of the other British officers, who ignored Major Fitzwilliam's glare.

"We are collecting them. We have surgeons aplenty, and they will be well cared for. We shall also bury the dead." Matthew's face hardened. "We request another meeting—tomorrow at noon—to discuss the exchange of prisoners."

"We shall be here, sir," Major Fitzwilliam replied.

"Your men are being fed and treated for any wounds. We expect equal treatment of our men."

"Of course."

"I remind you, sir, we speak of Lieutenant Catesby Jones and his men, also. Your tradition of kidnapping American sailors is what stared this war," Matthew said coldly. "I trust you understand me."

One of the British officers started to protest, but he was forestalled by Major Fitzwilliam. "I shall inform my general."

"Good. Until tomorrow, Major." With that, the Americans returned to their breastworks while the British dismounted and began their melancholy labors under a cold, grey, threatening sky.

IT RAINED THAT NIGHT, THE night the living buried the dead. In the American camp, there was jubilation and relaxation, despite an attempt at discipline. The enemy was beaten, they were alive, and the city was saved. Men still stood guard at the ramparts, but their hearts were untroubled for the first time in a month.

For the British Army, the suffering had reached a crescendo. General Pakenham was dead, and General Gibbs's sufferings ended as he joined his commander and friend in death. General Keane lived, just barely, but so many others did not. The cold, wet, hungry, dispirited burial teams trudged back to camp after interring hundreds of their comrades. The surgeons' tents were filled with the wounded and the dying. Dreams of beauty and booty had died on the muddy cane fields. All that remained was a desire to leave this hellhole—to go home.

The Royal Navy had other plans. Admiral Cochrane had not given up his dream to conquer Louisiana and bring the United States to heel. But the navy's way of fighting was not the army's, not when they had ships and bomb ketches. A squadron slipped anchor off Ship Island that night and made their way to the mouth of the Mississippi.

Chapter 25

The rains had stopped by morning. After breakfast, Matthew took Samson to the surgeons' tents to see if his strong, intelligent orderly could be of use. Entering the infirmary, he noticed the Ursuline sisters had returned to nurse the patients, most of them enemy British soldiers. Some of the Creole ladies of the city were helping. One carrying soiled linens was of particular interest.

"Anne-Marie!"

Anne-Marie Dansereau, in a plain grey dress, her curly black hair covered in a kerchief like a maid, turned toward the shout, the sheets in her arms forgotten. In a moment, she dashed over and fell into Matthew's embrace, crying on his dirty coat.

"Matthew, *mon amour*," she murmured.

Matthew said nothing; he hugged her tiny, soft body to his as if his life depended on it. No words were spoken—none were needed. Finally, Anne-Marie looked up, tears running down her face.

"I was so frightened," she said in English. "I did not know if... You are unhurt?"

Matthew cupped her cheeks. "Yes, I am well." He looked deeply into her large, dark eyes, and suddenly acted. Shockingly, in a tent filled with injured prisoners, surgeons, and nuns, Matthew kissed her. Not a quick brush of welcome, but one of relief and love and longing, of passion and promise. Anne-Marie responded in kind, her arms holding her lover close. A cough broke the spell.

"Monsieur, mademoiselle, je vous rappelle que vous êtes à l'hôpital —un peu de retenue, s'il vous plaît.[5]"

Matthew pulled away to behold an aged nun, shaking her head. "Forgive me, Sister, we…ah, forgot ourselves."

The nun said nothing, only raised her eyebrows. Blushing, Anne-Marie stepped away. The sister smiled.

"Bon. Mlle Dansereau, return to your duties." Appearing to expect nothing less than complete obedience, the nun left them.

Anne-Marie smiled shyly. "Sister Etienne was my teacher when I was a girl. She pretends to be stern, but I know she loves me. I must go, Matthew, but will you return?" Assured that he would see her for dinner, she glanced at Samson. "Samson! Have you been watching out for our major?"

Samson's wide, white smile lit the room. Matthew patted him on the shoulder. "Sam's been a fine orderly, never fear. But I think you need him now more than I do."

Anne-Marie grew serious. "The English—they will not attack again?"

Matthew looked out at the cots filled with wounded enemy soldiers. His face was hard and grim. "I do not believe they want another thrashing like this. But if they do, we will give it to them."

Chalmette Plantation

AT NOON, THE NEGOTIATORS MET again in the middle of the muddy battlefield. The separate British and American teams had completed their grizzly tasks, for the field was cleared of dead and wounded.

Matthew noticed a small British detail marching away from a lone oak tree. *That was a ceremony of some kind. Did they bury something or someone?* He looked at his opposite number. *No use asking. He would not tell me a thing.*

"My general wishes to begin the exchange of prisoners," Major Fitzwilliam reported. "He requires an accounting of all British

---

5   Sir, miss, may I point out that you are in a hospital—a little reserve if you please.

officers and soldiers held, including the wounded."

Interesting—he did not say "General Pakenham." I wonder whether we are right in thinking their commander is dead. "General Jackson assures you your men are being treated humanely, and your wounded are receiving the same care as ours. We, too, expect a full accounting of all prisoners, including those held by the British Navy."

"Of course. Here is my general's note." Major Fitzwilliam handed the paper to Matthew, who took a moment to read it.

"This is signed by 'the British commander.'" Matthew looked up. "Who is he?"

Major Fitzwilliam's eyes said nothing. "My commander in chief."

Matthew waved the paper. "I will take this to General Jackson, but I warn you he will deal only with the commanding general." Major Fitzwilliam nodded, and Matthew continued. "As of now, the truce is over. You are invaders and will be treated as such. Anyone who approaches our lines had best do so under a flag of truce, or they will be dealt with in the appropriate manner."

Matthew and his detail returned to Line Jackson. Once there, American cannons began sporadic firing on the British positions.

Conseil Plantation

"The Americans suspect Sir Edward is dead," James reported to General Lambert.

The general nodded. "Let us keep that to ourselves for now. The ceremony is complete?"

"Yes, sir. Sir Edward's heart is buried beneath the oak tree where he fell." James did not have to mention that the eviscerated bodies of both Pakenham and Gibbs had been packed in barrels of rum. They would be shipped back to England for proper funerals. The ordinary soldiers were interred in a common grave on Conseil Plantation.

"Now that the sad business is done, we must begin preparations for the evacuation, and we must do so under the strictest security. We shall work at night under the cover of darkness."

"That will take time, General," pointed out another aide.

"That is true, but we cannot take the chance that our intentions become known to the enemy, else they may fall upon us during the retreat." The occasional boom of artillery punctuated the general's observation.

"I cannot recover our guns, not with the Americans shooting at us," said Colonel Dickson.

"Leave them," replied Lambert. "It gives the enemy something to shoot at other than us." He turned to the two naval officers. "Once the road is done, begin the evacuation with the Ninety-Third. The Highlanders deserve to be the first ones out."

Fort St. Phillip

IN THE MIDDLE OF THE afternoon, Admiral Cochrane's bomb squadron took up positions downriver of Fort St. Phillip. A rough, strong structure under the command of Major Walter Overton thirty miles north of the mouth of the river, the fort had four hundred soldiers and sailors to service thirty-four various pieces of ordinance, ranging from six-pounders to thirty-two-pounders. Surrounded by swamps and marshes, it could not be taken by land forces. This considerable obstacle could only be overcome by naval gunfire, and the British were confidant they could do it.

The Royal Navy considered itself the most powerful in the world. Surely, they would sweep aside an insufficient, ramshackle, wooden garrison! With the destruction of Fort St. Phillip, the City of New Orleans would be defenseless before Cochrane's cannons. The city would surrender or die.

At three o'clock, the bombardment of the American stronghold began.

Macarty Plantation

THE MISSISSIPPI DRAGOONS SENT A steady stream of British prisoners back toward Line Jackson. Some were wounded, others were captured at gunpoint, but some sought out the Americans. They were weary and tired, cold and hungry, and they hoped their conquerors would have pity on them. A goodly number were Irish troops, claiming they fought for the British under duress.

"What do we do if some do not want to go back?" asked Matthew.

"Most shall, Major," replied Jackson, seated at his desk in his headquarters. "They have families back across the sea. But if any man wants to remain, I shall not deny him the blessings of liberty." The distant sound of cannon fire could be heard. He gestured to the window. "Do you hear that? The British Lion is not yet done with us. We must be vigilant. This war is not yet done."

Conseil Plantation

My dearest Meg,

First, let me assure you I am well. Providence has kept me safe and sound. With God's grace, I will hold you in my arms ere long.

By now, you know of the army's misfortune. So many of our brave, dear friends fell in battle. My heart is heavy, both for our losses and for the pain their families must now endure. If only I could be at your side to comfort you as you offer comfort to the other ladies.

I wish we had never come to this wretched place. We have no business here. England was not threatened by a few backwoodsmen across the ocean. Oh, how the proud have been brought low!

Rest assured that we shall carry on the best traditions of the army and that my thoughts are ever with you.

All my love,
James

Chapter 26

The rains returned with a vengeance, compounding the sufferings of the British.

Nothing was going well. The canal to Bayou Bienvenue had to be filled and the path rebuilt to expedite the withdrawal of the troops. The British wanted to keep this secret from the Americans, so the work was slow, and the rains slowed things even more. The soldiers were exhausted, so the escaped slaves who had fled to the British for protection were put to work on the road.

The lack of food was reaching a critical stage. Men were falling ill from cold and deprivation. Ammunition was in short supply, and the Americans were doing everything in their power to harass the invaders.

The American batteries continued their sporadic bombardment of the British positions. Few if any of the British guns were undamaged. Parties of enemy cavalry rode about, spying on them. Worse, casualties kept increasing. Every morning, a picquet or two were missing because the Americans persistently continued to send their Creek and Choctaw allies out under the cover of darkness to kill or capture them.

Macarty Plantation

THE PRISONER EXCHANGE NEGOTIATION CRAWLED on with little progress. The British wished to keep the news of the annihilation of the high command from their enemies, but General Jackson insisted to know with whom he was dealing and by what authority. Three days after the battle, Jackson received a letter from General Lambert.

"Lambert?" Jackson cried. "Who the devil is Lambert?"

All the others—Livingston, Carroll, Coffee, Lafitte, even Governor Claiborne, who had joined them—shook their heads in confusion. Jackson tossed the note back to Darcy. "I will deal only with the commander in chief! By thunder, this General Lambert will state his authority, or these negotiations are over!"

The fiery Tennessean hesitated briefly and calmed down. "It seems, gentlemen, that the entire British command has been obliterated. It gives one pause." He thought for a moment. "What does Major Overton at Fort St. Philip report?"

One of the aides stepped up. "Overton says he is under sustained attack, but to date there is little damage. Unfortunately, the British bomb ships are out of range of his guns. He requests large mortars to repel the invaders."

"See to it," General Jackson ordered Commodore Patterson, and then he turned to General Coffee. "What about the prisoners?"

"The few that will talk seem to indicate that the enemy is preparing to withdraw."

"Hmm. Are they evacuating or repositioning? We must find out." Jackson turned to Matthew. "Major Darcy, make it clear to the British representative that I will deal only with someone who has the authority to treat with me. And I want our sailors back!"

Chalmette Plantation

FOR THE THIRD TIME THAT day, Matthew met with Major Fitzwilliam in the middle of Chalmette Plantation. Rain dripped off Matthew's hat as the British officer and his escort trotted up, the horses kicking up mud.

"Your mounts seem well adjusted to our damp clime, Major," Matthew observed. Given their repeated encounters, the two officers had built an understanding of sorts. "Might they be some of our fine Louisiana horses?"

"They are, Major," Major Fitzwilliam replied easily. "We thank you for your generosity."

"Do not depend too much on our hospitality. We would take it very poorly if you carried them away once you leave us."

Instead of answering, Major Fitzwilliam held out a letter. "General Lambert's compliments to General Jackson, and here is his response to his note. General Lambert has full authority to conduct negotiations on behalf of the Crown."

Matthew tucked the message into his blouse. "On behalf of General Jackson, I thank you. So, when do you leave?"

Major Fitzwilliam's face revealed nothing. "I do not believe we said we are leaving. I, for one, like it here."

Matthew gestured with his arm back at the American lines. "In that case, why not come with me? I am sure my general would like to meet you."

There was a hollowness to Fitzwilliam's laugh. "Thank you for the invitation, but I must sadly decline. Allow me to extend the same courtesy to you."

"I would be happy to accept as long as I could bring a division of our finest boys with me."

"They would receive a hot reception."

"Good. We have a tradition of repaying such courtesies ten-fold, as I am sure you are now aware." Matthew's smile faded. "Your attack on Fort St. Philip will not succeed, and we want our sailors back. Tell your general that."

The strained camaraderie gone, Fitzwilliam's reply was cold. "Your opinion has been noted. Good day, Major."

With that, the details turned and rode back to their respective camps. Major Darcy would eat a hot meal with Anne-Marie that night, while Major Fitzwilliam could look forward to only a bit of cold ship's biscuit.

New Orleans

MATTHEW'S WELCOME AT THE MELANÇON house on Rue Bourbon was all that could be expected for a conquering hero back from the war. The fact that the war was not yet over and that Matthew denied he was a hero meant absolutely nothing to his friends. Their greetings were warm and affectionate, even from M. Dansereau. Anne-Marie, exquisite in a gown of indigo blue with gold lace, latched onto his arm and declined to release it. The two young people indulged in the pleasure brought from a lover's touch.

A jovial Emile Dansereau liberally ignored his daughter's impropriety.

"Emile," said Matthew, "I have brought Samson back with me." He nodded his head at the tall slave, fresh from his first bath in almost a month and immaculate in a navy coat and breeches. "I thank you for your generosity. My brave friend has given good service."

"But, what is this?" returned Emile. "Are the English still at Chalmette? Samson is yours, *mon ami*, until they are gone from our land!" He then grinned. "And you, Matthew? What shall you do when the war is over?" He pointedly looked at his hand, now grasped firmly by Anne-Marie, and raised his eyebrows.

"Papa!" cried his blushing daughter.

Matthew smiled. "I have some thoughts on that matter, sir, but until I am released from my service with the Federal Army, I think it premature to speak."

Just then, another man entered the house. "Henri!" cried Matthew. "Good to see you, *mon ami!*"

Matthew released Anne-Marie to take Henri Herbert's hand. Herbert still wore his militia uniform. The two laughed as only men who had faced deadly danger and lived can laugh.

"Welcome, Henri," said Madeline Melançon. "My house is full of heroes tonight."

"*Moi?*" Henri laughed again. "I fired my gun one time, managed to hit nothing, and took to my heels like the rest. Not bad for a coward, *n'est ce pas?* If surviving a battle makes one a hero, then I suppose I am, but I would never claim it to be so!"

"Henri, I am proud of you," Matthew had said. "You faced bad odds on the West Bank, yet you met your fears and did the best you could. No one could ask for more. You are a soldier as much as I. That is a fact."

"General Jackson does not think so. He has called us cowards."

Matthew's voice was firm. "The general was talking of the Kentuckians, Henri, not the Creoles. And I do not think he is being fair to men who had no weapons and very little leadership."

Henri nodded. "I thank you for that, *mon ami*, from the bottom of my heart."

Something had changed in Henri. Matthew could not tell whether it was the battle, but he carried himself differently. There was a new confidence about him. Perhaps it was his uniform.

"I did not know you were to dine here tonight," Matthew continued. "This is a happy surprise."

"He is here at our invitation. We have some business to conduct," said Philippe Melançon mysteriously

Matthew stepped back. "Then I should not detain you."

Emile slapped his back. "Ah, Matthew, our business is you!"

Philippe gave his wife a short nod. "Pardon us, my dear, if you please, but we men must retire to my study. I do not think we should be long." With that, Emile, Matthew, and Henri followed Philippe into another room.

"What is happening?" asked Anne-Marie to her aunt. "What is this business with Matthew?"

"Nothing but good things, my love." Madeline stroked her niece's hair. "They are just assuring his happiness and yours."

"Mine? How is this?"

"By seeing to it that Matthew remains in Louisiana."

January 12–17

VERY LITTLE CHANGED AT LINE Jackson over the next week. Negotiations between the combatants dragged on for days, and the weather remained foul. By January 15, General Jackson had enough information to be concerned about the British maneuvers. He ordered that a strong guard reinforce the troops on the Chef Menteur Road and asked Governor Claiborne to command them.

"We must keep them from Gentilly," Jackson said. He knew

that he could win the battle at Chalmette, but would lose the city at Gentilly.

What the Americans did not know was that the enemy was improving the trail to Bayou Bienvenue not for redeployment, but for withdrawal. Three days later, everything started to move. The road was done, and Lambert could begin the evacuation in earnest.

Meanwhile, the British suffered another embarrassment. The ten-day bombardment of Fort St. Phillip caused no appreciable damage to the American strongpoint. The Royal Navy did not attempt to force their way past the fort, unwilling to turn Admiral Cochrane's failure to seize victory out of defeat into a true catastrophe by losing ships. Instead, the squadron raised anchor and sailed away, ending the siege. It was another American triumph.

Lastly, negotiations had advanced enough that Edward Livingston, General Jackson's *aide de camp* and secretary, could draw up provisional articles for a prisoner exchange at noon on January 18.

Wednesday, January 18: Chalmette Plantation

LINES OF MEN CROSSED THE muddy fields of Chalmette. The group heading east, dressed mainly in red coats, was quiet or relieved. Passing them in the opposite direction were men in a riot of outfits, very few in anything resembling a uniform. These men were in much higher spirits. Some were singing.

In the center of the field, under flags of truce, were the representatives of the opposing armies. For the Americans it was Major Darcy, for the British, Major Fitzwilliam.

This was to be James's last meeting with the imposing, cocky Yankee, and he was glad for it. Soon he would be evacuating with the army, leaving this cold, filthy hell, and he was eager to once again embrace his Margaret.

Glancing at his opposite number, he had to quell a jolt of jealousy. The bastard was wearing a pristine uniform of blue and buff. He put the stinking soldiers of the king to shame.

Major Darcy pointed to one group of American prisoners, sailors by their appearance. "Ah, there is Lieutenant Catesby Jones and his men."

"Of course. We agreed to an exchange of prisoners, did we not?" James could not keep an undertone of annoyance from his remark.

Darcy chose to ignore it. Instead, he said softly, "You asked before whether my family was from the north of England, Major Fitzwilliam. We were, long ago. We gave up everything we owned and immigrated to Maryland after King James was overthrown in favor of Princess Mary and William of Orange. For us to maintain our rights, we were told to renounce our Catholic faith. We would not do so, so there was no place for us in England any longer. We moved to a place where our faith was not held against us."

"I am sorry to hear that. I would have had your people stay. There are many Papists serving the Crown—even in the army and navy."

Major Darcy chuckled. "You do not understand, else you would have not used that derogatory term. Can a Catholic vote in England? From what I have heard, they cannot. You still dislike and mistrust us.

"The entire structure of Britain is based upon class and titles and religion. Can a farmer become Prime Minister? Of course not. But here, any man can rise as far as his talents can take him. We are done with titles and nobility. Any man may stand for President —yes, even a Catholic."

"Could he win?" James shot back.

"Probably not," Major Darcy allowed, "but we have Catholics in our government. Men are not barred from serving; they only have to attract enough votes. We moved here so that we may seek our own destiny and not have our fate determined by others."

Major Darcy's offhanded remark struck at James's heart. His destiny had been forever altered by his decision to marry Margaret. He had been born into the aristocracy. Now, he was outside of it. He was not part of the merchant class or peasantry, either. He and Margaret were cast adrift between worlds.

He could force his way back into his class by great feats of arms. It had been done before; a hero was always welcomed by the *ton*. But James was no soldier. He was a farmer at heart. He had tired of fighting. He wanted to raise living things rather than kill his fellow man.

But how could he do that? Farmland was dear in England. Could his father be persuaded to allow him to farm on one of the family's estates? Could he bear to be his father's tenant?

Major Darcy's next comment brought James back to his present duty. "So, *Cousin*, when do you leave us?"

"I do not believe we said anything about leaving, Major. We like it here."

Darcy laughed again. "We are not blind fools, sir. We know your attack on our fort downriver is failing. Our eyes are everywhere. Tell your people that. Tell them also that those redcoats too ill to be exchanged will be treated with the utmost care. They will want for nothing until they are well enough to return home."

"As per our agreement," James noted. "We have promised the same."

Major Darcy nodded as the last of the prisoners crossed the field. "Our work here is done, Major Fitzwilliam. The truce ends when I return to my lines." He paused. "Your presence is an offence to us, and you will be treated as invaders until you either surrender or leave our land. I suggest you do one or the other soon."

"As usual, you are very direct, Major."

"This is a land inhabited by blunt people. It is our way to speak our minds frankly." Major Darcy paused. "I do not think we shall meet again, Major Fitzwilliam."

James, knowing Major Darcy spoke presciently, said nothing, working to keep his face as inscrutable as possible. *Damn their spies*, he thought.

"Safe journey, Cousin," Major Darcy said.

"Cousin," James returned.

The British party then rode back to General Lambert's headquarters to report that the Americans were aware of the next phase of the current operation—the withdrawal of the army from Louisiana.

AFTER THE SUN SET, THE British host began to move. The road to Bayou Bienvenue had been much improved, but travel on it still was an arduous task. The cannons were broken and spiked, and picquets covered the retreat. Those wounded too gravely to transport were left behind, surgeons volunteering to stay with them.

The rest of the army, the thousands of survivors of the battle, crept along the trail in the dark. With them came hundreds of escaped slaves, who hoped the British would take them away. For once, the British enjoyed good fortune. There was no rain, and a heavy fog shrouded their withdrawal. So thick was the mist that the Americans awoke on January 19 to discover the enemy gone.

After snaking through the swamp all night, the proud legions of the British Crown and their camp followers reached the end. They sat huddled in the mud and reeds on the coast of Lake Borgne, chilled to the bone, even with the pitiful bonfires that were lit. All eyes were on the lake, waiting for deliverance.

Meanwhile, General Jackson took no chances. He immediately occupied the Villeré Plantation on the nineteenth and set the dragoons to harass the enemy piquets. The British wounded and the surgeons left behind were brought to the hospital in the city. As for the army, a grand processional to New Orleans was held on the twenty-first, the first time Old Hickory had entered the city since the Night Battle. One thing New Orleanians were good at was throwing a party, and this one was spectacular. Nearly every able-bodied person was in the streets, hailing their heroes.

As much as General Jackson enjoyed the pomp, he knew the British were not finished. He expected they would try again to take the city, either through Gentilly or Mobile. Thus, New Orleans remained under martial law.

Monday, January 23: New Orleans

ABBÉ LOUIS DUBOURG OF ST. LOUIS Cathedral declared the twenty-third a day of thanksgiving for the deliverance of New Orleans. If anything, the celebration was grander than it was two days before.

Matthew and Anne-Marie were in no mood to participate in public celebration. They desired only time together, which accounted for their quietly walking the wards of the Ursuline hospital, visiting

Anne-Marie's patients. The hospital had swollen with the addition of the British wounded left behind. The English surgeons were welcome assistance for the local doctors and nurses.

Anne-Marie had a particular patient for Matthew to meet. "Private Masters, this is Major Darcy."

Private Masters still wore bandages on his face, but they were unstained as he healed. He managed a salute. "Major, Miss Dansereau has told me a lot about you."

"She has told me much about you, as well, Private," Matthew said after he returned the honor. "How are you faring?"

"I cannot complain, sir. Your people have treated me very well."

"I am glad to hear it."

Private Masters glanced about the ward. "Sir, I wonder whether you could tell me if the rumors are true that the British Army has left." His face showed his worry and fear.

"It is no secret. Your friends have been observed boarding their ships."

"Then, they've left us behind?"

"Rest easy, Private. We have exchanged those prisoners well enough to travel." Matthew waved his hand at the ward. "These men, like you, are too ill. Once you heal, when hostilities are done, you will be given an opportunity to sail to Jamaica or Barbados if that is your choice."

Private Masters' anguish turned to confusion. "My choice?"

Matthew proudly raised his chin. "The United States is a free country. Its door is open to any man who wishes to remain."

"Oh, no," Private Masters returned. "I want to go home! My family, you see, and…" He glanced at Anne-Marie.

She smiled. "Billy has many friends in Hertford, do you not, Billy?"

"Yes, ma'am, I hope so." He colored under his bandages.

"Ah, so that is how the land lies!" Matthew laughed.

"Not really, sir," Private Masters stuttered. He changed the subject. "You have been very kind to us," he said to both of his visitors. "I did not expect that."

"It is your government that is our enemy, Private Masters, not you," Matthew declared.

"I thank you anyway."

Anne-Marie patted his shoulder. "We must go now, Billy, but I will return tomorrow."

"Thank you, ma'am." Private Masters saluted Matthew again. "Sir, I hope this war ends soon. We should be friends."

"Perhaps, one day, we will."

Monday, January 27: Lake Borgne

JAMES FITZWILLIAM SAT HUDDLED IN the bow of the barge as it made its way across the choppy waters under grey afternoon skies. Over a hundred soldiers were with him, some of the last British troops to leave Louisiana. The sailors at the oars relentlessly kept up the backbreaking cadence, stopping occasionally to rest, drink, and eat.

For almost a week, the troops sat starving at the shore, waiting for their turn, as the navy barges moved the remains of the army sixty miles to the fleet. The soldiers surrounding James were impatient for the relative comfort of the troopships. Before, they found life on ship a curse—the food and water unpalatable and the congested hammocks uncomfortable. Now they anticipated these things as the greatest comforts of paradise.

James anticipated something far sweeter and softer—his Margaret.

Turning his face from the biting wind, he noticed the new hands among the sailors. A few newly freed slaves pulled at the oars clumsily. Curses from the coxswain were useless, for the newcomers understood only French. A few of the soldiers laughed at them, calling them stupid. But the sight haunted James.

The hundreds of escaped slaves who had accompanied them during the retreat pleaded to be taken along during the embarkation. After some discussion, the navy chose about two hundred of the most fit, all men, to feed their persistent need for hands aboard ship. The rest, men with families, women, and children, were left behind. It was expected that some would return to their masters, begging for mercy, while others would attempt to hide out in the swamps and bayous.

James would never forget the despair in their eyes as the last of the barges pulled away from Bayou Bienvenue. No matter what they did, he expected the slaves' fate would probably be the same: beatings, torture, or death.

Guilt roiled in James's belly. *What the devil have we done? No matter how hard those slaves' lives were before, our incursion into Louisiana has made things worse. They trusted us to protect them, and we did not. Now they are in danger.*

This whole operation has been a disaster. In our pride and foolishness, we thought to conquer. Instead, we have left our bravest in a common grave in this misbegotten land. And those slaves we abandoned are the latest victims of our arrogance! James dropped his face in his hands. *I cannot do this anymore!*

"Look there!" cried a voice next to him. "It's the fleet!"

James could not help but look up. Before his eyes was the huge British fleet. Never was there a sight more welcoming!

It took another hour for the barge to pull alongside the larboard of *HMS Imprudent*. As an officer, he was one of the first to make the climb up the side. No sooner did he step foot on the deck than his eyes searched for that face most dear to him.

Some voice mumbled, "Welcome aboard," but he paid it no mind. There, only a few steps away, was his angelic Margaret. An instant later, she was in his arms. Tears sprung to his eyes, to mix with hers. They wept together for love, loss, and thanksgiving as the world swarmed about them.

Chapter 27

The exultation in New Orleans following the victory soon faded. General Jackson disappointed the citizens by keeping the city under martial law.

Andrew Jackson was a confirmed Anglophobe, always supposing them capable of treachery. He expected that the British had not returned to Jamaica or England but were repositioning their forces to attack his country again. New Orleans was the most valuable target on the Gulf Coast. He had staked his life and reputation on protecting it, and he meant to do it, no matter the cost to his popularity. With no official surrender by the British forces, he kept the city battle ready.

Old Hickory was well nicknamed. His will was as hard and stubborn as the tree to which he was compared.

As it turned out, Old Hickory was right.

Sunday, February 12: Gulf of Mexico

ADMIRAL COCHRANE'S DREAM OF CONQUERING America had not died. Since the direct assault on New Orleans ended in failure—a failure of the army, in Sir Alexander's mind, not the navy—he decided to revisit his original idea of using the port of Mobile as a base. The army could then march overland back to Louisiana or strike northeast towards Charleston in South Carolina.

To take Mobile required the neutralization of the fort guarding Mobile Bay. Keeping with the British predilection for waging war on the Lord's Day, they launched a second attack on Fort Bowyer on Sunday, February 12. This time they did nothing by halves.

Fourteen hundred infantry supported with heavy artillery, ten times the number used five months before, was thrown at the earthen walls of the stockade. Outmanned and out gunned, the American defenders had no recourse but to surrender.

Offshore was *HMS Imprudent*. James and Margaret came up from their cabin to take the air and observe the progress of the assault. Captain Elliot was on the quarterdeck, standing at the railing and watching the flagship. Looking over, he invited the major and his wife to join him.

"Good day, Major Fitzwilliam, Mrs. Fitzwilliam. Quite the victory over the Yankees, what?"

To James's ear, it sounded as though the captain was taking some of the credit. "The Forty-Fourth recovered a bit of its honor," he allowed.

"What is the small ship near the flagship, Captain Elliot?" asked Margaret.

"'Tis a sloop-of-war, Mrs. Fitzwilliam—*HMS Brazen*, as fine a sloop as has ever sailed the sea. Commander James Stirling has her." Under his breath, he added jealously, "Lucky young bugger."

"You are keeping a close watch on her," James observed.

"She has undoubtedly delivered messages from the Admiralty. Well, Major Fitzwilliam," the captain smiled, "our next stop is Mobile, I should think."

A deep frown marred Margaret's pretty face. "More fighting."

"Indeed, madam," said Elliot in a careless manner. "How else can we put paid to these upstart Yankees?"

"Why?" she shot back. "Why are we here? Why are we fighting them? They have nothing we want or need."

"Madam, may I remind you that the United States declared war on us?"

"Does it follow that we have to fight? They are on the other side of the ocean! They cannot threaten us. Must we send more of our friends out to die? Does England need more widows?"

"Our national honor is at stake." Elliot glanced at James. "Your wife is very outspoken."

Elliot's condescension was too much for James after the month of hunger, distress, fear, defeat, and grief he had endured. His indignation unbridled, he stepped between his wife and the captain.

"Perhaps, Captain, if more gentlemen in authority were as outspoken as Mrs. Fitzwilliam, several hundred of our friends would still be alive. Her question is right to the point: Why the devil are we here?

"Ah, you cannot answer, for there is no good reason! The Americans declared war against us because we have never accepted their revolution. Believe it, sir, we were beaten at Yorktown, and we were even more soundly beaten at New Orleans! It was Agincourt all over again, except we played the part of the over-confident French, and General Jackson was Good King Harry!

"I saw, with my own eyes, our finest regiments, men who have forced Bonaparte's best off the field, utterly annihilated! And by whom, do you ask? Trained professional soldiers? No! Our ranks were thrashed by farmers, shopkeepers, lawyers, and slaves!"

James lost control, and in his rage, let loose his impotent frustration. "This entire campaign has been a shambles! Do you think we do not know of the fate of our invasion of New York? It was crushed at the shores of Lake Champlain five months ago! Admiral Cochrane's grand design was in disarray a full two months before we set sail from Jamaica. And now he wants us to take Mobile and continue this madness. Do you think for a moment that if we took the town, the Americans will let us keep it?

"This is not Italy or Spain, where soldier fights soldier and the civilians hide in their cellars. The civilians here *are* the soldiers. They do not follow the rules of war. They fight us from the front, from the back, from the top of the houses, and from behind the trees. They relentlessly hunt and kill us night and day without ceasing. They will not stop until they drive us from their land.

"The Americans have created a new race here. They are harder, more determined than any we have known. If we do not make peace with these people, we will be fighting them for a hundred years, and I should not be surprised that, at the end of it, it will be their

Stars and Stripes flying at the top of Westminster!"

Out of breath, James paused. It was at that moment he felt Margaret's hand on his arm. "Jamie," she hissed, "*enough.*"

It brought him back to sanity. The red mist was gone before his eyes, and he could see clearly about him. They were not alone; several of James's fellow officers were gathered about them, having overheard his tirade. The faces were a mixture of shock, outrage, disgust, and pity. As for Captain Elliot, his pale face changed into one of contempt.

"It seems Mrs. Fitzwilliam is not the only outspoken member in the family," he said with disdain.

In the stillness following Elliot's statement, Major James Fitzwilliam knew his army career was utterly exploded.

"Captain Elliot!" cried a midshipman. "Signal from the flag!"

Instantly, Elliot trained his telescope on the flagship. "What's that? RECALL?" He lowered his instrument in wonder. "The flag is recalling the troops from shore."

As one, the gathered army officers rushed the railing, gazing at Admiral Cochrane's flagship. "Look!" cried one. "A new signal is going up!"

Telescope raised, Elliot read the coded flags. "ALL OFFICERS REPORT TO FLAG." He continued to study the signal for a few moments while the others debated the meaning of the order. Finally, he cleared his throat.

"There is but one message *Brazen* could have delivered to cause such an upheaval. It seems, Mrs. Fitzwilliam, you have your wish. Unless I miss my guess, the war is over."

Hours later, Elliot's conjecture was confirmed. A treaty ending hostilities between the Kingdom of Great Britain and the United States of America had been signed in the Dutch city of Ghent. What was most shocking was that the document had been signed on Christmas Eve, December 24, and had already been ratified by Parliament. Orders from the Admiralty directed Admiral Cochrane to return to Port Royal.

Immediately, all soldiers ashore were recalled to the troopships. In a gesture of Georgian courtesy, Sir Alexander sent word of the treaty to General Jackson in New Orleans by courier boat. General Lambert and his chief aide were to sail on *HMS Brazen* for England with as many of the wounded as she could carry. The rest of the fleet prepared to return to Jamaica.

"I do not understand," said Margaret to her husband later in the privacy of their stateroom. "The war was over before the battle? All our friends died for *nothing*?"

Monday February 13: New Orleans

THE NEXT DAY, EDWARD LIVINGSTON RUSHED into General Jackson's headquarters with the exciting news of the Ghent treaty.

"General, I was on my way to the British fleet to investigate whether they still held some of our people and slaves, when the enemy apprised me of this extraordinary occurrence. Here is Admiral Cochrane's note."

Matthew, along with the rest of the staff, waited for their commander to read the communication in nervous anticipation, biting back their exuberance.

The tall, iron-faced general scanned the document. Jackson had recovered much of his health in the last month. His face was fuller and his color excellent. What had not changed were his demanding personality, abrupt manner, and cool confidence in his own observations and decisions.

"This is excellent news, indeed," he said. "But note here that the admiral writes only of the existence of a treaty." He held up the paper. "This is not an official announcement from Washington that hostilities have ended or even that a treaty exists. Mr. Livingston, did you not find the British attacking Fort Bowyer?"

"Yes, I did, General. But I must point out that they were in the process of recalling their troops to their ships."

"That does lend credence to this report," Jackson allowed. "While we may pray that what the British say is true, there is no guarantee that it is. We remain at a state of war, gentlemen, until such time as we receive word otherwise from our government."

The room deflated. Major Villeré, restored to his post, tentatively asked, "Should we send word to the governor that the emergency is over and announce the end of martial law?"

"Absolutely not!" shot back General Jackson. "I will not lay down my duties until official confirmation. The city remains under my purview."

"But, *mon General*, the martial law is very unpopular with the people."

"Major Villeré is right, General," added Livingston. "It has been a month since the battle and several weeks since the British sailed away. Everyone—the governor, the mayor, the legislature—they have all called for a restoration of civilian rule."

"Political preferences must be set aside in the face of military necessity," Old Hickory airily declared. "The locals may resume the governance of this den of sin and corruption when it is safe to do so, and they are welcomed to it. That is my last word on the subject."

THE JOY WITH WHICH WORD OF the Treaty of Ghent was received in New Orleans was indeed deflated by General Jackson's insistence on maintaining martial law. True to his word, he resisted the entreaties of the elected officials. In Jackson's mind, the war was not officially over. Technically, he was right and would not be moved.

The Creoles understandably could not fathom it. The English had run away. A peace treaty had been signed. There was no reason for military dictatorship. They quickly tired of the general's determination. What was once hailed as a hero's iron resolve now was berated as a tyrant's unbending willfulness. Among the leaders of discontent, to no one's surprise, were Bernard de Marigny and Wallace Anderson. In this strange way, General Jackson unified the Creoles and Americans; they all grew to resent Old Hickory.

THE TREATY OF GHENT REACHED Washington on February 14, 1815, ten days after the capital received news of General Jackson's spectacular victory at New Orleans.

The treaty was not a complete surprise. Envoys had been in negotiations in the Netherlands since August of 1814. The Americans were serious, for they sent Henry Clay and John Quincy Adams. The British Crown however assigned minor representatives. At first, the British demanded all the war aims Admiral Cochrane was trying to win by force. The Americans refused, and things were at a standstill.

Then matters changed. The British success at Washington was negated by the retreat before Baltimore and the failure of the invasion of New York. More importantly, both sides came to the realization that America was a larger trading partner with Britain than had been appreciated. Arrogant negotiating positions would not do; the feeling in both England and America was that, with the fall of Napoleon, the war needed to end.

So the British proposed *uti possidetis*—as you possess. The United States had conquered no land while the British occupied areas in the Midwest, so this was rejected. Finally, the parties agreed on *status quo*—everything as it was before hostilities. The American delegation quickly agreed and signed the accord on December 24. The British Parliament ratified the document on December 30, ten days before Pakenham assaulted Line Jackson.

On February 16, an overjoyed and relieved US Senate ratified the Treaty of Ghent. The War of 1812 was officially over.

Some observers claimed that because the Battle of New Orleans was fought after the Treaty of Ghent was adopted, Jackson's victory meant nothing. This was a complete misunderstanding of the accord. The parties simply withdrew to their borders. The treaty said nothing about the legality of the Louisiana Purchase. Great Britain and the Kingdom of Spain still did not officially recognize the transaction.

As it turned out, the Treaty of Ghent did not need to address the question of Louisiana. The British blood spilled at New Orleans did that and put to rest all complaints about the sale.

The United States of America now and forever owned the entirety of the Mississippi River watershed. Manifest Destiny was born on the plains of Chalmette.

Chapter 28

I t was a fine spring morning. Sunrise pierced the open French windows of the corner bedroom. A fresh breeze wafted the netting about the large, cypress, four-poster bed. From without, the sounds of the morning work of a plantation house could be heard above a gentle buzzing in a lady's ear.

Anne-Marie enjoyed the pleasant state of not-quite-sleep, a strong arm draped across her shoulder, a hand cupping her breast. She half-listened to the even breathing of the man in whose embrace she lay. April was still cool, so she wore a nightdress. She expected that, as the nights grew warmer and summer approached, she would forgo clothing entirely as she shared a bed with her husband.

Her husband! The thought brought a smile to her lips. Today was the two-week anniversary of her marriage to Matthew Darcy, retired major of infantry. Matthew was now a gentleman planter-in-training, apprenticed to the estate's current owner, Emile Dansereau, and most beloved husband to the heiress, Anne-Marie.

The wedding was held at St. Louis Cathedral. Anne-Marie would have preferred her parish church in St. Charles, but General Jackson indicated he would attend the ceremony if it were held while his wife and son visited the city. As the Jacksons were to leave New Orleans on April 6, the wedding date was moved to the middle of March.

The city needed amusement because the people denounced their hero for keeping New Orleans under martial law long after the battle. General Jackson only revoked his powers upon receiving official notice of Congressional approval of the Treaty of Ghent on March 13. Everyone knew since the middle of February that the war was over, and could not forgive the general for his obstinacy. New Orleanians, Creole and American, now cursed rather than cheered the name of their deliverer.

In this unexpected way, General Andrew Jackson united the various groups that made up the Crescent City as no man had done before. Everyone now disliked him.

Anne-Marie had little compliant, for it meant she would marry before Easter and not after as her father desired. She remembered little of the wedding in any case, save the incredulous picture of the general and his lady. Mrs. Jackson was as short and stout as the general was tall and gangly, and only good breeding prevented Anne-Marie from laughing aloud as the two took to the floor to dance a country jig.

Matthew's breathing grew quiet, and he began to roll over on his back. Anne-Marie reacted without thought, instinctively clasping her hand upon his, lest he release her. She was very comfortable and had no desire for him to move.

It was strange, she reflected. Two weeks ago, she could never have imagined that she would find herself in her current state. She loved Matthew, of course, and looked forward to being his wife. But she had only the barest taste of desire with little comprehension of its power. Now that she had experienced physical love, she was intoxicated with its various joys and delights. She now had an understanding of why young girls had to be protected from the ways of the world. Passion was a strong potion, indeed!

Her thoughts were interrupted by the lovely sensation of Matthew's lips on her bare shoulder.

"Good morning, *mon amour*," she said.

"It is a good morning, indeed." His voice was still rough from sleep. Between kisses, he inquired whether she had rested well.

Anne-Marie's response was to roll over and kiss him deeply, her arms entwined about his neck. His returning embrace was firm, and his strong, fit body excited her through the thin material of her nightdress. Desire reignited, Matthew's hands caressed her in the manner she loved. She felt him raising the hem of the nightdress.

"Matthew!" came a shout from without.

The lovers rolled apart with a painful groan. *"Papa!"* Anne-Marie hissed to herself.

Emile Dansereau continued in an annoyingly exuberant manner. "Come, Matthew! The sun is rising and so must you! The time for bed is past! We have work to do, and you have much to learn! You must exchange my daughter's company for mine. *C'est la vie!* You must come down for breakfast now, or you will go without! *Vite, vite!*"

"Papa, please!" cried Anne-Marie.

"Ah, you are distressed, daughter?" Emile laughed. "You cannot linger with your husband all day! You have things to do, as well. Such is married life! Come quickly for breakfast, or I shall eat it all!" They heard him chuckle all the way down the stairs.

Matthew lay with an arm across his eyes. "There are times I could strangle your father."

Anne-Marie kissed his fingertips. "Ah, I understand the feeling, *chéri*. Come, we must rise. Clementine will be in here at any moment, thanks to Papa."

Matthew sat up in bed, the sheet falling away from his bare chest. "Her last day. You must choose another maid."

"I know," she said as she slipped on a robe. Many things had changed at Dansereau Plantation. Anne-Marie's marriage had been but one.

Matthew had resigned his commission with the Federal Army. He now lived at Dansereau as Anne-Marie's husband, learning how to become a Louisiana planter. There were more responsibilities his occupation demanded of him than simply running a farm. A planter was a manager of slaves and a trader of crops and goods. He was also expected to be a community leader; that meant politics. Louisianans loved politics.

It also meant that Matthew would occasionally travel to New

Orleans to sell their goods. That foretold many weeks of separation in the years to come. Annie-Marie did not look forward to this. Wives did not go, for they managed the homestead in their husband's absence. In many ways, the planters' wives truly ran the plantations.

There was another disquieting subject. Some planters took the opportunity while living in the city to practice *plaçage*. Anne-Marie loved and trusted Matthew not to do so. They had spoken of it in the wake of Henri Herbert's abrupt departure. Matthew vowed he would never take a *placée*. He planned to stay at the Melançons during his trips to the city as her father did. Anne-Marie placed her faith in him, but she could not be a woman and not worry.

With exquisite timing, Clementine entered the bedroom moments after Matthew slipped through the door that connected his room with this one. Emile had abandoned the set of rooms he shared with Anne-Marie's mother upon his daughter's marriage. He took a room on the other side of the house, jokingly insisting that he was a bachelor now and that perhaps they should add *garçonnières* to the house. "Surely," he had smiled, "you will have sons, eh?" The remark led Anne-Marie to blush.

"What shall you wear today, *madame*?" Clementine asked as she opened an armoire.

Over the last two weeks, Anne-Marie still could not help smiling at the reference that she was no longer *Mademoiselle Dansereau*, but *Madame Darcy*. "The yellow dress, Clementine. Tomorrow you will be a *madame* as well. Are you prepared?"

Clementine's eyes shown. "Oh, *Oui, madame*! Tomorrow I shall be married and free! I cannot thank you enough!" Clementine was to marry Samson after Mass on the morrow. Matthew requested Samson's freedom in reward for the slave's service during the Battle of New Orleans. Emile granted Matthew's wish and more. Samson Freeman was kept on as assistant overseer with his own cottage and given permission to marry. To no one's surprise but Clementine's, he chose the young maid.

Anne-Marie bit her lip at Clementine's excitement. She hoped the girl understood that her new life was going to be very complicated and not always pleasant. As a freed slave, Mme Freeman could inspire resentment from the other slaves and arouse disgust from many whites.

Such is the world, Anne-Marie reflected sadly. *C'est la vie. Perhaps Henri had the right idea.*

Months before, Henri Herbert made an unexpected, shocking proposal. He mysteriously offered to sell his tiny Buena Tierra Plantation, his property adjacent to Dansereau, to Matthew at a ridiculously low price. As Matthew's funds were tied up at a bank in Virginia, Emile immediately offered to loan him the money, telling Matthew to reimburse him later.

The deal satisfied all of Matthew's desires. Dansereau Plantation would be inherited by Anne-Marie and eventually go to their children. Matthew would be only a caretaker in his mind. With Buena Tierra, he would a landowner in his own name. It was a small thing, true, and the two plantations would one day be combined, but the principle was significant to Matthew and, therefore, important to Anne-Marie.

The mystery of the unexpected offer was resolved a few days later. Henri Herbert had left New Orleans. His properties in the *Faubourg Marigny* sold and his servants dismissed, he had abruptly left for the Spanish territory of Texas. With him went Mlle Carmen Bellevue. The only thing Herbert left behind was a note addressed to Anne-Marie. It read in part:

I can no longer live as I have. I wish to embrace happiness as you have done, my dear cousin. Carmen and I journey to a new place where, hopefully, we will live together openly, where she will be my wife, not only in my heart but in fact. Our children shall bear my name and not be ashamed.

Forgive me for not attending your wedding. Forgive me for everything.

Oh, Henri, she thought at the time, *I hope you know what you are doing!* Anne-Marie was still troubled over Henri's choice. She disapproved of Henri's relationship with Mlle Bellevue. While she was happy that he would no longer live in sin, the price Henri paid for his *mestee* lover was high. She prayed Carmen was worth it.

Minutes later, Anne-Marie entered the first floor dining room. Matthew was already there, deep in conversation with Emile as they discussed the tasks for the day. The sight brought a lump to her throat. Her greatest desires were coming true.

Both men rose at her entrance. Once she took her seat, food and coffee appeared, and Anne-Marie enjoyed breakfast with the two men she loved most in the world.

After the meal, she escorted Matthew and Emile outside. Samson Freeman and the current overseer awaited them next to the horses. The tall black man was no longer in slave's rags but dressed in accordance with his new station: a brown coat over his white shirt and dark breeches and stockings. The hat on his head made him seem enormous, but the smile M. Freeman offered the mistress of the house showed he was still her brave and loyal Samson.

On an impulse, she held Matthew back a moment.

"What is it, my love?" Matthew was concerned.

"Nothing is wrong, Matthew." Her hands toyed with the lapel of his coat as she tried to distill her overwhelming joy into a few words. "I am just so happy that you and Papa are friends now."

"So am I." He ran the back of his hand down her cheek, sending chills down Anne-Marie's spine. "I am happier that you and I are…friends."

She gave him an impish smile. "Is that what you think of me? Your good friend?"

He leaned in to kiss her. "*Oui, mon amie très chérie.* My loveliest, dearest, good friend."

O thus be it ever, when free men shall stand
Between their loved home and the war's desolation.
Blest with vict'ry and peace, may the Heav'n rescued land
Praise the Power that hath made and preserved us a nation!
Then conquer we must, when our cause it is just,
And this be our motto: "In God is our trust."
And the star-spangled banner in triumph shall wave
O'er the land of the free and the home of the brave!

The forth stanza of *The Star-Spangled Banner*,
formerly *The Defense of Fort McHenry*, by Francis
Scott Key (1814). It became the official National
Anthem of the United States of America in 1931.

Epilogue

The world was never the same after the Battle of New Orleans. The War of 1812 did not end in America with a whimper with the Treaty of Ghent, but with raucous celebrations of the greatest victory yet of American arms, greater even than Yorktown. One could claim that the United States got their independence from Great Britain thanks to France's insertion into the American Revolution. But the young country won this great battle all on its own and against the best troops the British possessed. It was the Second American Revolution. The Yankees now feared no one. The desire of the United States of America was to stretch its hand of freedom from the Atlantic to the Pacific, from the Gulf of Mexico to the Great Lakes.

Without this victory, President Madison's successor, James Monroe, would never have dared issue the doctrine that bears his name. It declared that all of the Americas should be free from further European colonization and interference in its sovereign countries' affairs. It further stated that the United States considered any new European meddling in the Americas as a hostile act toward the United States. Thanks to General Jackson's masterpiece on a muddy Louisiana plantation eight years before, the Monroe Doctrine of 1823 made the United States of America, for all intents and purposes, master and defender of the Western Hemisphere.

Great Britain would claim the war ended in a draw. Failing to achieve any of its objectives and suffering one of the greatest defeats in its proud history made that belief suspect. Britain could no longer stand in the way of American expansion towards the Pacific. Its goal changed from hemming in the United States to retaining and protecting as much of Canada as possible. Britain also needed to promote trade. The merchants in London and Boston, Liverpool and New York, Plymouth and New Orleans desperately wanted to buy and sell goods. Within a few decades, Yankee dollars and British pounds would make the sworn blood enemies trading partners and eventually the closest of allies.

The Kingdom of Spain, a noncombatant, was perhaps the greatest loser of the war. Madrid's precarious position in the New Word had become a coffin, and the events at New Orleans were the final nails. It could not hold its colonies, and by 1833, all that was left of the mighty Spanish Empire in the Americas were Cuba and Puerto Rico.

Andrew Jackson became one of America's greatest heroes and rode his fame from New Orleans right into the White House. His followers created the modern Democratic Party. His name was celebrated across the nation—except in the city he fought so hard to save. Creoles excelled in holding a grudge, and it took almost forty years before they forgave Jackson his heavy-handed rule and renamed the *Place d'Armes* in his honor. Old Hickory did not live to see Jackson Square, and the author leaves it to the reader to decide whether Jackson would have cared one way or the other.

John Coffee served in President Jackson's administration, and William Carroll was elected Governor of Tennessee. John Adair, however, became Jackson's enemy over Old Hickory's complaints about the supposed cowardice of the Kentucky militia. Adair's spirited defense of his home state's troops landed him in the Kentucky governor's seat in 1820. Adair and Jackson would eventually make peace.

Jackson, Carroll, and Adair would not be the only veterans of New Orleans to achieve high office. Jacques Villeré succeeded William Claiborne as Louisiana's governor. The legislature rewarded Claiborne by electing him to the US Senate, but he died in November of 1817, only eight months into his term.

Bernard de Marigny de Mandeville continued to serve in the

legislature, but voters who tolerated his instability in the state senate would not trust him as governor. He eventually lost his fortune gambling and died impoverished in 1868. Left as his legacy was his *Faubourg Marigny* and the fishing village of Mandeville on the north shore of Lake Pontchartrain.

Edward Livingston continued to serve his state and country as a US Representative, US Senator, Secretary of State, and Minister Plenipotentiary to France. He passed away in his native New York in 1836.

The Brothers Lafitte swore off pirating after the battle. Dominique You married, entered local politics, and was given a hero's funeral in 1830. Pierre Lafitte gave all the appearance of being an honest businessman, but he often traveled to the Galveston base of his wayward younger brother. The dashing Jean could not resist the pirate's life, and by 1817, while supposedly working for the liberation of Mexico, he re-established himself as a smuggler. In 1821, the US Navy drove Jean Lafitte out of Galveston. He set up a new base in Cuba. Two years later, Jean Lafitte was killed in battle with the Spanish and was buried at sea.

The fate of the British survivors of New Orleans was a mixed bag. Much scorn was heaped upon the hapless Lt. Colonel Mullins of the Forty-Fourth Regiment. He was court-martialed and cashiered in 1815. He died eight years later, protesting his innocence to the end.

The architect of the entire operation, Vice-Admiral Sir Alexander Cochrane, rose to full admiral by 1819, became Commander in Chief, Plymouth, a senior command of the Royal Navy, and he was made Knight Grand Cross of the Order of the Bath.

Not everyone forgave Cochrane. As Lord Wellington commented in eulogy to Sir Edward Pakenham:

"I cannot but regret that he (Pakenham) was ever employed on such a service or with such a colleague. The expedition to New Orleans originated with that colleague... The Americans were prepared with an army in a fortified position which still would have been carried if the duties of others—that is, of the Admiral—had been as well performed as that of he whom we now lament."

Major-General John Keane survived the wounds he suffered at Chalmette. He served in several offices in the West Indies before his promotion to Lieutenant-General and did service in India. He was elevated to the peerage as Baron Keane in 1839.

Major-General Sir John Lambert returned to Europe in time to command the Tenth Infantry Brigade at the Battle of Waterloo, earning his Knight Grand Cross. He was eventually promoted to General in 1841, six years before his death.

Private Billy Masters survived his wounds, returned to England, ran a public house, and eventually married.

In 1818, records show that James Fitzwilliam, former major of infantry in the British Army, immigrated to the United States with his wife, Margaret, and settled to farm tobacco near Roanoke, Virginia.

The End

Definitions & Translations

ACADIENS   The original French settlers in the maritime
        provinces of Canada. After their forced exile from their
        homes, most ended up in Louisiana, where the word was
        eventually corrupted into Cajuns.

AMI   (French) Friend.

BAYOU   A slow moving stream or river. The term, used primarily
        in the Southern US, is thought to be derived from the
        Choctaw word "bayuk."

C'EST LA VIE   (French) That is life; so it goes.

CHÉRI and CHÉRIE – (French) A term of endearment to a loved
        one, male and female.

CREOLE   The term "Creole" has long generated confusion and
        controversy. The word invites debate because it possesses
        several meanings, some of which concern the innately
        sensitive subjects of race and ethnicity. In its broadest
        sense, Creole means "native"—or, in the context of
        Louisiana history, "native to Louisiana." In a more narrow
        sense, however, it has historically referred to black, white,
        and mixed-raced persons who are native to Louisiana. In
        short, the word means different things to different people,
        and more than one ethnic group arguably has a claim to
        the term.

FAUBOURG   (French) A neighborhood outside of a city.

FAUBOURG MARIGNY   The neighborhood of New Orleans,
        downriver of the *Vieux Carré*, built by the eccentric
        Bernard de Marigny de Mandeville. Free colored and
        freemen lived there, as well as the *placées* (see below).

FAUBOURG ST. MARIE   Also called the American Quarter, the neighborhood of New Orleans upriver of the *Vieux Carré* reserved for American emigrants. It no longer exists; in its place are the Central Business District and the Warehouse District.

GALLERIES   An outdoor balcony, supported by posts or columns anchored to the ground.

GARÇONNIÈRES   (French) Bachelor's apartment. In Louisiana plantation country, it was common to build separate apartments for the teen-aged sons of the owners, either attached to or detached from the main house. That way, the young men could drink and gamble with their friends without endangering the virtue of their sisters and other female relations.

HABEAS CORPUS   Latin for "you may have the body." Refers to the legal procedure that to hold a prisoner, there must be an alleged crime and that the court agrees that the authorities have the legal right to hold the accused. To suspend *habeas corpus* means the authorities can imprison anyone for any cause without a hearing or trial. In US law, *habeas corpus* may only be suspended in cases of national emergency.

LE GRAND DÉRANGEMENT   Literally, "The Big Trouble." The expulsion of the French Acadians from Canada by the British during the French and Indian War.

MARTEL, CHARLES (688 - 741)   The Hammer of the Franks, grandfather of Charlemagne, he was the greatest Frankish statesman and warrior of the Middle Ages and helped build the foundation of France.

MESTEE   An old French term, the offspring of a mulatto and a Caucasian (one-quarter black). Also known as a quadroon.

MULATTO   In 1814 New Orleans, the offspring of an African and a Caucasian (half black).

N'EST-CE PAS   (French) Is that not so?

NEUTRAL GROUND   In New Orleans, the French-speaking
Catholic Creoles and the English-speaking Protestant
American emigrants did not get along. The dividing
line between the two groups was a grassy strip along
Canal Street between the *Faubourg St. Marie* (where
the Americans lived) and the *Vieux Carré* (home of the
Creole aristocracy). This strip, the Neutral Ground, was
designated as a place where merchants and politicians
could meet in peace. To this day in New Orleans, medians
in streets and boulevards are called neutral grounds.

PLAÇAGE   A recognized extralegal system by which Creole men
entered into the equivalent ("veneer") of common-law
marriages with women of color and mixed-race descent
(*placées*). Men involved in this custom still considered
themselves free to enter into marriage with Caucasian
women while maintaining *plaçage*, while the *placées* could
not. They could only marry if the *plaçage* was terminated.
In any case, any offspring were considered legal heirs of
the fathers. The practice had peaked by 1803, and within
a few decades, it was abandoned in the face of American
emigration and criminalization of relations between the
races.

PLACE D'ARMES   (French) Military parade grounds. In New
Orleans, it was the large square in the center of the *Vieux
Carré* in front of St. Louis Cathedral. The *Place d'Armes*
was renamed Jackson Square in the 1850's.

PLACÉE   A woman engaged ("placed") in *plaçage* (see above).

RUE   (French) Street.

SCHOONER   A type of military sailing vessel with fore-and-aft
sails on two or more masts.

S'IL VOUS PLAIT   (French) Please; if you please.

SLOOP-Of-WAR   A type of military sailing vessel with twenty
or fewer cannons. Brig-sloops had two masts and ship-
sloops had three, and the primary sails were square-rigged.

TOUT DE SUITE   (French) Right away.

VIEUX CARRÉ – French for Old Square. It refers to the original settlement of *La Nouvelle-Orléans* (New Orleans). The district is now known as the French Quarter.

VITE   (French) Move quickly.

Bibliography, Sources, and Suggested Readings

Austen, Jane. *Persuasion.*

—. *Pride and Prejudice.*

Borneman, Walter R. *1812 – The War That Forged a Nation.* New York: HarperCollins, 2004.

Caldwell, Jack. *Pemberley Ranch.* Naperville: Sourcebooks Landmark, 2010.

—. *The Three Colonels – Jane Austen's Fighting Men.* Naperville: Sourcebooks Landmark, 2012.

—. *Mr. Darcy Came to Dinner – a Jane Austen farce.* Venice: White Soup Press, 2013.

—. *The Companion of His Future Life.* Venice: White Soup Press, 2014.

De Noux, O'Neil. *Battle Kiss.* New Orleans: Big Kiss Productions, 2011.

Dufour, Charles M. *Ten Flags in the Wind – The Story of Louisiana.* New York: Harper & Row, 1967 (out of print).

Pickles, Tim. *New Orleans 1815 – Andrew Jackson Crushes the British.* London: Reed Consumer Books, Ltd, 1993.

Remini, Robert V. *The Battle of New Orleans: Andrew Jackson and America's First Military Victory.* New York: Viking, 1999.

About the Author

Jack Caldwell is an author, amateur historian, professional economic developer, playwright, and like many Cajuns, a darn good cook. Born and raised in the Bayou County of Louisiana, Jack and his wife, Barbara, are Hurricane Katrina victims who now make the Sun coast of Florida their home.

Jack is the author of four Jane Austen-themed books. PEMBERLEY RANCH is a retelling of *Pride & Prejudice* set in Reconstruction Texas. THE THREE COLONELS – JANE AUSTEN'S FIGHTING MEN is a sequel to *Pride & Prejudice* and *Sense & Sensibility*. MR. DARCY CAME TO DINNER and THE COMPANION OF HIS FUTURE LIFE are *Pride & Prejudice*-flavored farces.

In 2015, the first of a series of four historical novels about New Orleans, titled CRESCENT CITY, will be published. THE PLAINS OF CHALMETTE begins the series, commemorating the Bicentennial of the Battle of New Orleans. To mark the tenth anniversary of Hurricane Katrina, three modern novels will be released: BOURBON STREET NIGHTS, ELYSIAN DREAMS, and RUIN AND RENEWAL.

When not writing or traveling with Barbara, Jack attempts to play golf. A devout convert to Roman Catholicism, Jack is married with three grown sons. Jack's blog postings — **The Cajun Cheesehead Chronicles** — appear regularly at **Austen Variations**.

Web sites: **Ramblings of a Cajun in Exile:**
www.cajuncheesehead.com
Austen Variations: http://austenvariations.com/
Facebook: https://www.facebook.com/pages/
Jack-Caldwell-author/132047236805555
Twitter: @JCaldwell25

The Crescent City Series
All available from White Soup Press

THE PLAINS OF CHALMETTE:
A Story of CRESCENT CITY (Jan. 2015)

BOURBON STREET NIGHTS:
Volume One of CRESCENT CITY (May 2015)

ELYSIAN DREAMS:
Volume Two of CRESCENT CITY (July 2015)

RUIN AND RENEWAL:
Volume Three of CRESCENT CITY (Sept. 2015)

Other Novels by Jack Caldwell
Available from Sourcebooks Landmark:

PEMBERLEY RANCH

THE THREE COLONELS – *Jane Austen's Fighting Men*

Available from White Soup Press:

MR. DARCY CAME TO DINNER – *a Jane Austen farce*

THE COMPANION OF HIS FUTURE LIFE

www.ingramcontent.com/pod-product-compliance
Lightning Source LLC
Chambersburg PA
CBHW030651260626
47157CB00007B/2589